Praise for *A Twist of the Knife*

'Wow! An absolute pleasure. Chilling, smart, funny, and what a voice she has'   Gillian Flynn, author of *Gone Girl*

'A crime novel that transcends the genre – a twisting, high-stakes story with characters so real and so recognizably human, that it breaks your heart a little. Brilliant'
Shari Lapena, author of *The Couple Next Door*

'Blown away. What else can I tell you?'
Linwood Barclay, author of *No Time for Goodbye*

'Brilliant, intricate, authentic and sometimes raw, this is a masterfully written story that'll quicken your pulse and challenge the grey matter too. Brigid Quinn is my new favourite female investigator. Loved it!'
Gilly Macmillan, author of *What She Knew*

'Brigid Quinn is the kind of FBI agent you have never met before, but will want to meet again!'
Peter Robinson, author of the Inspector Banks novels

'Becky Masterman is one of those skilled writers who makes the reader laugh, cry and think, all in the space of a few pages; and Brigid Quinn is as real as a character in a book can be'   *Promoting Crime Blogspot*

Becky Masterman created her heroine, Brigid Quinn, while working as an editor for a forensic science and law enforcement press. Her debut thriller, *Rage Against the Dying*, was a finalist for the Edgar Awards and the CWA Gold Dagger, as well as the Macavity, Barry, ITW and Anthony awards. It was also chosen by the Richard and Judy Book Club. Her books have been translated into twenty different languages. Becky lives in Tucson, Arizona, with her husband.

Also by Becky Masterman

Rage Against the Dying
Fear the Darkness

A
TWIST
OF
THE
KNIFE

BECKY MASTERMAN

WEIDENFELD & NICOLSON

A W&N PAPERBACK

First published in Great Britain in 2017
by Weidenfeld & Nicolson
This paperback edition published in 2018
by Weidenfeld & Nicolson
an imprint of the Orion Publishing Group Ltd
Carmelite House, 50 Victoria Embankment
London EC4Y 0DZ

An Hachette UK Company

1 3 5 7 9 10 8 6 4 2

A CIP catalogue record for this book is
available from the British Library.

ISBN (Mass Market Paperback) 978 1 4091 5548 5
ISBN (eBook) 978 1 4091 5549 2

Printed in Great Britain by Clays Ltd, St Ives plc

www.orionbooks.co.uk

For Del, Paulette, and Julie

Revenge, revenge,
See the furies arise.

JOHN DRYDEN

Prologue

The first execution I attended wasn't by lethal injection but by Old Sparky. That's what they affectionately call the electric chair at Raiford Penitentiary in the northeast part of Florida. It was in 1980, a few years after the death penalty was reinstated across the country. They had come up with the lethal injection cocktail by that time, but you were allowed to choose your method of dying.

I had nothing to do with catching the guy who was to be executed. The man who brought me there was a mentor who was dubbed Wooly Bully by the rest of my class at Quantico. With his full white beard, he was what Santa Claus would be like if Santa Claus was a son of a bitch. He said this should be part of my criminal justice education, that I should witness what you might think of as the final result of what I did for a living. Rookie though I was, it wasn't lost on me that I was the only agent brought here, and one of the first women hired by the FBI. That was when they made jokes like *On the way to a bust, the male agents check their guns, and the female agents check their lipstick.*

Call it hazing. Call it sexist. You can call it a field trip for all I care.

"The witnesses are now entering the witness room," I heard a voice say, and it continued throughout the entire event, like a macabre master of ceremonies.

We entered and sat in wooden pews, facing a room with glass partitions. Beyond the glass was a sturdy wooden chair, straps dangling from the arms, and straps hooked to the front legs. A metal cap was suspended like a halo over all. Two journalists were there as well. Another man sat by himself one pew ahead of us and to the right.

My mentor pointed to the man and whispered, "That guy? He's the father. The guy about to die killed his two kids." I could feel him looking at me from the corner of his eye. He leaned back and crossed his arms over his belly like he was about to enjoy telling a child he wouldn't get the football he wanted.

He had already explained to me how three executioners would be standing in a room off the execution chamber, each tasked to press a button that would deliver two thousand volts of current for three seconds, one thousand volts for seven seconds, and two hundred and fifty volts for fifteen seconds. The mechanism was set to deliver the current randomly from only one of the buttons. None of the three men assigned to deliver the current would know which button actually did it.

The warden's assistant stood by the window; I could see his face peering in and his lips moving as he reported everything he saw. His job was to stay on the phone with the commissioner, to report what was happening and to be alerted should there be a last-second stay of execution. There was always that dramatic anticipation of the final moment when the call would come in to stop the procedure.

Not this time.

The commentary, delivered in a sober yet matter-of-fact tone, defused the drama of the scene as much as it could. As if the actors wanted to convince the audience that the play was not real.

"The date is January 25, 1980. The time is now 12:13 A.M."

Why midnight, I wondered. What the hell difference does it make?

"The condemned man has been escorted from the holding cell into the execution chamber. He appears to be passive, and after some hesitation has seated himself in the chair. The guards have secured the straps around his arms and legs. Do you have any final words?"

The man in the chair had a round face and puffy eyes. He looked

2

out through the window at us and said, "I'm sorry, Frank. I take it back." As if Frank would say *Okay, then, never mind.* He tried to say more but only succeeded in making an absurd sound like the mewling of a cat, and he gave up.

The man sitting to our right and one pew ahead of us, who I figured was Frank, stared without comment.

The master of ceremonies went on. "These are the final words. Would you like to pray?"

The man's lips moved over and over in the same phrase, the words barely audible, the words hardly a prayer. "Going to hell. Going to hell. Going to hell. Going to hell." He might have continued like this forever if the executioners hadn't decided to move the agenda along.

"The assistants are now placing wet sponges on his head and his legs. This seems to have agitated the prisoner. One assistant wipes his forehead, either from perspiration or an excess of water running into his eyes. They are now securing a cloth over the man's head. Now they are placing a metal cap over his head and strapping it in place. The prisoner is trembling violently. The assistants have exited the room.

"The time is now 12:19 A.M. Permission requested to proceed with execution.

"Permission to proceed granted.

"Phase one. The body has gone rigid, seeming to rise above the surface of the chair for the seconds of voltage administered. There was a popping sound, which we thought was one of the bands breaking, but appears to be caused by the suddenly charged water. His hands are grasping the arms of the chair.

"Phase two. The body has already relaxed. I think we have a successful process this time.

"Phase three. No other condition to report. Current ceased.

"We are now into lapse time. He doesn't appear to be breathing.

"Four minutes."

Certainly the man's body was still and slumped, held in place by the cuffs on his arms and the metal cap strapped to his head.

"Three minutes."

None of us in the witness room moved. I think I remember breathing, but I couldn't vouch for anyone else.

"Two minutes.

"One minute.

"The medical examiner has now entered the room and is checking for signs of life. The medical examiner reports the condemned has expired on this date at 12:33 A.M. The warden has reported this execution to the commissioner, and we have been told job well done. The warden answered that it was a team effort and we were ready for the next one."

"So. What do you think, Jane Wayne?" my mentor asked.

I didn't mind that nickname as much as I minded Dickless Tracy. I rubbed the corner of my mouth where a nerve jumped. One person, somewhere, laughed.

We stayed for the autopsy, which was not my first, but the first I had witnessed from death by electrocution. It seems absurd to autopsy a man you've watched die, but it's part of the formal record keeping to which humans are so tied, perhaps in an attempt to protest that we are human after all.

I had been told there would be "some burn marks" at the site where the current entered. That was correct. The back of his right leg looked and smelled like pork after ten minutes under a broiler, and the top of his scalp was burned down to his skull. When the top of the skull was lifted, cranial hemorrhaging was noted in the record. Urine was taken to determine whether the man had been given drugs before execution, but none were found.

Manner of death: homicide by electrocution.

Homicide is what they put on the death certificate. That means one person killing another under any circumstances, although in this case sanctioned under the law.

Cause of death: cardiac failure.

It's a hard way to go, and not an easy thing to watch. Do you have any idea what it feels like to sit very still in what looks like a church pew and do nothing while a stranger dies violently fifteen feet away? To carefully control all your muscles that are getting messages fired from your brain to stop death? To tamp down that urge to do something. To save.

Many people in criminal justice are opposed to the death penalty because they know better than anyone else the flaws of judgment,

4

science, or law that can lead to a wrongful conviction. As for me, people joke sometimes about how vicious I am, how I support the death penalty to the extent that if I could I would make traffic offenses capital crimes. Well, I confess there were two times in my life, years later, when I relished watching someone die, one by my own hand. And for some I'd be pleased to pull the switch myself. But as a routine event, execution is more like putting down a sick animal. There's no pleasure in it, no thrills, only a kind of disgust that makes you cleave to a precise script from which you can detach yourself. You make yourself an actor in a theatrical drama someone else has written.

Yes, but can you take it, Brigid Quinn? Sure, I can take it. I tamped it down real good.

That's what an execution is like. It's what I witnessed thirty-five years ago, what I remember of every sight, and sound, and smell, like it was yesterday. I didn't want to know that man's complete story. I wasn't even sure he was competent. Having known some creatures that simply need to be put down, I'm not against the death penalty by any means. But anyone out there who ever suggests I get a morbid thrill from it, fuck you.

One

35 years later . . .

It is a well-established fact that stranger homicide is rare. Most murderers kill people close to them. This is a story about a man on death row for killing his whole family, and about the women who loved or hated him. This is a story about the lengths we go to seek justice as we see it. It's also about prisons, some made of stone. And along those lines, it's about the family legends we tell, to each other and ourselves, that imprison us. Heroes and villains, they all got family.

This story begins with my father. My mother had called me from Fort Lauderdale, Florida, to tell me that his bronchitis had turned into pneumonia, and an ambulance had just taken him from their assisted living facility to the hospital. I had to go. I had my ticket and I was packed.

But this story also begins with Special Agent Laura Coleman.

Here is what I saw in a room at Tucson Medical Center the day after she nearly died saving my life:

I saw the backs of three people who formed a cordon around her bed as if they could protect her from the world, the kind of family that hugged and kissed and were overly generous with their emotion. They were dressed in dark clothes. I had met the father and the mother, who was in some stage of Alzheimer's, several days before. The brother had just arrived. They turned and thanked me ten times and left for the cafeteria so Coleman and I could talk.

When her family peeled away from the bed I saw Laura Coleman, surrounded by things almost as pale as her face, the hospital gown, the sheet, the screen next to the bed. She was hooked up to an IV. She was thinner after going without water for more than twenty-four hours, not long but too long in a desert climate. Her bones cast shadows. A bit of antiseptic wash seeped through a gauze bandage covering the ear that had been stapled. I saw that her knees were supported on a cushioned platform to keep her ankles elevated after they repaired her sliced Achilles tendons. Her cap of curly hair formed individual coils from sweat and oil.

I felt guilty that I was upright, and only a little bruised. I looked down and noticed beneath my fingernail, despite the thorough cleansing, a speck of something that was likely not my own blood.

When I looked back at her I saw her eyes: at first gauzy from the sedative, but then they saw me.

Not me. The doctors, the family, they had distracted her momentarily, but I could see that my face plunged her back to where we had been the night before. She pressed her head back into her pillow as if she had been struck lightly.

I had been there with her, and even I had trouble dealing with it. This had been her first time of death, and what she had experienced, what she had witnessed, would have done in most agents, male or female. You don't just shake it off no matter who you are, and anyone who says you do lives in a comic book world.

I put my tote bag on the foot of her bed, moving slowly so as not to startle her, and gently so she wouldn't feel it in her ankles.

"You need to wash your hair," I said, to show her it was me, Brigid Quinn, and that this was a day like any other. None of that generic *are you okay we're concerned about you* bullshit. She would know that wasn't me.

Coleman started to pull her bedsheet to her chin and then must have thought how like a frightened child it made her look.

"I understand," I said. It doesn't take some kind of hooey-hooey New Age thinking to know that the violence we shared had linked us. "You'll get over it."

The terror left her eyes as she came back to the present and finally saw just me.

Coleman cleared her throat and changed the subject with small talk. "Willis. My brother, Willis, lives in North Carolina," she said. "I'm taking some leave and spending it with him in Hendersonville, in the mountains of North Carolina. It will be good." She said those words, but she didn't look enthused. "I worry about Dad having to deal with Mom by himself, though. It was one of the reasons I stayed out here."

"I can see you have good family. We should all have such good family." And then, being inept at small talk, I asked, "Has that jerk-off come to visit?"

The pain meds had her fogged somewhat, but she still followed me. "No. He wouldn't."

"Of course he wouldn't. I haven't told you that I tried to get him to believe that you'd been kidnapped. But he was more worried about having our conversation overheard by his wife."

"Let's l-let that go, Brigid," she said, stuttering the way she had the first time when she accidentally called the prosecuting attorney by his first name, and saw that I could tell they were lovers. "Nag me when I can fight back. Right now I'm tired."

Best thing to do for trauma is force yourself to review it over and over again until even you get bored with it. I said, "I know an excellent person in Asheville. It's a bit of a drive from Hendersonville, but he's worth it. He got me through a rough time once, and no one in the Bureau will know." I had already written down the name and phone number, and now reached into my tote bag where the piece of paper rested on top of all my other crap. I put the paper on her rolling bed table.

"Don't lose it. Oh, and I've already contacted him to let him know you'll be calling, so if you don't see him I'll find out."

"You're treating me like a rookie," Laura said.

Which she wasn't, technically. Coleman had been working for some years investigating Medicare fraud, following the money. But she had switched to homicide just before we met. Whole new territory for her;

8

hence her rookiness. With her encounter of violence still fresh, Coleman wasn't yet aware that she stood now at a crossroads, either living the present or living the past. Just because a bad guy dies in the last act doesn't mean he can't still pull you after him into the grave. At the time I wasn't aware of how this idea, that dying isn't always the last thing that people do, would affect Coleman and me.

"Any more advice?"

I realized I had gone into my thoughts and was about to picture Laura Coleman doing herself harm. I'd seen it happen to others, but not her, I told myself. She was too resilient for that. I came back to the room to hear her repeating, "Any more advice?"

"I've rethought what I told you about staying with the FBI. There are times when you walk away. This is one of those times. You've done your service. You've done a lifetime of service. After you've healed, after you've really healed, do something else." Despite my intention to stay tough, even in my own ears my voice sounded embarrassingly like a mother's, a little whiny pleading note in there somewhere. And no surprise; if I had ever had the ill luck to bear a child, she probably would have been Laura Coleman.

Her eyes and mouth went a little slitty despite the sedative, tightening the way they did when anyone got in her way. Laura never could control all those tells. Her look lifted me, because it reassured me that there she was, Laura was still in there. "Any other advice?" she repeated.

I knew when to back off. "Don't fall in love with the wrong man again. And always wait for backup."

She chuckled, just a small one, and probably for the first time in a while. My tendency to joke in the face of trouble wasn't all bad.

"That's it?" she asked.

"One more thing." I stopped to figure out how to put this.

"What's that?"

"Don't be me."

I hadn't spoken to Coleman in a while, and it had been a year since we'd worked that case together in Arizona. Last I heard she had moved from her brother's place in North Carolina to Florida, where she had signed on with the Palm Beach County Sheriff's Office, working on cold case homicide investigations.

On a day in June I called her from my home in the high desert north of Tucson to let her know my dad was in the hospital and I was going to be in Fort Lauderdale, and ask if she wanted to get together. Before I had a chance to do that, she told me she wasn't with the PBCS cold case squad anymore. Hadn't been there for seven months. Since we last spoke she'd gone to an Innocence Project fund-raiser and met a high-end criminal defense lawyer who wasn't part of IP but did some pro bono work for felons' appeals he thought had merit. He had hired her as an investigator. This was her third case. With that reluctance that showed how she took losing personally, she told me the first two had been unsuccessful. But she wasn't totally bummed, because those guys were guilty. It was a whole different thing to defend someone who was innocent.

"The attorney's name is William Hench. Right now we're working on an appeal for a man who's been on death row for fifteen years," she said. I could feel more than hear that intensity in her vocal cords, her voice a little higher pitched and raspier than usual, like she was trying to pretend she wasn't being gently strangled with a phone cord. She got that way when she was passionate. She was very passionate.

"Remember the Lynch case?" she asked.

Did I remember the Lynch case. That was what nearly got us killed, because she insisted on fighting to free a man she knew was innocent of serial murder even if he *was* guilty of necrophilia.

She didn't wait for the obvious answer. "This is the Lynch case again. It combines cold case with wrongful conviction. It's, like, what I'm meant to do with my life. We don't think this man did the crimes. But," she went on, "we're missing a couple of pieces of evidence. There's a thing with getting evidence released in Indian River County, and they've been stonewalling Will. I told him you might know some people in this area who you could put the pressure on. Will's heard of you. He was impressed that I knew you."

"Well, you're both in luck. What I called to tell you is that I'm coming over. My dad's in the hospital with pneumonia. Eighty-three years old and a smoker. I think he's got emphysema, too. No one there to help my mother except my brother, and he's useless. But we're not what you'd call a close family. I'll probably need a break from the hospital. Let's get together. Just think what fun it will be to talk out a case together again."

"I was thinking more like you could just make a phone call to some—"

"Nah. Who's the guy you're trying to get off?"

"Marcus Creighton."

Alarm bells. I didn't know everything, but I knew Creighton was guilty. Laura was going to lose. I remembered again Laura didn't care much for losing, and that made me question what she was doing working appeals. Then I remembered how the first time I met her she was so impassioned about a man's innocence she nearly leapt across the table at me in her effort to convince me she was right. But I didn't say any of that. I just said, "No shit? Seriously?"

"You remember the case."

I said, "That case was Casey Anthony huge. O. J. Simpson huge. Even if I hadn't been working in the area at the time, it was national news."

"Huge. The difference is, there was a stronger case against both of them, and yet they both got off. Seriously, who'd have thought? We think we can find evidence for Marcus Creighton that will, if not exonerate him fully, overturn the death penalty ruling for a life sentence. If he's proven innocent, the publicity will add to the current groundswell against capital punishment."

"It doesn't hurt that he's an upper-middle-class white guy," I said.

Silence on her end.

"I'm just saying I don't need a lecture," I said.

"Public opinion is turning, Brigid. Most legislators on both sides of the aisle feel the same way."

"But, Laura. Marcus Creighton."

It struck me that she might know me as well as I knew her when she said, "You think I'm deluding myself. I know what the odds are on this, but I think sometimes it's worth going against the odds, and I know you do, too."

"Right now I'm thinking I've always hated arguing over the phone."

"Well, don't then. Not until you hear what new evidence we're tracking."

11

"Tell you what, e-mail me anything you've got on the case so I can take a look. I'm coming in tomorrow afternoon, I'll stop by the hospital and then meet you at that Howard Johnson's on the beach in Deerfield."

So. Parents, then Laura. Good thing I didn't have any pressing cases to attend to in my investigation business, because I was clearly needed elsewhere.

I packaged up my firearm, took it to the post office, and shipped it to Laura's address because of TSA rules. Not that I was anticipating trouble.

Did I just say that? I always anticipate trouble. What I didn't anticipate, and what Laura didn't know at that point, was that the following day, around the time I was changing planes in Phoenix, the governor of Florida was signing the warrant for Marcus Creighton's execution by lethal injection.

Two

The next day Carlo, that's my husband, insisted on taking me to the airport. When I told him I could drive myself, he reminded me we hadn't bought a new car after I totaled mine around the same time I got shot in the leg. Not that he doesn't trust me behind the wheel or anything like that.

He let me drive, while he folded his long legs into the passenger seat like a praying mantis or some other unusually large insect. Our Pugs rode in the backseat, looking out the windows on either side of the car for a while before settling down to sleep. On the way to the airport we talked. About Dad's precarious health and what to do with Mom if, when, he died.

"Bring her to live with us," Carlo said.

"The hell you say. My family is nuts." I had turned his dusty Volvo east on River Road and found the desert sun positioned over the Rincon Mountains, hitting my windshield precisely midway between the wipers and the bottom edge of the sun visor. We spent a few moments in silence as I drove blindly, hoping not to hit a car I couldn't see.

Then I said, "They may have behaved at my sister-in-law's funeral, but you never know when somebody is going to throw something."

That was the one time he'd met my family, six months earlier. We've only been married a couple of years. Carlo was a Catholic priest turned philosophy professor, whose first wife died of cancer about five years before we met. He was my first husband. I may be able to kill a man with my bare hands, but when it comes to civilian life I'm what you call a late bloomer. I'm learning marriage by trial and error. It helps that I'm crazy for this guy.

We talked some about Laura then, her turning into an activist, and her latest passion for exonerating felons. Possibly more like abolishing the death penalty. Laura set herself high goals.

"I like Laura. I hope she succeeds," Carlo said.

I tried not to get up on my soapbox, but the thing is always sitting right there beside me.

"I like her, too. And because of that I have to convince her to stop tilting at windmills," I said.

"If there hadn't been a windmill, we wouldn't have Don Quixote."

I know I could have argued that, but we were nearing the airport. "You old softy, you don't even know what he's in for. The guy murdered his family, including a wife and three children. That's her asshole client."

Carlo was silent at that, but not because I had shocked his religious sensibility with the heinousness of the crime. He had been a prison chaplain at one point, and knew what it was like to have feces thrown at you, and to hear the confession of a man about to be executed. No, Carlo was silent because he was a retired philosopher. There were times when finishing a sentence took hours, days, in coming.

He sipped from a to-go cup of coffee dwarfed by his big hands. He said, "That's ugly. But if he didn't do it, I don't think I can imagine anything more cruel than to have your family ripped from you and then to be punished for it. If Laura is doing this, there must be a reason. You've got to respect it." The image of the man I had once seen executed flashed into my head. You know, those several dozen flashbulb memories that play and play and play.

As requested, Laura Coleman had e-mailed me a huge file on the Creighton case, including the complete court transcripts. On the leg from

Phoenix to Fort Lauderdale I opened my iPad and chose the first file because it was labeled PHOTOS. Photos are easy; you know, a picture, a thousand words, et cetera.

Well, sure. Why not start with the victims?

The mother: Kathleen Creighton, taken at a formal gathering with her lipstick fading on the bee-stung lips popular at the time, a glass in her hand, toasting the camera. Chin slightly up, not drunk enough to forget that little bulge below your jaw. An attractive man by her side, laughing in appreciation of nothing the way people do at parties. Marcus Creighton? What did it say about the Creightons that this photo was the one they used?

The others were school photos of the children, the last ones taken before they disappeared, or died, probably died.

The oldest girl: Kirsten Creighton, hair modeled after Jennifer Aniston's in *Friends*, a style too old for a girl barely in her teens. That Victoria's Secret pout that's supposed to look sexy without the child even knowing what sexy means. Trying on this person and that person. Whoever she was to be, ultimately, never was.

The younger girl: Sara Creighton, around eight years old, not yet practicing with a mask like her sister. Facing the camera dead-on, un-selfconscious smile showing a double gap where her lower teeth should have been, she reminded me of a drunk pirate. She was the clown in the family. If they ever found her skull there would be secondary teeth still in the jaw, forever waiting to erupt.

The boy: Devon Creighton, Sara's twin, a shyer glance than his sister, with lids half-shielding his eyes and a more tentative smile that probably covered gaps like hers. But this was a snap in time, like those flashbulb memories. You couldn't really tell who he was, whether he was the best soccer goalie on his elementary school team. The social stratum these kids came from, too rich for football and too poor for lacrosse.

School photos tell you everything and nothing. These were interchangeable with a million other little Americans in school photos. Only different, because there would never be high school graduation photos taken of these kids.

It was too early in the morning for a drink. I backed out of the photo file without looking to see if there were any of the crime scene, and decided on a court transcript.

CLOSING REMARKS OF DAVID LANCER,
FLORIDA STATE'S ATTORNEY

Ladies and Gentlemen of the jury. As I told you in my opening remarks, I'm David Lancer, and I have had the responsibility of prosecuting the case against Marcus Creighton on behalf of the State of Florida. Now I'm going to summarize the case we have proved. Here is how the detectives, forensic scientists, and crime scene reconstruction experts, all experts in their fields, reconstructed the scene at the home of Marcus Creighton, 2357 Oleander Drive, Vero Beach, Florida, on the night of April 30, 1999.

It is after midnight. Mr. Creighton has been away for several days on a business trip to Miami. Upon his return, arriving at the Melbourne Airport, where he picks up his car, he drives to the home where his wife and three children reside. In particular, a wife who has complained to her friends of the many arguments they have had over the sorry state of their finances, of the errors of judgment Mr. Creighton made that put his family at risk. She more than once threatened divorce. If she knew about his lover, it was the one thing she kept to herself.

Mr. Creighton has arranged for the children to be out of the house that night, attending a slumber party at a community center.

From this we can understand that he expected to find his wife home alone. Next events were planned even before he arrived there. Or perhaps he saw an opportunity and seized it. Whatever his mode of operation, when he walks into the master suite of his lavish dwelling, he finds his wife in the bathtub. She has, some would say foolishly, taken a sleeping pill prior to her bath, and is quite asleep. Perhaps he knows that this is common practice for her. Perhaps Creighton nudges her. Perhaps he perceives that she is out cold, and this is his chance to be with his mistress.

He has two choices: He can either push her under the water, and make it look like an accidental drowning, or . . . he opens the bathroom cabinet and finds her hair dryer. Plugging it into the wall socket between the sink and the tub, he sees that even the noise of the dryer does not awaken her. It's so easy, and the ease makes the temptation unbearable.

He tosses the dryer into the tub, and the water is instantly charged. Kathleen's body jerks with the current. Within less than thirty seconds she's dead. Perhaps he watched. Perhaps he turned away. But whenever he turned away, he saw one of his children, watching, too stunned to react, too frightened to even scream. The child had watched him watching their mother die.

The children had not gone to the slumber party after all. Let us imagine the child who saw this was a little girl.

Marcus Creighton is caught, but at what he doesn't know. Perhaps the child only saw her mother dead in the tub? Did she see her dying while he did nothing? Did she see her father throw the hair dryer into the water and then stand there doing nothing?

Does Marcus Creighton stop to question the child, and the child shrinks from his touch? Tries to run?

Impulsively, Marcus Creighton grabs the child and puts his hand over her mouth. What is he to do? What are his choices now? Somehow he binds the child, perhaps dragging her into the garage where a roll of duct tape rests on his workbench. He tapes the child's mouth and binds her hands, still horrified at the way this is playing out, not daring to think where it might lead. But this step is driving him there. He puts the child in the backseat of his car.

If anything is to be done, he reasons, it must be done completely and forever. He goes upstairs and rouses the other two children, one at a time, under some pretext of having to leave the house. They trust him. What child does not trust their father? And he leads them one after another to the same garage, the same duct tape binding them, the same car. Even now, they are more puzzled than fearful.

What then, ladies and gentlemen? Did he drive around for a while, weighing his options? Did he resist killing them or was it easy for him? Is it necessary to surmise what happened to the children after that? Where are the bodies of these children that cry out to you for justice?

There will always be questions which Marcus Creighton stubbornly refuses to answer, but let us address the answers we know for certain. Among the people providing testimony to this crime, you heard from Dr. Tracy Mack, a respected latent print expert, who developed the fingerprint on the hair dryer that, when questioned that night, Marcus Creighton told Detective Gabriel Delgado he had never touched.

You also heard from Detective Gabriel Delgado, who took Mr. Creighton into custody, and to whom Mr. Creighton insisted he had been with his mistress earlier that evening. You also heard Shayna Murry, the mistress whose peccadillo turned into horrific tragedy, deny he was with her that night, which places him at the house hours earlier than he said he was. We have also heard from friends of Mrs. Creighton who repeated conversations surrounding the state of their marriage.

The evidence is overwhelming. You have been told of the purchase of a life insurance policy on Mrs. Creighton, with Mr. Creighton as a beneficiary, twelve months prior to the death of his family. The State has presented a case that assigns motive, means, and opportunity to Marcus Creighton. Motive is the reason for a crime. Means signifies the way the crime was committed. Opportunity is the time and place that came together to allow the perpetration of the crime.

These three are necessary to convince you beyond a reasonable doubt, and the State has done so. The evidence is overwhelming. The defense may try to convince you that you cannot find a verdict of homicide for the three children because their bodies have not yet been found. This is erroneous. There are many precedents for homicide convictions in the absence of the body. The facts are plain.

Were it not for that child who saw his or her mother die, Mr. Creighton might have gotten away with the murder of his wife. Instead, he is accused of the crime of murdering his whole family. For this crime, the crime that all civilized cultures consider the most heinous, the State asks you to deliver not only a guilty verdict, but the death penalty. Thank you.

I felt my spine settle back into the seat, ordered a coffee with whitener as the attendant passed by, and leaned my iPad against the dropdown table in front of me.

Creighton did it. I was more certain than I'd ever been that he did it, and because of that, Laura would need me more than she realized.

Three

I knew David Lancer. Sure, he was a state's attorney, and his job wasn't to find the truth. His job was to get a conviction. He would call it winning. He was law enforcement's hero and had passable ethics.

But whether or not it was a just conviction, you can't take on the world. Guilty or not, Creighton wasn't one of the battles I was called to fight. Like that saying goes, *Not my circus, not my monkeys.* It's a Momism—she was full of platitudes that sometimes flapped through my head.

Mom, I thought. First Mom and Dad, then Laura.

June starts hurricane season, and even in the air-conditioned Fort Lauderdale airport terminal I could sense the tropical dampness I took for granted until I moved to Arizona. Without even looking I felt the tiny lines in my face disappearing, the cracks around my mouth filling in, while my hair doubled its body. My hand felt slippery on the plastic handle of my roller bag, and I tried to remember the last time I had sweaty palms.

Inside the terminal was nothing compared to the outside, though. I dragged my carry-on out the automatic doors and into the real humidity, making me feel like I'd been hit in the face with a warm wet cotton ball. After the dryness of the high desert my lungs had to work a little harder sucking in all that water.

Florida. It's a wet heat.

The feeling stayed with me as I made my way to the rental car terminal a short walk away, got directed to a self-effacing gray Accord, and drove north on I-95, not imagining how much time I'd be spending on this road in the coming days.

I grew up in this area. I left it to go to college and then Quantico and wherever that led, but had done some time working for the FBI in South Florida, too. Even with all the changes, I knew where I was. Every exit held a memory.

Sunrise Boulevard, where my family went to the beach. Every summer was greeted by the first sunburn, giving me and my brother and sister a back full of blisters the way crocuses announce the spring.

Oakland Park Boulevard, with the Wellman Building that showcased the largest selection of prostitutes in the state from its restaurant on the seventeenth floor. The two-story sex paraphernalia shop on the same block is a much later addition.

Commercial Boulevard, with the Denny's that had been there for more than forty years. It had first been a Mother Butler's that had more choices of pie than Howard Johnson had flavors of ice cream. I ordered the cherry pie there with a molesting scumbag just before I nailed him.

Also at that exit was St. Luke's Hospital, where my mother had spent eighteen hours in excruciating labor giving birth to me. There had been blood everywhere. Once Mom suspected I knew where babies came from, she would recount the story every year on my birthday, during the cake, as part of the celebration. By the time I turned eighteen I sort of looked forward to hearing the story.

St. Luke's was where Dad was now. That's where I was headed.

And if I kept going north this way I'd finally get to Raiford Penitentiary, where Marcus Creighton was one of four hundred men on death row awaiting execution, many for more than twenty years. The system wants to be real careful that they don't get it wrong.

Tourists see Disney World, Epcot, the Miami Dolphins football team, and Key West, but this is my Florida, the part where men kill their families.

Here ends the Quinn memories portion of our tour.

As I pulled in to the hospital parking lot, I have to admit, I wasn't all that worried about Dad. Maybe when you don't see a person face-to-face it's hard to picture what they'll look like sick. Instead, I was thinking about the big issues—Marcus Creighton, and whether Laura's instincts were as good as they used to be. Now I'd have to switch gears to the quality of the hospital food and why I didn't call more often.

Mom stood and walked toward me when I got to the door of Dad's private room on the third floor. There was the usual repelling force as of same-pole magnets between us, but I fought it and hugged her anyway. She was a little shorter than I remembered, and felt thinner, too. After the age of ten or so I could never remember her willingly touching any of us. All my memories of her involved cooking, sewing, cleaning, driving, those things that are meant to indicate that parents care when their absence would only indicate neglect.

She turned back into the room and I followed her to where she stood at the foot of the hospital bed. The television mounted on the wall was on loud and when I glanced at it I could tell from Alex Trebek's lapels that it was an old rerun of *Jeopardy!* Then I saw Dad lying with his back slightly raised, an IV attached to one hand and the television remote nestled under the other. Rather than shouting the answers as he usually did, he was listlessly hacking up his lungs.

At the full sight of him, my breath caught in the middle of an intake. Unpleasant little electric jolts ran down the surface of my skin from my sides to my legs. Physiologically, it was the same reaction I'd had the first time I walked in on the aftermath of a multiple homicide with an axe. But I'd never thought before now how perfect was the word "shock."

My father lived in my head as a roosterish sort of fellow, always ready to boost me into the air for a dive into the pool, or to teach me how to break an attacker's collarbone. People freeze in time that way. Now, bald head protruding from a body that didn't raise the sheets as much as one would expect, he not only didn't look like himself, he looked like something not quite human.

I felt bad that during the whole trip over here I'd been thinking about a case rather than him.

Mom ignored the coughing and shouted over the television, "*Look, Fergus. Brigid is here.*"

Note: Dad has excellent hearing. He just pretends to need us to shout when the TV is on. Mom doesn't argue with this.

Spent from the coughing, he hardly opened his eyes as he turned his head in my direction. I couldn't even be sure he recognized me. "Hi ya, Toots," he rasped generically, still trying to play the tough guy. Dad had retired from the Fort Lauderdale Police Department about thirty years before, but never stopped thinking of himself as a cop. We were all cops, of one kind or another. Except Mom.

Dad always let me get away with stuff that Mom couldn't get away with. So once I got my lungs going again I moved to the side of the bed, took the remote out of his hand, and pressed the mute button because I don't play that game. After that I didn't know what to do.

"Have you seen Todd?" Mom asked. Which was to say, Todd hadn't been to visit. Mom never said what she meant. It all had to be translated by the listener.

"Not yet. I just arrived and came straight here from the airport," I said. "How are you feeling, Dad? Mom said you just had bronchitis. Next thing, here you are with pneumonia."

In response he wrapped his arms around himself, holding his torso as tightly as he could, and had another coughing jag.

"That sounds terrible," I said to Mom. "What does the doctor say about this?"

"He's on an antibiotic," Mom said, her eyes darting around the room, as if expecting to find there what she should be doing.

I started to get up to get him a glass of water, but he gasped for air, coughed again, got it up this time, swallowed. I got him a glass of water anyway, and he took a good belt, swishing it before swallowing again. Recovered, he seemed to summon more of his old self for my sake. "Don't like water." He took a breath and wheezed his old W. C. Fields line, "Fish fuck in it."

Out of the corner of my eye I saw Mom flinch like she was counting the days he'd spend in purgatory for uttering that word. Dad started to hand me the glass, but lifting was hard and the glass settled on its own by his side and started to tip. I took it from him. "Could use bourbon," he said, and turned his head to wipe the side of his face on the pillow. I realized where I got my own bravado from.

I glanced at Mom to see if she had any reaction to that one. Having recovered from the F-bomb, her face was again as bland as I'd always known it to be, and when she spoke she was participating in a different conversation.

"Todd doesn't come to visit us much. He's busy," Mom said in more of her Mom Code. What that meant was *We're not as important as whatever else he's doing.*

" 'Scuse me a sec," I said. I went out into the hall and called Laura Coleman to cancel. But she wasn't answering. I left a message for her to call me, and then went to the nurses' station to find out what the hell was happening with my father. Finding no one there, I came back into the room.

Not wanting to be put in the same too-busy category as my brother, I didn't mention the Creighton case, or that I was going to meet Laura Coleman when I left the hospital unless she called back to reschedule. Instead, Mom and I talked over the bed, over Dad, the way people do when patients are very ill. Uselessly, we talked about everything but Dad: Carlo and the weather in Arizona, life at Weeping Willow Retirement Home when Dad wasn't sick, the possible whereabouts of Ariel, my sister, who we never heard from because she was in the CIA. I wondered aloud how we'd ever reach Ariel if *something happened.* Mom didn't know.

A nurse came in, checked the fluids, took Dad's temperature. I looked at the board on the wall where the names of the health care providers were listed. "Dettie?" I said.

"Short for Bernadette," she said, and smiled warmly enough. I introduced myself and shook her hand. Asked for details to put her on notice that someone had Mr. Quinn's back. With a glance at Mom, Dettie responded with what she knew, elevated temperature, chest x-ray showing bacterial pneumonia, nothing else. I managed to drag out of her that Dad was stable. She left, and I tried to seize on the comfort that she was acting like business as usual, wasn't calling code blue. Wasn't mentioning hospice.

To try to rouse Dad a bit, I did ask if he remembered anything about Marcus Creighton and the murder of his family. Usually keen to talk any kind of crime, Dad failed to be roused this time, only said he couldn't remember it. This lack of interest in death, more than anything, told me how sick he really was.

"Have you eaten lately?" I asked Mom, thinking I'd take her somewhere, bring her something. In our family food is the answer to so many questions.

"Yes" was all she said.

Dad felt for the volume button on his remote and pressed it with no effect because the mute was still on. Pressing and pressing, he said, "Dinner was supposed to be here at four. The service is bad."

Him speaking in complete sentences was a small thing, but I felt a sense of hope. I stood, feeling antsy and wanting to do something useful, anything. "Should I go hustle up someone for you, Dad?"

"He ate," Mom said, and pointed at a tray on a sliding table against the wall on the other side of the room. I walked over and picked up the reddish brown lid, revealing some sort of chop suey thing, a plastic cup of fruit cocktail, and too much of it left over.

"Are you staying at our place?" Mom asked.

I tried not to sound like a guilty child. "Mom, all you've got is the couch, and the one time I slept on it I couldn't move the next day because of my back. I got a room close. I'm, I'm really tired from the trip over, so I'm going to go check in now. But did you drive over? Do you need a ride home?"

"I have the car. I'll be leaving in a while. Are you coming back?" Mom asked, struggling to keep the question light, the *I don't care if you come back* tone at just the right pitch.

I leaned over the bed and over her chair so she wouldn't have to stand up, and kissed both of them on the side of the face as I had been taught to do. My own pitch off a bit, with more of a bite in my own tone than I intended, I said, "Of course I'll be back. That's why I'm here. I'll see you tomorrow."

Four

I took the newer image of Dad with me over to the Howard Johnson's on the beach in Deerfield. How pitiful he was, how weak, how in and out of himself. Todd didn't care. I wasn't even sure Mom did. Or if she did, how she could handle the health care maze.

Did I care? Somebody needed to care. It was the right thing to do, coming here. I might not have felt like the best daughter at that point, but at least I felt righteous. I reminded myself to find out who his doctor was and get in touch first thing in the morning in case some Quinn attitude was necessary.

I had regretted agreeing to meet Laura Coleman, and I felt torn. But there she was, punctual as ever, standing on the sidewalk in front of the hotel waiting for me. In her left hand she held the case that contained my weapon of choice, the snub-nosed FBI revolver, that I had over-nighted to her address. Her right hand almost made a fist. Her stance looked like she was preparing to get punched in the gut with a log. She hadn't changed a bit, other than appearing more tense, more level nine than her usual level six.

I gave her a hug instead of shaking hands and then, stepping back to take a better look at her, said, "It's good to see you. You look healthy. But tense."

She had hugged me back, but her first words were, "I just got a call from Will Hench. The defense attorney? He wanted to make sure I was coming into the office first thing tomorrow. He sounded like he was trying not to be upset but didn't say why, like he didn't want me to lose sleep. So I'm a little stressed."

"What you heard in the attorney's voice might not even have to do with this case," I said.

I got my roller bag out of the trunk and balanced on it the case she handed to me. As always, the closer I got to my loaded weapon, the better I felt.

She walked in with me to register. While the reception clerk took my credit card and handed me a plastic key card for a room on the second floor, I examined Laura in my peripheral vision. She had cut her hair shorter than I remembered it. Now the tight curls clung to her skull, making her head look like a Persian lamb coat my mother used to have. She had gotten buff, too. Even her forearms were defined.

"You been working out?" I asked.

"Nothing better to do while I was taking time off."

When we turned away from the counter and walked to the elevator I could feel rather than see her limp, not pronounced, but there. The result of her wounds. But even with the limp she walked like someone you better not mess with, her shoulders purposeful, committed to forward movement even if the route was over your corpse. I didn't remember her quite this way.

"How long are you here?" Laura asked as we walked.

"About a week. I hope."

"Did you read what I sent you?"

Half my mind was still at the hospital, and I was a bit testy. "I'm fine, thanks for asking."

"So what did you think?"

"I think you're not listening."

Laura stopped walking and stared at me, realizing finally we were on different pages and neither of us the kind who turned them easily.

In a second I remembered how much and how little I knew Laura's story. Daughter of Mormons who had uncustomarily stopped at two children. Happy childhood, probably. Ballet lessons and tutus. Learning how to be a homemaker. Groomed to be a good wife. So she goes into the FBI instead. What was it with that? Who was she really? Did she know?

She touched her fingertips to her upper lip as if stopping the words. She said, "I'm sorry. I've got that call from Will on my mind." She forced herself off her own track and onto mine. "How is your father?"

"I understand, believe me," I said. "Tell you what, how about you let me put my bag in my room first. Get a little something to unwind. Seeing Dad in the hospital was weird; he's always been so robust."

"I'm sorry," she said again, and I knew she meant it.

Laura left me at the elevator. I got to my room and dropped my bag, knowing enough not to push my advantage by stopping to unpack it but at least taking the time for a quick pit stop and washup after the flight. I unlocked the case, drew out my pistol, and loaded it with some rounds that I'd sent in my checked baggage. I put the gun in my sizable tote bag, thick canvas with a plastic bottom so you couldn't see it sag too much where the gun rested. Slung the tote over my shoulder. Better and better.

When I came back down Laura was waiting at the elevator, leaning against a chrome and glass table with a monstrous turquoise ceramic vase holding those foofy things that aren't found in nature.

"I haven't taken a look at the ocean in a while," I said. "Care to walk out onto the pier?"

We stopped at the outside bar, where music blasted louder than I ever remembered. We got our drinks in plastic cups, me a Scotch over ice and her a lemonade.

"I thought you were a vodka drinker," she said.

"You're not an alcoholic if you like variety," I said.

"All due respect," she said, "bullshit."

The entrance to the pier was just fifty feet or so north of the hotel. We took our drinks there, and I paid the three-dollar fee to a guy at a counter behind which hung light fishing tackle in case you forgot anything. We went through the turnstile and walked over the rough wooden boardwalk on pilings that had miraculously survived every hurricane for as long as I'd been around. The pier extended straight over the water a good football-field in length. Benches as rough as the pier itself were

28

placed in the center at equal distances, and a two-slatted railing ran on both sides, splattered with pelican poop and fish guts. Dingy pelicans with beaks down to their bellies waiting around for handouts completed the scene.

Laura pointed to one of the benches now and then as a good place to sit, but I made us walk all the way to the end and stopped to smell and feel the salty onshore breeze, more noticeable here than when I first arrived. I put my tote bag safely between my feet and leaned on the rough wood armrest grooved by tropical storms and bugs. I looked down at the incoming tide that nibbled at the barnacle-covered pilings. The sun was setting at our backs, and the breeze finally felt a little cooler, a little dryer.

I thought about how Dad used to bring the three of us to this spot to fish. No matter how grouchy he was at home, he always seemed relaxed and jovial out here, and it didn't even matter whether we caught anything. Just letting him teach us how to cut the mullet and double-punch it on the hook so the fish couldn't take it easily was a fine thing. He didn't get angry if we did it wrong. In later life I wondered if it was getting away from Mom that made him feel better.

Then I pointed to her ankles. "Is there much residual pain?" I asked.

"Some," she said. "Come on, I thought we were here to talk about the case."

"It's only been a year, Laura. Someone your age thinks a year is a long time, but it's not."

"You're doing that condescending thing," she said, but not like she wanted to pick a fight or anything. It was just a friendly observation like *Oh, you changed your hair.* Maybe she really was okay.

I said, "All right. On point. How'd you get involved with all this?"

"Will told me he got a letter from Creighton, who found out online he does pro bono work. At first I thought the way you do. But do you know Tracy Mack?"

"Old Dick Tracy?" Some nicknames make more sense than others. "The fingerprint examiner. I saw him mentioned in the trial transcript."

"Is that what they called him? Well, he had the leading piece of physical evidence in Marcus's case, and he was indicted a month ago on multiple charges of erroneous, and likely fraudulent, findings."

"Shit. We always knew he was a little confused about his role in the criminal justice process. He fancied himself as a crime fighter more than a scientist. How many cases are they looking at?"

"Thousands."

"Good God."

"Yeah. The Florida Innocence Project has been flooded with letters from inmates Mack put away. Creighton sent them a letter, too, but they didn't answer, they're so overwhelmed. Will wants to get ahead of them, at least get a stay of execution so we can recheck the evidence, and follow up on things that weren't used in the trial."

"How were prints damning evidence if the crime scene was in his own home?"

"One print. On the electrical plug on the hair dryer. You know those rectangular flat plugs about one and a half by two inches? But Marcus said he never touched his wife's hair dryer. Ever."

"Is the man stupid? It would have been smarter to testify that he used it all the time so it didn't prove anything. Or at least that he didn't remember."

"It wasn't actual testimony; it was more like a blurt the night of the crime. The detective asked if he'd touched the hair dryer, and he blurted that he never had used it, ever. After his arrest he was questioned about it and he stuck by that. Then when Mack said his print was found on it he tried to backtrack, but it didn't sound good."

"Where was his defense in all this?"

"He kept telling Marcus there wasn't enough evidence to convict him. The thing is, Will had shown the print as it was originally developed to an independent examiner, Frank Puccio, before he even agreed to take the case. Puccio said there aren't enough matching points that you could prove the print is Creighton's. Now that Mack has been indicted, they'll probably let the guys with lesser convictions sit in jail. Most of them will just run out the clock and get released before the prints are even retested. But Marcus should get attention because they're always real cautious with capital cases. Too high profile."

"They don't want to look bad, killing innocent people," I agreed.

"Right. We get all our evidence together on Marcus and file an appeal for a retrial. And no, you don't have to tell me I'm jumping the gun on that."

That wasn't what I was jumping to at all. Marcus, I thought. She kept saying that, not Mr. Creighton, or Creighton, but Marcus.

"What do you think of him?" I asked, taking a casual sip of my drink and staring at the horizon to avoid her thinking what I was thinking.

"Think of him?" she asked.

I looked out of the corner of my eye and saw her brush a hand over a copper-colored birthmark on her temple. I knew her well enough to know this was a tell when she was hiding something. I wondered if she was hiding this thing from me or herself.

"Yes, think of him," I said, and nudged, "What's your read?"

I could see her picking through possible responses in her head before choosing "He presents very well."

I snarfed lightly. "You spend two years at Quantico and 'presents very well' is the extent of your profiling?"

Laura held up one index finger with which to indicate I should shut up. "I haven't spent all that much time with him. Been focusing on the evidence." She changed the subject. "Will is doing the paperwork. What I'm trying to do is get the hair dryer so our independent guy can redevelop the latent and examine the rest of the appliance. Now that Mack has opened the door for us, maybe we can find another print that would exclude Creighton altogether. Best case, point to the real killer."

"Where's the evidence?"

"There's where you could help me. It's being held at the Indian River County station. They're stonewalling."

"How?"

"They said they lost it. Then they said they destroyed it. Then they said they'll look for it. Then the appellate judge said it probably wouldn't prove anything."

"Sounds like the legal shell game. You want to get what you need but play along so the judge won't just say no dice. What you say, sounds like they didn't destroy the evidence after the trial." I considered her. "You really think it's worth it, huh? You're hot for this."

Laura stared up at the sky a moment before answering. I think my nagging was wearing her out. "Brigid. Here's what it is. Cold cases, you solve them and the victim's still dead. Even economic crime, you seldom recover the money. But exonerations. Hey. You save a life."

"But," I said again. I had remembered Lancer's summation of the state's case, this mistress named Shayna Murry who denied he was with her while his family was getting murdered. "You've still got the fact that his mistress blew his alibi."

Laura threw the remaining ice from her drink into the water, put the flimsy plastic cup on the wooden railing, and telescoped it with the flat of her hand. "Did I say we had other evidence besides the fingerprint? Oh, we've got Murry taken care of, too."

Five

"The fingerprint is only half of what we're basing the appeal on," Laura said, opening her third little package of oyster crackers, leaving the crumbs and plastic wrappers strewn over her paper place mat with one of those ubiquitous maps of Florida on it, alligators and the Magic Kingdom out of proportion relative to the phallic outline of the state.

Laura had agreed to tell me the rest at the Tale of a Tuna across from the hotel. We both ordered seared tuna and brown rice. I ordered a glass of chardonnay, tasted it, and added some ice cubes from my water glass. Laura frowned. "You put ice in your wine?"

"Only when it tastes like this." I was half paying attention to what she was saying and half doing a little profiling of my own now that we were face-to-face. What I could see in the light over the table was that she had dark rings under her eyes, as if she hadn't been sleeping. That coupled with the strain in her voice and the new lines in her forehead told me she had that disagreeable combination of anxiety and fatigue, strung taut and worn out at the same time, and that she was putting a hell of a lot of energy into not showing either. I wouldn't have thought she could be more intense than the last time I had worked with her, but there it was. Like she had something more personal at stake. For the time being I didn't go there. "Okay, let me catch up with you. Give me the skinny on Creighton's story the way he tells it."

She reconstructed the story as follows:

Marcus Creighton, forty-two years old in 1999, had a fine home in Vero Beach, Florida, a couple of hours up the coast, nestled between the ocean and the Indian River, which took over for the Intracoastal Waterway for that stretch.

Marcus had three fine children, ages eight to fourteen, of whom he was said to be fond, and a wife he didn't care for as much. He said they never argued. They never did much of anything, and an argument now and then might have lessened the boredom.

Their home was maybe a bit too fine. On prime coastal property, in an upscale area, the residents of which made self-referential jokes about being "Very Very Vero." What made it Very Very? Dog breeds like Petit Basset Griffon Vendéen and Coton de Tulear. In strollers.

Up the road a bit, in a less upscale neighborhood in a town called Sebastian, Marcus kept a twentysomething mistress who spent her time making art from trash, what she called "assemblage." Maybe Shayna Murry had loved him at some point, or at least he thought so.

It got a lot worse. Besides a marriage that had also soured, and a house that he couldn't afford, and losing his shirt in the tech-stock market, Marcus had a wine import business that was about to go bankrupt due to the competition from the big chain stores. Under pressure, he said he had been to visit a short-term lender in Miami, to plead for more time on the quarter mil he had borrowed. He said he had lied at first about why he went to Miami, because he thought the money problems might make him look bad. He was right; they made him look very bad.

He had taken out a life insurance policy on his wife less than a year before.

"Did he give you a reason for that?" I asked.

"He said she was a serious alcoholic and had had a couple of bad accidents. He thought it was a responsible thing to do."

The Fateful Night According to Creighton: That afternoon Marcus lucks into an earlier flight from Miami to Melbourne, the closest airport to Vero Beach, about thirty minutes north of his house. He isn't expected home for a while, so he stops to visit Shayna for a little comfort. They spend several hours together in her house-slash-studio, and he doesn't pull up to his more palatial residence until close to one thirty in the morning. Wearily, he kicks off his business shoes and shrugs his black suit jacket onto the couch in the living room and heads to the master area of the house, which, he is surprised to notice, has lights on. Kathleen, his wife, usually does not wait up for him.

When he sees the bed empty, neatly made, he goes into the bathroom and finds her in the Jacuzzi tub. He turns off the bubbler and sees that her hair dryer, while plugged into the outlet by the nearby sink, is resting on the bottom of the tub.

"Wait," I said. "Is her hair wet?"

"Pretty dry. It was humid out, but the house is air-conditioned," Laura said.

"Hair dryer submerged."

"I'm already ahead of you on that one. The first examiner, I mean Tracy Mack, said it would have been a waste of time to look for prints on the submerged part of the dryer, and the defense never questioned that. Frank Puccio says it's possible, especially given advanced techniques. Okay. So, Marcus calls nine-one-one. At first when the paramedics arrive, he's just upset. But then he calls this community center where he thought his kids were spending the night, something called a lock-in, and is told they never showed up. That's when he goes hysterical, at least apparently, and the cops get called. They do an Amber Alert to find the kids.

"When he's questioned he panics. That's when he confesses he was at his mistress's house until well after his wife's 'accident.' But the mistress blows his alibi when she says he wasn't there at all that night."

"That's what I'd call being blindsided. Do you trust the mistress?"

"I never trust a mistress. I know, I was one once, remember?"

I did remember, and how it always reminded me of all I didn't know about this upstanding young woman. I asked, "Motivation for lying?"

"I've gone over the textbook possibilities: Bribe. Threat. Revenge. Nothing yet. And I've tried repeatedly, but I can't get her to talk. But that doesn't matter, because I think we've got her on perjury."

"How so?"

"During her testimony she said Creighton called her from his cell phone that night and said, quote, 'If anyone asks where I was, tell them I was with you.' I kept going over the transcripts, and it finally hit me. Called. The defense didn't use cell phone evidence."

"That's typical. No one considered the potential evidence of cell phones in the nineties. I was working an abduction case in '97 and watched a cop use the victim's cell phone to call his office. Sometimes it's still hard to get it accepted."

"That's right. But Marcus says that he didn't call Shayna that night. She already knew he was coming over."

"His word against hers."

"Agreed. But what he did do is try to call his house *from* Shayna's. On his cell phone. So if we can find the records that match to a cell tower near her, we can show what time he was at her house and prove she was lying under oath."

"What are the chances after all this time?"

"They're good. I did some homework and found out the same company still owns his service. They're looking right now."

"Who was his attorney? Didn't he raise objections at any point?"

"Ronald Croft. Public defender."

Public defender: not incompetent, just overworked and underpaid. "Why didn't Creighton get decent counsel?"

"He says he wasn't thinking clearly. All he was thinking about was where his children were and why no one was looking for them."

Laura stared at the remains of her fish, like it was all the fish's fault, or like the fish had the answers.

I thought of Carlo, how everywhere I turned there seemed to be these people who spoke to me like Jiminy Cricket. Sometimes it works, but sometimes it doesn't. Rather than go all Old Wise Woman on her, it made so much more sense to convince Laura of Creighton's guilt, and allow her to move on.

"What about contract murder?" I asked. "Creighton hires someone to do the deed for him, takes a convenient trip to Miami for part of his alibi. Then when he comes back he heartlessly screws his mistress while his family is being killed."

"I already thought about that," Laura said, attention back and cylinders firing.

I grinned. The woman had a fine mind to go with that passion. "I just bet you did."

"Will and I talked out every angle over and over before he took the case. The medical examiner put the time of death, given the temperature of the water and how it affected the body, no sooner than midnight. If you had everything planned so carefully, would you have arrived within an hour and a half of the murders?"

"Are you sure he's an intelligent man?"

"That's a good question. I can't tell you what he was like when he went in. Can you imagine what it's like to spend fifteen years as a condemned man?"

I'd seen them and I remembered. After nine years Billy Wallace had no teeth from grinding them in his sleep. After just two years John Hughes tried to commit suicide by falling off his bed onto his head. "Yes, I can imagine," I said. "They go nuts. I think there's an official term for it."

"Well, Marcus Creighton didn't. The way he tells it, some literacy volunteer gave him a copy of a book about King Arthur called *The Once and Future King* shortly after he was put in his cell. He was struck by something Merlin said: 'The best thing for being sad is to learn something.' So Marcus, when he wasn't working on his appeals, he set about learning things. He learned chess, playing the game in his head. He read the classics. Now he's working his way through the modern literary canon. He says it keeps him relatively sane. You wanted a profile. I don't think he's merely highly intelligent. I think he's heroic."

Ignoring the fact that her eyes were glistening as she finished, and the contour of her shoulders had softened, I said, "All right, then. Except for thinking with his dick, I think any normal man of good intelligence would have arranged to miss his flight in Miami, stay the night there, and get home the next day. It's a much neater alibi than the mistress. I wouldn't have trusted the mistress for an alibi. It would just make me look bad."

"Exactly." Laura looked like she was about to say *Gentlemen of the jury, I rest my case*. "Then, if you could plan a murder so carefully, so cold-bloodedly, would you drop the ball when it came time for your defense? And on top of *that*, if it was a contract killing, why would he have not said that when he saw his case going south? Gone state's evidence on the actual murderer? Made a deal for a lighter sentence? So many questions it makes my head spin. Except for the lame alibi, the prosecution's case was very weak, and it's driving me crazy that they rushed to conviction."

Laura had said very much the same thing when someone had confessed to a crime she was certain he hadn't committed, and there was much less certainty with that case than there was with this one. What to do? Support her wholeheartedly, distract her, or keep rubbing her face in what she already knew, the capriciousness of the system that could just as easily lead to Marcus Creighton's death?

I said, "If you can stall the death warrant. If you can confirm the phone records. If you can reassess the fingerprints. If you can get a retrial based on perjury and flawed forensics. If Marcus Creighton is innocent."

Under the weight of all the ifs, she looked a little more defeated, but she was nothing if not a fighter and was suddenly back for another round. "We can try. But listen, if none of that works for you, there's also one more thing I haven't mentioned. Have you heard about the progress with touch DNA?"

"I know defense is in love with it these days, because there are so many cases where you don't have body fluids to test. You talking about where he was said to touch the hair dryer?"

Laura gave a cautious nod.

"You really think those skin cells will be viable after so many years?"

"Again, the odds are hard to call, but some time ago they developed touch DNA found on JonBenet Ramsey's pajamas twelve years after her murder. They don't know whose it is, but they know it was no one in her family. The evidence finally cleared them. Technology has gotten better since then. So yeah."

"I'd forgotten about that. Must have been around the time I had some problems of my own."

"If Marcus is telling the truth about his not touching that hairdryer, and if we can capture some DNA from it . . ."

Two more ifs, I thought. But I couldn't deny she had a point.

Six

Laura urged me to come to Hench's office in the morning, and I really wanted to see if he had anything new to say about the case, but I waffled, saying I'd have to see how Dad was and let her know first thing. I didn't have positive feelings about Dad's condition, but you never know. I forced one of my sleeping pills on Laura with the command to get some rest for God's sake, then went back to my room, where I laid out the same pair of travel slacks I'd worn on the plane and a fresh cotton blouse. Via FaceTime I found out that Carlo was doing well without me, and wasn't going to eat the chili I left in the fridge for him. Somebody told me that leaving food for your husband was treating him like a child, and maybe that's so, but like I said, I'm still learning how to do this marriage business.

"I thought you liked my chili," I said.

"I'll have it tomorrow."

"So what did you eat?"

"Do you really care what I ate?"

"No. I just like the sound of your voice and want you to keep talking."

"You talk. What's happening over there?"

I told him about Dad first, then said, "Remember how you said Laura must have a good reason for taking on this case? Well, what if the reason is that she's fallen in love with a condemned man?"

Carlo briefly pressed his lips together and shut his eyes, blocking out that possibility. When he opened them again he said, "That would be very bad."

When we disconnected I called my brother, Todd.

"I'm in town," I said.

"Cool," Todd said. Pause, then, "Listen, about that thing with Gemma-Kate."

That was as close to an apology as I was ever going to get, for the phone conversation where he called me the slang term for part of the female anatomy. Not even in our family is that what you'd call a term of endearment. I said, "There's no problem with that thing. We were both—"

After the events of a few months before, there had been plenty of more reasonable conversations about Todd's daughter, who had come to stay with us, and I'm sure Todd talked about it with Mom and Dad, so it wasn't totally creepy that we didn't discuss it now. We were both nuts at the time, but now I felt a little regret at the way Gemma-Kate was pushed into the shadow. Another story, another time.

"That's right" was all Todd would say. Rather than say *Oh, we must get together* he asked, "How long will you be here?"

"I'm not sure. Maybe a week."

"Have you seen the folks?"

"I stopped there first. Dad looks really sick. You need to go see him. Mom is asking."

"I will."

"Todd, what do we do if he dies?"

"Bury him, probably," Todd said.

I felt a little click in my heart. "That's not funny, even for a Quinn."

"Not meant to be. You know I hate the old bastard."

"We're going to have to talk about this at some point, and don't think you'll be able to just shove the surviving parent at your big sister."

"Isn't that why you're here?" he asked.

"Mostly." I explained the other reason for my presence. He got more engaged in the conversation then, other people's murders being so much easier to talk about than familial responsibility. He was aware of the Creighton case, though he hadn't worked it. He knew the guy up in Vero Beach who did.

"Solid?" I asked.

"Solid." Todd cleared a minor frog from his throat. "Well, not directly, a friend of mine knows him."

So when did Quinns start having friends? The throat frog told me that the friend was female, and likely more than a friend. I was curious. "When I get back from seeing Creighton's attorney and Dad, do you want to have lunch or something? With your friend? Once I get more information I might have some questions."

Being needed was even one step better than murder shop talk. He quickly agreed.

I turned on my iPad to read a little more of the court transcripts so I wouldn't look too ignorant the next day if I went to see William Hench. Tracy Mack would be a waste of bullshit. I wanted to see what Shayna Murry, the other damning piece of testimony, had to say.

TESTIMONY OF SHAYNA MURRY

Shayna Murry, having been duly sworn, was examined and testified as follows:

By Attorney Lancer:

Q: Ms. Murry, would you please tell the court why you're giving testimony today?

A: I was Mr. Creighton's mistress.

Q: Would you please point to the person in the courtroom to whom you're referring?

A: (Points to Marcus Creighton.)

Q: Thank you. How did you meet?

A: The Creightons were decorating a house in Vero Beach, and happened to see my studio up the road in Sebastian.

Q: Did they buy anything?

A: No. Not that day. But Marcus, Mr. Creighton, stopped by a week later and said he wanted to commission a gift for his wife's birthday. Nothing I had in the studio, but something different, and would I work with him on it.

Q: Please tell the court about your collaboration with Mr. Creighton.

A: At first he came by the studio. Then he started taking me out for lunch, wonderful lunches up in Melbourne in restaurants that had private rooms and the waiter knew his name and discussed the wine with him. I grew up dirt poor and he made me feel like Cinderella. He was so kind and handsome, older than me, but in a Sean Connery kind of way. It wasn't sleazy, and he was no more of a flirt than any other guy. At first we talked about art. Then he started asking me personal questions about my life. What did I do for fun? And then, I must have a boyfriend, what was my boyfriend like, was he an artist, too? After a while we stopped pretending to talk about art.

Q: Please be more specific.

A: I became his lover.

Q: Thank you. How long did your affair go on?

A: About a year. But the pattern, having lunch and then going back to my place for sex, it began to feel like a dead end. I only saw him once a week and it wasn't enough. Once I told him I wanted to wake up beside him, and he got this look on his face like someone had stabbed him. I should have been smart enough to stop it then. What happened after was as much my fault as his.

Q: Would you please describe the last time you saw Marcus Creighton before today?

A: Marcus showed up around two in the morning and pounded on my door. It was raining, and he was soaked. I let him in and gave him a towel to dry off. After he wiped his face I could see the water wasn't just from the rain. He was crying.

Q: Then what happened?

A: I asked him what was wrong. He . . . he said he loved me. He had never said that word before. He went down on his knees. Seeing him cry, and on his knees, he was always so strong.

Q: What did you answer?

A: (no response)

Q: Please, Ms. Murry, you're doing fine and you're almost finished. What did you answer?

A: I told him I . . . loved him, but he was married. I said we should never have started. I started to cry, too.

Q: How did he react?

A: Then he said, I can get a divorce and we can start again like everything was new. And I said, Marcus, you've got three kids. And he said, I can still keep a relationship with them, you'll like them. And I said, they'll hate me. I started out as Cinderella and I'd end up like the wicked stepmother.

Q: And what did he say? The words as precisely as you can recall them, please.

A: He said . . . oh God. I thought I could do this part. I'm not sure I can.

Q: That's all right, Ms. Murry. You take all the time you need.

A: He said, he said, I don't care about anything but you. I'll do whatever it takes to have you. He got up off his knees and patted my arm like I was one of his children needing reassurance. Then he repeated those words. Then he left.

The Court: Ms. Murry.

Murry: I'm sorry. (unintelligible)

The Court: Ms. Murry, would you please repeat for the record?

Murry: I can't get those words out of my head.

By Attorney Lancer:

Q: One more question, Ms. Murry. Would you please tell the court on what date you had this meeting with Mr. Creighton?

A: It was April twenty-third.

Q: Please let the record show that this meeting was seven days before the murder of the Creighton family. Ms. Murry, was there any other contact with Mr. Creighton within the seven days after your meeting?

A: (crying) One. He called me the night of the murders and said, No matter what you hear, tell them I was with you.

If the Marcus Creighton that Murry described was really who he was, I didn't like him much. This transcript made me more concerned about Laura falling for another unobtainable jerk. Yet there it was, Creighton's Get Out of Jail Free card. If they found the phone records, and the records showed he didn't call her at all, but instead called his home number *from* her place, she was lying. I started to have some what-if thoughts that were very unappealing.

Seven

Walking down the hall to Dad's room the next morning, I passed a sign that cautioned me to be quiet because rest was healing. Unfortunately that wasn't the case with Dad. I could hear voices coming from his room when I was still about three doors away. When I got there, the nurse was yell-talking to him the way people often do with the elderly. He was yelling back as well as he could, given the condition of his lungs. Apparently he was much more alert than the night before, and I had hope.

"Mr. Quinn, all you have to do is hold this in front of your face, put your mouth on the stem, and blow as hard as you can."

"You blow it," he said. "I want my breakfast."

"Fergus, stop acting like a baby and do what the nurse tells you to do," Mom said. She was standing next to the bed, leaning over him like she was about to take the blower from him and do it herself. I wondered what time she had arrived. Had she spent the night there?

Did I really grow up with this? "Hi, ya'll," I said.

The women turned to me without having time to drop the same glares they had used on Dad. He looked relieved to see me. And spent from the yelling. "Brigid. Tell these two I don't need to blow in a god-damn tube."

"You sound terrible. Blow in the goddamn tube, Dad."

He wheezed. "Make me."

What a child would say. There was something about this two-year-old in an eighty-three-year-old body that set me off, Quinn-style. I took the device from the nurse and shoved it at my father. He grabbed it out of my hand and swung it against the opposite wall, missing Mom's face by about six inches. She reared back with the long practice of avoiding projectiles.

Things stopped. I had one of those flashbulb memories, other swings, other ducks, loud fights while Ariel and I played Drug Bust Barbie and Todd whimpered in his playpen.

Then another flash of my last routine mammogram and how the technicians had started asking routinely: Is anyone at home hurting you?

Did they ever ask Mom this? What did she say? Of course not, she would say, because he never actually connected, he only threw things. When I was growing up, this wasn't considered abusive. Very little that went on with married people was considered abusive.

Time started up again, and I happened to connect with the nurse's eyes. She frowned. Times had changed. I felt ashamed of my family.

As if she noticed my shame, which made it worse, the nurse said, "Sometimes this happens with what he's on. How about you both go get a snack or something." She lowered her voice as if Dad couldn't hear. "It may be better if there's no audience."

Mom set her mouth in that way she could and followed me out into the hall. I leaned against the wall, but she stood rigidly at attention. She was one of those elderly women who never sagged in any way.

"Did you have a nice evening with your friends?" she asked. The woman could have written *Passive Aggression for Dummies*.

After translating her question, I ignored it, as I did most often. "How is he doing today?"

"The doctor said he's got about a quarter use of his lungs," she said. "Pneumonia on top of emphysema on top of all those years of smoking. It's a wonder he still has that much fight left in him."

I thought about him throwing the breathing thing across the room. All the throwing I had seen. I asked, "Does he still throw things?"

I wouldn't have thought it possible, but she stood straighter. "Throw?"

"Like the time, I guess I was about eleven, the Thanksgiving turkey burned and he hurled that metal chair at the wall so hard the legs stuck in the wallboard."

"I don't remember that."

I doubted that was true. "Honestly, sometimes he acts like a cartoon character."

"Mmm." The way her head was turned I could tell she was only half paying attention, one of her ears fixed on the open door behind us, waiting for the shriek of the nurse. I wanted to distract her.

Anybody else grow up comparing people to Warner Brothers cartoon characters?

"Yosemite Sam, or maybe the Tazmanian Devil. We used to be scared of him even though he never did anything to us, just blustered. You were never scared of him, though. Like in the room just now."

"I learned how to stay out of his way," she said, looking toward the room so it seemed she was partly talking to herself.

It occurred to me that I couldn't remember the last time I was alone with my mother, talking. There were always other people in the room. Dad was always there. That and the hospital setting made me say things I never had before. I had visited many women in a setting like this, trying to get them to speak to me through opiates and split lips. The way Mom put things made habit kick in.

I asked, "How long did it take you to learn?"

Mom looked down the hall again, and I couldn't tell if she was thinking of my question or just ignoring me. So I didn't ask the other questions, and maybe never would.

The nurse came out of Dad's room. She looked fatigued. "You can go back in now. If you want."

Eight

I talked to the respiratory therapist and got the usual runaround. Primary care physician? Yes, but not the one looking after Dad now. A specialist? A pulmonologist, maybe? Infectious disease? On call, she said, but who I really wanted was the hospitalist.

What the hell is a hospitalist?

I finally got what I was assured was the right information, and gave my name and number to the person at the nurses' station, explaining I was the one he or she should talk to. I made sure my parents weren't in fighting mode and told Mom I'd be back in just a little bit. I made her write down my cell phone number in case she needed me, and asked for hers. She said she didn't have one, but Dad had a phone in his room.

After calling Laura to tell her I was definitely available, I picked her up. She lived in a condo, a two-story boxy thing in west Pompano Beach, close to I-95 so she could get to work easily. I had volunteered to drive to put the miles on the rental but also because I wanted to see where she lived.

She was brushing her teeth with one hand, gesturing me to come in with the other so she could go finish up. When I asked her if she had figured out what was up with Will Hench, she shook her head and walked into her bathroom, still brushing.

While I waited I checked out her living room, which included an elliptical trainer, a set of free weights, and a ten-pound medicine ball.

Like in her house in Tucson, the other furnishings were spare to the point of nonexistence. Most of it was too shabby for her to have bought new. It looked like a college kid's apartment. The only thing I recognized was her desk, a big heavy pale oak thing. She must have been particularly fond of her desk, because she brought that with her. I remembered working at that desk when I used her house in Tucson to hide out in. The surface was bare except for a Charles Dickens novel. I just knew if I opened the top right drawer I would find her pens and pencils lying side by side in order of their length, and her list of twenty or so unique random numeric passwords taped under it.

Rigidity is maybe not such a good quality to have when you're dealing with people on death row. Not that I'd say Laura was rigid. Okay, maybe I'm saying that. Just a little.

I opened the next drawer down. Her office supplies in this one included a semiautomatic, a can of pepper spray, a stun gun, several rape whistles, and brass knuckles. Jesus, even I didn't have brass knuckles. I looked over my shoulder to make sure she hadn't seen me snooping, and shut the drawer.

There was something different about the top of the desk, though. An ugly gash in the wood peeked out from the side of the blotter. I lifted the blotter with my index finger and saw that the gash extended across the top of the desk a good ten inches.

"I'm ready," she said behind me, as I let the blotter drop. She picked up the copy of *Our Mutual Friend* and took it with her.

William Hench's office was on the fourth floor of a modest building in immodest Palm Beach. We got to the suite he shared with a couple of other attorneys, and Laura gave our names to the receptionist, who took us straight to his office. He wasn't in it, so I took the opportunity to look out his big clean windows onto Olive Avenue. Then Hench walked in, introduced himself, and showed me a chair in front of his desk. Laura stayed standing behind the other chair with her arms crossed, coiled in preparation for what he might say.

Will was technically a whippersnapper in my view, early forties, which meant young enough to still have the passion that brought him into this field, whether for the money or the justice. Nice enough suit, and what actually looked like a piece of Chihuly art glass on his bookshelf, so the justice must have been profitable enough. He gave me the fake smile. I didn't have to wait long to hear why.

After the accepted offer of a coffee, which he fixed for me himself—it felt more like a delaying tactic than hospitality—he sat down behind his desk and looked at Laura with a bad-news look, the kind where you try to telegraph it without having to actually say the words.

While I was noting this, he was already at the back end of a sentence. ". . . new law the governor signed, the Timely Justice Act. The name puts a positive spin on it, but essentially it's bada boom bada bing, and you're dead, all right? The law sets a deadline for appeals so we don't have enough time to get reversals in cases where egregious mistakes were made. Plus, it gives a maximum of thirty days to execution once the death warrant has been signed." Hench sighed, and apparently knew he couldn't keep the information from us any longer. "Laura, I got the call late yesterday that it's been signed."

"When?" Laura asked, as loudly as a ghost.

"Five days."

Laura's arms quickly unfolded and her hands shot down to the back of the chair so you kind of got the feeling the support of the chair was necessary. I wanted to help her sit down, but I thought if I tried she'd smack me. She managed to say, "I've . . . never . . . heard of—"

Hench raised his hands, palms facing us as if he were surrendering, and said, "I know. I never have either. It feels like someone is expediting his execution just because we're going to leverage the fingerprint examiner's fraud. They're afraid if this works it will start a domino effect with other cases. Man, I don't want to be responsible for Marcus Creighton's death."

"Has he been told?" she asked him.

"I'm sure."

While he had been saying all this, Hench's expression slowly fell in sync with his words until by the end I could see his weariness making the lines already in his face a little deeper, even gravity turning against him.

Laura appeared to recover from the initial shock and was already jumping on her horse and riding off in all directions. "I need to go to him today," she said.

Raiford is a five-hour drive north of Palm Beach and would take the whole day. I thought about Mom and Dad. But for now I focused on Hench instead. "Do you really think you can stop this?" I asked, not voicing my personal opinion.

"How the hell should I know?" he snarled, and then shook his head as if trying to get the useless anger out. "Sorry, but I can tell from your face you're thinking we're idiots. It's par for you people. But that's how it is. It's defense. We try to see justice done. Sometimes we succeed." He glared at me as if he anticipated my response and got to it ahead of me. "Or maybe we *are* all just idiots. But the world has to be made aware that forensics is not infallible. We need to show that some cases are built on forensic mistakes and flawed witness testimony."

Laura had re-coiled her arms and started to pace like we were wasting daylight and her next move would be out the door. It nearly was until Hench stopped her.

"Just wait a second, Laura. We know what the evidence is. We have less time to line it up, and right now we only need enough to make a case for a stay of execution. We can do this." His eyes gleamed with spirit and maybe the excitement of the chase as he slurped his coffee. "And I've got a possible ace. I've got a TV interview scheduled."

"Local station?" Laura asked, turning back into the room and leaning across Hench's desk.

"National. It's a tremendous opportunity," he said to both of us. "Maybe the publicity will give us a little more leverage." He made a brave gesture of giving a one-two punch. "Can't hurt," he said, and to Laura, "But don't let up on what you're doing. Any bit of evidence, an excluding fingerprint, the phone records, will support the stay. Best case is I have something to offer on-air."

"How much time do we have?" Laura asked.

"The TV slot I was offered is day after tomorrow, airing on the six o'clock news, filming in the morning at a local studio. Apparently it's a hot topic because it will be the first execution following the passage of that law. If we can make it public, we can make it political. Our chances are better that they'll back down."

Laura didn't say anything but tucked her thumbs into her blazer pockets, which to someone trained in body language said everything about whether she gave this idea a thumbs-up.

Will said, "They would have been willing to schedule it for tomorrow, but the other person they want to get can't make it until the next day."

"Who's the other person?" Laura asked.

"Alison Samuels."

"Well, isn't that just the most idiotic thing you could do," Laura said, taking her hands out of her pockets and throwing them in the air.

"It's that controversy thing they do now where they're hoping we start to yell at each other," Hench said, more to me than to Laura. "It's the only way they'd agree to the interview."

"Who's Alison Samuels?" I asked.

Will shuffled some papers around on his desk, but tentatively, as if he feared the woman was hiding under the pile and would jump out at him. "I'm on my way up to Tallahassee," he said. "Laura, would you please tell Brigid about Madame Defarge?"

Nine

We'd gotten into the car before I finally murmured something vague about the drive to Raiford and my promise to go back to the hospital.

Laura tried not to look like she was asking for anything as she said, "He's not in Raiford. They built a new prison for the overflow. It's just about forty-five minutes from here, west of Jupiter."

When I didn't say *oh, well, then* immediately, she said with hardly any ice in her tone, "But no problem. Really. Just take me back to Pompano to get my car."

That would have added two hours to her trip, and I got the sense those two hours were precious to her today. I declined and headed north instead.

On the road I had Laura call the hospital so I could tell Mom I'd be a teensy bit late getting back. Laura was able to get to the room, but no one answered. Mom definitely needed a cell phone. I had Laura call her apartment at Weeping Willow and, with no answer there either, left a message that I'd be back in the afternoon and reminded her of my cell phone number.

What with thinking about my parents, I forgot to ask Laura about Madame Defarge.

Jefferson State Penitentiary was much more high-tech than I remembered Raiford being. There weren't fenced runs staffed by guard dogs, for one thing. They had been replaced with higher-tech surveillance.

I might point out that Florida is ahead of Texas in the number of prisoners on death row, more than four hundred at last count, and only trails behind California. However you look at it, the statistics aren't happy ones for convicted felons. But no one has been able to come up with a better way to warehouse them.

The warden had received my preclearance request from Will, and approval from Marcus Creighton. We got through the first checkpoint with Laura's ID, parked in visitor parking, signed in (Laura grunted as she did so), handed over our weapons, and were shown into a waiting room preparatory to meeting Marcus Creighton in a private room. We didn't have to do the glass partition thing.

A guard, who Laura introduced as Wally, came to meet us, said hello to me, and turned back to Laura. "You were just here," he said.

Laura's face flushed. Flushing is odd in a woman who owns brass knuckles. "I don't think—" she started.

"Yeah, just a few days ago. You'd been coming about once a week," Wally said.

Laura was silent, so Wally turned to lead the way. We followed behind him. We walked through clanging door after clanging door that, even in the short time the prison had been around, had all been painted layer upon layer until the surfaces of the bars looked deceptively malleable.

If the General Population cell block was a zoo, with a thousand animals all shouting at the same time, and the only place on earth where you could smell communal bad breath, let alone the expected urine stench, death row was something else. "Row" didn't begin to describe it. The number of prisoners housed here needed much more than a single row.

We walked down a wide hallway that looked up to a ceiling forty feet above, where fluorescent lights, some flickering, cast a blue-white glow over the pale green cinder-block walls. Solid metal doors with slots in them just big enough for a food tray spanned the three stories of cells above us. If the cells weren't full, somebody was planning for a future boom in the prison industry.

And yet it was quieter than General Population. Here the prisoners didn't need to do subhuman things like make shit bombs out of their own feces and lob them at the guards. No, this was where the worst were housed, men who no longer had to prove how bad they were in order to survive. The metal doors that kept these men contained didn't ease my feeling that I was breathing in evil, that I was being coated with it. This might not be the lowest level of hell, because I'd already been there and I knew what it looked like. But this was easily the vestibule.

"How is Marcus Creighton getting on?" I asked Wally, to provide a sound other than that of his slightly out-turned feet in rubber-soled shoes squeaking like a mallard on the glossy linoleum.

"I've liked him," Wally said. "He's educated. Refined. And you know, who hasn't thought of buying that ticket to Bali, wiping the slate clean, and flying off the next day?"

I felt myself controlling my eyeballs so they wouldn't roll.

A few more steps and then, "Is there extradition from Bali?" Wally asked no one in particular without turning around.

No, I thought.

"Sure there is," Laura said.

Wally thought about that some. "Mr. Creighton had a bad attack today," Wally said.

"I noticed Alison Samuels was here. She has a dog." Laura turned to me. "Sometimes the inhaler works and sometimes it doesn't." And back to Wally. "How bad was it?"

"We had to take him to the clinic and get him a shot of epinephrine. You're right, it was when that Samuels woman came to visit. God awmighty, I don't know what zone that woman lives in, but he was still wheezing like he couldn't get the air out of his lungs in order to take the next breath, and she just sat there asking him questions like he could answer if he really wanted to. Like maybe she thought he was pretending to be sick. She even stayed till after he came back from the clinic."

We got to the interviewing room, where Creighton was seated at the far end of a rectangular table. His wrists were cuffed. His hair was wet, which meant this was shower day. Was that the last time he would shower before his death? He wore an orange T-shirt over blue pants. Regular prisoners wore blue shirts. At this prison it was the orange T-shirt that said you were a death row prisoner.

"Hey, Marcus."

"Wally," Marcus wheezed. He sounded worse than Dad had the night before.

"You're a popular guy today," Wally said.

"Guesso," Creighton said. He forced his breath out with some difficulty, drew in another with the same effort, and asked, "Howz daught's gradu . . . wheez?"

"She was pretty hungover but managed to make it up to the stage. I'm about done with this crap."

I do not think that the fact that Wally was expressing his familial dissatisfaction to someone who had been convicted of wiping out his own was lost on anyone but, apparently, Wally.

Marcus let the subject drop. Laboring over another breath in preparation for the next few words, he said more clearly than before, "Please. Bring inhaler? And that thing?"

"Are you allowed to use it again so soon after the shot?"

Marcus gave Wally a thin smile, and we all acknowledged the absurdity of keeping a man safe on death row, and Wally left us alone.

Laura sat down on the side of the table, and I sat at the other end to have the best vantage point to see them at the same time. Creighton nodded politely at me, seemed curious, but then focused on Laura. That left me the freedom to observe him.

Pale as sandstone, either from lack of sunlight or his asthma attack, he reminded me of a splendid ruin, its surface crumbled by time and the winds of fortune, but showing all its former glory through the wreckage. He still had all of his hair, thick and wavy but totally gray, like mine. Besides the shower, he had shaved, in preparation for either us or another guest. His prison attire looked clean and hardly wrinkled. That's about all he had to work with, but he was one of those men whose handsomeness survived no matter what, so you could understand how at least two women had once been in love with him. He seemed to be aware of all this, and ran his fingers through his hair because that was the only part of him he could do anything about. With every gesture his hands moved in tandem because of the wrist cuffs.

"I'm due for a haircut," he said, his breathing beginning to normalize. "Did you get a chance to bring that book?"

"I'm sorry, I forgot it in the car. Distracted," Laura said, her head tilting to the side and her voice sounding softer than I'd ever heard it before. "I could—"

"Never mind, next time," he said, shaking his head.

Laura's hand almost went to her throat but then passed over the birthmark on her face instead. This may have been her most honest expression of the confidence she had in Creighton's case. If the man realized the irony in what he said, that there might not be time to read another book, he ignored it.

"I still have a ways to go with . . ." he said, trailing off. Laura would know which book he meant because she had brought it to him. They could speak in the half sentences of intimates. Creighton took off his wire-rimmed prison glasses and pinched his shirt around them to rub them clean. The cuffs made this awkward, but he managed.

I asked, "Do you like to read?"

He seemed pleased to talk about anything but his case, and said, "I didn't use to, but I find it makes the time bearable."

"What do you like to read?" I asked.

"Long books."

"Alison Samuels was here," Laura said, forcing him toward business.

"That's right," he said, wheezing less with each breath, and better able to speak as long as he breathed after every few words. "I'm in demand. Like that show. Wally told me about. *The Bachelor*. It's still on, right?" Trying to engage Laura on a topic that would make him appear he had much more time than five days.

For the first time I noticed he had a white five-by-seven card before him on the table. In an absentminded way the fingers of his right hand curled and straightened so that they moved the card up and down, up and down.

Laura's voice took back its usual edge. "Why do you see Alison Samuels, Marcus? Even if she didn't upset you so much, she's got a dog. They should never let people in to see you if they have pets. Just refuse to see her." Laura turned to me and said, "Marcus reacts to animals the way some people react to peanuts. It's a real problem for him."

Thinking of Al and Peg at home, and whether I might have some Pug residue on me the way killers have gunshot residue on them, I drew back in my chair.

"Is she still telling you she's looking for your children?" Laura asked.

Creighton looked like he was forming his lips to repeat *That's right*, and then, maybe thinking too much repetition might make him sound crazy, he nodded and smiled to reassure us that he was not. "She's working very hard," he said. He moved the card up and down, up and down, in front of him.

"Marcus," Laura said, "is that another picture you've got there?"

For a second he looked like a child caught passing a note in school. His eyes drifted to the side and his hand went flat over the card, though he couldn't possibly hide it. I looked at the hands at rest. Though the knuckles were somewhat swollen with stress arthritis, the hands were still that combination of elegance and masculinity. I thought of Carlo and wished I could be away from here, sitting on our TV room sofa with his hand resting lightly on my leg, listening to him talk about a book I didn't understand.

Laura's own fingers crept forward over the table toward the card. "Could I see it?"

He shook his head no, and besides the refusal it communicated, the shake seemed to bring him back from the person most of us succeed in hiding most of the time. "I'd really rather not, Laura," he said. He slapped his hand on the card like it would win the jackpot and smiled. "You tend to be a little discouraging."

"Marcus, that's just cruel." Laura looked at me again. "Samuels brings him photographs of exploited children who might be his. She thinks if he didn't kill them, he got rid of them somehow, sold them or something. You know you can say you don't want to see someone," Laura said, turning back to him. "Why talk to someone who doesn't have your interest at heart?"

"My interest," he said. "Sometimes I think she's the only person who cares. She knows my children are alive. She's looking for them. I have reason to believe she'll look for them even after I'm dead." His hand pulled the photograph closer to him. An expression, sad and disappointed, slid down his face. "You don't even think they're alive."

"Marcus. We've gone over this. I don't have any opinion at all about your children. My job is to find the evidence that will get you a new trial."

He rubbed his mouth with his hand and was contrite. "I'm sorry, Laura. Of course you are, and you're doing everything you can for me. I'm so sorry."

Putting aside talk of the children's survival, a talk they must have had before, Laura said, "I'm here today because I wanted to reassure you face-to-face that we, Will and I, we haven't given up. I've got good news. The same cell phone company still owns the service you used in 1999."

He seemed to read the look on her face and responded with cautious excitement. "Is that good? You look like this is good news. I could use some."

Laura explained the significance of the phone records and how I was there to help get the hair dryers. "This is Brigid Quinn, and she's going to help us. She has some connections."

Now he really saw me, and the man who had mastered calculus put two and two together. Ran his fingers through his hair again. "I usually don't look this hopeless," he said to me, trying for a small laugh and almost getting there. "It's the asthma attack. And the somewhat disappointing news about my upcoming execution. I promise you, most of the time I look like someone worth saving."

"It's okay. I've seen worse," I said, trying to observe him with all I had. I've been caught by liars when I wasn't expecting it, but this was one of those times when I thought a person was lying and I was just looking for proof. It would make this part of my trip so easy.

"Do you think you can help?" Creighton asked, and to disguise any real hope that might have crept into his question, he added a flippant "I'd really prefer not to die."

A voice came over the loudspeaker: "Counting time. Counting time." Wally interrupted us just then by poking his head in the door. We all looked up. "Just counting," he said.

"Here," Creighton said, and Wally seemed to enjoy the little joke that Creighton delivered without humor. Then Wally's face lit up with a remembered thing, and he took an inhaler out of his pocket, as well as something that looked like a small book. Wally left both within Creighton's reach. When Wally left, Creighton took a hit off the inhaler.

He was silent after the "here." No matter how much you learn, when you spend twenty-three hours a day in a cell, and the twenty-fourth standing in line for the phone to talk to your attorney, counting time, and using the inhaler, having conversations with more than one person may overwhelm. Creighton looked momentarily fatigued, and let his head drop slightly like that of a mechanical toy whose crank had run out. Then he lifted it for another go.

He was like this the whole time we were there, in and out of himself, fighting to appear to be a man who was not on death row, and sometimes succeeding. I pictured those concentration camp prisoners who ran around the compound trying to show that they were healthy enough to be worth keeping alive. There was something noble, something courageous in this, and I admired him in the same way Laura did. Then I gave myself a mental shake, because sympathy wasn't my reason for being here.

Marcus must have been thinking while I was, because he spoke in a continuation of his last remark. "It's not the dying so much as the waiting for it. Did Wally tell you they're going to move me into another cell this afternoon? It's called a death watch cell. They watch me to make sure I don't kill myself before they do."

Laura's energy seemed to swell then, to give hers to him as if they were two cells of the same organism and the conveyance of her life force to his was actually possible. I knew this Laura well, a woman who could not countenance failure of any kind. She leaned toward him until their heads were closer than I would have liked, and said, "Marcus, the reason I drove up here today is to show you how convinced I am that this isn't hopeless. You just keep hanging on, because there are a number of us working on your behalf. I swear I won't let anything happen to you. Do you hear me? I swear this, Marcus."

Creighton laughed, this time more of an echo of a sound that came from the back of his throat as from the back of a cave. Yet he seemed to be the calm one, making cocktail-party small talk, while Laura became more agitated as he went on. "One of the things I've learned is that the gazelle doesn't spend its life in fear of the lion. The fear just kicks in when the chase starts. But humans, humans live in terror of what's going to happen."

"Marcus," Laura said.

"Dogs are the same way," he said. Like a teacher, he lifted his index finger to punctuate the most important points of his lecture. "They get all anxious and trembly when a storm comes, but they don't worry about the storm that's coming tomorrow."

"Marcus," Laura said.

"We've never had a dog. The kids have always wanted a dog, but I've got this asthma."

"Marcus," Laura said.

Creighton got that look a person gets when someone they're talking to isn't understanding, and they want to be understood more than anything. He started working his jaw side to side. He opened the little book to show that it was actually a photo album, and as he paged through it, lingered here and there to touch one of the photos, I saw another man emerge, one who forgot to pretend that a meeting on death row was not uncommon, who forgot we were there for a different reason, even forgot where and when he was.

"See, this is the one they want. It's a standard poodle. It's not the actual dog, it's a picture of one, see? Sara put it in this album along with the other pictures when she gave it to me for Father's Day. They say I should at least go to a breeder and just test it to see if it's true that poodles don't have fur, they have hair like us."

When he stopped talking, his jaw started up again, that little grinding motion that showed how hard he was fighting for control. He had let his hand come to rest on the page facing the one with the poodle. "Here, look—"

"Marcus, we can't—"

Giving up on Laura, Creighton asked if I'd mind if he sat closer to me. When I said that was okay, he got up from his chair and sat down in the one at my end of the table.

"See, here's one of me with Devon," he said. "He likes model cars, and when I sat down to help him, I found out I did, too. It's as if he inherited a trait I didn't know I had. This is Sara, see, she's draped around

61

my neck like a cat. She always does that. She wants to be sure she gets her share of my attention." He flipped two more pages. "This is from our trip to the Grand Canyon. See Kirsten standing there with her foot out and that sullen look kids put on? And see, she doesn't know I'm goofing off behind her, pretending like I'm going to fall over the edge. But she's a good kid, a responsible kid. Very reliable."

"Marcus," Laura said.

"Laura?" Creighton said, and looked fondly over at her as if he had just arrived in the room and was surprised and pleased to see her.

"Mr. Creighton," I said, "do you want me to help you? Do you want to stay alive? Because an honest answer to that question will determine what happens next."

Creighton focused on me. He shook his head the same way he had before, as if he was shaking the crazy out of it, to get a grip on being normal enough to be allowed to live. He took off his glasses again and pinched them between the folds of his shirt to clean them, something a sane person does. "Yes. Yes. Yes," he said. "But what can I tell you? What can I say? I didn't do it? Would you believe me?" He put his glasses back on and raised his cuffed hands off the table in some gesture of supplication with a smile at the folly of it all. "Give me the magic words that will convince you."

"It's not us you need to convince. Or at least not Laura. Can I ask you some questions?"

"Anything," he said. "And I'll answer them honestly because that's all I've got."

"You obviously loved your children. Did you love your wife?"

Creighton didn't seem surprised. "I hated her. She was a drunk. She kept threatening to divorce me, but I didn't want to share custody of the kids. Didn't want to be one of those dads. And I didn't want them to have to live alone with her. She blamed the drinking on me, but I knew it wouldn't stop if I was out of the picture." He laced his fingers and leaned across the table in my direction. "Do you want more honesty than that? Well, I imagined her dying in much the way that she actually did. When I found her body, there was a moment when I had the thought *This is luck*. Then the children were missing and I thought I was being punished for being glad she died."

"Why didn't you try to get better defense?"

"I thought I could convince the detective on the case that they shouldn't be wasting their time on me. They should have been looking for the kids. They did an Amber Alert immediately but called it off when Shayna blew my alibi. Couldn't they see how crazy I was? I was going nuts and no one was doing anything. I begged them. I even told them maybe Kathleen's death really was an accident, and the crime was that the kids had been abducted on their way to the community center. Nobody listened. Have you any children?"

"No," I said.

"Maybe you can't understand the horror of that time, knowing that with each minute my children could be closer to death, and the very people sworn to protect them were doing nothing. Nothing. Then I was in the system, I'd been assigned a public defender, and that was that." Creighton looked as if the agony was now, that moment when he tried to make someone believe him and no one did. His breathing got labored again, and he took another hit off the inhaler.

"You don't have to keep talking if it's hard," Laura said.

Creighton put up a hand to show he was okay.

I thought it would help to change the subject for now. "What about Shayna Murry?"

Even so long after last seeing her—and that was when she was on the stand betraying him—his eyes still softened. "I was in love with her. And I'm certain she loved me, too. She was coached. I've spent all these years wondering why she lied about my being there that night." He smiled at me, his breathing controlled. "How am I doing so far? Are the words magical enough?" He waggled his fingers in a sleight-of-hand way, making his shackles jingle.

"So far, you're convincing," I said. "Why do you think your children are alive?"

He took as deep a breath as he was able. "I didn't in the early years. I stopped hoping. I told myself they were probably dead, and I spent some years mourning. Then Ms. Samuels suggested they weren't. She said anything could have happened. That they could have been shipped to Thailand. Especially the twins, she said. Exotic sex." He pressed his midsection against the edge of the table as if it could press out the pain.

"I think at first she wanted to hurt me by saying this, to trick me into saying I'd buried them somewhere. But while it was awful, it was hopeful, too. I wanted to live again. Find them. If I seem a little . . . off . . . it's because there's not much else to do here, besides the reading, than think. Sometimes the thoughts make me crazy, but I can't stop them."

"Mr. Creighton," I said, "what will you do if Laura and Will get you a stay of execution? What will you do if you're exonerated? If you're let out of prison after all this time?"

"Find my children," he said, without having to stop and think. "Help Alison Samuels find my children." He clutched his hands on top of the table and gazed at me in all sanity, as if his words were all there was between him and despair.

Laura reached across the table to touch the hands, then, glancing at me, drew back.

"We need to go, Marcus," Laura said. "We have a lot of work to do for you."

Whether or not he was paying attention, she explained how the paperwork was all done in anticipation of getting the two pieces of evidence. How Will Hench would use what he had to get a stay of execution within the next five days, then file an appeal based on perjury and flawed forensics with the next higher court. She would continue to be the investigator for him. She promised again that he wasn't going to die in five days. And promised again.

Creighton, for one, at least pretended his confidence in Laura's assurances, and didn't ask any more questions about the case. Instead, he pushed the photograph album in her direction, but kept his fingers on it as if he couldn't decide whether to really give it up. "Would you take care of this?" he asked. "I wouldn't want it to get lost. In case."

Hesitating a bit more, he finally decided to pull his hand back, and stared at it as Laura sighed, put the album into her briefcase, got up from the table, and announced her intention of leaving into the intercom. She tried to say good-bye, but professional though she was, her voice broke on the "bye," swinging it up to a higher pitch.

And my reaction as I sat there watching him? On death row for murdering his family. No matter what kinds of evidence to the contrary Laura and Will said they had, I had arrived at this meeting convinced of his guilt. I was leaving with a mixture of instinct that he didn't do it and a fervent hope that he did.

That feeling of hope? The reason I hoped he was guilty was because only that, and nothing less, would justify what society had done to this man. The alternative was unthinkable to me: an innocent man, waiting for death, while tortured by the obsession that his children were out there somewhere. And if they were still alive, no one but him caring that they were being hurt.

Ten

Laura was quiet, running her finger lightly over the cover of the little album that Creighton had passed to her. I turned the ignition and put the air on to cool the car down, but didn't drive off immediately.

"Is he always that way?" I asked.

"He's been lovely, really. Appreciative, and . . . and engaged . . . and more positive than I could ever be in his circumstances. It's just the news today about the execution actually being scheduled that threw him." When I didn't respond, she said, "You think he's dissembling."

"I didn't say that."

"That's what you're thinking."

"What gets me is, why so certain the children are alive? So certain. But that business with him talking like it's sixteen years ago."

Laura said, "It's years of wanting something so bad he's convinced himself," but then her face clouded. "For all I know they still could be alive. I don't know."

She opened the album and started to page through it. I looked, too, having been too far away at the other end of the table to see it well.

The album was the kind with clear plastic sleeves, one per page, each holding a five-by-seven photo. The cover had been decorated with mul-ticolored sequins, glued on to spell "Happy Father's Day." At least originally. After all those years, most of the sequins had fallen off, with "H pp ath 's Da" remaining, the rest of the letters filled in with spots of white glue where the sequins had been.

Laura opened the album. The first photo showed two babies, one blissfully sucking on his toe. Maybe he had just discovered his foot. As she continued to turn the pages, I saw a rough chronological progression, two bigger babies in a top-of-the-line double stroller, with an older but still-small child reaching up to the bar to push them. The three children, two on tricycles and one on a two-wheeler, in a row facing the camera. A group photo at the beach, all five of the Creightons building a sand castle. Mom in happier times. A fishing trip, the younger children in those orange life preservers, the little boy holding a fish that wasn't much bigger than the feathery lure in its mouth. Maybe Lake Orange.

The pictures were pretty much the same as would be found in any well-to-do family's collection. But here is what was different about this album, now that I was able to take a closer look:

There was fifteen years of body oil from a man's fingers on the clear plastic covering each photograph. The way you could tell was that, over the years, the oil attracted the grime of the prison and left spots of rough, raised dirt stuck to the pages. Of course, that would only happen if the book had been handled hundreds, thousands of times. Other, less dense spots showed on top of the faces. There some of the grime had been rubbed away.

He had touched their faces repeatedly.

All the pages were that way, spotted with the dirt of the prison years.

I put the car in drive and headed away from the prison. "Did Creighton ever show you this photograph album?"

"Never. Even though he used to talk to me about them, for purposes of my getting him exonerated, he always said to keep the family out of it. He said he didn't want people to see his emotion and think it was an act. He was always very firm about not including anything about the children in his appeals. It made me respect him."

And more than respect him? I wondered. Laura let her fingertips settle onto the same spots on a photograph where his fingers must have touched. It looked like it was the closest she could allow herself to come to touching the man himself. She said, "Brigid, does a man who keeps this in his cell, looks at the pictures as much as he must have looked at them over the years, who talks about his children as if they were still alive, who gives the album into my keeping in order to keep it safe after his death—is that a man who killed his children?"

No. No. Or only if he was insane with guilt. But not even that, because, while he might have been standard death-row crazy, I didn't sense anyone could pin a psychiatric label on him. No.

I said, "I have to tell you, it troubled me when you made that promise to save him."

"But what do you think? Do you still think he's guilty?"

"I wish to God he was."

"You're not answering," Laura said. "Say you don't think he did it. Say it flat out."

"All my instincts say he's not guilty, but that doesn't mean you'll win the case. Laura, I have to know that you fully realize, even if we get the evidence you're looking for, if the Law wants someone dead, it's pretty hard to stop it no matter what the evidence. I want you to say *that* flat out."

"I understand," she said. "But you have to understand I'm going to fight like hell."

I turned to look at her as she said that, and watched her mouth get thin and straight with judgment, and I hated that. So I said, and this was pretty much the truth, same as what I had said before, "I tell you, Coleman, I trusted you once before and you were right. Maybe this time you're wrong. But right now I can say I think it's a good thing, what you're doing."

We were coming to I-95, and as I pulled onto the ramp there was thunder, and lightning, and then a deluge that felt like being followed by a waterfall. I slowed a bit and glanced at my watch. Yep, in Florida in June you can almost set your watch by the afternoon storm.

"Should we pull off the road?" Laura asked.

She was clearly not a Floridian like I was. "No. Two miles from here it will stop. That loan shark Creighton borrowed from. Do you have a name?"

"Manuel Gutierrez," Laura said, gripping her knees and watching the road for me.

"No shit? I know Manny Gutierrez. I wonder if he's still alive."

No response, just the stare through the rain.

"Then tell me about Madame Defarge," I said to distract her so she wouldn't worry about me getting us killed.

"Will keeps calling her that, and I haven't had time to google it."

"Madame Defarge is a Dickens character. She knits a stitch for every aristocrat who gets guillotined during the French Revolution."

"So it just means that Alison Samuels is bloodthirsty."

"Doh, why didn't I think of saying it that way. Tell me about her. Why did she give Creighton that photograph?"

"She's the spokesperson for the Haven, that group that helps with retrieving missing and exploited children. She tells how she ran away from abusive parents, got involved in prostitution for a while, but got out of the game when she was nineteen, pulled herself up and got a graduate degree in sociology, working some bona fide job nights while she did it. She's been with the Haven for three years, came up the ranks fast, made a name for herself. Last year when she was going over some old cases, she got interested in finding out where the Creighton children are buried, or whether they even died that night. She has this idea that Marcus had given them to someone and they've been working the sex trade because Marcus saw them as baggage that would keep him from getting Shayna Murry. Only he didn't have the balls to kill them. Something like that. Crazy."

"But why the obsession with the Creightons? There's lots of other cases of missing children and runaways."

"None in Florida where three children disappear overnight and their bodies are never found. They're seen one day and then gone. Apparently she has aged photographs of Devon, Sara, and Kirsten and compares them to photographs she finds online. She shoves them in his face and makes horrible suggestions about what became of them, and he continues to let her in. She's feeding his obsession that they're alive, and he wants her to find them."

"That's pretty sick."

"He wants to believe her, that the kids are alive. The only good thing about her is that she keeps him from giving up. Otherwise it's like—"

"Like trying to push a freight train with your shoulder? Or like trying to fill up his lungs for him?"

Laura took a deep breath. I think it reassured her that someone else had felt the same. "Exactly like. You know."

The mention of lungs and the slowing of the rain made me call the hospital again. Mom answered this time, and I tried not to beat myself up for not being there when she was always there, as if we were in competition. Sure, I cared, I worried, but I could not sit there. You can't just sit there breathing for the other person. You have to come and go from the hospital room.

Right? Am I right?

Yet you think about them while you're away, and when you find yourself not thinking about them, you feel guilty. Or you wonder if you've somehow sealed their death sentence with your momentary lack of caring. Superstitious crap.

Where was I? Oh, right. Mom said Dad was resting, weak but not in too much discomfort. Just weak. I said I would be there by the late afternoon.

I hung up and noticed we were approaching I-95. The rain had stopped.

"How far to the Creighton house?" I asked.

"Not far. But there's nothing to see."

I knew we both had our reasons for heading back to Fort Lauderdale, but a different route wouldn't take that much more time, I told myself. I talked Laura into stopping by the Creighton house. Something compelled me to go there, like a pilgrimage.

Eleven

We made a turn at the second Vero Beach exit. We were driving east now, past open land that turned into outlet malls that turned into fields again, past the haggard Wabasso Bait and Tackle shop, its rough wood and rusted metal roof holding stubbornly against the tropical storms that routinely blew in off the coast.

Laura pointed out that if we turned left on Highway 1 we'd come to Shayna Murry's old place. "She still in the area?" I asked.

"Yep. I tried repeatedly to get her to talk to me, but nothing doing. She's sort of broken. She works at a place called Cracker's Café that's not too far from her studio."

"Art career didn't go so well, I take it?"

"No. She's different now from what she was at the trial. If what she said was true, it's a hell of a burden to carry with you the rest of your life. Thinking you might have been responsible for a family dying. Even if it's not true. People look at you and that's the story they see."

And with that mental mountain-goating that sends you skipping from one idea to the next, I asked, mostly myself, "Why did the kids not go to that slumber party?"

We didn't have time to talk that part out because the rusticity of the west gave way to the opulent east as we crossed the tall bridge over

Indian River, the body of water that takes over the job of the Intra-coastal Waterway in this part of the state. At Laura's direction I made a hard right into an area called Pelican Shores.

Three houses down the street she pointed out her window. "There it is." I was rewarded with the sight of nothing. "What?" I said.

"I told you there was nothing to see."

"I didn't know you meant that literally."

"The bank couldn't sell it, even on prime waterfront property. People too squeamish. So about ten years ago the neighbors all pitched in to buy it from the bank, bulldoze the house, and make a little park. I've seen pictures, though. It was gorgeous. Another stupid thing Marcus did, having that house custom-built."

"Lemme take a look since we're here."

We headed to the backyard, walking over a grassy rise that might have been the living room. I have to admit that little nerve in my neck, the one that warns me of danger, jumped a bit. I don't know if it meant I could feel the violence that had once occurred between the walls that would have enclosed me, or whether it was that little thrill at something I didn't know. I don't think it was ghosts. Whatever still haunted this place couldn't hurt anyone unless innocence is terrifying. No, the feeling coming through the soles of my shoes was just sorrow, plain and simple.

I realized I had been holding my breath as we walked over the ground that had been the house, and the rush of air that filled my lungs now was almost a gasp of relief.

There was a wide expanse of deep water, deep enough for the thirty-foot sailboat going by as we watched. Across the water, a dense stand of pines blocked the view of anything beyond. In the crook of a dead white tree there was a nest big enough to be seen even from this distance.

The inlet was at dead low tide and gave off the summer stench of rotting vegetation. Compared to the urine smell of the prison, and the antiseptic smell of the hospital, it was decent.

Call me selfish, but right at this moment, in this lovely spot, our backs to an invisible house where there'd been wholesale slaughter, I needed to not think about hospitals or prisons. About sickness or death. It's important to wrest these moments out of time, when you detach from the bad things.

"Look." As we stood, an otter swam up to the end of the dock, trusted us, somersaulted, and disappeared. Okay, maybe it wasn't quite Disney, but still, the otter saved me. Believe it or not, for all the rank odor, and the history, it was a place that eased my heart, and I gotta say, this heart is not easily eased.

"Did you see the otter?" I asked.

"Uh-huh." But she had pulled out her phone while I was looking around, and now connected to Wally back at Jefferson. "Thanks for taking care of him, Wally. You're a good man. How's he feeling? Okay, I'd sure appreciate it if you keep an eye on him. Tell him again this isn't over. Would you tell him that? Good man."

Apparently the place wasn't having the same calming effect on Laura. She said, "Maybe Alison Samuels is right. Somebody tried to fake an accident and one of the kids walked in. Very obvious. So they took the kids with them. Maybe they didn't have the guts to kill children and risked giving them to a trafficker. Maybe they ended up in Thailand. Maybe their organs ended up—"

"Did you make any friends at your brother's place in North Carolina?"

"Make friends?" Laura seemed to climb out of her own brain and notice me for the first time. "Brigid. The time right after Tucson was rough. You noticed that gouge in the top of my desk. Did you wonder why I didn't have any of my other furniture from the Tucson house? It was because one night I went nuts and trashed the whole place. Took a knife to the sofa cushions and smashed the glass coffee table." The side of her mouth twitched like she was trying to be flip but failed. Then she got a grip again. "But just as I'm telling you honestly about that, you have to believe I'm okay now."

I wanted to tell her I hoped to never see her photo with a small wedding bouquet on the cover of a tabloid, but I didn't think she'd be amused. So I just said, "And you'll be okay no matter what happens to Marcus Creighton?"

As mild a question as that made her reflare momentarily, but she said, "No matter what."

I didn't believe her. "Did you ever skip rocks when you were young? Probably not, growing up in the desert. Dad showed us. Watch."

I found a good stone that was flat enough on the bottom, drew back, and flicked it like a Frisbee. It sank like a stone. I tried again, failed. "I guess it's not like riding a bike." I tried again and got one skip. Skipping stones makes you think, and I thought about when I'd first met Laura back in Tucson, that affair with a married man, someone unobtainable like Marcus Creighton. What you saw with Laura Coleman wasn't all there was.

Still facing away from her I said, "When your life is devoted to saving people, pity can get confused with affection. I know, because it's happened to me. Laura, you're going to have to put a lid on the emotional involvement with your client. It's showing."

There was silence, and when I turned to her she was standing, again, like somebody getting ready to be punched in the gut with a log. Instead of denying it, she said, "You're damn right I'm emotionally involved. You don't have to be in love to care desperately for someone in trouble. That's what emotions are. Jesus, Brigid, haven't you ever had any feelings at all?"

I started to comment that I hadn't actually said anything about being in love, but the flashbulb memories went off again as I thought about all the times I'd gotten involved, then tamped down those feelings, and wondered again if I had any left. Laura took my silence for contrition.

She said, "I'll let you have this time, Brigid, but don't you ever fucking bring it up again."

There was nothing more I could say except, "I'll stop hovering now. Reboot?"

She nodded, turned, and walked across the grass without looking back. I started to follow her, then stopped another second and stared at where the house would have been. I felt the story, the woman drowsing in the bathtub, the hair dryer on the edge, the person coming in and taking the opportunity.

Which child saw it happen? Even if I wasn't in this for Creighton, whom I, too, was pitying despite my best intentions, I was in it for the child who shouldn't have to watch her mother being electrocuted.

· · ·

I'd familiarized myself with the case, met the accused, and paid hom-age to the victims at what was left of the crime scene. Now I wanted to keep the peace.

"Okay, I'm in the game. What do you need me to do first?" I asked.

Apparently she'd been honest when she said she'd let it go one time. "You said you had connections. What about with the Indian River physical evidence room? Get them to release the hair dryer?" She asked me if I knew Derek Evers, the caretaker there.

I was hoping she'd say that's who it was. "Evers. Evers. Nope, can't say as I do. But I know people who know him, maybe some pressure in that way."

"Let's go by there now. Double-team him."

"Better I go by myself, drop a few names without you hovering around to make him lose face."

"You're talking about a twenty-four-hour delay. We don't have that much time, and I can't see you driving up here again tomorrow."

"Look, I know Will said he wanted something for the interview, and if I can get the hair dryer tomorrow we'll have time for Puccio to check it. I know we're under the gun, but I'd prefer to see Evers when I've done my homework, maybe make a few calls. We just have the one chance to do it right. Tell you what. Let's drop in on Manny Gutierrez. Sur-prise him. I'll get you home in time to hustle the cell phone records. That's more promising."

"How do you know him?" Laura asked.

"Manny Gutierrez was investigated by the FBI for racketeering and Medicare fraud. But they could never build a credible case against him. Smart man, too polished for a hoodlum. You had to admire his talent."

"How do you know he lives on A1A?"

"Just assumed."

I headed south on A1A, keeping my eyes on the road, but I could feel Laura's eyes on me, knowing me better all the time, and because of that not bothering to comment.

Twelve

Manny Gutierrez had one of those properties that straddle the road, house on the ocean side, tennis court and boat dock on the Intracoastal side. With a white marble box of a house, and a sad angel presiding over a fountain in the middle of the circular drive, it looked something like a mausoleum.

We parked the car in the drive between the angel fountain and the front door. As we approached the house, I spotted surveillance cameras hidden under the second-story balconies, and motion-activated spotlights trained on optimum points around the yard.

One of those chimey doorbells echoed through the interior when Laura pressed it.

No one came to the door. I waved at the surveillance camera as the intercom attached at the side of the door fuzzed on.

"Gutierrez residence," a deep goon voice said.

"Would you please tell him Brigid Quinn is here?"

"I am so sorry," said the goon. "But Mr. Gutierrez is incapacitated and is not entertaining visitors."

"That's a fine long sentence you memorized there," I said. "But would you please give it a try? We just want to take a look at him."

"Mr. Gutierrez is not available for viewing."

The fuzz sound went dead.

Laura was trembling with fury over our dismissal as we walked back to the car.

"Relax," I said. "Not everything is a battle, Coleman. I figured he wouldn't let us in. Mostly I just wanted to let him know I was in town. Throw out a little bait and see if the fish takes it. Now it's his move."

Laura ignored me. "I investigated so many bastards like him when I was doing financial crime. Insurance fraud, collecting Social Security and Medicare off dead people. And they get away with it because we're only able to track down a small percentage. Manuel Gutierrez. Am I right, or am I right?"

Even though I'd been prepared to be disrespected, I wasn't liking it much either, so my response may have been harsher than intended. "Oh, grow a set, would you?" I said, forgetting my intention to keep my trap shut. "Not everyone gets punished for what they've done."

Laura said, "Can't help wishing they did."

"I hear you. But this is the real deal out here. If you want justice, go watch old episodes of *Law & Order*."

Okay, okay, I know sometimes I lose patience and open my mouth and crap like that comes out. I dropped Coleman back at her place, parting with her on slightly less than the best of terms.

It's about six. I brought two turkey sandwiches and ate mine an hour ago. Now I'm considering eating Mom's, only because she doesn't want it and I don't have anything else to do. Dad's sleeping, his ragged breath the only sound in the room, countered by unnecessarily loud voices out in the hall, punctuated by that *squeechy* sound of rubber-soled shoes that reminds me of the guard's step on death row.

Mom is staring impassively at Dad from a chair at the foot of the bed. I wonder if she's thinking anything or if she goes blank. I'm in another chair by the side of the bed with my feet up on the lower part of the metal sidebar, staring out the window, having given up on conversation. I've been running the day through my head and wondering why Marcus Creighton was so sure his children were alive. If they weren't killed that night, what happened? Could they be saved even now? You think he's innocent, don't you, Quinn? They put away an innocent man. No. Wait for the corroborating evidence before you go Full-On Coleman. But we've only got five days to get that stay of execution.

I will not look at my watch. That would be indelicate.

I called the hospitalist, Dr. Jason McGee, twice. He hasn't returned my calls. I left a written message at the nurses' station, too. This is pissing me off.

What has been easier than this? That time I happened to be near ground zero of a bomb blast. I wasn't hurt myself, but I was able to assist the paramedics. I look at Dad. If he had a sucking chest wound I might actually be of use here. Otherwise, I just sit and wait.

I'm not good at sitting and waiting. It's not my thing, my forte, my strong suit. I don't hate my parents; they never hurt me. But how do people do this, year after year of dealing with illness? Listen to yourself, it's only been two days. Three?

Suck it up, Brigid Quinn, you ungrateful little shit. This is not about you.

No wonder Todd doesn't want to be here. He did this with his sick wife, with Marylin. I don't give a fuck if he had enough. He needs to visit Dad. I'll tell him that to his face when I see him in the morning.

I feel bad, wanting to look at my watch.

I really don't want my father to die, but would you say that's because I love these people? If I do, why am I feeling so hateful?

Thinking about my father dying makes me think of Creighton. Creighton. I need to keep Creighton alive, at least until we know the truth.

The truth makes me think about Derek Evers. Contrary to what I told Laura, we had a history, Derek and me. Here's what you need to know, and forgive me if I don't use names.

There was this guy I worked with some, a detective in the Tequesta County Sheriff's Office. He was such a good man. Good family man, with two daughters.

One day the detective called me. Said he had no one else to call and would I meet him. We met at that Denny's on Commercial Boulevard that I mentioned. We both ordered pie. Cherry. He didn't eat his, just let it sit in front of him. I didn't eat mine either, once I started listening to him.

He'd been working a case of child sexual abuse. The father. Mother in denial. The child had told her teacher, and the kid was taken out of the home and put in custody. The kid was in the second grade, so they called in a specialist to interview her. What my friend didn't know was that the specialist had a bad track record. During the grand jury it was brought out that in two cases the specialist had bent the rules a little, fudged the interviews. It called into question the eight-year-old's testimony, which was all they had. For once the grand jury, which will usually indict a dead dog, failed to do so. The child was given back to the parents.

"You were certain?" I asked.

"I swear to God I was certain," he said.

"That's good enough for me," I said.

"It's not good enough for that kid," he said. He tried to eat a forkful of his pie but dropped the fork and stared at it. This was the case that would break him. "God doesn't give you anything you can't handle," he said to the pie.

Given what I had seen God dishing out to people, I had grown disenchanted with that line long before then, and blurted, "Then why do people commit suicide?"

Not a day goes by that I don't wish I could take this back. Two days later I found out my friend had eaten his gun.

I swore I'd get revenge on the man who had abused his daughter and caused the death of a good cop.

First, I managed to get the scumbag who had started this whole thing to meet me alone at the same Denny's where I'd met the detective who failed to put him away. The man was arrogant despite my telling him I was going to watch him for the rest of my life and take him down. How are you going to do that? he asked. You'll see, I said.

He scoffed, made some comment about double jeopardy, and left me with the bill.

Criminals always assume they're the only ones who don't play fair. Laugh out loud. I put on a pair of latex gloves and took a fresh roll of tape out of my tote bag. I pressed it against the things on the table I'd noticed him touching, and stuck the tape to a five-by-seven-inch piece of acetate.

I took the tape to Derek Evers along with some really bad pictures and told him to hang on to it all. You see, I'd known for a long time that Derek liked to take a little off the top here and there, money, cocaine, small things that wouldn't be noticed. I'd been keeping this intel to myself for a while, thinking to use it when I needed to. Evers knew I knew about him, and could prove it. He agreed to cooperate.

Then I waited. It took a couple of years, and the daughter was ten by the time I acted, but I made sure everything was set up just right and then nailed the guy on charges of distribution of child pornography across state lines using the postal system. In so doing I transferred the prints to the photos, and Derek entered them into the evidence log on my say-so. At trial Derek testified to the chain of custody.

Sentences weren't as stiff in the nineties for that kind of thing, and the guy would have gotten out of jail in another two years if he hadn't been murdered. I'm sure you've already heard what happens to child molesters in prison.

So I know what you can do with fingerprints to convict a guy.

That's me, and that deed I did once was not lawful, but it was righteous. I bet you would have done it, too. Right?

PS: I followed the life of the daughter, and she's okay. She's okay.

Thirteen

The next morning after I checked in with Carlo I called Laura. She was still stressed but in forward motion, working on getting a game plan going with Will for his interview, and trying to push for finding the physical evidence so he'd have something compelling to present. I told her I'd talk to my brother and attempt to talk to Tracy Mack. Maybe a different face, my own, would be useful. I assured her I would then wrest the hair dryer from Derek Evers.

I was torn, but telling myself that Dad was stable, I had the feeling that Creighton was in the more imminent danger. With the certainty that Mom wouldn't understand Derek Evers taking priority, when I called her I said I was going to spend some time with Todd and would be over to the hospital as soon as I could. Definitely by the afternoon. I told myself I wasn't escaping.

When I went downstairs to the HoJo's restaurant, Todd and his colleague were waiting for me at a table in the back. They both sat in chairs that faced the door. The other detective, dressed in civvies, a button-down shirt with flowers on it and jeans, sat with her knees spread wide, that position that makes a man look either like his balls are too big or else his shoulders are so wide he's in danger of toppling over. When I got close Todd stood up and gave me a brotherly hug, which feels like being hugged by a fire hydrant. At five foot seven he's the tallest in the Quinn family and may be the healthiest, having gone largely unnoticed during his childhood. He was sweaty as usual, and I sat down, consciously not swiping the side of my neck, which had come away from him dampened but was starting to feel cool and dry in the air-conditioning. I had an unsisterly thought about whether he sweated more during sex or just maintained.

Todd had told me he was bringing the colleague who might be able to provide some information. Now he gestured toward the woman and said, "Madeline Stanley."

I took the hand she held out to me and let her grip mine harder. "Brigid Quinn," I said.

She gave me a small quick twitch of the corners of her mouth. "We met at, at the funeral," she said. "So many of us there, I wouldn't expect you to remember."

She was polite enough, even though she had that thing going that so many women do who are trying to make it in a man's world, copying the little things guys do to show they're strong. The way she sat as if she had cojones, her handshake, that twitchy smile. Some women use that coping skill, putting on the tough broad; others turn up the feminine juice to get what they want. Some splendid few are just themselves. It's hard to be ourselves; we're that conditioned to be what others expect. The masks are natural. I flashbulbed to the execution I'd witnessed thirty-five years before. *Can you take it, Brigid Quinn?* And wondered, of all the kinds of women I'd been, which kind I'd been most of the time since then.

The two already had coffee poured, and I took a mug and helped myself from the pot left on the table. As I did so I noticed they both crossed their arms at the same time as if their guts might reveal a secret they shared. You don't have to be a cop to read body language. I wondered how long they had been lovers, whether Todd had had an affair going before Marylin died six months before.

Even if he wasn't my brother, I wouldn't judge him. For one thing, life is hard enough with the plentiful judges we've already got. For another thing, the things I've done don't qualify me as a good judge. For still another, Marylin was sick with multiple sclerosis for the last twenty years of their marriage, and Todd must have done a good chunk of his mourning long before she died. You had to cut the guy some slack.

Now they were both in a happy time, and were yucking it up pretty good while I placed an order for poached eggs and grits on dry rye. But the yucking was partly for show, and I could feel their wariness. Cops are so defensive sometimes.

"You need to go see Dad," I said.

"You didn't bring your girl with you," Todd said.

I took a sip of coffee while I considered him. "That's pretty insulting even for you, Todd. She's Special Agent Laura Coleman. She's busy."

"I heard Laura Coleman has been sniffing around, and not picking up much of a scent." Madeline was smart, maybe smarter than Todd, and despite her cordial greeting it quickly became apparent she had arrived at the restaurant with a self-protective chip on her shoulder. "I just came with Todd because I thought it would be nice to see you again. Other than that, I've got nothing for you."

"Let me just catch up a bit. You were with the Vero Beach Police Department at the time of the Creighton crime, right?"

She couldn't help but look surprised that I'd done my homework. "That's right. I moved here about four years later. It was definitely a good move."

"I imagine so." I kept my eyes carefully off of Todd, feeling a double entendre in every phrase.

"I hadn't made detective yet at the time. The case was handled by a colleague I respect, Gabriel Delgado. He tied it up quick and neat. So what's with this sudden interest? It wasn't a DNA case. That means you got something on the investigators or the legal guys. So who're you going after, Delgado, the forensic examiner, or the prosecutor?"

I was here to get information while giving up as little as possible. I said, "No, apparently the only DNA that would have cleared Marcus Creighton was in the mistress's vagina, and it doesn't appear that Delgado was all that interested."

Madeline thought I was just being funny. "Damn, that's what he did wrong. He forgot to subpoena her vadge," she said, with one of those little shoulder bumps against Todd.

Todd smiled, and then caught himself smiling.

I said, "Maybe he forgot a lot of things." I wasn't smiling.

Todd and Madeline rearranged their faces in a flash, as if they were working a mass fatality and the media had just arrived on the scene.

Madeline tried not to sound snappish when she asked, "So what are you after him for, corruption or just plain incompetence?"

I stopped and took a breath, not wanting to let the conflict escalate. On the other hand, I could have tried cajoling, but I didn't have the time. Besides, Todd boffing her made her practically family. I decided on "Oh, stop taking it personally. We've got a case that someone thinks got screwed up somehow. I respect the person who thinks that. I'm just trying to get at the truth before a man fries. Cool your jets and tell me your perception of the case. It was huge. You guys must have talked a lot."

"It's been a long time," Madeline said.

"Mr. Creighton knows that. He's spent more than five thousand days alone in an eight-by-ten-foot room. Have you known Todd all that time, or did you just hook up when you got to town?"

Todd looked clueless at my question, but Madeline was a woman after all and she got it. Sex makes a person vulnerable in ways they never see coming.

"There was no screwup." Noticing that her mouth had gone a bit dry, Madeline ran her tongue over her front teeth and brought her attitude down a notch. "Okay, here's what it is. Creighton is broke, and the only thing between him and his loan shark is a two-million-dollar life insurance policy. Conveniently, while Creighton is out of the house, his wife is electrocuted and his children go missing. His mistress is his alibi, but she denies he was with her that night. He leaves a fingerprint on a hair dryer he swears he never used."

"All this I know. What do you think about the examiner being indicted?" I said.

Madeline turned to Todd. "What is this, an interrogation?" And back to me. "We're all trying to do the best we can. These days we're all under attack. Police brutality, they yell. Shoddy science, they yell. Fucking ACLU and the liberal media. I'm trying to be polite here, but I'm getting a little tired with the effort. You don't expect this kind of treatment from someone in the business."

What kind of treatment? I just asked about the indictment. But I ignored the bluster and kept to the issue. "So you think the fraud charges are unfounded."

She bypassed that by going back to Creighton. "You're not going to find anything. It was a slam dunk of a case. Judge gave the prosecution a free ride, and the defense was in way over his head. If that new law—"

"The Timely Justice Act," Todd said.

"If the Timely Justice Act would have been enacted fifteen years ago, Mr. Creighton would be dead and we wouldn't be having this conversation. So in that respect, he's one lucky man."

"One lucky man," I repeated, not asking her if she'd ever visited someone on death row who might be innocent. I'd finished my breakfast and had enough of Madeline, so I stood up to leave. She stood, too, and this time when she shook my hand I noticed the small spare tire around her middle. Or maybe what's a spare tire on males is now called a muffin top on women.

I could have been a lot meaner. I could have told her, except for the extra weight, how much she resembled Todd's dead wife.

Fourteen

Even if he hadn't been indicted, Tracy Mack was still retired, and at home. Before I went down to the underground parking garage I called his number, and when a raspy voice answered, I hung up. I looked at my watch. It was a long shot, and I knew what my priority was that day, but this wouldn't take that much time, and you never know if you don't try. I went to the Imperial Point housing development, which was considered imperial when it was developed fifty years ago. Now not so much. While the entrance still sported a straight line of royal palms that had been impressive in their day, the houses were all single story and modest by today's bigger and better standards. Luckily they didn't have gated communities in the sixties, so I was able to drive right up to Tracy Mack's house without warning him.

I went up to the door and rang the bell.

Nobody came. I supposed he could have left the house since my call. I walked around to the garage and peeked through a window in the door. Car in there, and parked in the middle, which meant he only had one. Lived alone.

I called his number again, and this time when he answered I said, "My name is Brigid Quinn. We haven't met. I'm not here to hurt you. Look through your peephole and tell me if I look dangerous."

I stood back from the door to reveal my short stature, my prematurely white hair, and my most winning smile. I even held my arms out and tried to let my triceps sag a little.

There was a long pause during which I felt observed, and then he opened the door.

I got a whiff of closed-up house, a combination of cigar smoke, onions that had been fried long ago, and flatus. Tracy Mack stood there in a T-shirt and workout pants with elastic at the ankles. White socks.

"You don't look like a reporter," he said.

"I'm not." I had a business card ready and handed it to him. "I need your help," I said.

He took the card with one hand, and with the other extracted the very soggy, tooth-chomped end of his cigar out of his mouth. The thought of anyone touching that with their lips turned my stomach a little, and I have a very strong stomach. After taking a deep breath I stepped inside the door while he was studying my card.

"I recognize your name from somewhere," he said.

"I used to be in law enforcement, and worked a lot of cases in South Florida."

A memory slipped across his face. "Brigid Quinn. Now I remember. FBI." He plugged his cigar back in his mouth.

He didn't invite me further into the house, and I was just as happy to stand in the foyer with the door open, letting in some fresh air. I took shallow breaths while I scanned the living room and saw a half-finished jigsaw puzzle on a card table and a laptop on a small desk. All his play and work right there. Maybe his whole world.

"You're retired?" I asked, to put him at ease until I could get to the good part.

He talked around the cigar out one side of his mouth and couldn't seem to resist engaging in the human contact. "You could say that. I'm working on a book."

"What's it about?"

"It's a history of forensic science."

"Let me know when it's done. I have some contacts."

That's not true, but it always works. He unplugged the cigar, an indication that he was more interested in whatever I had to say now that I might be of use to him. But enough beating around the bush.

"Right now I'm here because of Marcus Creighton," I said.

"Who's Marcus Creighton?" he asked.

"A man you testified against. He was convicted of killing his family based partly on your testimony."

He might not have remembered the name of one of the many thousands he had put away, but you could tell he knew where I was going and that he'd been had.

"I'm not talking to anyone," he said, and plugged the cigar back in. He started to push me out the door, but I had seen the muscles tighten in his right arm and knew it was coming. I blocked the door with my body.

"I'll call the cops," he said as he pressed the door against me, his cigar threatening.

I turned my face to avoid it. "That won't do you any good," I said. "I used to be one, remember? Look, Mr. Mack, Creighton has been scheduled for execution. He's going to die in four days, for God's sake. Do you realize if you reverse your testimony even now you can save his life?"

Appealing to his sense of decency didn't help. Maybe he was low on that particular sense. He looked at me with a tired hate, though he eased up on the door some. "I would have thought we'd be on the same side," he said.

"I was never on a side. And if I was, it wouldn't be yours," I said, losing my patience as I recognized he didn't have the heart I was hoping to find.

Mack said, "I know, I know, the business about calling me Dick Tracy. Well, maybe I'm not so different. It's not my fault. They pressure you."

"About Creighton, you mean? About that fingerprint being his? Who pressured you?"

"I'm not saying anybody pressured me. Maybe I'm just admitting to myself that when you're in doubt, you give the prosecution what it wants. And after thirty years of rendering that service, I get repaid with an indictment. Go talk to my lawyer."

This time he caught me off guard, pushing me off balance and out the door. Before he slammed it I managed to say, "Do you think it'll be easier or harder to find a publisher now that you're indicted?" Then I left, with nothing accomplished except having the last word.

Fifteen

First stop near Vero: When I first met Derek Evers at the Indian River physical evidence storage facility I thought he was there as part of Bring Your Kid to Work Day. Turned out he was in his early thirties and in charge of the facility. So diminutive, and so slight, he probably bought his clothes in the boys' department. Here it was more than twenty years later and, except for graying at the temples and sporting a goatee to force his face to look older, he hadn't changed much. He certainly hadn't gained a pound, and he still really needed that belt to cinch in his pants, which puckered around his waist.

"Brigid Quinn," Derek said warily. At his post, guarding the stacks of evidence boxes, he was always mildly wary without giving an obvious reason, like a librarian always expecting you to tell him your books were way overdue.

"Derek! It's been forever. How the hell are you?" I didn't want to come across all King Kong on him, so I didn't ask him if he'd kicked the habit. But just the same his eyes narrowed with suspicion. The books were way overdue.

"Our business is done. I don't owe you anything," he said.

"Our business is never done," I said quietly. "Hey, looks to me like you've been hearing about what's going on. The Creighton case. What a mess, huh?"

"Seems pretty straightforward to me."

"No, it's a mess, all right. Listen, I have someone investigating—"

"I know. Laura Coleman."

"That's right! Laura Coleman. She really needs that evidence, Derek."

"Have you got a written request?"

"Derek, Derek. Don't waste time. I know William Hench filed the paperwork. First you said you couldn't find it. Then you said it was destroyed. You can whisper to me, very softly, that you just don't give a shit and didn't bother to look for it."

"That's not it," he said.

"Then what is it?" I asked.

"Why do you care about what happens to one man on death row?"

"I don't, actually. I just don't like a good person like Laura Coleman to get the runaround from someone like you. It goes against my sense of justice."

"That hair dryer won't tell you anything you don't already know. It won't change anything. He's going to die."

"Look for it. Evidence storehouses are big, but this one isn't that big. And it's not like there are vans filled with stuff waiting for you to check in. It's Indian River, for God's sake."

"What if I say no?"

"Well, then we talk about another issue, don't we?"

"You wouldn't."

"Yes, I would."

"You realize if I go down, you go down."

"Shh. Don't even talk about it when we're alone. Derek, I'm sixty years old, and I've been living in a gray zone for most of my life. Maybe it's time I went down for something. Maybe it's time I stopped trying to outrun my past. Maybe it's time for both of us."

Derek took one of those gulps where you try not to look like you're gulping so the other person knows just how nervous you are. His Adam's apple, always a little more prominent than most, bobbled. He knew if I talked it wouldn't just mean losing his stupid job so he couldn't play video games during the day. It would mean prison time.

"They don't want it found," he said.

"Who doesn't? The state's attorney because it will cause too much trouble and his caseload is already full? Or the appellate judge who just rubber-stamped the death warrant? Is it laziness, incompetence, or something worse? Or does it even matter who told you to stonewall? Personally, I couldn't care less."

"They'll give me a hard time."

"They can't touch you. They wouldn't dare. Now me, I can touch you. Hard. I made sure to keep my own chain of custody on our little project just in case we ever came to this point. And we're here."

"I'll look for it," he said.

"I don't see you looking for it. I see you just standing there." I looked at my watch. "When do you expect to find the evidence, Derek? Should I wait, or should I come back in, let's say, an hour?"

"Give me two," he said, pretending that he had to search that hard.

I let him hold on to this shred of his dignity. That's how you forge good relationships. "Great. See you in a bit, but call me if you find it sooner."

I gave Derek my cell phone number, left the facility. Now for the third person on my list.

Sixteen

FROM THE DIRECT EXAMINATION OF DETECTIVE
GABRIEL DELGADO BY ATTORNEY LANCER

Q: Did you detect evidence of any foul play regarding the children? Overturned tables, bedsheets dragged onto the floor.

A: None of that. The bedclothes were rumpled, but you couldn't tell if they were slept in that night, or if the kids just never made their beds. If they were at home, the children seem to have come downstairs and left the house under their own steam. It appeared if there was an adult present at the time, they trusted him.

Q: And when did you begin to be suspicious of the defendant?

A: Almost immediately. I sat him down and questioned him about his activities in the hours preceding the death of his wife and disappearance of his children.

Q: Is this kind of questioning typical?

A: Oh. Yes. You know—

Q: For the sake of the jury . . .

A: In so many cases where there's a suspicion of foul play in a death investigation, in the great majority of cases the killer is known to the victim. I asked Mr. Creighton why he had been

out of the house. He said he had returned from a business trip
to Miami. I asked him what the business was, and he got cagey.

Q: Cagey?

By Attorney Croft: Objection.

The Court: Can you use another word?

A: Evasive, I mean. He didn't want to tell me what the business
was.

The building was on Fiddlewood Road, off the main drag to keep it more
discreet because in Vero no one wanted to think about crime unless they
had to. The building blended cunningly with the old Florida style of the
rest of the city, white shutters accenting pastel yellow walls. A small
sign whispered that this was the Vero Beach Police Department.

I parked in a visitor's parking space and walked inside to a tasteful
lobby.

"I'm here to see Gabriel Delgado," I said to the receptionist, who, in
a thick polyester long-sleeved shirt, forest green, large, that fought
against her curves and barely won, was clearly not Very Very Vero.

"Do you have an appointment?" she asked.

"Is he here?" I smiled.

In an effort to preserve the small-town goshness, there was nothing
for her to do but smile back. For all she knew I was rich, and the rich
needed to be treated just so.

"Yes, he is," she said through her smile.

I handed her my card.

She took it and disappeared down a short hallway. I heard her knock
on a closed door and enter. She came out again quickly, followed so
closely by an older than middle-aged man, I knew he would have gotten a thrill if she stopped fast.

She managed to get out of the way in time, and he stopped on a dime
in front of me as he said, "Brigid Quinn. To what do we owe the honor
of your visit in our humble township?"

Obvious from the start how he was able to keep his job. He was
smarmy. But it would have been unnecessary, he was that hot. Yes, yes,
yes, I know I said older than middle-aged, and that should eliminate the

possibility of hotness in some younger minds out there, but this guy was hot. You know the classic image of the arrogant bullfighter? Black hair combed back? Body sleek and powerful as a whip? That.

I imagined lonely Vero housewives staging home burglaries just so he'd come over and dust for prints on their underwear drawer. Breaking a window at the back of the house. Calling him. Coming to the door breathless wrapped in a towel when he knocked. "I'm sorry, Detective Delgado, I never dreamed you'd come this fast! Do you always come this fast?" And blushing, "I mean, I mean . . . I'll be in the bedroom just over there getting dressed. The window is there. I don't see anything missing, so maybe it was just vandalism."

Hey, my sexual development was influenced by watching *Peyton Place*, many decades before *Real Housewives*. Feeling a little visceral flutter, I admit I stopped to take a breath before I spoke. "I know you're probably swamped, but may I have just a teeny moment of your time?" I asked, matching his southern gallantry.

He stepped aside and put out his hand with an ever so small bow to show me back to his office. I felt a little thrill going through the door as if it led to his bedroom, and simultaneously wanted to hide my wedding band and show it. Other women my age feel like this, right?

He shut the door.

He gestured me to a not-uncomfortable chair in front of his desk and, instead of going around to the back of the desk, turned another chair to face me. He crossed his legs, leaned back with his elbows on the arms of his chair, and made a confident steeple of his fingertips.

"You actually do know why I'm here, don't you?" I said.

"Of course I do," he admitted, bobbing his head to the side to deprecate his former pretense. "Madeline and I are very old friends. She called and told me to expect you. But that doesn't mean I'm not excited to meet you. I only regret I never got to work with you."

"Not a lot happens in Vero Beach, I imagine."

"This is true. So when you begin asking me what I remember about the Creighton family murder, you'll find I remember everything to the last detail. It was not a terribly grisly case, no mutilation or decomposition. Just an electrocuted woman in a bathtub and three missing children.

But when a man wipes out his family it makes national headlines. I was interviewed many times. Going over the information again and again is part of the reason I remember it all, I suppose."

"It was an easy case, apparently."

"Ah yes, I think I'm on record for closing a murder case in the quickest amount of time. I took Marcus Creighton in for interrogation the morning after the murders, when Shayna Murry blew his alibi. He was so stunned by her not lying for him, he couldn't offer any other. I arrested him on the spot, even before the forensic evidence came back with his fingerprint on the hair dryer that killed his wife. The thing I regret the most is that he hid the bodies of the children so quickly and so well we were never able to find them. This haunts more than one of us who was involved."

"Was he offered a deal?"

"Life without parole if he led us to the children."

"But he didn't take it."

"He insisted he didn't know. He was hoping for an acquittal based on the lack of bodies, or at least for less than a life sentence. That's what his attorney advised."

I said, "I suppose Shayna Murry's testimony did it more than anything. That call she reported from him, 'If anyone asks tell them I was with you.'"

"That's right. You and I both know trials are won on the strength of feeling more than fact. What the jury heard was that men should never put too much trust in a woman's love. That was the evidence." He stopped to convey with his eyes a second of sadness for a lost romance, then shifted back. His timing was superb.

"Did you ever consider that Shayna Murry could have been an accessory if not an accomplice?"

"If it was anyone else but Shayna Murry I might consider it."

"Why not her?"

"Do you know anything at all about her?"

"I haven't met her."

Delgado shook his head. "You know runaway kids? Well, that time it was the parents. Her no-good parents ran away from home when

Shayna and her brother were in their teens. They left them five hundred dollars in cash and that little house that Shayna still lives in."

"Okay, hard-knock life, sorry for her, et cetera. But just stick with me on this. Shayna Murry as accomplice."

"And then chickened out and made herself appear oblivious to Creighton's plan? Okay, could happen. But if she could countenance doing such a thing in the first place, she would have been strong enough to keep up the lie. The reward would have been great. She could have simply moved in and taken over the life Kathleen Melissa Creighton had not appreciated. Instead she lost everything. If you only saw her now . . ."

"Why do you say Kathleen Creighton had not appreciated her life?"

"I think she was an unhappy, or at least dissatisfied, woman. She knew her husband was having an affair." He glanced away. "At least this is what her friends reported."

He even remembered the victim's full name after all these years. Did he lick his lips when he said it? "Did Kathleen Creighton ever have you investigate a burglary?" I asked.

"I'm sorry?"

"Oh, nothing." And then in the same casual tone, slipping it in to catch him off guard, I said, "Did you pressure Tracy Mack into calling that fingerprint on the hair dryer a match to Creighton?"

In a millisecond his expression flew open and shut. He managed to keep his mild accent, though the steeple he had maintained throughout our conversation fell from his fingertips. He tried not to rush the questions. "Why would you ask that? Have you spoken with him? Did he tell you that?"

"Yes and no," I reassured him. "He didn't mention you at all."

Seventeen

Partly to kill time until I knew whether I'd need round two with Derek Evers, but also on the slight chance that I had a better shot at Shayna than Laura had, I drove the short distance to Cracker's Café.

Sebastian, Vero Beach's lower-middle-class neighbor, nestled unapologetically, almost with a smirk, beside the wealthier enclave. This area was more of the Florida Keys flavor, waterfront restaurants with names like Squid Lips, and ice-cream parlors housed in crumbling cottages, their strawberry aroma blending in the humid air with the smell of the fish house next door.

Cracker's Café was on the main drag. Like the rest of the town it expressed a reverse snobbism. A sign outside said FOR FINE DINING, GO ELSEWHERE. A Ford pickup, more rust than red, was parked outside in a lot with faded parking stripes. Maybe an early eighties model, it could have rated as a classic if it got the respect it deserved. Cracker's was the kind of place that has several kinds of pie made on the premises and stacked on a stand under a clear plastic dome. Oh, and a counter with vinyl-topped aluminum stools.

The way you could tell the place wasn't just your generic diner was the decorations. At least a dozen whips hung on the walls, some looped and some extended almost to their limits. Dark leather on dark walls.

The lunch rush must have been over. Only one booth taken, a middle-aged man and woman who munched in relative silence. At the counter a tall scruffy guy argued mildly with a shorter scruffy guy on the other side. The taller one looked youngish or middle-aged, depending on how old you are. The shorter guy was definitely a geezer. The argument was over money, but it sounded like one they had often, and both already knew the outcome.

Instead of a booth I chose a table where I could view the entire place as well as the front door. Covering the table was a plastic cloth with sunflowers and roosters on it. I rested my elbows on it and then drew them away because the tablecloth had that sticky feel and smell of one that's been washed recently with a stinky dishrag.

The couple watched me with interest as if I was the floor show. The two guys arguing, which included the words "mahi" and "wahoo" at intervals, ignored me.

I waved at the couple. They quickly looked down at their sandwiches.

The waitress approached, and I got my first look at the woman who destroyed Marcus Creighton.

Shayna (as her name tag said) was petite to the point of being elfin in both form and feature. She was the sort of woman who you suspect might be attractive to certain men who've denied something taboo deep in their subconscious. Was Marcus Creighton one of these men?

"Coffee?" she asked, lifting the carafe she carried.

"Lovely," I said. "What kind of pie do you recommend?"

"The cherry is good."

"What else?"

She looked at the stand on the counter, squinted to see better. "Peach and pecan."

"Is it fresh peaches or canned?"

She looked at me like I had a smudge on my nose. "Fresh. Straight from Georgia."

I bobbed my head in a quick nod. She wrote that down and went back to the counter, not bothering the geezer for the order but getting one of those thick white plates out, lifting the plastic cover from the pie stand, and easing a piece of peach out of the top tier. She brought it back to me by the time I had added cream and a little packet of fake sugar to my coffee.

"What's with the whips?" I asked, waving my hand across the walls. "I haven't seen anything like this since *50 Shades*."

She snickered at that, apparently accustomed to satisfying tourists spilling over from the more popular attractions several hours west to Orlando. "It goes with the name of the place, Cracker's. That was what they called the herders in Florida because of the sound their whips made. That was in the early twentieth century when most of Florida was agricultural. Sam has quite a collection."

"Ah, thanks." While she was talking, I observed more than listened. The premature stoop of her shoulders matched by the sag in her face suggested that she was still weighed down by the burden of Creighton's conviction, not to mention the fact that she was the killer's mistress, the woman who had seduced him to violence, the destroyer of a family.

And one of the victims.

It would have been a big load for anyone to carry, but for this tiny creature it seemed especially hard. She had wanted to be an artist; maybe she even thought her involvement with Creighton would give her some level of celebrity. But in the end her bad decision on a boyfriend had made her nothing but a waitress in a backwater café. Whatever her motivation at the time, she couldn't have foreseen what it would be like to live maybe another half century with drudgery, remorse, and guilt. Life is so much longer than it seems when you're twenty-nine.

I had been ready to see an opportunistic parasite. Instead I felt bad for the little thing. I pushed on her anyway because that's what I do.

"By the way, Shayna. I heard Marcus Creighton will be executed in four days. How do you feel about that?"

It had been a long time since I'd felt this much tension associated with a piece of pie. The rest of the people in the room caught the feeling, too, as if they were like those aliens in *Invasion of the Body Snatchers*, a single organism with identical reactions, or something creepy like that. I exaggerate; it was just that everyone in a town this size knew each other and their history.

Shayna didn't respond, only shot a look that looked like a warning toward the counter. When I looked in that direction, too, I saw both the scruffy guys looking at me. Without saying anything, Shayna disappeared down a hall with a sign over it that said REST ROOMS, where I assumed she was going to try to pull herself together and process the news I'd given her.

While I waited, the older woman in the booth across the way looked at me with a sour little smirk that said I was in for it now. The two men who had been arguing at the counter arrived at my table and pulled out chairs on either side of me. Looked like we were going small-town noir.

My phone rang, but I gestured to the chairs, letting the gentlemen know they were welcome to join me though they had not asked. Attentive to them, I snapped the phone open without looking at the caller. Let everyone here wonder if this call was about Creighton.

"Derek!" I said.

But it was Laura, with news.

"They sent the cell phone records to Will's office, Brigid. There weren't that many."

Those days people didn't spend all their time checking weather or Facebook, and I bet Creighton's phone didn't even have texting capability. "So tell me."

"It was easy. Shayna Murry testified that he called her and said 'If anyone asks, tell them I was with you.' There's no call from Marcus to Shayna on that date. Okay, so maybe he used a different phone. But here's the thing: There is a record of him calling his home number like he said he did. It's linked to a cell tower in Sebastian. Incredibly lucky that they even had a cell tower in Sebastian then."

"So she lied," I said. I took some pleasure in realizing that no one in the café knew who she was, except maybe someone who had lied. I wondered if she was leaning against the wall in the hallway that led to the bathrooms. Listening. Maybe now she would talk to me.

"She lied," Laura said. I got the feeling she would have liked to squeal but was keeping her voice controlled after my warning about her feelings showing.

My heart thumped on Laura's behalf with the excitement of that moment when you've followed a hunch and now you're damn sure. I looked to my right at the shorter of the two scruffy men watching me as I said, "This is hopeful. I say we try to get this guy out."

Professional or not, I heard Laura whoop spontaneously. "Did you get the hair dryer from Evers?"

I told her I was sorry I hadn't yet accomplished my part of the job, but needed to get off the phone because I was sure a call was coming soon.

I left the phone out on the table and put out my hand to each of the scruffy guys in turn. It seemed impolite to keep calling them that. "Hi, I'm Brigid," I said, and waited for the polite return of names. Which did not come. "Who might you be?" I prodded gently, getting into cracker-speak.

The taller of the two was leaning back in his chair, balancing on the two back legs while his hands held the table. He had lit a cigarette while I was on the phone with Laura and would keep one hand out for balance when he took a puff with the other. He put the cigarette in the ashtray on the table. "Erroll," he said, after a time. "This here's Sam."

"This your place, Sam?" I asked. I took an appreciative bite of my pie. The aroma of the peaches had under-notes of fried meat and menthol. "The pie's terrific."

"It's been better," Sam said, trying to maintain what I guessed was a threatening demeanor while conflicted by the pride he took in his pie. He swiped his hand through the air, either in a gesture of disdain for my poor taste in pie, or trying to clear the air of Erroll's smoke so as not to ruin my dining experience.

Erroll said, "I'm here because I sell fish to Sam."

This reminded Sam of their argument. "Can't put wahoo on the menu. Tourists don't know what it is. They think it's the Internet. Nobody'll order it."

"Call it something else, then," Erroll snapped, and then ignored him and said to me, "Which way you headed?"

The words were southern good ol' boy, but the tone was more like *Get yer ass outta here*. They were looking for the way to get the old broad gone without hurting her.

"Nice place," I said after taking another lip-smacking bite of pie. "This whole area is nice. I grew up in Southeast Florida, but I went to school in Tallahassee. I remember tubing down the Ichetucknee with a case of beer. Hell, I remember what it was like before Disney World. You?"

Sam said, "I wouldn't mind having the days back again when I could take a line down to the lagoon, catch a bigmouth bass, and cook it up right there on the bank with some swamp cabbage."

Erroll shifted irritably in his chair and let the front legs bang to the floor while I nodded my agreement.

"I know," I said. "Once Orlando took hold you got developers coming in, so the coast from Miami to Palm Beach is now creeping all the way to Jacksonville. Just in the past twenty, thirty years. Every little spit of land, every island—"

I looked to Erroll to include him in the conversation, but he was looking at Sam like Sam was an idiot. I had to agree with Erroll, if any of us were going to make any progress, someone was going to have to be more direct. I asked, "Is Shayna coming back?"

"Shayna," Erroll said.

"The woman Marcus Creighton killed his family for. I wanted to talk to her about him."

"She went home," Sam said, back with the program. "She's sick."

"Uh, yeah, we really want you to leave her alone about that Creighton," Erroll said. "It's bullshit." His voice stayed neutral, but I could sense the muscles in his shoulders tensing. Mine tensed in response. I made my right hand into a fist and let it hang beside the chair. *If he spreads his knees to stand up and come for me, I've got good leverage to bring my right fist up between his legs. Nothing fancy.*

"I just wanted to ask her a few questions," I said.

Erroll said, "But you know, we did that for years. After a while this whole town got real tired of news people, and those true crime television shows—"

"But I'm not—"

"I don't give a shit what you are. It's about time they fried that cocksucker who took advantage of our girl. You come to this town, you deal with everybody here. Understand?"

Then my phone rang again. Sam jumped a little, and Erroll's muscles got harder. I unballed my fist and flipped the phone open, but not without looking at the caller this time.

I said, "Derek! You found it. Listen, I don't want to get near it. I want you to follow proper chain of custody and send it to . . ." I got out my pad and gave him the address of the independent fingerprint examiner that Will had retained. "Repeat that back. What? Clothes, a shovel, what kind of crap is that? I don't care about the other stuff, I want the fucking hair dryer. You don't find it and I'm coming over there and starting a shitstorm the like of which hasn't been seen since the great turd tornado of '63. You'll be sharing a cell at Raiford with someone who knows what you've done. I'll make sure of it. You got that? Good."

I hung up my phone and looked up at the two men, who were looking at the old broad with different eyes now.

I said, "What?"

Eighteen

I got out of Cracker's Café without any information, but at least without starting a brawl, so I counted that as a plus. Headed home with thoughts shifting from Marcus to Dad and back again, like that Pong thing in the first Atari game. Full-on monkey brain without any more profit than I had in Vero. But the progress in the Creighton case was also a plus, right? Finding the cell phone records that showed Shayna Murry had perjured herself. Having an opposing interpretation on that incriminating fingerprint. Then I remembered what I'd told Laura, how it doesn't matter what kind of logic or law you bring to bear, the appellate judge could just say no.

Then back to what Will Hench had said, "but you try to see justice done anyway." At least I had Derek Evers on the ropes; it would only be a matter of time before he came through with the hair dryer. Would be a good day if I found Dad feeling better, sitting up and taking some nourishment.

The afternoon rain hit again, but I didn't even slow down.

It was still raining when I got off I-95 at the Commercial Boulevard exit. I found a Walgreens and purchased a cell phone to give to Mom. Also an umbrella.

And arrived at the hospital around six. Despite what I had told myself about the level of involvement with my parents, the self-centered tedium of sitting in that room, I still approached it on hyperalert, ready for a monster to jump out at me. How odd, I thought, totally calm in that café not knowing what two grown men might do, but now my heart pounding harder and harder the closer I got to his room.

With this in mind I nearly ran into the priest, dressed in black with a white stole around his collared neck. He carried a little black box in front of him.

"Oh my God!" I said, nearly shoving him aside in my frenzy to get to Dad's bedside, but he was a large priest and couldn't get out of the way fast enough even if he wanted to.

He looked startled, then said, "It's all right, my dear. I'm not here for last rites, I've just given Mr. Quinn his communion."

He stepped around and out of the room, leaving me to consider how my heart appeared to be looking for a way out of my chest. Wondering if it meant that I cared after all. When I'd calmed down some, I walked in and found Todd standing next to the bed.

"There," Todd said. "Happy now?"

Dad was lying there, totally out of it, paler and bonier than ever. I stroked a skinny shoulder that protruded from his hospital gown and felt the joint. His hand had turned purple from the IV needle. Blood bruises marked his forearm. "He's in a coma? I thought he just took communion."

"He did. Then he went back to sleep. Don't wake him up."

I knew Todd was saying this for his own benefit rather than any healing power sleep might bring Dad. I wasn't in the mood for arguing.

At that point Mom emerged from the bathroom. So I wouldn't forget, I got the cell phone out of my tote, plugged it into a wall outlet to charge it, and showed her how to use it. From phrases she used, like "newfangled gizmos," I'd say her ability to learn this was in doubt. Funny how you get used to doing something like tying your shoe and then wonder about it when you're trying to show someone else how to do it.

It took us a while, practicing from my phone to hers, what buttons to press to speed-dial me and how to make sure it was charged and why to keep it on. How to turn it back on in case she accidentally turned it off.

Todd left while we were doing that. I stayed for several hours.

· · ·

Finally heading to the hotel just after sunset, I called Carlo, who was three hours earlier than me. Wanting to keep the conversation from the battlefield light for the home front, I joked about Mom trying to learn how to use a cell phone, and the run-in with the good ol' boys in Sebastian. I meant him to laugh, but he didn't. Carlo expressed concern for my safety, which I pooh-poohed vigorously before I switched the topic to weather. Arizonans like talking about the weather because there is so little of it.

"Did it rain there yet?" I asked. June mostly bakes, and the monsoon rain comes in July.

"No, it's just hot," Carlo said with the terminally cranky fatigue of summer. "How about there?"

"We're getting the three P.M. thunderstorm pretty regular, but in between rains it's so hot and humid my elbows are sweating. I'm never going to make cracks about dry heat again."

"This is too long. I miss you."

"I miss you, too, Perfesser."

He asked me how Dad was doing, then about Laura. I was uncustomarily distracted by all this and finally thought to check out the car behind me as I usually did when driving. It was dark, but I could make out a large upscale vehicle. I wondered how long it had been there.

"Gotta go, honey."

"Is everything all right? Your voice sounds edgy all of a sudden."

Like I was going to say *Oh shit, I think someone is following me* when they probably weren't? I adjusted my voice. No need to worry him about nothing. "Just worn out, and I shouldn't be on the phone while I'm driving in the dark. Love you, talk tomorrow, 'kay?"

I hung up and focused my eyes on my rearview mirror. The car continued to follow me east on Hillsboro Boulevard, light after light. Not too alarming; it was a well-traveled crosstown street. At the Hillsboro Bridge the raising light went on, and I got sandwiched between the car in front of me waiting at the drop bar and the car behind me.

Not that there was anywhere I could go, but I didn't switch off my ignition as I usually would.

A tourist would watch the gigantic drawbridge go up and admire the several luxury yachts and a sailboat crossing through on the Intracoastal. A Floridian would curse at being stopped for six minutes and swear to get the timing better next time. Instead, I took the opportunity to lift just my eyes to my rearview mirror and study the vehicle behind me.

Black Mercedes, late model, I'd guess E-Class from the grille. Made for comfort, not sex appeal. Pricier than some, but common as sand in this part of the world. Guy with very wide shoulders driving. Blazer, white shirt, and tie, which I could make out because the day-bright lights on the bridge made the shirt glow in contrast to the jacket and tie. A baseball cap. Not wrong, and not quite right either.

The drawbridge finished its slow descent, the arm went up, and the line of cars that had grown since I stopped continued its progress across the bridge.

Better safe than sorry, Mom said inside my brain. Rather than make the left turn on Ocean Boulevard that eased into A1A and the entrance to the hotel, I turned right instead. So did the Mercedes.

I drove down the two-lane road hemmed by high-rise condos on the beach side, to my left, and quaint old fifties-style motels on the right, blue neon pelicans with VACANCY signs. I drove five miles under the speed limit to encourage the car to pass me, but it didn't. Either the driver was a senior citizen who always drove this speed, or I was definitely being followed in a kind of slow-speed chase.

I didn't want to let him know where I was staying, of course, so I looked at my options. No left turns possible, but if the car followed me down any one of these dinky side roads to the right, it would be too coincidental. The roads were dark, and he had more of a chance of getting aggressive without being seen, but that was my only choice.

At the last second I whipped to the right without braking, and because I was only going thirty miles an hour I managed to mostly stay on the road, just snagging the small plot of grass in front of the Flamingo Harbor Motel.

In my rearview mirror I saw the car jam on its brakes, its taillights stopped midway through the intersection. A horn honked, some driver who didn't appreciate almost rear-ending him. I sped up and kept going, and made the third right before he could back up and follow. The driver behind him helped delay that move.

After a few blocks heading north, I turned left and then turned right again like a fox leaving a confusing trail for the hounds, watching for that Mercedes along the way. I kept expecting to see his headlights behind me at every turn, with a feeling that I was playing a large-scale game of Pac-Man. But oddly, and this made me more suspicious than if I had seen him, there was no sign of him ready to gobble me up. If that was the case, he'd given up too easy.

Still watching every side street, I finally made my circuitous way to the hotel. I would have valeted, but couldn't see anyone on duty and didn't want to leave my vehicle parked for long under the well-lighted portico where anyone driving by could see it. So I pulled around the building and into the underground garage. I wanted a space close to the elevator, but so did everyone else, apparently. I finally found one about six aisles away.

Parking garages at night. What a cliché, huh? There's a reason for that.

There was more shadow than light down there, and no one else around, so I pulled my weapon out of my tote bag and held it dangling against my thigh as I walked toward the elevator. The gassy smell. The dampness. The now-familiar *squeech* of my sneakers that had become theme music behind the whole Florida visit echoed against the dank concrete walls. I disapproved of the sound because it made it harder to hear more important sounds.

I heard the catch of a car door that wasn't slammed shut but gently closed. I wasn't sure where the sound came from because of the acoustics down here. I ducked down between two cars—not SUVs, in which case I wouldn't have had to duck. Where's an SUV when you're not trying to get out of a parking space? I looked out around the back fender of a Honda and saw my man leaning up against the concrete wall next to the elevator. Same dressed up below the neck, same baseball cap above. He was looking around, a little too curious for a parking garage, like what's to see? Yet too relaxed and in the open to be an assailant. Still, the man was like a Miami Dolphins defensive end who was just a little past his sell-by date. Good two twenty-five, two fifty, and at least six two.

I tried to assess the situation, figure out my options, deal with this bum. I didn't know what his own objective was. Rape or similar assault, robbery, or sent specifically after me by someone who knew me when I worked this area, someone with an old grudge? With his body mass about three times mine, I preferred not to deal with him hand to hand unless I had to. I could still kill him, but after the day I'd had I wasn't in the mood.

I eased out from behind the car, gun drawn. I said, "Put your hands by your side."

He did. "There's noth—"

"Shut up," I said. "Step away from the elevator."

For a regular Joe he seemed a little too comfortable with this kind of scenario, standing in front of the muzzle of a weapon in a parking garage. He pushed off the wall slowly with his foot and took one slow step after another. "If you'd—"

By this time he was within about ten feet of me, angled with his right side forward, likely disguising something under his jacket on the left. "Jacket off," I said. "Very slowly."

He did that, revealing a side holster with a Glock. He smiled, almost apologetically, when I saw it. He started to drape the jacket over his arm.

"Drop it," I said.

This was his first protest to my instructions. "But I'm—"

"Drop it," I said. "And one more word and you're dead."

He dropped it, on the oil-and-tire-tread floor of the garage. "It's a nice jacket," he said, with more regret for the jacket than concern for his life.

"Oil stains will come out easier than dick matter from your pants. Now I want you to use your index finger to release the strap on your holster. That's good. Now your index finger and thumb to remove your weapon. Slowly. I'm watching, and I'm feeling strangely alert."

He did as I said and stood holding the gun before him with two fingers like a smelly diaper.

"Shut up," I said again, just in case. "Now gently put the gun on the floor, and then kick it over here."

He did, but not far enough. It stopped midway between us. He stepped forward, but I gestured for him to stay where he was.

I said, "You were following me. But you knew I was staying here. How is that?"

"When I saw your erratic route, I figured you spotted me and were just trying to give me the slip. I figured you'd be here sooner or later."

"How did you know I was staying here?"

"I followed you here yesterday. When—"

I said, "You're not the kind of person who works for himself. Who sent you?"

"I've come from Manuel Gutierrez," he said, sounding a little sheepish that we had come to this pass without him being able to identify himself.

I remained on alert, but silent. That encouraged him to go on.

"He'd like to see you. Now, if you're free."

"Who are you?"

"My name is Glen Slipher."

"You're not very good at the task you're currently performing. This makes me suspicious, because I would think Manny Gutierrez would be able to afford better. What kind of work do you usually do for him, Mr. Slipher?"

"I'm Mr. Gutierrez's accountant," he said, and repeated, "He'd like to talk to you."

"You're a very large accountant. Why didn't you say that sooner?"

"You didn't give me a chance." He inadvertently glanced at the sound of tires that had a heavier *squeech* than my shoes had made.

"Terrific. You bring another accountant for backup?" I asked, not daring to avert my eyes from him and the gun on the ground, which was closer to him than I'd like.

"No. I'm alone."

The door belonging to the car that must have pulled in to a spot somewhere behind me opened and closed, making no attempt at secrecy. Or wanting to make me think it was making no attempt at secrecy. I'm suspicious that way.

I cocked my head slightly to the right as hyperawareness rippled over my skin. "Swivel around me so we're facing the guy coming this way."

As we did this I stayed conscious of his gun on the floor. Maybe he was paying a visit from Manny Gutierrez, and maybe he wasn't. We waited.

A youngish man, in twentysomething uniform of shabby jeans and a vintage rock band T-shirt, clearly lost in his own thoughts, got all the way past Glen the accountant before he saw me and the gun. He slowed despite his best intentions.

"Evening," I said.

"Evening," said the accountant.

Youngish man didn't answer, just picked up the pace and headed on. I figured he thought, little woman with a gun, looked like she had things under control without his interference. This was South Florida, after all.

"I'm not going anywhere with you," I said.

He nodded. "Mr. Gutierrez told me to anticipate that possibility. He said you'd prefer to follow in your own car."

"He remembers me."

"He said you've had a long association."

I stepped forward to bend down and pick up Glen's weapon. "I didn't like the way Manny disrespected me when I stopped by. I'll see him another time, and I'll give this back to you when I do."

"I might have a second one in my car," he advised helpfully.

"I may be paranoid, but I'm not ridiculous," I said. "What else did Gutierrez say?"

"He called you a tough cookie. He said that with great respect, of course. That you were little. Very small in stature, but nonetheless dangerous, he said, and I should use every caution or you'd likely kill me before I had a chance to speak."

"Why didn't he just let us in the last time we were at his place? That's no way to treat an old friend."

"He only wants to see you, not your associate."

"And why not just call me and invite me over?"

"Mr. Gutierrez doesn't like to use phones. Anytime, anywhere, any way."

"Yup, that's Manny. Tell him he should suck it up, buy a phone, and call me on it. Then when he's not using it he can stick it up his ass."

Now you might be saying *Why stop by his place and then tell him to go to hell?* This is how you do it with Manny Gutierrez. I wanted him to know I was in town, but couldn't make it look like I needed him. I would go on my terms, in my time.

Nineteen

Next morning I told Laura I'd meet her at the recording studio and planned to get there after Will went on the air, but I showed up a little too soon. I identified myself and was directed toward the control booth, and ran into him coming out of the greenroom, followed by Laura. He gripped my arm and steered me out of earshot of Alison Samuels, who followed close behind with a remarkably large German shepherd by her side. The dog wore one of those service animal please-don't-touch-me-when-I'm-working jackets.

"Did you get the physical evidence released?" he asked. "Can I say we have it?"

"Yeah, I did. You can. You go out there and give her hell, Will."

He looked at me doubtfully, but he was being nudged into place, waiting his turn to go on. We were ushered into a tech booth, where two aggressively ungroomed guys sat in front of a board with a thousand identical levers that moved up and down. A window that reminded me of the execution chamber looked onto the filming area. Low platform, high table. Bright lights, two cameras. The host, a warmth-exuding woman who introduced herself as Joy Ferenz, appeared on a screen in our booth and also in the room where Will Hench and Alison Samuels sat at the high table.

Laura's phone rang, and she answered it despite frowns from the person who had herded us into the booth. She hung up without explaining who it was, but I knew it was Marcus because of the way she reassured him. Telling him to stick in there, that Will was getting the stay of execution. From the sound of her voice it was hard to tell whether she was lying more to herself or to him.

"I hope they don't start yelling," I said, about Hench and Samuels.

"I hate it when they yell over each other," Laura said.

"Are we live?" a woman's voice said, and then Joy Ferenz's smile expanded across the whole screen. "Welcome back to our program," she said. "Next up we have Alison Samuels, Florida spokesperson for the Haven, a national organization for missing and exploited children, and William Hench, attorney for Marcus Creighton, who, in three short days from now, will be executed for the murder of his family in 1999."

She quickly described the Creighton case, the dead wife, the three children never found. Then the camera panned out to show Will and Alison sitting very straight and looking like they did this all the time. Either that or they were both so passionate about their missions, they neglected to realize anything but those missions. No interviewer, no cameras, no world beyond themselves. Or more precisely, no world beyond the people they were trying to save.

I had the opportunity to observe Alison Samuels from this vantage point. She looked taller than me, so she was either as tall as Will or long-waisted. She had her hair at that length where you can't tell if she needed a haircut or not. She was unattractively tan, as if she spent a lot of time outdoors without sunscreen. She seemed like the kind of person who would benefit from a makeover if you could talk her into submitting to one. Everything was in her eyes, which somehow shifted to convey her affirmation, her anger, or her contempt. A lot of contempt.

"She doesn't look all that bad," I whispered.

"That's because you can't tell her baseline emotion is Pissed Off," Laura whispered back.

Joy Ferenz didn't focus directly on Hench and Samuels to start. First she ran a couple of clips that were intended to show them at their best, starting with Hench. He walked beside a black man dressed in denim pants and a denim shirt buttoned up to his throat. A voice-over told how

Brent Ford had been in prison for thirty-five years, convicted of the brutal (like when is it not brutal?) rape and murder of an elderly white woman in Palatka, Florida. DNA tests not only exonerated Ford but connected the murder to another man already serving time for a similar crime in Alachua County.

Cut to Alison Samuels. I half expected her film clip to show her leading some sleazy pedophile into the same door from which Brent Ford had exited, but the producers avoided the obvious and went for the heartwarming human interest angle instead. She was shown sitting on the floor in what looked like a playroom with that monstrous German shepherd and a small person whose face was obscured.

Then back to the real Will Hench. "As you say, the execution of Marcus Creighton is scheduled for three days from today. But we're convinced he's an innocent man. We have two pieces of evidence that we feel are sufficient to get him a stay of execution." Without waiting for a question from Ferenz, Will briefly explained the cell phone records and the *fraudulent* (he was going full bore here) fingerprint interpretation.

Whether it meant she was unimpressed, it was hard to tell, but while he spoke Samuels ducked down behind the counter as if she was hardly paying attention.

"We need to get a look at her face while Hench is talking. Can you get her to look up? Show a little reaction? Something that will look like reaction to what he was saying?"

"She just keeps bending over to pet her dog."

"Well, somebody get her to look up at least once so we can edit it in later."

Will couldn't hear the conversation in the control booth and kept on. "We're convinced the forensic examiner who testified regarding Creighton's fingerprints on the hair dryer lied. And we have evidence that one of the key witnesses perjured herself. All we're asking for is a stay of execution until we can look at the dryer for other prints that will definitively exclude Creighton."

Joy Ferenz's face was inserted in the screen. "How would you respond to Mr. Hench's request, Ms. Samuels?"

Alison looked up casually from her dog. She gave a smile that was only gentle, and at odds with her words. "Forty-five thousand children under the age of eighteen run away every year," she said. "One in seven runaways falls prey to sex traffickers. The market is large."

Even a professional like Joy Ferenz had a glimmer of uncertainty in her eyes. "And how does this—"

"Operation Cross Country. This was a national sweep in which the Haven joined with the FBI in trying to locate some of the three million children, male and female, who have been pressed into service as prostitutes. We retrieved more than one hundred and fifty children and arrested nearly three hundred pimps." Her smile failed, and her next words were tinged with not triumph but sarcasm. "The operation was considered a great success."

"What does this have to do with Marcus Creighton?" Will finished the host's question, failing at any attempt to disguise his indignation.

Samuels's voice stayed noncombative. "It has to do with missing children. Marcus Creighton knows all about missing children, doesn't he? And he may actually know where three of them have been for the past sixteen years. I'm simply establishing who the real victims are and who the criminals."

"What the hell. Get a shot of the dog."

"This is offensive," Will said, shifting in his chair as if he wanted to leave but knew that leaving meant losing.

Turning her face to look in his direction, but other than that still not reacting, she said, "Offensive." She smiled at the word. "Did you hear that yesterday a fifty-six-year-old man in Dania was indicted for buying another man's twelve-year-old daughter for twenty dollars and a bag of dope?"

Alison turned back to the camera rather than looking at him. "Did you know that girls who have been forced into prostitution often can't get a legal job because they have a criminal record? I find this offensive. I find it so offensive that I'm giving my life to fighting against it. And I have a story to tell you. No, it's not about my own life spent as a child prostitute. It's not about Marcus Creighton's children or the other three million children who are missing today. It has to do with a man who was walking the beach one morning and saw an elderly gentleman picking up starfish that had come onto shore with the high tide and been left there as the tide receded."

"What the fuck?"

"What do we do with this?"

"Beats me. Keep it rolling and we'll figure out what to edit later."

Like Will, Alison couldn't hear the conversation in the control booth and had kept going. "As the younger man watched, the gentleman took each starfish and threw it as far into the waves as he could. When asked what he was doing, the man explained that unless they made it back into the water, the starfish would surely die.

" 'Have you looked down the beach?' the young man asked. 'There are starfish as far as I can see. You can't save them.'

"The old man picked up another starfish, looking a little weary now, but summoned his vigor and threw it far into the water. He said, 'I saved that one.'

"I saved that one," Alison Samuels whispered again.

"Whoa. She's crying. Get a close-up."

The host couldn't stop the story in the middle, so she had let it play out before finishing, with her voice breaking on a sympathetic "Yes, you did. Thank you both for joining us this evening."

Ferenz was doing her wrap-up while the techs messed with the board and said things like "We'll cross-cut." Then Ferenz turned off-camera and said so we could hear in the control booth, "Is this weird? I don't think we'll get any better from these two. Let me know if it hangs together in some logical way. Otherwise, what else we got?"

Samuels was already up and on her way out, her dog striding beside her, until she saw Laura and me in the control booth. Ignoring Laura, she said, "I know you." She studied my face. I felt like a photograph that couldn't look back.

"I don't think we've met," I said. I put out my hand, and the dog's eyes flickered, his nose twitching in my direction.

"Friend, Larry," she said.

"Brigid Quinn," I finished.

"Oh my God," she said, turning within a second into a fangirl sort, taking my hand and pumping it longer than typically advised. "Now I know, I've seen your picture." In another second she had the presence of mind to let go of me. "At the Haven they still talk about that massive kidnapping-for-hire ring that you cracked. I heard so much about you, but you left the area, moved to—"

"Tucson," I said.

Samuels glanced now at Laura, who was, if possible, more tense than before and wanted us to move along already. Samuels said, "But why are you here. With—"

"Agent Quinn is assisting with the Marcus Creighton case," Laura said. "And if you'll excuse us, we have a few things to do."

Alison Samuels turned her attention to Laura with something like anger that morphed into something like satisfaction. The wildly disparate expressions on her face were those of a young person, flitting from emotion to emotion, all equally intense.

When she had gone I said, with undisguised admiration, "The woman is a pro. Samuels had the last word, and ran out the clock like a basketball team two points up and fifteen seconds left."

Laura said, "Did you see what she did? She didn't give a shit about Creighton. She dismissed Will like he wasn't there. All she was interested in was the value of the program in promoting her organization."

"You're right, I saw the tactic," I said. "By going after the bigger story of child exploitation, she made Creighton's case for one man seem insignificant. Excuse me a second."

I wandered out of the booth and into the hall, where I called Derek Evers. "Last chance," I said when he picked up. Silence on both ends, and I wasn't going to be the one to break it. When he finally told me he had all the evidence I wanted, I said, "You're not jerking me around this time. You got the dryer? I'm talking the dryer. Good. What about that address I gave you, you still have it? Repeat it. Okay. And listen, Derek, that fucking thing goes missing at any step along the way, you're finished. Chain of custody, got it?"

Will came up behind me and was either too angry to notice I was on the phone or didn't care. "They'll probably scrap the whole segment. The bitch sabotaged me."

I gave him a thumbs-up, for what he didn't know.

Twenty

I called to let Mom know I was running late but would be there shortly. She didn't pick up her cell, so I tried her apartment number. She was there. She said she forgot the cell phone at the hospital.

"Go visit Dad if you want. Not me. I'm tired and I came home."

Her voice was so thin and airy I had to strain to hear her. We always took care not to put pressure on Mom, and the effort of her having to take care of Dad this way, running back and forth to the hospital, was beginning to tell. I told her I would go sit with him instead.

No one would have known if I hadn't, but I played it on the square and visited Dad. He was sleeping, though, so when Laura called to tell me Frank Puccio hadn't yet received the hair dryer, I called Derek from the visitor waiting area down the hall.

He didn't answer; no one did. I left a message and waited. I waited for three hours, with Laura calling back approximately once every twenty minutes. Did I mention that doing nothing but waiting wasn't my favorite thing?

On the last call, I was able to tell her: Derek had indeed sent the evidence, but not overnight. Probably by sailboat heading south against the Gulf Stream. God damn that little weasel, he got me.

Laura yelled that I should do something.

"What can I do, drive up to Indian River and scream at him?" I asked. "Find the package in transit and rob the shipment?"

"We're running out of time," she yelled. "We have to have that evidence."

I felt for her, believe me; it felt like my gut was being smashed between frenzy and despair, but what good would it have done to share this? I said, "Calm down. The phone records, remember? I think that's more important."

"Don't tell me to calm down! A man's life hangs in the balance and all you can do is *think*."

"You're being unreasonable, and you sound hysterical. Where's that old Coleman professional restraint?"

There was a shout, and then I heard the sound of something breaking.

"Did you just throw something?" I asked.

She didn't answer that. "Restraint," she said. "Brigid Quinn is advising restraint."

"Oh. Well," I said.

By this time it was late afternoon, and I was starving for lack of lunch. Wanting to feel like I wasn't letting at least one person down, I drove over to Mom's, picking up a couple of burgers from a drive-through.

I found her already in her nightie and her old snap-front housecoat with the big pink hibiscus flowers on it. I made a mental note to get her a new housecoat for Christmas. There were crumbs on the counter in the tiny hallway kitchen, and Mom was always very neat, which told me she had eaten something in her apartment rather than go down to the dining room. But the crumbs didn't give me a clear picture. Could have just been toast.

"Junior Whopper with cheese, your favorite," I said, unwrapping one for each of us. "Fries and a strawberry shake, too."

She didn't say anything but looked grateful almost against her will. She sagged into her recliner, and I sat in Dad's, facing the television, which was turned on to an old Fred Astaire/Ginger Rogers movie. We munched in silence, and when we were done I cleaned up the smelly hamburger wrappers and took them to the garbage chute down the hall so they wouldn't stink up the place.

In the hallway I called Carlo on my cell, only to connect and tell him there was no real news.

"None here, either. We got a notice from the homeowners' association. There have been some cases of graffiti in the neighborhood. And Peg got a thorn in her paw. Pretty boring."

"Did you get it out okay?"

"Yes."

I said, "I can't think of anything nicer than to be bored with you."

When I got back to the apartment, Mom hadn't moved. As in, her fingers were in the precise position on the arms of her recliner. I sat back down.

We watched another movie while I thought about Creighton and whether we'd actually get the stay of execution, let alone a new trial, let alone an exoneration. How many more years he'd have to be in prison while all that happened. Thoughts veering from him to Dad and back again.

I asked Mom if she had the old photograph albums I remembered looking through on countless occasions myself, trying to get a handle on our family and my place in it. She pointed to the hutch crammed into the small space that was the dining area of the apartment, and I found the two albums in the bottom drawer.

I spent a little time looking, and remembering. Then something made me say, "Mom, if something happened would you be all right?" *Please say you'll be all right.*

There was a silence. It was like there was something going on at her end that had never been there before, or at least that I had never noticed. Did she know what I was thinking as well as what I was saying? Had she always? Were mothers that way?

"Sure, I'll be all right," she said, saying what I wanted her to say. What she knew I wanted her to say. But she picked at the arm of the chair as she said it.

I turned my body the way I used to so that my back was against the arm of the chair and my legs hung over the other arm. I slurped the rest of my milk shake and balanced the empty plastic cup against my stomach. "He's been a hard man to live with, hasn't he?"

I could feel her thinking *Here we go again*, but she said, "None of us is perfect."

"Remember how he used to try to turn Ariel and me into boys?"

"It's a little soon for memories. You might want to save them for the wake," Mom said. She sounded angry now as well as tired. I liked that bite in her tone, I wanted to spur her on to some emotion, any emotion, and if I couldn't get affectionate reminiscence I'd settle for anger.

"Do you ever wish he was dead?" I asked.

She managed to keep control. "That's a mortal sin, even to speak those words. Even to think them."

"Then what about divorce, ever think of that?"

"That's a mortal sin, too. Have you completely forgotten your catechism?"

I shouldn't have fanned her flames any more than I had already, and certainly not when she was down like this. Then again, what the hell, I was a Quinn, so I said it. "What about hating him, is that a mortal sin?"

"I never said I hated him."

There was another long pause, as if she'd gone too far that time and didn't know how to get back. She had said more than she wanted to say, and only this forced contact over Dad's ill health, and my persistent questions, had brought her to it.

"Did you ever love him?" I pressed.

She finally turned to face me and leaned her elbow on the arm of the chair as she did so. "Why are you suddenly asking all these questions?" She came as close to shouting at me as she ever had. Tired past her limit. I didn't back down.

"What is it with you two?"

She settled on "None of your beeswax."

Ah, the old beeswax defense.

But then later, when I insisted on spending the night, she didn't resist, not even when I told her I'd sleep in Dad's bed.

I walked into the one bedroom, where they still had the antiqued French provincial bedroom set with twin beds. The Dick Van Dyke bedroom set. The little bed table held the beds apart as if it was a boxing referee. Dad's dentures were in the glass next to his bed where they'd been ever since he went to the hospital. The water was getting filmy. On Mom's side there was a rosary I remembered playing with as a child. Blessed by the pope it was.

I didn't want to appear insensitive, but I couldn't stand the thought of Dad's teeth grinning at me all night, so I took the glass into the bathroom and left it by the sink. The place was so hot I considered sticking my head under the faucet, but instead found a blanket in the closet and put it over Mom's bed.

"What are you doing?" she asked.

"I'm turning the temperature down because I don't want to die of heat stroke in my sleep," I said, going to the thermostat and taking it down ten degrees from the eighty-five where it was set.

She was already in bed fingering her rosary when I came back. I got one of Dad's old T-shirts out of the single dresser in the room and changed into it in the bathroom. As far as I could recall, the last time I was naked with her was when I needed a diaper change. I had never seen her body.

I got into bed and reached for the lamp on the nightstand to turn off the lamp. Some light still came in through the venetian blinds that overlooked the parking lot, casting a slatted shadow across the wall.

The smell as I lay down on Dad's bed was that singular odor that identifies a person no matter how young or old they are, the scent caused by years of breathing through the night. This scent was perspiration and old-fashioned hair oil with undertones of bourbon. It wasn't that bad, kind of comforting actually, but I turned the pillow over just the same.

There was no sound for a while other than the occasional clicking of the rosary beads, no louder than a moth beating against tinfoil. Then it stopped.

Flashbulb memory of slumber parties in school, whispering secrets in a dark that knocked down barriers. I thought about the slumber party that the Creighton children missed. Their dad. My dad. Then my thoughts came back to the room. Thoughts are like that, real travelers.

I put my hands out and felt both sides of the narrow mattress. Thoughts ran again, this time to what they had ever done in these beds. No, I wouldn't ask that. But kisses? I tried to remember them kissing and came up with that thing where bodies stay apart and both pairs of lips extend out to barely touch. Once a year on anniversaries, and then only at someone's urging. What other touching?

Is anyone at home hurting you? This was part of my job, after all. I had seen so many cuts and bruises in so many states of injury and healing, and in places one would never think to find them. Maybe I had it too much on the brain, but what's oddest is that I had never before applied it to my parents. Is that odd?

"Are you awake, Mom?"

"Yes."

"Did Dad *never* hit you?" I strung out the words in such a way that I could almost be saying it would be unlikely never to have been hit. Not a big deal, Mom.

Silence.

"When he threw things, I mean."

"No."

I tried to make it easy for her. "By accident, I mean. A vase or a book?"

"No."

The nos were coming pretty regular, but they didn't have a lot of resistance in them, and I had the feeling that in the dark I was melting the beeswax. "What about cheating, Mom?" I tried to keep the words as soft as possible. "It's okay to say, cops have that reputation."

The longest silence yet, and then "No," whispered so softly, even now I can't be sure I heard it. Even if I heard it, there was something about it I couldn't believe.

"Did he ever hurt you?" A different word, hurt is, from hit.

I thought I heard a quick intake of breath, more like a sigh than a gasp.

"No," she said, with the breath. The word sounded so matter-of-fact, like we were talking about whether she had ever traveled outside the country, or eaten raw oysters.

I didn't believe her. I held my breath waiting to see if she would say more, but there was silence again. Silence, but so far she hadn't cut me off.

I had asked these questions of so many women, but never my own mother. Maybe I didn't want to know after all. For now, change tack. "You've never complained about anything."

"Mothers don't do that to their children, bring them into the battle. It's not fair."

Battle. "Did Dad play fair?"

"Go to sleep now, Brigid. You wore me out. I'm sleepy."

I waited for a long time to hear the sound of steady breathing that would tell me she'd fallen asleep, but I must have been the one to go first.

Twenty-one

The way Mom was the next morning, I had to doubt whether that conversation ever happened. Brisk and brusque as ever, after we called the hospital to find out Dad continued stable, she made me go down to the dining room for breakfast, where we sat at their usual table with two other old women. No more opportunity for honest conversation. No conversation at all; the two women with identical white poofs of hair sprayed into plasticity had nothing to say, and I ran out of energy with my own attempts.

My phone rang, and I took it out of my pocket. Laura. Maybe she wanted to yell at me again. I started to get up and take the phone into the lobby, but Mom said, "Answer it here. The old ladies are listening more than you think, and this will probably give them their thrill for the day."

So I did, but tried to keep my voice down so the adjacent table couldn't hear. "Hey, Laura. What's up? You mean Will's interview actually did some good? Are you shi—kidding me? Bones? Seriously? Where did he say they found them?"

I was aware of the whole room going silent. Even the waitstaff froze in place.

"Have you called the sheriff's department in Vero? We'll need a cadaver dog." I closed my eyes. "I don't think so . . ."

When I disconnected, I looked at Mom. Her eyes, in which I'd just today noticed the sadness, almost twinkled. She said, "Go."

"No, I'm not."

"What are you going to do, hold my hand? I'll go over to the hospital later. When you get to be my age, bad health is your main source of entertainment."

I pretended to pick at my toast, and now I was the one who wasn't saying what I meant. "I hate to leave you."

"No you don't."

I didn't know what to say to that, and was aware of the two old women sitting on either side of me. The glitter in their eyes told me there was nothing wrong with their minds. This was better than a daytime soap opera.

Mom sounded a little gentler when she spoke next. "Honey, listen to me. You left a long time ago. Longer than you think you did."

But then she opened her eyes wider over the edge of her juice glass, making me feel as if she'd just given me permission to run along and play.

Laura and I met the others at the Vero Beach police station by midmorning, Staci Kuhl along with the construction guy. Kuhl was a human remains searcher, the kind of person who, when you looked at her, you somehow saw *dog* in her eyes. It was a kind of goodness in the raw. The construction guy was introduced to us as Richard Hiatt. You can always tell an ex-marine. They're always too something, too short or too tall, too good-looking or too ugly. His body looked like it couldn't get any taller so he did his best to get bigger.

Next to Kuhl was Chili Dawg. About one foot off the ground and wiry around the muzzle. Breed? I don't know, maybe what they'd call a dachsypoo. Chili had won awards, but it wasn't for her looks.

Laura looked at the dog doubtfully, and Kuhl was used to the look. "Don't even go there," Kuhl said. "Chili has investigated collapsed buildings that a full-sized shepherd couldn't fit in. She's a pro."

The six of us, Staci Kuhl, Gabriel Delgado, Richard Hiatt, Laura, me, and Chili Dawg, piled into Kuhl's SUV and drove to the site where Hiatt had seen the bones. I felt we could trust his memory; he remembered he had been eating a tuna sub that day, sitting under the shade of the half-completed bridge they were building to get to the island. If Hiatt hadn't offered so much information as we drove, including that he moved from the North when his wife got a job in Vero as a paramedic, that he was happy to leave the cold, and that she made more money than he did, I would have talked more with Kuhl on the way. Kuhl would probably have explained to Laura that there was a chance the bones would have been covered by either bridge pilings or asphalt, and that we'd never stand a chance of having it all dug up.

Luckily, Richard Hiatt remembered pretty specifically what part of the bridge he had been leaning against when he spotted something protruding from the sand. He said at first he thought it looked like a bone, but then he thought it was just a shell or something. The place wasn't so much a beach as the sandy lip around the island, and the waves that came ashore in sync with the boats going by had eroded the soil some, even at that time. He talked mostly to Delgado, maybe because he was the only other male in the group.

When he was finished describing that day when he sat in just this spot eating his tuna fish sub, he leaned against the piling and appeared satisfied that he had our undivided attention. He would, after all, think of us as "important people." He would have more interesting things to tell his wife that evening than she ever had to tell him, no matter how many heart attacks and traffic fatalities she had covered.

Laura pulled three T-shirts from a plastic bag. One was hot pink, one was navy blue with Spider-Man on the front, and the third was black with JUICY COUTURE written on it. They had been left with the evidence after the searchers stopped using cadaver dogs to hunt for the children. I thought about how those dogs would now be long gone themselves and whether in some afterlife they might have finally found the children. The others in the group were more about reality.

"The records show these were picked up off the bedroom floors, probably unwashed, typical kids," Laura said.

Kuhl nodded in a polite but dismissive kind of way and did not take the shirts. "How long ago did you see the bones?" she asked Hiatt.

"This would have been . . ." I could tell he was pausing for effect, but let it go when he saw we were all more fascinated by Chili. "Two years ago. It was the first part of the development process, and you can see they're still adding houses. Do you want me to show you exactly—"

"No, thanks," Kuhl said. "Better if we do it this way." She looked down at Chili, who was looking up at her as if ready for a game. "Chili, find!" Kuhl called, emphasizing each letter of each word.

Chili took off at a run, through a large concrete pipe that had been placed there to prevent further erosion, and peed against a sign warning passing boats NO WAKE.

"Why didn't you mention the bones again?" Kuhl asked as she watched.

"Like I said, if I thought they were really human bones I would have said something. And I never heard about the missing kids until my buddy mentioned it last night, that interview on TV. I only moved here from Pittsburgh the year before I started working on this site."

"The remains would have been here for over a decade at that point," I said. "Do you think it's possible Chili can find them?"

Kuhl snorted. I could almost think Chili did, too. She ran past Richard Hiatt in one of her passes over the area, and the guy reached out to pet her.

"Please don't do that when she's working," Kuhl said. But then she looked doubtful despite her apparent confidence in Chili. "If there were still some bones left when you were here two years ago, and they were close to the surface, it doesn't necessarily mean there'd be some now. This is a very unstable environment. They could have washed away."

Chili kept her nose to the ground. After a few passes, during which time we might have all been holding our collective breath, she paused and cocked her head to the side. "Show me, Chili," Kuhl said with the same careful pronunciation as before. But Chili didn't appear to have reached a definite conclusion. She sniffed closer to the spot, almost digging her nose into the wet sand, then moved a step or two up the slope. She scratched a bit, sniffed, and moved another step

"Ah, probably an odor plume," Kuhl said.

Chili had been moving step after step further up the slope of the bank. About ten feet from where she'd first paused she took a good drag, and only then started to bark. It was an annoying yippy kind of bark like you'd expect from a small dog. Grass had been planted on the spot, to make the area more attractive and to further hold back the erosion.

"Chili. Find," Kuhl repeated. Chili gave a louder yelp and lay down next to the spot.

"Humph," Kuhl said, taking a step back and holding up both her hands like that was that. She turned away, went back to her van, and returned with a small plastic spike.

Kuhl asked Chili, "Are you sure?" Chili barked.

Hiatt was in a carnival mood, all excited suspense, like he was watching another television show. But the fact that we were looking for little ones made it different for the rest of us. Because of this we felt anticipation, sure, but it was anticipation covered by the shroud of small lives lost in violence, a life never lived. It wasn't fun, it wasn't exciting, it was deathly sad, where we were.

I sensed these feelings were in the breath Staci Kuhl drew as she again asked the dog, "Chili, are you sure?" The dog barked again, and she gently placed the marker into the sand near the spot Chili indicated.

"Are you positive there's something down there?" Delgado asked.

"Yes. Yes and yes," Kuhl said.

"And it's human?"

"Yup. Well, can't swear it's bones, but I can swear that human remains have been here. Chili hasn't been wrong yet. My job's done. Secure the scene and call in an anthropologist."

Chili yelped again, more commanding this time. Kuhl reached into a small bag hanging from her shoulder and withdrew a rubber toy. It looked like a chicken mermaid. "You love you some merchick, don't you?" Kuhl said, and passed it to Chili, who squeaked it with an air of triumph.

"You got anyone in the area you can get?" I asked Delgado.

Delgado nodded and pulled out his smartphone, saying while he dialed, "University near Orlando has a good forensic anthropology department. Hey, Hank? Gabe Delgado in Vero. I think we found bones." He explained what was going on, then smiled. "I figured as much," he said, and disconnected. "Henry Aggrawal. I sent him the coordinates of the scene so he'll get here via GPS. I got his attention. He's canceling a class, and he'll be here in an hour and a half."

"You say he's good?" Laura asked.

"One of the top five bones guys in the state, board certified. He testified at the Anthony trial."

The construction guy was listening with interest, pleased to be part of it all. "I know where we can get subs," he said.

Instead Delgado thanked Hiatt for his civic service and told him he'd call if he was needed anymore. Delgado quickly secured the scene and got a nearby officer to come stand guard. Then at my suggestion, "seems appropriate," we dropped Hiatt back at the police station, picked up our own vehicles, and drove over to the Cracker Café.

Turned out Shayna wasn't there, and Sam, the owner, objected to Chili. But Staci Kuhl muttered, "Service dog," and when Sam looked like he thought she was suckering him, Delgado assured him it was the truth. Sam trusted Delgado, apparently—that small-town connection again.

We all ordered and ate in relative silence, everyone concerned with their own thoughts. Gabriel Delgado was a little different now than when I had seen him before. He didn't seem to want to meet my eyes, or Kuhl's or Laura's for that matter, just kept them roaming the restaurant and fixed them on his roast beef sandwich when it arrived.

I could only imagine what he was thinking, about how he had missed finding the children, and whether he might have given up too soon, whether he could have saved them if he hadn't wasted time trying to get Creighton to tell him where they were. And how they were still waiting to be found, like silent witnesses. Just because Delgado was a little smarmy didn't make him a bad person.

I said, "Detective Delgado, if these are the Creighton children, it proves that the whole family was wiped out that night. There was nothing you could have done to stop it."

He cleared his throat by way of acknowledging that, and chewed his sandwich. Kuhl shared hers with Chili, who sat between her and Laura.

Laura just had water, and she only drank half the glass and watched the rest of us eat.

"Actually, Brigid, you might be wrong there," Laura said, not looking at Delgado. "Maybe they weren't killed immediately. Maybe they were taken to a secondary scene and held there, even for several days until the killer was confident the law was stopping with Marcus Creighton."

Delgado made a sucking sound in his throat as if Laura had punched him in the gut and he was trying to keep his sandwich down. Before I could step in to referee, she added, "Once I've helped clear Marcus Creighton, I'm going to find who really killed those children."

Delgado finished swallowing, then wiped his mouth with his napkin and looked at Laura with unasked questions on his face. Like he wouldn't risk asking what had her so convinced Creighton was innocent, because she just might tell him. "Getting a little ahead of ourselves, I think" was all he said, keeping his voice as mild as he could, trying not to sound defensive given that he was the one who put Creighton on death row.

Laura said nothing, but the battle lines were drawn.

We finished in less than half an hour, and while Delgado gallantly took out his wallet to leave money on the table for all our lunches, I went over to the counter and asked Sam where Shayna Murry was. He looked a little wary and was exceedingly polite. I gathered that he figured me being with Delgado changed the rules of engagement. Maybe he didn't want me to let Delgado know he and the fish peddler had come across all tough guy with me.

He said she'd taken a couple of days off, the way she did sometimes when she got depressed. "She fiddles around with her sculptures," he said.

"Isn't that a hardship on you, for her to not come in?"

Sam waved his hand around the place. Two tables were taken besides ours. "Typical lunch hour, I don't really need her. I just have her here as a kind thing to do. She's a nice girl, pretty good worker when she isn't running off after her nutso brother."

"Nutso brother?" I pressed.

He nodded. "Erroll. He's a nervous man," he said, finally choosing the word.

"Ah, that's the brother Gabriel Delgado told me about," I said, feeling another piece of information fall into place with an almost audible *clink*. Erroll was the man I'd seen at the restaurant, and the brother Shayna took care of when their parents deserted them.

Not seeming to notice my surprised interest, Sam nodded. "I buy fish off'n him for a good price. Every so often I just have to run him off when he needs gentling, but it's worth it."

On the way back to the site, Delgado pointed out Shayna Murry's house. We went by too fast to get a good look, but I marked its location and got an idea.

Henry Aggrawal showed up about fifteen minutes after we arrived, with Oliver Brach, the medical examiner out of Jupiter, following close behind. He was there as the legal witness in case human remains were found.

Aggrawal was one of those guys, more common in the South than anywhere else, who came across like a good aw-shucks country boy who had accidentally stumbled on his PhD in physical anthropology. Brach was just generically young, with none of the distinctive markings that make aging interesting. He was the kind of man you want to say "Hello, son" to when you're introduced.

Chili led Henry to the spot as if the marker Kuhl left there wouldn't have been a good enough clue. Then Chili and her handler left.

"I'm going to go easy," Aggrawal said. "I figure with erosion there would be less ground now then there was when the remains were first buried, so they might be even closer to the surface than you say they were."

Aggrawal put on latex gloves and laid out a small tarp a bit away from the spot. Then he got down on his haunches with a small trowel and started digging a square trench around the area. He placed every trowel full of dirt on the tarp for later searching.

Brach stood over Aggrawal and asked quiet questions about the process. You could tell this was new for him.

Both with different issues at stake, Delgado and Laura kept their eyes fixed on every move Aggrawal made, without his seeming to be aware of them. When he was finished with the trench, he got out another tool, this one more of a paintbrush with hard bristles. He scraped away the dirt carefully. Looked.

"It's cloth, canvas. Maybe a tarp." He eased more dirt away and found an edge at which he pulled gently. Pulled something brownish yellow out of the hole. "It's human, all right."

At that, Brach bent onto his haunches beside Aggrawal, who went on, "Stained by the tannin in the soil. I'd reckon it's been here for well over a decade. It's a clavicle."

"The age. Can you tell the age?" Laura asked.

"Definitely juvenile," he said. "This is going to take some time. Gabe, you want to call in some help, that would be great, and I'll just keep working."

Delgado made the calls to get extra law enforcement to help document and monitor the site.

Laura stood by, staring at the spot as if her eyes could make it all go faster. I wished she would say something, cry, moan, something. It would be good if she could get rid of some of what was coiled up inside her. At the same time, I knew she would not.

I put a hand on her shoulder to nudge her out of her tunnel vision. "Coleman. We don't know for sure if it's them," I said.

"It's them," she said, her face giving nothing away.

It struck me that, except for her blowing up when she found out Evers hadn't overnighted the physical evidence, Laura had been taking great care to hide her emotions from me. My telling her to keep a lid on them was partly to blame. Yet in those two words, *It's them*, she couldn't disguise the grieving voice of a mother.

Twenty-two

It's not like on TV where it takes five minutes including commercial breaks. Many times watching a forensic anthropologist at work is like watching a paleontologist unearth a wooly mammoth with a tooth-brush. But Aggrawal made surprisingly good progress while I sat under the shade of the bridge and watched fish jump.

He carved a trench the width of a trowel around the whole perimeter of the supposed bodies. The dirt from the trench made a sizable pile on the tarp.

The others all reacted when he exposed what served as a burial shroud, some canvas tarp or a sail from a boat. He cut the ropes tying it together while leaving the knots themselves intact at both ends, and peeled it back the way the flesh is laid open in an autopsy. I had got up from where I was sitting and watched him first examine the remains, then begin drawing out some of the bones and placing them in paper bags after numbering them with bits of sticky notes. There was no bad smell. It just had an earthy aroma as if it was in the long process of turning into soil the way all flesh does.

Aggrawal was focused, so I asked Brach what we had.

"The bones are commingled, and best he can tell at this point we're definitely looking at multiple juveniles," Brach said. "See, there's some clothing fragments. Only one skull intact. The others are in fragments, either from blunt force trauma or maybe the heavy construction equipment rolling over the spot. There's part of a mandible."

Laura's head jerked and she made an *awww* sound that everyone pretended not to hear. For my part, I went back to that night and wondered what the children saw, and whether they could tell us now even though we'd violated the spot they'd come to rest in.

"Whoever did it wanted to do it fast and didn't consider destroying identifying evidence," I said.

Delgado agreed. I pried Aggrawal's attention from the remains by bending over, hands on knees, face close to his. "Can you see anything that identifies the clothing?"

He didn't look up at me. "No, it's a mess."

"Something, a brand name." I turned to Laura, partly to force her attention off the goop that was in the tarp. I knew that what she'd seen before was bad, but not as bad as this. "I can't remember if companies were advertising themselves that way in the late nineties. Or that blingy stuff on T-shirts?"

Laura ignored me, and Aggrawal was just annoyed. He stopped and looked up at me with some impatience, losing his southern drawl. He pointed with his trowel. "Did I say this is a mess? All the bug carcasses and matted fur and practically liquefied clothing and bits of remaining flesh that fell away from the bones, you can see it's like a rotten black pudding here. The tarp surrounding it, the dampness of the area, the ambient temperature up to ninety-five degrees, it's like sixteen years in a Crock-Pot." He jerked his thumb in the direction of the water lapping at the shore. "And you see where the water is? With searise, and erosion, and the tides, even though the remains look securely encapsulated, I might have to go into the water. I promise the moment I find something I'll let you know."

"What about shoe rubber? Like a flip-flop?"

"Let the man do his job," Delgado said, but gently.

"We don't have time for DNA analysis," I barked gently back, but they ignored me. Of course they did. They knew it wasn't my circus, or my monkeys either. I heard Mom's refrain behind the thought.

Thinking of Mom made me think of Dad, and I called the hospital. Mom answered this time, sounding tired again, and said he was breathing funny. I said breathing funny how? And she said just funny. I said what about sending for the doctor. She said the doctor was coming in a while. I wanted to go, but Laura wouldn't, and we only had the one car. She kept a careful eye on each bone as it went into the bag. Like they were her own bones and she didn't want to lose count.

We stayed till the tide started to come in and it got too dark. Aggrawal wasn't satisfied that he got all the remains and was going to come back the following morning. We were both quiet on the drive back, me worrying about Dad breathing funny and Laura probably thinking about what she was going to tell Marcus but not daring to discuss it with me.

I was at the hospital with Mom listening to Dad breathe when I got a call from Laura.

"There's already something on the news," she said. "How does that happen?"

"Easy answer, fuckin'—sorry, Mom. Richard Hiatt, construction guy. He was pissed that he didn't get to play forensic scientist and called the local station."

"You're right. He's being interviewed right now. Everything about the bodies, and the Creighton case, and they did the background and connected it to Marcus's execution. Like it's a done deal."

"He doesn't sound so funny anymore," Mom said.

I looked out the hospital window to the east where I knew the ocean was. Except for that walk on the pier I hadn't been near the beach, and there was my hotel right on the water. I decided that's where I needed to be the next morning. Take a break from everything, Dad, Mom, Laura, Creighton. I was standing next to the whiteboard where the hospital staff listed the names of those on duty. I picked up the marker hanging by a string next to it and absentmindedly started doodling on it to detach a little from Laura's intensity. I do doodle, but it's limited to a few cartoons I once learned: a monkey, a toucan, and a dog.

"You probably shouldn't do that," Mom said. Her lips got thinner.

"We need to tell Marcus ourselves," Laura said.

"Laura, we don't even have confirmation that it's the children."

"Multiple juvenile bodies in the ground over ten years and less than twenty. Vero Beach. No other missing children at that time and place. Who else could it be?"

"Did I tell you the doctor is going to come back tomorrow to check on him again?" Mom asked.

"Yes, you did, Mom. We need proof. What we need is to tell Marcus before someone else does. Tomorrow first thing."

I had gone through my repertoire of doodles by that time, and, thinking about whether Dad was actually Yosemite Sam or maybe Foghorn Leghorn, I branched out and tried Mickey Mouse.

While I was doing a bad job on Mickey's ears I asked, "Did you talk to Will today?"

"I told him the remains had gone to Gainesville for sorting and interpretation. That I'd stay on it in case they found anything that we can use. All he has right now are the phone records and the opposing opinion of the independent examiner on the fingerprint."

Laura was still trying to stay cool, and you had to know her to hear what was behind "Brigid, the hearing is tomorrow!"

"We were going for the stay before we had the remains, remember? We always knew the best we could hope for was the phone records and Puccio's opinion on the print. But you know what might help? If Marcus can confirm it's his children, maybe they'd give us time to examine that new evidence." I stared at my doodling. Memories loop forward as well as backward, and link to each other in unlikely ways. "Or maybe Marcus has already given us what we need. Do you have Creighton's photo album handy? And do you own a magnifying glass? I thought you would. I'll pick you up tomorrow morning. Bring it with you."

As soon as I hung up, Carlo called.

"Hi, honey," I said, keeping my voice light as I looked over at Mom. She was staring at me, her lips getting thinner. On all sides except home I felt engulfed in other people's pain.

I responded to Carlo's question with "Oh yeah, everything is going well here."

"You can't talk right now, can you?" he asked.

"That's right. No news, but I'm having a visit with Mom right now. I'll call you again tomorrow, okay?"

Mom's lips got even thinner and then disappeared altogether.

Twenty—three

I knew it was a long shot, but as we headed up to Jefferson Pen, Laura got on the phone with Will in Tallahassee who got on the phone with the guys in Gainesville where Aggrawal had taken whatever he had found before the tide came in and started saturating the ground in his excavation site. Will begged them to stop worrying about defleshing the bones or any other scientific protocol and instead look through the mess for any plastic or metal objects that might have been on the children's bodies the night of the murders. Plastic not so much, but metal might have survived.

"They say sure would help if they knew what they were looking for," Will said.

Laura had examined every photo the night before, and now while Will had her on a conference call with Gainesville she described roughly a dozen items while paging through the little album to make sure she didn't forget one. There was Kirsten showing off a wristwatch in front of a Christmas tree. I glanced over. "I bet it's a Swatch; they were popular in the nineties. But there were lots of styles, so describe it in detail. Maybe that will help. And look for pierced earrings." Both Kirsten and Sara had them, but they weren't unusual, just studs. Still, they went on the list.

"What about these jeans?" Laura asked, spotting something she had not in her first go-round. "They have an odd triple snap thing."

I said, "I remember those. They're Cavariccis. Maybe the snaps survived. Chances are they were in their pajamas but still."

In a photo of the three kids standing in front of Cinderella's Castle at Disney World, Sara was wearing a trinket on a black string. Laura looked closely at it but couldn't make it out. "A bumblebee?" she asked. "Look for a bee," she said more loudly so Will and Aggrawal could hear.

"What about shoes?" Will asked over the speaker. "We know an expert who can identify shoes by the tread."

"We don't have any shoe tread to compare it to." Laura tried not to yell with impatience and pretty much succeeded.

"No shoes," Aggrawal said.

It was a ghoulish scavenger hunt—I pictured Aggrawal fishing through the sludge with tweezers—and Laura and I felt certain that if we won, Marcus Creighton would get to live. At least while the remains were examined thoroughly.

Gainesville understood the importance and was working for us. Will called when we were still a half hour's drive from the prison to let Laura know that several items had been found. A wristwatch was in there, but it was so mangled it would take some time to analyze what the brand was.

And then the anthropologist described a corroded pewter figure of Dumbo the elephant, ears outstretched in flight.

I knew that image, and I knew what Laura would have mistaken it for. "That's the bumblebee Sara is wearing," I said. "Tell Will they should keep looking, and send them our photo for analysis to confirm Dumbo, but I'll bet we've got a match. Those are the Creighton kids."

We were ushered into a smaller room than the one we were in last time, in a different building. This was the building where executions took place, and Marcus Creighton had been moved to the death watch cell. Wally, the guard he'd known for so long, who had been his friend on the inside, was not his guard here. If Wally had been there, he would certainly have seen the news and told Marcus about the bodies being found. The guard who took us to the meeting room looked like even if he knew about the bodies, he didn't care. No names were exchanged. Too little time was left for politeness, but Creighton didn't seem to recognize this.

Marcus greeted Laura, and, with a screw-you-and-the-prison-rules glance at me, she put her arms around him and drew him close. He was passive through it, his arms barely lifting in response, but over her shoulder I saw his chin lifted and his mouth opened as if he was receiving a sacrament. I wondered how many years had passed since he was last touched.

Even this gesture didn't tip him off that something about our visit was not good. He sat back in his chair a little dazed from the human contact. Then he pulled himself together once more and said with a wink, "Hello there, Brigid Quinn. I still don't want to die."

"I don't want you to die." I winked back.

"There must be good news," Marcus said, searching our faces for a sign of more. "You got the stay." He rubbed his hands together, making the cuffs jingle, unable to suppress his hope.

Then Laura first told him about finding the bodies of the children, succinctly and without showing any of the emotion I warned her about. Caring more for him than herself.

At first all he did was blink. Then he rubbed his hand over his unshaven face. When he didn't speak, Laura told him more about the burial scene, on the shore of an island that had been undeveloped at the time of the murders. That's how she spoke of it, murders. Trying to break through his denial. Each word she spoke carefully and slowly, but as she spoke she took his hand, a hand so unresponsive it could have belonged to a corpse.

Not responding, not looking at either of us, Marcus moved his jaw from side to side, grinding his teeth.

"Marcus," Laura said, "do you understand what I just told you?"

He managed to rub his stubbled face again, and for a moment it seemed that was all he could manage.

Then, "It's not them," he said, finally.

"We think it's them, Marcus," Laura said.

"Think? You think. What proof do you have?" he said. His voice was soft and weak, but there he was, rising to the surface again. I had seen him do this the last time, sinking and rising and sinking again as despair and hope tossed him about in their wake.

Laura gestured to me to confirm what she said, but I shook my head.

"How do you know it's not them, Marcus?" I asked. Even now I had some small hope that he would confess and I could let him go to a justified death. "Do you know where they are?"

His voice grew stronger but not angry. He said, speaking slowly and patiently as if I was a half-wit, "I told you, no. That's why Alison Samuels is looking for them. Because I don't know where they are. I keep telling you I don't know where they are. You don't listen."

Laura took the photo album, open to the photograph of the children posed in a line in front of Cinderella's Castle, and slid it in front of him, saying, "Tell us about this picture, Marcus."

He was only too happy to talk about something other than dead bodies. "I took them to Disney World for the twins' eighth birthday."

"How long was that before they . . . before this?" Laura asked.

"Their birthday is March tenth. We always joke that it's appropriate the twins were born under the Pisces sign. It was a great trip, a whole week. We did it all, Epcot, SeaWorld, stayed at the Polynesian resort." Marcus's smile faded. "I think it was an apology for screwing up their lives. It cost me a bundle that I didn't have, but now I'm grateful I did it."

"They don't look here like they thought their lives were screwed up," I said, in a stop-that-nonsense voice.

Something didn't seem right about the chronology, though. The photo album was a Father's Day present, and by that date they were all dead. It made the album feel ghostly. I asked.

Creighton said, "Sara was so cute. She remembered making this for me the year before and would add pictures as we took them. She added these a few weeks before she disappeared."

I asked, "What about their mother? Was she with you?"

"She didn't want to go." He sounded very sad at that, as if it had happened yesterday.

Laura, who was sitting close enough to Marcus to reach the photo, pointed to Sara. "It's hard to see, but we know Sara is wearing something around her neck. Do you recognize it?"

Marcus nodded at Laura's question but didn't answer it. "Have you talked to Alison Samuels?"

"Not lately, no," Laura said with a frown.

"So she doesn't know what you're telling me."

"I think she might, Marcus. It was on the news."

"You must tell Alison Samuels to keep looking, that they haven't found my children. Will you do that for me? Please? I don't know if she'll come to see me again, so you have to get to her."

Laura put her hand over her mouth involuntarily as if she could not bear to be the person who would force him to acknowledge the truth. But then she forced the hand away, took a breath, and said softly, "Marcus, just for now, could we talk about Sara's necklace? Do you recognize it?"

I watched Creighton's eyes come back into focus and appear to recognize Laura. "I don't have to recognize it. I remember everything about it. Each of the kids, Kirsten included, got to pick out a souvenir. We saw this little Dumbo character made from pewter in one of the gift shops, and Sara asked me about it. I promised her we'd rent the movie and watch it when we got home. We did, and I remember she rubbed the little Dumbo and asked if you could make a wish on it. Sometimes when I look at this picture I wish I had asked her what she wanted to wish for. But I never did. I played along, told her any wish would be granted as long as she kept Dumbo close to her. She said she'd never take it off," he said. "You know how little girls are, so over the top with their emotions. Never, ever, take it off! I can hear her saying that. But of course kids, they don't know what never ever means."

Marcus Creighton stopped talking, finally, and stared at the reluctant truth in Laura's eyes. He made the connections. He said, "Oh my God, she never took it off."

Twenty—four

Leaving Marcus felt like leaving someone alone for the first time after their children's funeral. Laura told me she wanted to stay with him a while longer. Alone, she said, with a defiant lift of her chin that would tolerate no opposition. I felt the frustration of a mother who's certain a boy will break her daughter's heart and can't do a damn thing to stop it. But then I figured Laura couldn't hurt any worse than she did already, and any of these visits might be her last chance to say what was on her mind. In her heart. I told her I'd meet her in the parking lot in half an hour. An hour, she said.

Rather than just sit, I drove the car east into Sebastian and made a quick dash into one of those tourist shops that sell beach supplies, orange-flavored fudge, and refrigerator magnets shaped like dolphins and flip-flops. I bought a sun hat.

A few minutes later I was parked in front of Shayna Murry's yard. Her studio-slash-house was right on U.S. 1, the main road, so people driving by would see it. If there were any doubts that I had the right place, I was reassured by a small wooden sign, worn to the same dull finish as the house, with the fading words MURRY CREATIONS painted on it.

The house itself was a one-story boxy thing with a metal roof, but it sat on enough property to make a small urban park. There was a stand of old oak trees behind it, and nothing for a goodly distance to the north and south. The wooden siding on the house at one time might have been painted a vivid iris; it still looked that way under the eaves, but the weather had turned most of it to bleached denim. Old Florida rusticity in spades.

What made Murry's house more distinctive than others of its ilk was that all the windows were covered with cheap plywood. When I put on my hat (and sunglasses, too, why take a chance?) got out of the car, and approached to look around the yard, I saw the wood was warped and the nails used to fasten it to the house were rusted.

Just in case I managed to make it inside, I walked the whole perimeter of the house to see if there was a back door. It's good to know your exit options. Nothing back there except for a small unboarded window and the dense stand of trees that began about fifteen feet out from the back wall.

Had Shayna boarded herself in during some hurricane years before and never bothered to remove the boards? Or was there another reason for the self-imposed barricade? Escape from public scrutiny? Depression? Fear? Those boards gave me more food for thought regarding Shayna Murry's current state of mind than anything I'd heard or read so far.

Rounding the front of the house, I noticed a rusted bicycle turned into a planter leaning up against the wall. Not terribly creative, that planter. I went up the steps onto the once-white front porch and knocked on the door.

No answer. But when I stood close I could hear what sounded like a hot air balloon being filled. Awful tight space for a hot air balloon. I knocked again; still no answer.

I tried the handle on the door, a quaint metal lever that might have been part of this building from the start. You needed a key to lock it. Unlocked. I had a feeling this was a part of the world where that was not uncommon. Besides, Officer, the sign out front promised something like a gallery inside, so I felt justified opening the door and walking in.

I expected to see more items like the bike inside. The room I walked into seemed to take up most of the building. And it was filled with what an artist might find meaningful but what I, at first glance, could only see as crap.

Shayna Murry was standing in one corner of the dim room, lit up by sparks surrounding a yellow-to-blue flame. She was dressed in a flame-retardant apron and cap, with gloves and dark goggles. So intent was she, and so loud the blowtorch she held against some hulking piece of rusted metal, she didn't hear me enter. She didn't even hear me when I spoke her name.

I used the time to look around more carefully and saw, amidst the strips of aluminum siding, and metal objects that looked like their stop previous to this had been in a junkyard or on the side of the road, and even some dead palm fronds, some real art. Hanging on the walls were shields that somehow blended ancient Rome with early twentieth-century art nouveau, and an abstract piece that would have been an intricate brooch if it hadn't been three feet in diameter.

The only light came from naked bulbs attached to a ceiling fan set on high. With the windows boarded, and the heat from the blowtorch, and the June temperature, and not even a window unit for air-conditioning, it was no wonder her face was running with sweat when she finally turned off the butane or propane or whatever dangerous gas she had in that thing. It made a loud *pop* that made me jump.

She turned to me and screamed.

"Soooorrry!" I said, raising my hand and waggling the tips of my fingers to show I was a harmless sort. "That noise scared me."

"It's just backfire. Not dangerous. How long have you been stand-ing there?" Shayna asked, no longer terrified but still unnerved that she hadn't been enough on guard. I myself would be a little less on guard when she put down the blowtorch.

"Just a few minutes," I assured her. I gestured around the room, dropping the silly-woman shtick. "This is real art, not some dilettante artsy craftsy shit. This is intelligent."

At that, Shayna stripped off her goggles and gloves. She was appar-ently used to the heat in the place, because she left on her apron. She glanced at the door as if trying to gauge whether I could block her dashing out.

"Who are you?" she asked when she saw the unlikelihood of either

her escaping or me disappearing. "I mean really. And don't bullshit me because I recognize you now even with the hat and glasses. You were at the café the other day. You might guess I'm visual that way, being an artist and all."

I stripped off my hat and glasses in turn. I said, "Did you hear they found the Creighton children? It was on the news."

She finally let go of the blowtorch, but that was because it slipped out of her hand and clattered to the floor. Even shocked as she was, she had the sense to turn off the gas and the oxygen tanks. Clearly this had taken her by surprise. Was it because she knew they were dead or, like Marcus, thought they were still alive?

"Are they sure?" she asked.

"There will be some confirmation testing, but yeah, it's certain."

Shayna looked like she was starting to ask a question, then closed her lips, and when they reopened it was to ask another. "And you're telling me this, why?"

I knew I could get more information from her if she thought I was on her side. "Because I've done some investigating since I last saw you, and I think Marcus Creighton did it. A woman I've been dealing with on the case, Laura Coleman—have you met her?"

"She camped out on my doorstep a few times, but I wouldn't talk to her."

"Her. She's pretty obsessed about this case, and I'm trying to prepare her for his death, and what I want is to find better proof of his guilt. Something that will convince her without a remaining doubt."

Shayna appeared to be buying my story. I wiped a trickle of sweat that tickled my cheek. "And look, could we step outside to talk? It's only ninety-five degrees out there."

Shayna took off her apron, and we went outside to the front porch. There were no chairs out there, so we sat side by side on the top step. The offshore breeze on my face from the ocean that was only a quarter mile away made me aware of how much I'd been sweating. I wiped my palm on my jeans and offered it. Didn't help; it was a damp handshake on both sides.

"My name is Brigid Quinn," I said. "What did you have against Marcus?"

148

"Why would you say that?"

"I read your testimony."

Shayna shook her head, the kind of gesture that indicates distaste rather than disagreement. "I was so young. So confused. The fact is, you know when they talk about being swept off your feet? I get it. It's never happened to me before or since. I met him at a time when if I bought gas to get to the grocery store I wouldn't have enough money to buy food when I got there. Then I meet this guy who stole my electric bill out of the mailbox so he could pay it himself. But it wasn't even the money. Sure, he was rich and I was poor, but there were the little notes he would leave on my pillow, and the tulips . . . he knew I liked yellow tulips better than roses. He listened to me, and remembered little things. He was so charming, so handsome. Have you . . ."

I nodded. "He still is. Fifteen years on death row tells, but he's still got it."

"And I was the one everyone said made him do it. It was like they blamed me."

"Is that why the boarded-up windows?"

Shayna's face wrenched, and then she got it back under control. "What about the children? Tell me more about the bodies. Do you know how they died?"

"We will. When the police first questioned you that night about whether he'd been to see you, you didn't know why they were asking?"

"No." Even now there was a mix of anger and despair in her voice. "I just answered honestly, and it broke my heart when I found out. I know I didn't sound like I still loved Marcus in court, but the prosecutor said it would be better if we slanted it that way, that he was a total creep who had taken advantage of me. He said it wouldn't be a lie because in a way it was true."

"How much did money have to do with it?"

"What do you mean? The fact that he had it and I didn't? I said—"

"No. I mean the fact that he didn't have as much money as you thought he had."

"You think I would have thrown him under the bus for that?"

"Did he tell you he was in financial trouble?"

Shayna wasn't sweating as much as she had been inside the studio, but she was still a little steamy. I got the feeling she was sorry she had sat down like this, and was now figuring out how to get the latest news on the Creighton kids while getting back inside the house and locking the door.

I repeated, more softly, like it was just idle conversation and I didn't really care about the answer, "Did he tell you he was in financial trouble?"

I guess she decided it couldn't do any harm to answer at this late date. "There was one night about six months before the . . . murders when we'd shared a couple bottles of wine and had sex on the beach. I asked him why we didn't do it on his boat anymore. He said he sold the boat. Then he said, 'I'm in one of those situations where I'm worth more dead than alive.'"

"He was talking about assets," I prodded gently.

Shayna nodded. "That was when I found out he had borrowed money from a loan shark, and had a term life insurance policy on him and his wife, the kind that pays double for accidental death and dismemberment."

Keeping my voice just as gentle so she wouldn't be tipped off, I said, "Why didn't this come up at the trial?"

Shayna jerked her head in my direction. "Wha?" she managed.

"In the court transcripts. I don't have them with me, but it was something like, Prosecutor: Did you have any idea that Marcus Creighton was in financial trouble? You: No, I had no idea. Something like that. That's not just about feelings, is it? That's a statement of fact."

Shayna paled, trying desperately to remember what she had said back then. Whether I was just lying for some purpose she couldn't see. Stuttering a bit as she tried to get out the words, but raising her tiny chin in defiance, she said, "I don't care what I said. Maybe I remembered it all wrong. I'm sticking by my testimony, and there's nothing you can do about it. Marcus Creighton killed his family. And I had nothing to do with it."

"I didn't say you did." I got up from the porch and dusted off the back of my jeans. I still would not reveal the cell phone evidence that was more proof of her perjury. Better save that for later. "There's more, Shayna. I know you're a liar. Probably not about being in love with

Marcus Creighton; that sounds right. But about other things. I don't know why you're lying, but we've got better proof of it than what you just gave me. I'm here to tell you you'd be better off coming clean now than before Marcus Creighton is retried. Because then you won't be in a position to make any deals."

Her face was closed off. She'd had years of practice. She might process what I said later, and come around, but for now all she wanted was me gone. Yet she wanted something else even more. "Wait. You said you'd tell me about the children."

I shrugged. "I think you already know it's the children. And you know where we found them."

"But I don't!" she sobbed.

I almost believed her then. I almost felt bummed about tricking her like that, but then I thought of Marcus Creighton's face when we forced him to acknowledge his children had been found buried in a shallow grave.

One last try. "Shayna. There's a man who's going to die because of you. Shortly after midnight tomorrow. Someone who genuinely loved you. We've got a case for appeal, but you're the one who put the nail in his coffin, and you're the only one who can pry it out. If you come forward now you can stop his death. Tell me what happened that night. Tell me what you've known all these years. I promise you it will feel good to say it."

Shayna didn't speak but instead started to tremble, and then started to shake. She got up off the step and, weaving like a drunk, using the doorjamb for support, went back into the house. I got up, too, and started to follow. I stopped when she reappeared, blowtorch in hand. It was on full blast.

"Get off my goddamn property," she screamed and cried at the same time, a little spit popping in the flames.

Twenty-five

On the drive home Laura kept wiping her nose on the back of her fingers as if I wouldn't know her tears were leaking despite her best effort to hide them. I handed her a Kleenex from my tote and muttered something about summer allergies. She didn't say what had happened when she was alone with Creighton, and I didn't ask. I told her about how I had cornered Shayna Murry and got the feeling from our conversation that she was like Tracy Mack, Gabriel Delgado, even Todd's girlfriend Madeline Stanley, knowing more than they were saying. Laura was unresponsive, lost in her own thoughts and leaving me to mine, which, as always, turned to Mom and Dad.

I would go back to the hospital, I told myself after calling Mom on the cell phone that she still did not answer, but before that I needed an hour with no one and nothing in it. After I dropped Laura off at home and got back to the Howard Johnson's, I walked across the street and down to the hot sand that, barefoot, would feel like walking across hot coals. I kicked off my sneakers when I got to the water's edge and in doing so felt the unaccustomed stiffness in my muscles. I stretched my arms behind me and felt the resistance. Oh man, I needed to work out. I tested my leg where I'd been shot some months before. Wondered if my back could take a run like in the old days. Tried a few tentative steps.

Not too bad. The soft sand both cushioned the impact and created a challenge that I knew was good for me. Up down up down into the thin sheet of water that was the farthest point of the waves. I hadn't been back so long that I couldn't still smell the salty fishy smell.

I passed a few jellyfish washed up on the beach, looking like blueberry chewing-gum bubbles, and hoped to avoid their invisible tentacles that could be stretched out twelve feet in any direction and give a painful sting even when the jellyfish itself wasn't attached. I passed a wad of netting. A filtered cigarette butt. A small dead fish. Danger and death all around, but then a tern ran into the receding water, so light its feet hardly left a mark in the sand. It picked up something I couldn't see and ran back up the beach ahead of the next wave.

The eighty percent humidity might have made the running rough, but it was balanced against the drop in elevation, coming from thirty-five hundred feet where I live in Arizona to sea level. Huffing just a bit, but knowing it would pass as the endorphins kicked in, I headed along the water's edge toward a small group of people standing solemnly in an uneven circle, looking down.

I remembered Alison Samuels's story about the starfish and thought how weird that would be. Then I thought of a photograph I had seen in one of Dad's homicide textbooks when I was six years old. The face of a man who had been in the sea for two weeks. His head looked like a white balloon. The photograph had never really left me, and my psychologist friend has suggested that I went into law enforcement because of it. He thinks I've spent my whole life confronting that image before it could get me. Hunting for it rather than turning my back to avoid it and letting it creep up behind me. It may be that the memories of events before the age of ten are the memories that stay implanted most firmly for the rest of our lives. They make us who we are. There had been many times before now when I wished I'd never seen that photograph.

Please, nothing awful this afternoon, I thought. So often in my life it had been something awful, and a dozen of those images flashed through my head before I came up to the group.

I laughed out loud that it was neither a floater nor starfish. It was turtles.

Some mother turtle, after enjoying wild aquatic sex, had crawled up onto the beach late one night, dug a hole with her flippers, and deposited roughly fifty eggs the size, color, and shape of Ping-Pong balls. She had covered up the hole with the sand she dug out of it, and then the bitch had headed back to sea without so much as a *Good luck, kids.*

Some mothers were like that. Some mothers, like mine, said that children should be like cookies; you should be able to throw out the first batch. Some mothers got in the bathtub with a glass of wine after taking a sleeping pill, leaving three children untended, undefended. Unalive.

Stop it, Brigid. Just stop.

Then, without trying, my attention was hauled kicking and screaming back from the internal vision of a crime scene to the real sight of about fifty baby turtles, each about the size of a silver dollar, following the same path as their mother.

The other people who had got there before me, most in T-shirts and shorts, each out for their own morning walk or run, had instinctively formed a rough cordon on both sides of the nest, leading to the water. No one seemed to be in charge. Without waiting for an invitation I lined up with them, and we watched the slow progress of the little feet and shells, with heads like a plug of licorice, over the sand. Some few of the turtles got confused and pointed their licorice plug in the wrong direction, west to where they'd be run over by cars or find themselves trapped against a two-foot-high concrete wall running along the sidewalk. One of my fellow turtle watchers put himself in charge of these. When he picked them up, he didn't carry the turtles all the way to the ocean. He only brought them back to the vicinity of the nest and got them started in the right direction. One can only do so much to change the world, and then the world has to take care of itself.

A woman dressed in a long gauzy skirt flapped it and yelled *"Ha!"* at several seagulls who were also witnessing the activity, probably with breakfast in mind.

I bent down and picked up one little guy who had gotten himself stuck in the depression left in the sand by someone's foot. His paws scrabbled uselessly and continued to do so until I put him down outside the footprint, where he gained traction again.

A half dozen of the turtles made it as far as the water's edge and stopped, too exhausted to go on. Someone tried picking them up and putting them in the water, but they were too far gone and didn't try to swim. You can't save everyone. But most of the fifty made it at least into the water, where more would be food and who knows how many would survive to breed again. The ones who made it swam for a few seconds with their heads above water. In the afternoon sun their heads looked even blacker against the surface of the water, interspersed with the diamonds cast by the sunlight on the small rippling waves.

It would be nice to say they looked back at us, but we're talking biology here. Over the course of a minute they were gone, without so much as a thank-you, and our role was finished. The seven of us stood on the beach, watching as if we could still see them. No one cheered. We looked around as if we hoped we could do it again, but there were no more turtles. I waved; what could you say, after all? It wasn't until I started back to the hotel that I realized I'd gone a good twenty minutes without an ugly picture in my head.

My cell phone rang. Wanting the peace to last a little longer, I looked at my watch. Three P.M. It wouldn't be Carlo; he was three hours earlier than me and always had lunch at precisely noon. Mom? I scowled to myself and answered it.

It was Laura. The tears that had finally burst their dam made it hard to talk, but she managed to tell me that nothing had done any good, a capricious judge had denied the stay of execution, and on June 23, 2015, at twelve o'clock A.M., Marcus Creighton would be put to death. I checked my watch. Thirty-three hours from now.

Twenty-six

Will had gone ballistic, Laura said, and was already on his way to appeal to the governor, the same one who had signed the Timely Justice Act. I admired Will for his perseverance.

Right after Laura, my phone rang again. Used to be this didn't happen when you were at the beach.

"Brigid, it's Mom. I'm at the hospital. I think it's bad." Her voice sounded like an old woman's, that weak reedy whisper, and it struck me that she had never sounded quite so elderly before.

Why do things happen this way, bad news on bad news, like it's a plan, the goal of which is to fuck you over?

"What happened?" I asked. "Was it the breathing?"

"I don't know. I wanted you to know we're in a different room."

"What's the number?"

"It's on the fourth floor now" was all she said. "I think it's intensive care."

"Did you call Todd?"

"Not yet."

So I'd have to call Todd, too. I had a fuckin' innocent on death row with his execution scheduled, but I still had to play the part of the oldest girl. Oh, and excuse my language. When I get stressed I get angry.

I called Todd on my way to St. Luke's, and he just said thanks. I made it to the hospital in short order and got Dad's room number from the front desk, got up to 416 in no time.

Dad still had a private room. He was pretty unresponsive, eyes not quite closed, his nose and mouth covered with a nebulizer. I wouldn't have thought my heart would break a little when I saw him like this, without that fight, but it did. I never realized how important the fight was before now. Mom was there, too, with a paper in her hand.

"What did they tell you?" I asked.

"Nothing," she said.

"They didn't tell you why he's here." I sat down on the corner of the bed and pointed to the paper she held. I said, "What do you have there, some explanation of what's up?"

"It's that thing you said we should sign. Living will."

"The Do Not Resuscitate order? Did they give that to you?"

"No. I brought a copy from home."

"Why? Good God, he doesn't look like he needs life support."

"I don't know" was all Mom said.

I left the room and went to the nurses' station, which was only three doors down the antiseptically gleaming hallway.

"Status of Fergus Quinn, room 416," I said. Okay, maybe I snarled it, but only a little.

The nurse at the desk, protected behind a bank of black-and-white monitors, looked up at me with no sense of urgency. "Excuse me. You are?"

"Brigid Quinn. Daughter."

"I'm sorry, I'm not authorized to—" she started, and looked back at her computer monitor, a response I would have ignored if I wasn't already pre-pissed at the Florida criminal justice system, not to mention health care in general.

"My mother is in room 416 with my father, who was brought to intensive care. No one told her why. Right now she's sitting there holding a living will and wondering if he's about to die. So you get me a doctor or whoever the hell can tell us what's going on. Otherwise you're going to have to call security."

She kept an eye on me as she picked up the house phone and called someone. Luckily for the hospital he was on afternoon rounds and just one floor away. A white coat and stethoscope marked him as he strode down the hall toward me.

"I'm Dr. McGee," he gruffed, towering over me so far he couldn't have got in my face if he bent from the waist.

Ooh, scare me with your white coat, will you? "I need to know the status of Fergus Quinn in room 416. Why is he in intensive care?" Not bothering to lift my chin, I stared at where his eyes would have been if he wasn't invading my personal space.

"I'm sorry. Are you a doctor?" he asked, without an obvious smirk but with an edge I knew too well.

"Is sarcasm now a treatment protocol?" I asked, keeping my own voice mild.

He looked startled, scowled, and then fired off, "The patient had been on oral beta-lactam plus macrolide, but the strain of bacteria was resistant and there was risk of sepsis. So we moved him here for extra monitoring and put him on IV beta-lactam, plus aminoglycoside, plus quinolone as an added precaution."

I could tell he was attempting a smackdown, physician-style. Intimidate the ignorant woman with medicalese she'd never understand.

"Antibiotic-resistant bacteria. Sepsis. Three-drug cocktail to blast it." As I said that, I tapped the lapel of his lab coat, not hard, but just enough to show he had not achieved intimidation. He backed away, but slowly so as not to let it look like he was cringing.

"Now. Prognosis," I said, looking him in the eye.

"His lungs are like tissue paper. But there is some hope that he'll pull through this. Small, but I should be able to give you a better picture within the next forty-eight hours."

"May I have your card," I said, without it being a question.

He hesitated, then took out a little case and handed me one. "Can I answer any other questions for you?"

"Just one. What other drugs you got if this doesn't work?"

"I'm afraid this is our best and final recourse," he said, with something of a sympathetic tone.

"Thank you, Doctor," I said. We stared at each other a moment more, both, I hope to think, finally seeing actual people. I was the one to turn first and head off back down the hall.

"They're doing everything they should," I said to Mom when I got back to the room. I translated what the doctor had said, short of the sobering prognosis. When Mom got upset she got an attack of colitis, so we tried to protect her, for our own sake as well as hers. "So you can put the DNR authorization away. No matter what you say, it makes you look eager."

Mom looked like her mind was elsewhere, and I started to bend down and take the sheet of paper from her. But she gripped it tighter and looked up at me. "You think I don't know what this means? You're saying it makes me look like I want your father to die? Why do you joke about everything?"

"I'm sorry. It's how I deal with stress," I said. "Let me take care of the form. We're not at that point yet. When did you eat, Mom? I can get you something from the coffee shop."

"Oh, that's okay," she said. She looked around, but nothing in the room was any different from the other room he'd been in, the IV pole, the bin for waste linens, the metal rails on both sides of the bed. "You were born here," Mom said, making it sound like it was this very room.

"I know. Eighteen hours of labor. Blood everywhere. I was there."

Her wandering gaze focused on me, and it was suddenly the gaze of the woman I'd always known, in control and kind of hard. "Of course you were there. I get it. You and the other kids always thought I was such a dim bulb. That I didn't know you were making fun of things I said and did, right in front of me. Well, you know how smart you all are? You don't think you got that from your father, do you?"

I wanted to defuse her before one of us said something we'd have to apologize for. I used the response they taught me in anger management counseling that I had momentarily forgotten out at the nurses' station. "I hear you, Mom," I said.

She stared at me for a long time while I waited for her to murmur something agreeable. But she said, "I don't think you do. You've been asking questions lately, so I'll be honest and tell you a little something. From now on I'd like you to know I'm not a joke."

• • •

At least there was nothing more to be done on Creighton's behalf. I spent most of the rest of the afternoon in that hospital room, being a good daughter. I watched Dad's ashen face, remembering how he used to wrestle with the three of us at once. Even with those odds we sort of felt like he was a tame lion and there was the chance of accidentally being killed.

I tried calling Carlo on the home phone (he refused to get a cell), but he was out. I was glad. Sometimes when you're depressed the last thing you want to do is spread it around. I left a message saying enough, that Dad was in ICU but stable. I started to mention that I would be attending Creighton's execution the following night, but couldn't manage to say it. So I just said don't worry, and don't return the call, I'll be out of touch the next day but will call when I can.

He tried calling, but I couldn't bring myself to answer. I hoped he understood.

I stayed at Mom's place again that night, telling her that if Dad stabilized I would be away the next night, but back by the next morning. She was listless, staring at an old Carole Lombard movie on the Turner channel, and didn't ask what would take me away at night.

Twenty-seven

The next day is a blur for its sameness, my recollection dulled along with my senses. I drifted in and out of the hospital room, bringing food that wasn't eaten, and called Todd to let him know what was going on and that he would have to look out for Dad, and Mom, too, while I was gone. I gave him Mom's cell phone number, made him promise to call her every hour and stop by the hospital the next day. He promised. I made sure he could contact me if Dad's condition changed. That done, I decided it would be okay if I was with Laura when Marcus Creighton was executed. It had to be okay.

Laura and I drove up to Jefferson Penitentiary in the evening. The long summer sun stayed up until after nine, and the only talking we did on the way was Laura on her phone, with Will, with Wally, and steeling herself not to break down when she spoke to Marcus. I heard her say, "No. I know. No, Marcus. No." When I asked what he said, she tried to tell me, then admitted, "Nothing that made sense."

A little later she told me that he had asked Wally for a pen, some paper, and an envelope. He wasn't allowed to have it, but Wally gave it to him anyway, and kept watch over him so he wouldn't stab himself with the pen. He reported that Marcus used a hardcover book as a writing surface, and wrote for what seemed to Wally a long time. But Marcus didn't address the envelope and ask Wally to mail it, as Wally expected him to do. He stared at the letter a long while, then put it down on the bed beside him. Wally took the pen and went away.

Wally had volunteered to be with him on his last night, and been given permission. They say you can tell the quality of a man by the loyalty of his friends.

Later when Laura called Wally again, he told her he saw Marcus touching the words in the letter he had written and counting them out loud rather than reading them. "I don't think he can focus on the meaning of the words, but he doesn't want to just sit and stare."

"I wish I could be there with him," Laura said.

It was a long drive.

I talked Laura into stopping at a Waffle House for something to eat. I was the only one to order some eggs and sausages, but even I, inclined to stress eating, had lost my appetite. Laura clutched her coffee mug between her hands, keeping her phone on the table, in easy reach of that improbable call that would say Will had succeeded, that the governor had granted a reprieve, keeping Creighton alive until we could take further action. She had the phone in front of her rather than to the side, so she didn't even have to move her eyes to look at it.

"Laura," I said. "Coleman. It's eleven. It's okay to let go."

"It's happened this close before, Brigid. I've read about it, not just movie stuff but actual cases where the stay came real close to the execution. There's a lot of pressure on the governor. He could change his mind."

"Coleman. Stop. Did I say it's late? Everyone but us is sleeping."

Mind skipping, losing connection to the thoughts she'd just had, she said, "I talked to him."

I didn't remind her I was there in the car during the call. All that mattered was letting her talk.

She said, "He was allowed one call, and I was the person he chose to call. I kept offering hope of a last-minute stay, and all he wanted to talk about was what he was eating."

I knew why. The last meal was the saving grace of banality in the face of existential terror. To avoid extravagance, the food to prepare the last meal must cost no more than forty dollars and must be purchased locally. "So tell me. What was he eating."

Laura scowled at me.

"Tell me."

"Okay, I'll play your psychological game of Distract Coleman. At Wally's urging he ordered a Thanksgiving Day kind of dinner, roast turkey and stuffing, cranberry sauce, and sweet potatoes with melted marshmellows. And that green bean casserole with cream of mushroom soup. And pumpkin pie. With whipped cream. He didn't eat it. Is that what you wanted to know?"

"Did the green beans have those fried onion things that come in a can?"

"I don't know." She hadn't bothered to look up while she spoke, continuing to stare at the phone. Without looking at her watch, she said, "I think it's time to go."

Three media vans were already parked outside Jefferson Penitentiary, lights strong enough to light the whole parking lot, their accompanying broadcasters speaking to the cameras pointed in their direction when the cameras weren't panning around the facility for establishing shots. A larger contingent of people who opposed the death penalty stood silently with lighted candles. From the license plates on some of the cars, you could tell they had come from some states away.

We went to the same building where we had last seen Marcus. I noticed this time that it had no windows. I don't have a clear recollection of how, or what happened in between, but then we were standing outside Creighton's death watch cell in the hall leading to the execution chamber.

A radio and television were positioned outside the cell bars, a special benefit for those on death watch. It did not appear that Marcus used either of them.

Two guards in uniform stood near, both male, one of them Wally. "He was a gentleman," Wally said, already speaking of him in past tense. "Dignified and all. Not like some of the maniacs we have in this place."

"Were you able to give him something?" Laura asked.

"The doc can give out Valium."

"Did he?"

Wally unlocked the door and kindly kept his voice as casual as possible, like he had tickets to a game and they were running only slightly late. "Marcus, time to go."

Marcus was already standing, the fingers of his left hand on the wall of the cell as if he was ashamed to be thought unsteady. His face looked like he was drawing up his remaining perseverance from the slippers he'd been given, and it was barely enough. How I admired him in that moment. What did he feel? I couldn't imagine.

Will Hench was already in there, standing by Creighton's side. He didn't look like a tough attorney. He looked every bit like a man ashamed of his own failure to do anything good.

Will was allowed to walk Marcus down the hall. Laura and I followed. Except for the guards and those whose job it was to kill him, and a minister, there was no one else. Wally made the usual announcement, without gusto.

"Dead man walking."

Marcus started to hyperventilate at that, his first reaction to what was about to happen. He was neither noble nor brave nor cursing the world that put him here. He was merely in forward motion. The walk was blessedly short. Will knew to leave Marcus at the threshold of the execution chamber. The chamber was small, and contained only a padded table with straps, and a machine with plungers and lighted buttons against the wall. There the minister blessed him and stepped away. It did not appear that Marcus noticed him. A man in a suit and latex gloves waited by the side of the table.

I guided Laura into the witness room. Instead of the pews I remembered from Raiford in 1980, there were those metal-legged chairs with vinyl seats and backs, and faux-wood arm rests. The color of the chairs was dark to match the dim lighting. The glassed-in room where the execution would take place was more brightly lit, giving me the sensation of viewing an aquarium.

"I asked Wally if he had a sedative," she whispered to Will when she sat down beside him. Right at the end, powerless but still wanting to do something. I could hear them whispering about the hair dryer and the cell phone records and the remains, Laura asking why this and why not that, why he was here instead of in Tallahassee, Will saying they'd done the very best they could and now was the time to stop fighting.

After a decade and a half of the media forgetting his existence, they were present to cover the end of it. One reporter from each group must represent a news organization that covers the county in which the condemned inmate committed the crime for which he or she is sentenced to death. Twelve reporters maximum are allowed. Two places are always reserved for the Associated Press and United Press International–Radio. Five reporters were ready to tell the world what happened this day. At least two of them had still been in high school when Marcus was convicted, so they'd needed to be briefed before they came.

There was no family left to mourn him, and no one left to cheer. If Marcus had parents who had somehow survived the tragedy, they had abandoned him. This was often the case with people on death row.

There was a digital clock on the back wall of the execution chamber. It said 23:56. Four minutes to go. Laura's eyes were still on her phone, which nestled in her upturned palm, like a small bird she sought to protect.

An intercom connecting the execution chamber and the viewing room was on. We heard the warden ask if there were any last words.

Marcus faced us and tried to say something that might have been a thank-you but was interrupted by a coughing fit. He gave it up and just winked, only a muscle twitched in his cheek and made it look like a facial spasm instead.

Laura's phone went off.

The intercom didn't go both ways, so dying men couldn't hear any cries or curses as they succumbed. Laura jumped up, grappled with her jacket pocket to retrieve her phone, and answered it. Marcus saw her do that, and saw the look on her face. Courage at an end, he dropped to the floor in a faint. I heard a suppressed shout from the back of the witness room but didn't bother to turn.

As the guards stooped to revive Marcus, Laura said, "Hello, hello, hello," into the phone. Her face paled, and her lips turned white at the edges. "Hello," she said one more time. Then she turned off the phone. She stayed at the window then. Will had jumped from his chair at the same time Laura had, and stood behind her without touching her.

I have known many moments of cruelty in my life, the kind where you think the universe has created new and inventive ways to torture a person. But never one more cruel than this.

The rest happened quickly. There was no drama in the scene, just quick efficiency to shorten the time of any more terror Marcus might experience. The flash of hope followed by hopelessness unnerved him finally, stole all the fortitude he had managed to build up for this event over the preceding days and weeks and months, and sedated or not, his whole body shook as they placed him before the table that stood upright for him. His knees kept buckling, and a garbled mutter came from his mouth that might have been repeated apologies, as if the worst thing about the process was the difficulty he caused his executioners. Embarrassing himself. The shaking made it difficult to strap his legs down, but they finally did and then lowered the table until it was parallel to the floor. They strapped his shuddering arms to pads that extended from the sides of the table, the kind of extension that phlebotomists use when they're drawing blood.

Now Marcus was gasping for air. His head strained on his neck, and his torso arched. The guy who was supposed to insert the needle said, "This shouldn't happen. What's wrong with him?"

Wally answered, "He's having an asthma attack." Probably against protocol, he rested a hand on Marcus's shoulder. I think he was trying not to cry. "There you go, buddy, we're nearly there. For God's sake, Phil, get on with it, would you?"

The executioner had his back to us so we couldn't see when he placed the needle into a vein as quickly as he could and taped it down. But we could see the back of his head as he nodded at Wally and the other guard, posted on either side of the mechanism against the wall.

Marcus's chest continued to heave as he struggled to let out the air in his lungs. No one told him again to calm down. They hoped the drugs would take care of that soon enough.

I sat there watching how quickly the mechanized death went into Marcus Creighton.

One: sodium thiopental to induce the coma that would end his fear forever. He still tried to force air out of his lungs, but his head was no longer straining, his torso was no longer arching off the table.

Two: pancuronium bromide to paralyze him, including his diaphragm, which cut off his breathing. His muscles went slack.

Three: potassium chloride to make his heart quiver to a halt.

There wasn't even time for me to flash back to a similar circumstance, those memories that came back for every given instance. Even if the death hadn't gone so fast I probably wouldn't have thought of anything. I had witnessed the death of someone who'd committed the crime, but never sat watching a man who I knew was innocent die by someone else's hand less than fifteen feet away from me, and not done something. Jumped up, beaten my hands against the glass. Rushed into the room and cut down the three men doing the deed. Saved him.

All I could do was beg that it worked quickly this time.

From the depression of the plungers to the check for a nonexistent pulse, it took seven minutes for Phil to declare Marcus Creighton deceased.

Twenty-eight

It was a textbook killing, no glitches except for Marcus collapsing and his asthma attack. That is to say, nothing that the executioner did was wrong. The drugs worked. All in all it was not a dignified, or meaningful, or high-minded death. It wasn't the movies with emotion or symbolism or swelling background music; it was mere physiology.

Will lifted his hands reflexively in her direction, then stopped and whispered, "Laura," and again, "Laura." But not loudly enough, because she didn't turn from the window where she was staring at Marcus Creighton's body. No matter his motive for entering this field in the first place, no matter whether Will had witnessed his share of executions, like the rest of us he was immobile in the face of grief. He turned to me. "You were right. I shouldn't have let her become involved," he said. "She's not as tough as she'd like you to think."

"We're friends," I said, not trusting myself to comment. "I got this."

"I'm supposed to be back in Tallahassee at a hearing in the morning, but I can stay a while, all right?"

"I got this," I repeated.

"I'll be back in just a few days. Let's stay in communication, all right?" I nodded. Still without trusting himself, without daring to speak to Laura, he said good-bye and left.

Whether or not she sensed Will's presence, or absence, and didn't trust herself with it, Laura turned from the window to face me. She was without any affect at all. "What I just did to him, just there," she said. She looked at me as if expecting some sort of lashing about how, with the cell phone alarm, she had made Marcus's final moment even worse than it needed to be.

"It's a singular thing, this," I said. "No matter how strong you are, and no matter what you've seen before, you can't tell how you'll be."

There are a few tells you can't control no matter how controlled you are. Like dilating pupils, blushing, and trembling. Laura was unable to stop shaking no matter how detached her words when she said, "I've never done this before. What happens now?"

That broke my heart as much as watching an innocent man die. Are you surprised that I put it that way, that my heart was breaking? As if someone had taken it and stuffed it down my windpipe, where it hurt as it beat against the sides. You can never tell about a person. This execution was a singular thing for me, too, and a furious shout stayed packed inside me without hope of release.

I needed to be the strong one and managed to speak. "Sit down a minute. No, not there." With a hand that annoyed even me with its slight trembling I gestured her to a chair a distance away from the window where she couldn't see Marcus. Without appearing to know what I was doing, she obeyed me and sat down.

I found Wally outside the execution room. He was standing quite still, head bowed and hands folded before him in the stance of prayer, but when he saw me he pretended that he'd been looking for me. "There's no one else to say. Do you have any stipulations for disposition of the body?" he asked.

"No. Just do the usual."

He made a note. "Cremate. Spread the ashes?"

I nodded.

"Check," Wally said.

"What about effects?" I asked.

"He had a few things. He already said he wanted them sent to Laura. Do you have her address handy?"

"Is the box ready?"

He nodded. "He packed it himself. But I found some bits and pieces under his cot, and I didn't want to throw anything away, so I threw it in and sealed the box."

"Give me the box. That letter he wrote last night. Was it for her?"

"I don't know, I don't remember seeing a letter." He sounded apologetic. "I got him to shave this morning. A little pride, you know? He looked good."

The gurney was passing by on its way to take Marcus off the table. I stopped one of the guys, who looked fairly upbeat compared to the rest of us, as if his main thought was that he was glad it wasn't him in there. I said, "Do me a favor, guys, hold it right there until I get someone out of the witness chamber."

Laura and I walked out of the darkened room into a night ablaze with the lights surrounding the media circus. Will had been snagged before he could get away, and we heard him saying to three cameras, ". . . a travesty of justice. The state executed this man before we were able to prove his innocence so that it wouldn't be forced to pay him reparation for his fifteen years in prison. And so people wouldn't look bad. You tell it, you hear me? It was all about politics and money."

Laura cringed at the sight of the knot of reporters around Will.

"I can do what I have to do, but I can't do this. The media thing," she said. She had the shaking somewhat under control, but in the way she spoke I could tell her teeth were still chattering.

We kept a slow pace going to the parking lot so we wouldn't draw attention. The night in the middle of the state was airless, hot, and humid, and I felt trickles of perspiration before we were halfway to the car. And then we saw Alison Samuels leaning against hers, a couple of spaces away from mine, and it felt like someone had turned up the heat.

Laura saw her but had no words in her. I couldn't stop myself from saying something. "I guess you already gave them a line, right?"

Alison didn't answer that, just looked at, no, examined Laura's face with something like curiosity before finally saying, "Yeah, it was the justice is served blah blah blah line. But I didn't come for the publicity. I wanted to make sure the family was represented. I stood in for them." Her voice shook not a little, and I got the feeling it took much effort to sound that heartless. She cocked her head at the news vans, and at the reporters who were still clustered around Will Hench. They'd keep the cameras rolling and the questions coming, hoping to later harvest a good fifteen seconds of raw emotion. "Aren't you going to say something passionate for the cameras?"

"Were you there? Did you see it?" Laura asked, and she said it without harshness, but with some kind of puzzlement that Alison could be this cold.

Alison's eyebrow raised slightly. "I came in once he was strapped down and left right after they declared him dead. But hey, I'm not vengeful. I just wanted to make sure justice was done. Like I said."

I got the sense that Laura wanted to go and wanted to stay in equal measure, to say something to make Samuels feel some part of what she was feeling. That rage you feel when you're in pain and someone doesn't honor it.

"We could have exonerated him. We might have even been able to find out the real killer. But you," Laura spat. "It's people like you who caused the death of an innocent man."

"Poor Mr. Creighton," Alison said.

At the sarcasm Laura sprang forward, and I thought she would surely pummel Alison Samuels. I gripped her arm, not firmly enough to stop her but hard enough to get her attention on what she was about to do. "Careful, the sharks can smell blood, Laura," I said, and to Alison, hoping to shame her into ceasing her cruelty, "This isn't necessary."

Laura caught herself and said, her voice shaking again with the effort of not attacking, "You didn't know this man."

"I didn't know the man?" Alison laughed, or maybe coughed. At least she was back in control. I got the sense that, like me, she was well practiced at it. "Shit, at the end of the day my biggest problem is that I've known too many of him." With that she was finished with Laura. She got in her car first and drove away.

We followed, and as we pulled through the front gates that opened before us, I thought about the call Laura had received at the precise moment that Creighton stood facing her.

"Who's the stupid idiot who called your cell phone?" I asked.

"It was a recorded message from the service provider." Laura started to laugh at the absurdity of it, then made a sound that reminded me of

171

some small animal. "I'm an idiot to have imagined a stay of execution would come to my phone." She held up her hands and watched them shake. "I feel nauseated. It's like that time when you and I—"

"It's the adrenaline aftermath. You'll be all right," I said. Some people cry. Some people curse. Some people just fold up their hearts, at least at first.

Laura crossed her arms over her stomach and did none of those things. When she turned to look at me, her voice had a little envy and a little despair. "Oh yeah. Brigid Quinn. The rock."

I closed my eyes at her, and when I opened them I was relieved that they weren't even damp. "It's not easy being a rock, Coleman. And you have to be very cautious, because sometimes you might want to not be a rock anymore, but you find out after a while you can't be not rock."

Twenty—nine

It was one A.M. in Arizona, four A.M. in Florida. Everybody I knew was sleeping, and that sounded wonderful. Back at my hotel before sunrise I fell onto the bed still clothed, intending to fall asleep at will like a good soldier. By five A.M. I admitted failure and eyed the sleeping pill on my bedside table next to the bottle of wine. That would be really stupid to take a sleeping pill right now, I thought. Then I popped the pill, and with the bottle silently toasted the action character I most admired before taking a slug. More power to ya, Reacher.

It was noon by the time I could fight my way back from oblivion. To get rid of a chemical hangover, I took a long shower and put on fresh clothes. That had only a minimal effect, so I called Todd first to ask how Dad was because I couldn't take any surprises just then. Todd said he didn't know what was going on.

"Todd. I just got back from Creighton's execution. Laura Coleman was a mess." I didn't mention that I was a little messed up, too.

"Brigid. I can't take sick people anymore. I can take them alive or dead, but not in between. You want to be there for Dad, more power to you."

FaceTiming with Carlo was a little better. He seemed to understand my delay in contacting him better than I did. If he had been worried, he didn't put it on me. I couldn't remember when we'd spoken last or what message I'd left on the home phone, so I covered it all. "Creighton's dead. Laura's emotionally wasted. Dad's in ICU because his condition worsened. I'm so tired my bones hurt. And I've spent most of the last five days either in a hospital room or the inside of a car. And have I mentioned I'm tired of driving?"

He didn't offer any platitudes or comfort, just observed, "I can see you're holding on tight, O'Hari."

"Sorry to whine. I can take it," I said.

"I know you can. For once I wish you would stop taking it. You look like you could use a good cry. I don't think I've ever seen you cry."

"I cried about a year ago when I thought I was going to lose you. You weren't there to see it, but I got good and drunk, and I had a great case of the whisky remorses."

"Did it feel good?"

"No, it sucked. I'd rather just tamp all this down. From now on I plan to do that until I'm around ninety and then implode."

I made him laugh. One good thing in the day.

I tried reaching Laura on and off. She wasn't answering her phone. Then I spent the rest of the day at the hospital, making up for all the times I hadn't been there for my parents. Not just this go-round, but *all* the times. Mom was right when she said I'd left a long time ago. I'm talking years. Just because your parents aren't the Cleavers doesn't mean you don't feel guilty. Dad was still not out of danger, but he didn't seem to be getting worse. In a way, that described Mom, too. There was the same listless hospital patter, how are you feeling Dad did they say whether he's responding to the antibiotics did you eat are they walking him does he get respiratory therapy in ICU did you sleep last night Mom have any lunch can I get you something (please say yes and give me a reason to get out of this room!) anything good on TV? But then as I watched Dad I thought about, no matter how fragile his hold on life, how much better it was than seeing Marcus Creighton's corpse. Second good thing in the day.

Then there was nothing else to talk about. It made me sad to guess that there never had been. Remembering how awful it was to sit there with them, nobody speaking, as if we were watching over the corpse laid out at home, I had brought the photo albums with me that I'd taken from their apartment and left in the car.

As with most families, most of the pictures were of me because I was the eldest, and the frequency of photos lessened with each child, until for Todd there were damn few. I asked Mom some questions about the pictures, about the ones I couldn't remember. Then I got to the end of the second book and saw the photographs of Christmas. So many of them were Christmas, that silver tree with the plastic disc rotating in front of a light that changed the color of the tree. You could say we weren't classy, but we weren't the only family who had that silver tree.

I remembered that Christmas. Dad got us all our own fishing rods and tackle boxes, filled with hooks and sinkers. Even little Todd, aged six, got one. We were pretty excited.

I turned the page of the album and that was it. A couple of dozen blank pages. No more photographs after I turned ten. I'd never thought about that before. I started to ask Mom, but she had dozed off. She looked like she was too exhausted for the doze to do any good.

Then I dozed off, too. When I woke I felt like the effects of the early-morning sleeping pill had finally lifted. I woke Mom up and, feeling more tender about the living for some reason I couldn't fathom, insisted on driving her home. I even put her to bed.

It wasn't late, and my body clock was now royally screwed. I left Mom a detailed note about how her car was at the hospital, and she should rest until I returned the next day. Then I left to pick up a bottle of vodka and a pizza. I kicked at Laura's door while I balanced the bottle, the pizza, and the box of Marcus Creighton's effects.

When she finally answered my kicks I took a look at her face. "You should have a good cry," I said.

"Here's how it's going to be," Laura said, not opening the door all the way. "You can come in if you say are you okay, and then I say I'm fine. I'm not up for jokes," she said. "If you say a single snarky thing I'll shoot you."

"Aw, Coleman," I answered. "Am I that bad?"

She stood her ground. The things I was carrying felt heavier. "No jokes," I said. I felt an urge to hold up two fingers in a Girl Scout pledge gesture, but even that felt too close to a joke.

Laura opened the door and let me in. I put the vodka and pizza on the kitchen counter and placed the box on her desk. I noticed that the photograph album Creighton had given her during our visit was there and open to a picture of the family on a boat, all the kids in those clumsy orange life preservers, with grins showing baby-tooth gaps that could likely be matched to the jaws they found.

Laura folded up at one end of the couch, picking holes in a crocheted yarn pillow that looked like her mother might have made it. Her computer was on, running what seemed like a continuous loop of the news reports of Creighton's execution, the finding of the bodies, the history of the case, and on and on and on. Her thousand-yard stare was fixed on something beyond the computer screen.

"Drink?" I asked.

She came back long enough to shake her head.

"Pizza?" I pressed. "It's got anchovies."

Nothing.

In the airplane safety talk, they always tell you to put on your own oxygen mask before helping the person next to you. So I walked into the little kitchen and went through the cupboards to find what could almost double as a cocktail glass. I wasn't particular. I've used bud vases more than once. I opened the freezer door and took some ice from the automatic ice cube maker with my left hand. Opened the vodka and poured a decent shot. Stirred the ice around in the glass with my index finger. I wiped my finger on a towel lying on the counter and wandered back into her living room area. I could feel the sadness in the room so strongly I didn't want to sit down and let it get on me.

"So how's your father doing?" Laura asked, her fingers still picking at the yarn pillow.

Even without crying, she looked like she was starting to develop those little running cracks like in a cartoon character who gets hit by a dropping anvil just before she falls to pieces. I wanted to say I told you so. I wanted to remind her that when I first arrived I told her she was rushing it, that it takes more than a year to get over the kind of trauma she had experienced in Tucson before jumping into a case where an innocent man's life hung in the balance and her heart was at stake.

But I didn't say any of those things.

I said, "I think the first time it hit me like this wasn't when I was in mortal danger. My first time was more like the Marcus Creighton business. I was taken to watch a man being executed in the electric chair at Raiford. I didn't feel about him the way you felt about Creighton, but there's something about just sitting there, doing nothing, while a man dies. You want to react but you don't. Everything in your brain says stop it, but you hold in check all those muscles that want to react. You just tamp it all down, and you don't realize the effort that goes into it. The tamping stays with you your whole life. It doesn't start from square one the next time; it all has a way of stacking up, one on top of the other, so it doesn't get any better, only worse. You try to protect yourself from this. You keep working out, and when that doesn't work anymore, you try yoga. You go to movies. You drink. You find what will protect the human being in your core, and you do that. Because if you leave yourself vulnerable, it will kill you."

"The rock, huh?"

"A granite callus on your soul. I don't recommend living this life."

I took a sip and put my glass on the coffee table. I knew things were bad then because she didn't get me a coaster.

"What do you mean, how I felt?" she asked.

"Felt?"

"About Marcus. What do you mean, how I felt?"

"Oh, I don't know. Maybe that business about being too emotionally involved with a case."

"That's not what you meant. You meant I was in love with him. Didn't you?"

I could feel her ire rising. I said, "I thought we were going to keep this easy." Maybe I was still a little disoriented from lack of sleep, feeling cranky. "You wanna pick a fight? Is that how you want to handle this? Who would think I'd forget that option?"

"Didn't you?"

If that was how she wanted to go . . . "Remember that married prosecutor you were having an affair with in Tucson? You've got a pattern, Coleman, of falling for men you can't have. I don't know why that is, but you need to come to terms with it."

Laura got up from the couch and, with her fists clenched, looking ready to take the argument to the next level, began to pace the room. "What do you want me to do right now, Brigid? Do you want me to fall to my knees and shriek *Why God why*?" She laughed at the melodrama of it. "Would that work for you?"

"It's nothing to be ashamed of. We've all been there, when love rears its ugly head. Just admit you were in love with Marcus Creighton. And consider. Even if you never told him, maybe he knew. Maybe he played you. Maybe he was so desperate he let you think whatever you wanted."

"You're still trying to prove to me he was guilty?" She stopped pacing. "You can be incredibly cruel, you know that?"

"This is news?"

Laura's eyes darted around the living room until they came to rest on the medicine ball placed neatly next to the elliptical trainer. She picked up the ball and, in a rage I'd never known from her, threw it at my head. With my feint that would have made Mom proud, she missed, and left a crater in the drywall an inch deep. We both stared at the crater as bits of gypsum drifted to the carpet.

"How about that?" she asked with a quaking voice.

"Not bad for a beginner," I said, trying not to let my voice shake with its own anger at nearly having taken a fifteen-pound projectile in my face.

Her fury unspent, she picked up my glass from the coffee table and threw that at the same wall where the medicine ball hit. Shards of glass splattered with the remaining vodka.

As for myself, watching the violence, I felt a perverse mix of compassion for her pain and satisfaction that I was right. It was like a parent telling a child she was sure to break her favorite doll if she continued to play with it that way, and then seeing it come to pass. And it reminded me a little of home. "Welcome to my world," I said, standing my ground for her sake.

But disgusted at the outburst, both with me and with herself, she went into her bedroom, presumably for some tissue to blow her nose loudly enough for me to hear from the living room.

In her absence I went to her desk, where I had put the box of Marcus Creighton's personal effects. In the top drawer of her desk was a box cutter. I knew Laura would have a box cutter specifically for opening boxes. I used it. We might as well hurt all the way tonight, for I doubted I would have another chance to get behind the person Coleman showed the world. Right on top was that letter, the one Wally said he hadn't seen. Odd.

I held it up when Laura returned to the room, but she ignored me and went into the kitchen. I followed her and got another glass out of the cupboard for myself, poured a little more vodka. For her part, Laura reached over the fridge to that little cupboard that no one uses. Pushed to the side, just close enough for her fingers to wiggle it forward, was a bottle of port. She used a towel to wipe off the cake of dust that had formed on the sealed cap and neck. She removed the cap and left it off, though I don't think she had its breathing in mind.

In another cupboard, the one with glasses, she again reached high up and took a red wine glass, the kind with a monstrous bowl, from a set of four on the top shelf. She had to dust that off as well, and then poured half the bottle into the glass. The thought of drinking that much port made even me a little sick to my stomach. She reached into the freezer, threw a few ice cubes into the glass, and swished it.

"You should eat a little something with that," I said.

She opened the pizza box, took out a slice, and finished it in half a dozen bites. With her mouth still full she said, "Happy now?" At least that's what I think she said.

Pizza only works so fast. By the time we returned to her desk the port was half gone, and the effects of that on a brain that had no alcohol resistance, plus not having eaten anything for at least a day, could already be seen. She could have made a Guinness record for time to inebriation. Laura swiveled her chair out from her desk and sat down while I remained standing, the envelope in my outstretched hand. "Might as well get it over with in one fell swoop," I said.

Laura took it listlessly and opened it, assuming as I did that it was the letter Marcus had written to her the night before his execution. So she looked understandably puzzled when she saw the letter was typed, and then she looked terribly hurt, and then angry. "It's from Alison Samuels," she said. She scanned it. "It looks like this was her first contact with Marcus, introducing herself."

She read it aloud.

Dear Mr. Creighton,

My name is Alison Samuels. I work for an organization called the Haven. Because of my affiliation with that organization, though I wasn't working for them at the time of your conviction for the murder of your wife and children, the case was so sensational that it was still being talked about when I joined them three years ago. I had the opportunity to view photographs of your children that were used to search for them. Others gave up the search, but there was something about your case that would not allow me to give up. I am obsessive by nature, and do not easily give up on any of the children I seek.

I never forgot the faces of your children. While I'm sure you've spent all these years regretting your actions, carried out under who knows what circumstances at that time, I feel you must have arrived at the conclusion that you deserve your penalty. Whether you actually killed the children, or whether you abandoned them to someone, their souls still died, even if their bodies are alive today.

As for the purpose of my writing: In the course of my job I've come into the possession of a photograph that may be one of your children. It is a photograph of a boy I found recently while doing internet searches on child pornography websites. The child appears to be fifteen years old in the photograph which would have been taken seven years after his disappearance in 1999. I obtained the photograph on record of your son and aged it to fifteen. The photograph I have appears to be your son.

I would like to show you this photograph and get your opinion. With your execution pending I would suppose you willing to speak with me and perhaps shed some light on what happened to the children. Perhaps this information would help me to trace the location of the boy in the photograph.

Her voice cracked here, and I took the letter out of her hand and continued.

Again, perhaps you did not kill your children, or at least not your son. Perhaps some horror at what you were doing made you stop at him. Perhaps you paid someone to do the deed for you, and they profited from this child instead of murdering him. His name, you'll recall, was Devon. Please think of him. It is a sad circumstance to imagine him being given up and degraded in the way this photograph suggests, for at least seven years, and maybe even now.

I think he was a sweet boy at eight, according to the photograph I have. At fifteen he is handsome, though thin and stooped. I can see the despair only in his dead eyes. Was his life cut short by bondage or by death? If he is still alive he would be twenty-four now, but he is still your child. How can this boy tear my heart apart, but leave yours intact?

You'll find my card enclosed with this letter should you agree to meet me and look at the photographs. I would bring them with me.

Sincerely,
Alison Samuels
The Haven

I picked up the envelope from where Laura had dropped it on the desk and found three photographs inside. Marcus must have agreed to meet her that first time, and she left the photos with him. The first was one of Devon as a child, taken standing next to what might have been his first two-wheeler. He had that dopey fakey grin that kids give you when you say smile.

The second photograph showed the boy in the first, only aged to somewhere in his teens.

The third photograph in the envelope was a closer-up shot of a boy. This one seemed to have come from an Internet site. That third photograph I won't describe. There's no purpose in it. I'll only say that it could very well have been the same boy, except that he wasn't smiling anymore.

Laura had slipped down into her chair, head on the back, legs stuck out under the coffee table so her body was in a straight line at a forty-five-degree angle, eyes staring up at the ceiling, blinking. I put the photos on the desk, lining them up in order, youngest, then aged with bicycle, then the one from the porn site. This business seemed to go on and on. Big mistake, giving her that letter.

"She was mistaken, Coleman. We know the boy is dead now. It's all done."

"Maybe it wasn't a mistake." The words came out slowly, carefully chosen, as if she was thinking them for the first time and hardly believing them. "Maybe Samuels knew that kid wasn't Devon. It was as if she wanted to twist the knife, as if she took out all of her hate for men who hurt children on him."

"Oh, come on, Coleman. You can't just make up stories and call them true," I said.

"Or maybe I know." She crossed her arms tightly the way I remembered crossing mine at a time when it felt like all of my bones were trying to jump out of my body. "Ever think of that, Brigid? Maybe I know Alison Samuels better than anyone."

I let her keep drinking her port while I paged through the rest of the photograph album once more. It told a story like any other book. Except that this story was only happy, no sadness, no conflict. It was Christmas trees and birthday wrapping paper and playing with plastic toys in the tub and learning how to ride a bike and swim with flippers in the pool and fishing, just like the Quinn family album. And like any other book, it simply stopped in time like a freeze-frame of life.

Then Laura started voicing her thoughts again, without looking at me. "Did you ever want to kill someone, Brigid? Did you ever get so fucking furious at injustice that the thought of taking a shotgun and *blam* exploding someone's face is the only thing that keeps you from actually doing it? I don't mean that you're so horrified by your thoughts that you turn away from them. It's more like the violence comforts your mind, you know what I mean? Imagining it all. When you feel this impotent rage, imagining it feels almost as good as doing it. It feels good."

I couldn't decide what was healthier for her, depression or rage. Laura closed her eyes and looked a little dreamy as if she was watching a scene play on the inside of her eyelids. If it was for her own benefit, her thoughts might be heinous. But this way she could call it justice. Sometimes when you're angry at the whole world, you pick out one piece of it for your reckoning.

· · ·

Laura opened her eyes and sat up. Using her hands as much as her sight she searched around the desk, then got up to do the same on the kitchen counter, and the coffee table that had nothing on it.

"What are you looking for?" I asked.

"Keys. Car," she said.

Laura always kept her keys in her purse. This was how I knew she was pretty drunk. I wondered if she would go into the desk drawer where I knew she kept her weapons, but she did not. I picked up the box cutter and discreetly moved it under a couch cushion. I was about to grab her purse, which lay in precisely the same spot it always did, on a small table in her front hall. But she remembered and got to it before I could. I wondered what was in the purse besides her keys.

"Where are you going? Let me drive," I said, but she was already out the front door and into the parking lot of the apartment building before I could grab my own tote, thrust less neatly on the dining room table.

By the time I grabbed it and followed her, Laura had gotten into her own car and was pulling out of her parking space.

I don't know where she intended to go, but halfway out of the parking lot she passed out in the car and rolled to a stop against the curb. I managed to wake her up long enough to extract her from the driver's seat, and got her to a patch of grass.

"Nobody cared enough to do something," she slurred.

"You cared," I said. "Come on, sit up."

"Not enough. Not enough to make everyone else care."

Then she passed out again. I'm pretty strong, but after twenty-four hours without sleep, lifting one hundred and thirty pounds of dead weight was beyond me. It was either bring her a pillow or get some help. By this time the lights were off around the complex, and I risked the supposition that Laura wasn't chummy with her neighbors. So I called Todd.

He was asleep rather than screwing Madeline, thank goodness; otherwise he might have been crankier. As it was, he answered the phone with a sleepy, "What?"

"I've got Laura Coleman passed out in her front yard. Can you come help?"

"Throw some water on her."

"I tried that," I lied.

He agreed to come, and, leaving her safely on the lawn, I pulled her car back in to its parking space. Then I sat beside her. The sky was typically cloudy in June, and I couldn't even imagine where the constellations would be that Carlo had taught me to see in the desert this time of year. The only thing I could spot for sure was Venus. But even a few miles in from the coast the offshore breeze cooled off the night, and there weren't more than a few mosquitos to swat before Todd arrived.

Between the two of us we got Laura into her bed, took off her shoes, and drew a sheet over her. "Poor kid. She's not used to drinking, and she hasn't had water. She's going to feel like hell in the morning."

"Sometimes that's not a bad thing," Todd said. "It takes the edge off the real hurting." He was wide-awake now and asked if there was anything to drink in the house. I poured him a vodka over ice in a blue plastic tumbler, which was the only other glass Laura had.

I picked up the bigger pieces from the glass Laura had thrown at the wall. Then I nosed around in Laura's laundry room and found a whisk broom and dustpan. While Todd and I talked, I cleaned up the broken glass that had sprayed out from the wall where it hit.

"So, Todd," I started, "this Madeline Stanley. What does she see in you?"

"Come on, Brigid, don't give me trouble."

"I'm not. Not really. You seem less angry to me than you used to be. And we all know you did your time."

I whisked the smaller pieces of glass into the dustpan and tossed them in the garbage pail under the sink. Then I got a wad of paper towels and dampened them.

"I still love Marylin," he said. "For me it wasn't doing time." That's as cozy as Todd would get, and he changed the subject. He indicated the bedroom with his chin. "What's the story with that woman?"

"She's bent out of shape over Marcus Creighton being executed."

"Why?"

"I dunno, why do Greenpeace activists risk their lives for a porpoise? The thing is, when I met Laura she was a passionate righter of wrongs, and she's just being herself." What I didn't bother to tell Todd was how this passion was intensified if you happened to fall in love.

"Where was she going tonight?" he asked.

I concentrated on running the wet paper towels over the tile floor to make sure I captured any small shards that had missed the whisk broom. I knew to do this from experience in my youth.

"I'm not sure where she was going," I said. "She was all about wanting to kill someone, and then she passed out."

"Who?"

"I don't know, Alison Samuels maybe. It was that kind of mood where anybody would do."

The wall would have to wait for some Spackle to fill the crater made by the medicine ball. I didn't know if Laura had any. We always had some on hand on a shelf in the garage, to patch up the holes that Dad made when he put his fist into a door.

Finished with the cleanup, I got a little drink for myself and settled back down on the couch. "You ever witness an execution, Todd?"

"No," he said. "Not that many death penalty cases for me at all."

I said, "I'm starting to rethink the death penalty thing."

He took a sip of his drink and still didn't comment.

"Come on, talk to me," I said.

Todd gave an impatient grunt. "It's understood that you're ready to deal out death as soon as you strap on a gun. The ultimate penalty, that's just paperwork."

"You ever doubt a case?"

"I play my position," Todd said.

"You're hedging. I asked, do you have any doubts about any of the guys who are still in prison because of you?"

"The word they use is *reasonable* doubt, isn't it? Not *any* doubt."

"I know, I know. But the science is moving so fast. In half the cases where there's DNA to test, the people are exonerated."

"I told you, that's not my position to play. I investigate, I arrest. It's not my job to decide who lives and who dies."

"But."

"Stop pushing me."

"But."

Todd's face hardened with the effort of not remembering something. I could tell because he finally said, "You want a but? Okay. *But*, there have been a few times I testified when I was damn glad I wasn't the judge." He thought some more. "Like God. I'm damn glad I'm not God."

Thirty

I slept on the couch that night with the help of the vodka and, around six A.M., with Laura still sleeping, I called the intensive care unit at the hospital for Dad's status. They must have gotten instructions about me, because they were very polite and told me he was still alive and still breathing on his own. I told them I'd be there in the afternoon. They said thank you, as if I was warning them.

Then I turned on the shower in Laura's bathroom to get it hot, dragged her out of bed, and pushed her through the door.

"I hate you," she mumbled.

"Good, we can use that. Don't come out till you've showered and put on some workout clothes," I said, shutting the door. While I checked in with Mom at the hospital (Dad maybe a little better, good, I'd be there in the early afternoon) I nosed around a bit, pocketing just one picture of the three kids, and an extra set of house keys that Laura had in her top desk drawer. I took those in case I needed to get back into her apartment fast at some point, in case for some reason she decided not to answer the door the next time. Not that I thought she was suicidal or anything.

"How did I get an anchovy in my hair?" she asked when she was dressed. "And why are my car keys in the bed?"

"I think you were going to kill Alison Samuels, but I could be wrong," I said. "Come on, we're going."

Laura groaned, but was still in too weakened a condition to protest. I got a couple of water bottles from the fridge and a handful of protein bars from her pantry, loaded her into the car, and let her direct me to her neighborhood gym. On the way she tried to talk.

"That was really stupid last—"

"No talking. Not yet." I unwrapped one of the protein bars and handed it to her. "Here, eat this."

She took a few bites, chewed listlessly, and said, "Oh jeez, I'm gonna throw up."

"Well, let me know if I should stop. Hertz frowns on vomit in their cars."

We got to the gym without incident, where I steered Laura gently toward the ellipticals. Nothing rough, just twenty minutes level seven. I did it, too, on the machine next to hers, where I could monitor her progress. "Keep your rpms over a hundred," I said when she started to lag. "Those tendons doing okay?"

She didn't speak, didn't even look in my direction, just nodded, her whole focus on the circles her feet made on the pedals. The perspiration was coming now, even in the cold temperature of the gym. I could smell the soured port wine from four feet away. After a while a stray endorphin even made her smile. "I take it you have some experience with hangovers," she said.

"Some. Okay, enough warmup. Let's see what you got."

We moved out of the area with the cardio equipment, bypassed the fancy machines, and ended in the free-weight room. There were a couple of guys in there, one of them displaying his loud grunting technique more than his strength.

I walked past the rack of weights to the corner where the boxing gloves were thrown in a box and picked up a set that would fit Laura's hands. I didn't intend to spar with her. She was in such a mood that I thought even with a hangover she could actually hurt me. So I picked out the pads for myself and held my palms out to receive her punches.

"I get your point," Laura said. "We don't have to do this."

"Humor me," I said. "Come on. Cross. One-two-one-two-one-two."

She couldn't resist giving it her all; she was disciplined to the point of obsessiveness, remember? After a couple of dozen crosses I did a variation with uppercut, a dozen more. Good thing I had myself firmly planted or she would have knocked me over. She was sweating profusely now. The wine aroma had grown fainter. We took off the gloves.

"We done now?" she asked. "I've been thinking."

"Bad sign." I led her back to the free-weight rack and picked up a fifteen-pounder, did a couple of curls in a silent challenge, and handed it to Laura. She put it back on the frame, picked up a twenty-pounder, and did the same.

"Show-off," I said to her. "Now you can talk."

Only she couldn't talk so much while she was curling, and I kind of knew that, so I waited until she finished another ten reps on her left arm and we walked to the bench-press table.

"I'll spot first," I said, and she sat on the table. But she didn't lie down immediately.

"Marcus Creighton was a flawed man," Laura started. She looked at me as if she expected this was the moment I'd go all Wise Old Woman on her.

"What weight do you want?" I asked.

She glanced at the rack and lay back on the table. "Oh, let's go with the seventy-five. I think that's all I've got left in me."

With little effort I hefted the weight and slid it onto the bar extending from one side of the table to the other, over her chest. Laura grasped it, took a breath that filled her whole lungs, and released it as she raised the barbell slowly, with good control.

"You probably knew more about him than anyone did for the past decade," I said. "I'll bet you know the name of his boat," I said, wanting to introduce more peaceful thoughts.

"He told me once, I don't remember just now." Then memory clicked. "*Sea Breeze*. It wasn't creative. He never brought it up except to say they had a boat that he had sold when money had gotten . . . son of a bitch."

She sat up.

"Brigid. Something." Laura blinked, as if that would help her get to the spot in her mind where something important was hidden just beyond her reach. And then she got there. "The place where the children's bones were found. The bridge to that place was only built two years ago. Sixteen years ago it was an island. Inaccessible by car."

I had done this myself. Thought over and thought over and thought over scenarios until I got one I liked. It could drive you crazy, and I wanted to help her stop, even if it meant incriminating Creighton. "Coleman. He could have gone by boat."

"I told you he didn't own a boat by that time."

"He rented one. He planned things in advance and had it waiting at the marina."

"Okay, you want to go with that story, let's go. We both know that Shayna Murry was lying about him being at her place, because of the cell phone call and because Marcus wasn't stupid enough to take the chance that she would lie for him and be the willing alibi for him murdering his family. So he comes home from her place in the late evening. We know it was late enough, after dark, because the children had all gone to bed and the wife had taken a sleeping pill. He had the wife's murder planned well in advance of that evening, but hey, if he had planned everything in advance he would have done a much more logical job of getting rid of the kids. No, one of the kids sees him, and now he has to quickly improvise. Somehow, oh never mind how, he kills them all, leaves the wife in the tub, and loads the children into the trunk."

I said, "Laura, stop it. It's over."

Laura had got off the bench by this time and was pacing back and forth in the weight room as she spoke. "He drives to the well-lighted marina and manages to put all three bodies into a boat without being seen. No, that's not it. He drives to the nearest marina and is able to rent a boat in the middle of the night. If anyone had checked the marinas, would they have found a record of the rental? Good question. So then he takes the boat, runs it three miles to the dock at the back of his house, and loads the bodies in there where there's more privacy. He's remembered to bring a shovel, too, so he can bury them."

I parked my butt on the bench and watched her go back and forth, but said in one of her passes by, "You're just making up stories, Laura. I promise you there's no good to come out of doing this to yourself. You have to stop."

She barely took notice of my words with "Not stop. He runs the boat out to the island, totally undeveloped land with soft sand close to the water's edge, but far enough up the bank so the tide won't uncover the bodies. He can tell the high-tide spot from the lack of vegetation. There's no place to dock, so he drops anchor and wades to shore. He digs the grave, just one big one, cutting through the grass with the shovel. It has to be deep to bury three bodies. When it's deep enough, he wades back to the boat.

"Three trips, one for each body? Or maybe bring the twins at once to save some time. Then he runs the boat back to the marina, drops it off in its sloop, still without being seen, gets in the car . . . oh, right, he remembered to bring a plastic tarp to put on the front seat so he wouldn't get it wet with his clothes. He's such a cold-hearted killer he even re-membered to bring a towel. Then he drives back to the house, calling nine-one-one on the way. No, wait. He's all wet, and would have to change into a similar shirt and trousers once he got back to the house. He puts the wet things into a plastic garbage bag and hides it somewhere, I don't know where, figures he'll destroy the clothes later. They're never found. He places a dry pair of shoes next to the couch where he had thrown his jacket upon coming into the house. At the last minute he remembers the shovel in the trunk and hangs it up in the garage.

"Now you tell me, Brigid. How long?"

"It doesn't matter. Can't you see it just doesn't matter anymore? We lost."

"We've only lost if we don't figure out who actually murdered that family. How long?" she demanded.

I couldn't know where this would end, but she was right, and I admitted it. "Hours," I said. "Just hours and hours. I have to clock it myself, but four . . . five?"

"Even if he hadn't gone to Shayna Murry's house, but done anything else at all after coming back on the five o'clock flight, and arrived home after nine o'clock on a summer's night when the sun would finally be down, there's no way Marcus Creighton would have the time to kill his wife, load his children into the car, drive to a marina, get a boat, come out here, bury the bodies, take the boat back—"

I put a hand up to stop her narrative. "You're looping. I get it." My brain was tumbling over on itself, looking for a way for Laura to stop arguing the case for Marcus Creighton, to end this craziness. And if I had to prove Creighton guilty, so be it. She started to speak again, but I interrupted her.

"Hold on a second, I'm thinking, and I'm not as fast as I used to be. Let's look at every single angle. What if he did the deed before he ever left on his trip?"

"Kathleen had only been dead for a few hours when her body was found."

"What if he killed Kathleen that night, then the children, then hid the bodies and buried them at a more convenient time?"

"Let's say he did that." She kind of stammered that, and I could tell she was so excited her teeth were chattering. "Even with small bodies, where do you hide all three? Plus, there was no convenient time. First he was questioned. Then the crime scene techs were all over the place. His alibi was blown the same night, and he was taken into custody the next morning. In the meantime he was watched so he couldn't get away."

I almost laughed with the insane feeling that I was getting sucked back in against my will. "Could Murry have been an accomplice who buried the bodies? And then she chickened out?"

"Even if she had the guts, she'd have the same timing issue that night. And if the bodies were hidden at her house? No, we've already agreed that killing the children wasn't part of the original plan. Something went wrong. And there was no way they could have communicated about it. Creighton was being watched so carefully he couldn't take a dump without the cops knowing about it."

If Laura's eyes had been like blood yesterday, today they hardened into ice. "The key thing is, if Creighton didn't kill the children, he didn't kill the wife. The case falls apart. But no. They wanted to believe the mistress so bad because that made the case very easy. They didn't want to see anything else."

"And the contract with a paid killer?"

"We went over all that, remember? We decided Marcus would have turned him in." She stopped to think. "And sometime around the murders, up to the day before, there would have been a suspicious number on his phone, maybe someone we couldn't identify. I don't remember seeing anything suspicious in the records. All I remember is that he called his wife's cell from Miami the afternoon of the crime."

I watched this woman who had done a one-eighty in front of my eyes, going from immobilized depression to an almost manic state, pacing wildly, talking fast. She had repeated the facts as she saw them for what may have been the third time, and it was tiring me out. But what can you do? It felt to me like even dead Marcus Creighton was still pulling at her, as if he was drowning and clutching on to her.

She brought my attention back with "I'm all right, Brigid. You can go home now. Go back to . . ."

"Carlo," I said.

"Carlo. Listen. I need to go home and ice myself." She forced herself to look at me and smile reassuringly.

I looked at her, trying to get under the smile. Thought about the colleague who ate his gun. "And when you say 'ice yourself,' you mean . . ."

"Soak my ankles in a bucket of ice water, for Pete's sake! And I'm not going to murder Alison Samuels, either. Go home. Or take care of your parents or whatever you need to do."

"Are you sure?" I said. Of all the qualities I might have inherited from my mother, I've hated that one the most. What is someone going to say, after all? No, I'm not sure? Laura answered my question with a small sigh, and I backed down.

"Speaking of parents," I said, "I do need to get over to the hospital again."

With some doubts, I dropped Laura off to spend the rest of the day with an ice pack and her continuing obsession, preparing her prosecution of someone she didn't know and her defense for the trial of a man who was already dead.

Thirty-one

I walked down the hall and into Dad's room, still composing my excuse for not being there first thing in the morning and finding it insufficiently compelling. So I was faintly relieved to see that Mom wasn't there either. Then I remembered she was at home, that I had driven her home myself, the evening before. I wondered where my brain was. And why she hadn't bothered to call me.

I'd call her and go get her, but for now I watched Dad, sleeping, his same limp-puppy look that I'd seen the day before, but maybe a little better color, or it was just my wishing. This was the first time I remembered being alone with him in the hospital. Hospital, hell, this was the first time I remembered being alone with him. I studied his face closer, trying to see a man rather than the image of the father, and wondering if I would like him better that way.

His eyes opened so he was starting back at me.

"Is your mother in the room?" he asked.

"No. She's at home right now. Are you in pain?" He reached out for me, and I held his hand with its nails thick like an animal's claws.

His body may have been weakened, but all his life was still in his eyes. "No," he said. "I wanted to tell you when she wasn't around. Your mother. She's unnatural."

I had no idea what was going on inside that mind of his, but I responded the way anyone would, whether or not they were talking to their father. "Aw, Dad. No she's not. She's natural."

"I never hurt any of you, did I? Tell me that."

I remembered all the ways that a child can be hurt. I was glad I could answer honestly, "Well, there was that time Todd was wetting his bed and you—"

"Besides that."

"Then, no. You yelled a lot, you threw things, but I don't think you ever hurt us. Per se."

"What the hell does persay mean?"

"Dad, is there anything you'd like to tell me? Anything at all?"

He looked concerned. "Why? What have they told you?"

"Nothing. Just that you're responding to the new antibiotic."

Dad breathed a sigh, but it sounded like it came from the very top of his lungs. I wondered if they'd told me the truth at the nurses' station or just had instructions to say whatever they thought would get rid of me. I stroked his arm, and wondered when I had ever touched him so much as I was touching him now.

Dad said, his difficulty breathing chopping up his words, making me remember Marcus Creighton after his asthma attack, "It's just that. When people start asking. You questions it feels like they. Think you're going to die and. This is their last chance for. Answers."

That was kind of a thoughtful thing. Was I doing Dad an injustice by thinking of him as only a two-dimensional cartoon character? Was there some depth in him that I hadn't seen? Something of wisdom, of a small good? Or even great bad?

"You're not going to die," I said.

But he was drifting back to another point. "I wasn't a. Bad father, was I?"

"You were an excellent father," I said, thinking of Marcus again, and wishing I could stop that little tug in my heart. "Better than most."

That didn't seem to satisfy him, though, and I tried to think of something more comforting. But then I wondered if he was totally off his rocker, because he followed up with "The devil in his might. He couldn't catch a bite."

I remembered that poem, if you can give it so highfalutin a name, from when we went crabbing. We wound string around raw chicken necks and, holding on to the string, threw the chicken far out into the canal. When we felt a little tug, we'd pull in the chicken slowly, luring the crab after it into a fishing net. He'd say that poem softly as the crab came closer and closer.

Going wherever his mind was, I held his hand in mine and finished for him, "So he fished and he fished the whole feckin' night. He fished so hard that his arse got sore, and that's why the devil don't fish no more."

Dad's eyes shifted then, and I suspected that the whole poem had come out to disguise what we had been talking about, because he had the same Mom Radar the rest of us had. Aware of her at the door of his room, I looked up to catch her face sad, unspeakably sad.

I felt like I'd been caught. "Mom," I said, a little too loudly. "I was just about to come get you. How did you get here without your car?"

"So many Weeping Willow residents come here, there's a shuttle," she said.

"Dad seems better today," I said.

"The doctor called me at home. They're moving him out of the ICU today. They'll keep him for another seventy-two hours, then they're going to send him home." She kept it together until the word "home" that came out like "ho-oh." Then she pressed her lips together for the "mm" and started to cry. It was the first time I could remember seeing my mother cry.

Thirty-two

I had told Carlo I was tired of driving, yet after leaving the hospital there I was, heading north along the beach road. I didn't want to go back to the hotel, cold and lonely. I couldn't go to Laura for solace because she was dealing with a pain greater than my own.

I tilted my head to one side, imagining Carlo's big hand on the side of my face, but he was twenty-five hundred miles away, and no technology could produce the comfort of his touch. For most of my life I hadn't missed this, and now the thought of going without was unthinkable. Maybe I drove to punish myself. And to think over and over what I could have done differently. Is there any relationship with more potential for cruelty than that of a mother and daughter? Men don't remember what was said yesterday, but then you get two women who remember every nuance of every conversation of a lifetime and don't hesitate to throw them into the argument.

The one thing I could always count on was that Mom would be Mom. That role was somewhat varied. I could take Passive-Aggressive Mom. I could take Quietly Critical Mom. I could take Mom as Pious Saint. I might not have particularly liked any of those characters, but she adhered to them in a script that both of us had known since I was at least ten years old. Dad and the rest of us, we could spin out of control at the drop of a hat, and hats dropped daily. But not Mom. No matter what the character she played, Mom was always the one in control.

Now, in the midst of everything, Mom was crying. It was the one thing I couldn't take. Sounds small of me, doesn't it? Well, I've promised to tell the truth in these stories as much as I'm able even if it makes me look bad. Recently I'd had plenty of experience with people emoting all over the place. Not Mom. I'll tell you, I hadn't had any experience in handling this Mom.

I had made an effort, tried asking questions: Are you stressed? Are you just relieved that Dad is out of danger now? When she didn't answer, I tried putting my arms around her. She pushed me away, her tears getting angrier. I patted her shoulder, and she brushed my hand away, too. She sagged against the wall, threw her eyeglasses on the unoccupied bed close by, and rubbed her face hard with both hands, spending a little more time drawing her fingers out over her eyelids, a last-ditch attempt to rid herself of the tears. Then she looked at me the same way Laura Coleman had after Creighton's execution, with something too close to hate. She said, "Would you please go away now? Would you all just go away?"

Besides Dad, I was aware of being the only other person in the room. I understood that she meant the whole of us, Dad and Todd and Ariel and me, so different from her. I thought of how she had heard Dad and me reciting that silly poem together, and in a flash it came to me, what I thought this was. So this is what I heard myself say: "Sure, Mom. I'll get out of your hair. You take it easy. You know what I bet this is about? You've just always been a little jealous that all of us got along with Dad better than with you."

That dried her up before I could realize what I'd said, and say I was sorry. I apologized. She told me that was all right, but I could tell from the hardening of her expression that I had struck too great a blow, and there are those words you can't ever unsay.

So I left as she told me to do, got in the car, and drove blindly north, overwhelmed with Mom-guilt, hating myself for being such an insensitive idiot, because with everything that had gone on I was all out of whatever she needed from me.

I drove for two hours and found myself nearing Vero Beach. I remembered that time I'd visited Shayna Murry. As long as I was doing some damage, I thought I'd see her again, describe the execution, and watch her face to see what it would tell me. This was something I was good at.

When I called Cracker's Café and asked if she'd seen the news lately, Sam said he didn't know, she still hadn't come to work.

"Since when?" I asked.

"Since before the execution, I guess," he said. "I don't know, I lose track."

What was she feeling about Creighton's execution, I wondered. Was she relieved now that the long journey had reached what she thought was its destination? If so, I would give her a little something to worry about. I would tell her Laura Coleman wasn't stopping her investigation.

Just like last time, I knocked at her front door, and there was no answer.

The door was unlocked just like last time.

I pushed open the door, only this time, instead of finding Shayna working with her blowtorch, oblivious to the rest of the world, I found myself pushing against a stench that pushed back at me.

Shayna.

I turned my face from the interior of the studio and took a deeper breath of the fresher air outside. Then I covered my nose and mouth with both hands and ran in. I thought briefly that I should have had a gun in hand, but then I would have to give up one of my hands to hold it. Besides that, no real need to worry about some bad guy being in there. He wouldn't be able to stand it any better than I could.

Several steps into the place I tripped over something in my path and fell to my hands and knees, sucking in much more air than I wanted. I went back outside for another breath, then returned, this time noticing that a piece of art, the huge metal medallion that I had seen on the wall the first time I was there, was on the floor.

I had some fleeting notion of the rest of the room I ran through, dim because of the boarded-up windows, the makeshift gallery with I-don't-know-whats spread about, works in progress, works mounted on the walls, more rusty metal, some cypress knees. I can't tell, though, if what I'm remembering was from that day or from the previous visit I'd made to the place.

No one was there, but I saw a dried brown palm frond pushed across the entrance to a hallway, and I followed that trail. Each breath through my mouth was as small as I could make it because I could even feel the odor in my mouth.

There were more rooms at the back. Living quarters. Nothing in the tiny corridor of a kitchen, but I knew she was somewhere. I had to breathe again but again tried to keep it to a minimum. As I ran down a short hallway, the smell grew to a truckload of ground round left out long after its use-or-freeze-by date.

I found what I was looking for in the bedroom. The door was partially closed, and I kicked it open with my foot. Then I saw what I took to be Shayna Murry, long gone. She was crumpled against the wall under where the window was boarded up like in the front. I say "took to be" because she was no longer easily recognizable as the woman I had met.

When Delgado got out of his car I said, "She's been dead for some time, so if I was you I'd call the ME and both go in once at the same time. The room where I found her had a window unit, but it was off, so the whole place is hot. I'm sorry I must have corrupted the scene some."

Delgado stopped to call the ME and then told me to wait where I was and started into the house.

"She's in the bedroom down the hall," I called after him.

He was able to tolerate it a little better than I could, was in there for several minutes. But he still reeled down the front steps when he returned.

I said, "I think it's homicide."

"The ME will take a closer look. I didn't see any gunshot or stab wounds."

"There was that metal sculpture on the floor, and the palm frond across the hallway. Looked like a struggle," I said.

"Did you see the glass?" Delgado asked.

"No, I missed that. Shattered?"

"A plastic glass on its side next to the body. Like she dropped it."

"You thinking heart attack?" I asked. Coming this soon after Creighton's execution, I wondered.

He shook his head and wiped his sleeve against his forehead, sweatier than the day called for. "Hard to tell. Usually I'd do the initial death scene investigation, but for this I'm going to call in a team. They'll want impressions of your shoes and prints to exclude you, so stick around, okay?"

"I didn't touch anything. Moved the bedroom door a few inches. Oh, I tripped on something that was on the floor."

I waited around for the ME to come and examine the scene and the body on-site. Dr. Oliver Brach and I recognized each other from when the bones of the Creighton children were found. He might have been curious about why I was at this scene, too, but his questions were only about my discovery of Shayna Murry. I knew enough about situations like this that, not being the investigator at the scene, not even in active law enforcement, I ghosted it. Just stayed unobtrusive, didn't offer anything except to answer Brach's questions.

Brach and Delgado left me sitting in Delgado's cruiser with the AC on, smeared a little Mentholatum under their noses, then went in the house together. I was impressed by how much longer they were able to spend inside the house than I did, but then this was their job, so they didn't have much of a choice. By the time they emerged, both the meat wagon and a forensic van had arrived, the first to take the body away and the second to go over the scene. I gave them my prints and shoe impressions to exclude me as a suspect.

I submitted to another round of questions, why I was there, what time I had arrived, did I know when anyone had last seen her alive, again did I touch anything, did I walk anywhere but in a straight line to the bedroom. I was so well-behaved they didn't mind my asking some questions of my own.

"Could you tell how she died? Strangulation? Blunt trauma? I couldn't see any blood, not that I spent much time looking."

Brach shook his head. "I'll know better when I have her on the table and cut away her clothing. There's nothing apparent, but it's often that way once decomposition sets in."

"Holy moly, it was bad in there. How long since death, do you figure?"

"The more time elapses, the harder it is to say. Could be as little as forty-eight hours."

"With that much putrefaction?"

"In that house, this time of year, you can go from dead to bones in two weeks."

During this conversation I had been standing there forcing air out my nose in hard little puffs to get rid of the smell of one hundred and twenty pounds of bad meat. It can get so bad the thought of putting your head under water and sucking it through your nose is actually appealing. Brach noticed and gave me some of his Mentholatum to smear on my upper lip, which helped a little.

Delgado looked at Brach. "Natural? She's in some kind of physical distress? That piece of art on the floor in the studio, could have been dropped. She tries to make it back to her room where her cell phone is to call nine-one-one. Goes off balance and pulls the palm frond onto the floor." You could see on his face that this was playing out in his head, hopefully. I wondered if Delgado was still as much out of his league as he was with the Creighton case. Why did he hesitate to call it homicide?

"I'd seen that sculpture before, hanging on the wall near her workbench. Now it's on the floor across the room. It was a defensive maneuver."

Delgado gave in. He said to Brach, "We treat it as a homicide until you determine cause of death."

Brach nodded. "Can't rule out sex crime. I'll do a swab and see if there's anything that hasn't been contaminated."

Delgado nodded, too, which made me forget my intention to remain silent. "You know it's not a sex crime," I said to Delgado.

Brach looked at me with an enhanced interest, while Delgado went poker-faced.

I said, "Way too coincidental. This is connected."

I could tell Delgado knew what I was talking about, but Brach said, "Connected?"

"To the Marcus Creighton case," I said to him. "To the bodies of the children you saw. To the execution two days ago."

Then they both got cautious. I didn't think I'd find out any more information until the crime scene techs got finished with the place and Brach did Murry's autopsy. Delgado agreed to share information he got, and I agreed to let him know if I thought of anything. He seemed very amicable, maybe overly so.

I could feel the smell of decomposition wafting off my clothes, so I rolled down all the windows of the car when I got in and cranked up the air-conditioning full blast. But before I could be on my way, the old Ford pickup I'd seen outside of Cracker's Café pulled onto the grass not far from me.

I recognized Shayna Murry's brother even without the truck. He left his door open. Shock competing with his forward motion, he stumbled with the gait of a drunk man trying to run. He fell to his knees once on the way to the gurney, pushed up with his hands, and kept on. None of that palpable aggression I'd felt in the restaurant, but a little boy scrambling to his sister before they could put her into the ambulance.

I turned off the air-conditioning so I could hear better. I also scrunched down in the seat a bit, thinking that if he saw me it could cause trouble, that he might somehow blame me after our meeting in the café, if he remembered it.

He cried, "Stop!" and everyone did. He swiveled his head around, trying to fix on the best person to tell him that wasn't his sister. "You didn't tell me." He said it as if they had made a mistake in protocol and therefore his sister could be alive.

"It's not the kind of information we give over the phone," Delgado said. "I'm sorry, Erroll."

Erroll was shrieking now, raising his fist as if he would pound on the body bag, and then realizing that's just not what you do. Instead he scrabbled at the zipper before anyone could stop him, and he actually got it halfway down.

Relief washed through his face and voice when he saw what was once her face. "It's not her," he said. "It's not her."

"Aw, Erroll, I'm sorry. It's her."

"She has bags on her hands. Why does she have bags on her hands?" He shrieked the words as if the plastic bags they used to preserve any evidence under her nails was worse than anything. Delgado grabbed him by his wrists and turned the man to himself so Erroll wouldn't be able to see any more.

"When was the last time you saw her, Erroll?" asked Delgado, his voice all sympathy and probably sincere. Surely he couldn't be digging for anything. This was Shayna's brother.

"A few days ago, where she works," he said, turning back and wiping away from the black bag some saliva that had trickled down from his mouth. "What happened to her?"

Brach stayed suitably quiet and let Delgado answer.

"We're not sure," he said. "Let us take her in and let Dr. Brach here see what's what, give us a report. I'll tell you everything we find out. In the meantime, you stay away from the house, okay?"

Erroll looked closer at the house now, where the techs were following Delgado's instruction. "You're putting tape up. It says crime scene on it."

Delgado glanced in my direction inadvertently. I decided it was time to go.

Thirty—three

I pulled away from the area, parked a ways off, and just sat there, temporarily too stunned to consider my next move. Family was forgotten as Shayna Murry's corpse set off alarm bells that hadn't rung since Laura Coleman had been abducted the year before. No one believed me then, and I wondered if this time they would.

Because it had not ended with Creighton's execution. Someone was out there, and thirty years of finely tuned intuition told me they weren't finished.

The afternoon rain hit. No place does rain like Florida. Even with the windshield wipers going full tilt you couldn't see out, but contrary to what others might do, that got me moving again. Like I've said, every Floridian knew either the downpour would let up by itself in ten minutes, or it wouldn't be raining at all a block away. Whatever the case, you didn't just wait. Only tourists waited like depressed ducks.

I even called Laura while I was driving, having to speak loudly and get her to do the same over the hail-like pounding of the drops on the roof of the car.

"Shayna Murry's dead," I shouted.

"What?"

"Shayna Murry's dead."

"I heard you. How did you find out?"

"I found her dead in her bedroom." I described the condition of her body. "It's a homicide."

"How?"

"I don't know. But I know."

I explained how the ME couldn't see any wounds but it looked like there was a struggle, like she ran into the bedroom to escape and then realized she couldn't get out that way.

"What about Delgado?" she asked. "Was that creep at the scene?"

"Aw, don't be so judgmental. I called him."

"What did he say?"

"At first he was going along with a sex crime scenario, but I stopped him. You and I know this isn't random."

Rather than respond to that as I expected, cursing Delgado or saying *Damn straight it's not random*, she paused, as if she was weighing what to say next. Then she finally asked, "How long was she dead?"

"Could be as little as forty-eight hours."

"That much decomposition?"

"ME said yeah, this part of the world, this time of year, no AC, you go from dead to bones in two weeks."

Just as I knew they would, the clouds started to break and the rain slowed. "Hold on a sec," I said. Then a minute later, "Gimme a footlong Veggie Delite," I said.

"What?" Laura asked.

"I'm in a Subway. I have to have something to get the smell out of my nose. Whole wheat, please. No, no cheese. No animal products." I lowered my voice and turned from the counter. "Hold on a sec, I don't want to talk any more in here. Extra jalapeños. No guacamole." I couldn't take guacamole just now.

I paid for the sandwich and a bottle of water, tucked them into my tote bag, and walked back out to the car, picking up where we left off. Predictably, the rain had stopped.

Laura's voice said, "What were you doing at Shayna Murry's house?"

"Long story. But the main reason I'm calling is to tell you this obviously isn't just a cold case anymore. And I don't think Shayna Murry is the end of it. You're going to be needed."

I unwrapped the sandwich and bit into it, glad for the cleansing feel and the lack of any meat smell. Veggie Delites had saved my sanity on more than one occasion.

I swallowed, and suggested to Laura that she do whatever it took to get official again, and expect a call from either Gabriel Delgado or my brother, more likely the former. Laura sounded good with that, and I thought this would get her off the Creighton loop while doing something of benefit to protect live people.

Then I called Todd.

"Quinn," he answered.

I told him what had happened, filling in anything he might have forgotten re Shayna Murry as witness for the prosecution and how many people might know we'd caught her in a lie. I repeated what I'd said to Delgado and Laura, putting it out there to get everyone thinking. "Delgado seemed resistant, but what do you think of the idea that this isn't over?"

Silence for a beat, while both of us counted up the other possible Shayna Murrys, then, "That's a leap, Brigid."

"What can I say, I'm worried. I don't think it's isolated. How many people you got down there in your jurisdiction? Tracy Mack? Manny Gutierrez? The state's attorney, whatever his name is? What about people who weighed in after the fact? Alison Samuels from the Haven, she went on national television and practically said she wanted Creighton dead. What you gonna do, wait and see?"

"I can't just call Delgado out of the blue."

"You should at least talk. Find out who's living where. Your—what about Madeline Stanley. Old friends, right? She can put the bug in his ear that he might even be in danger because he was the detective in the Creighton case. Have her reach out to him."

He snarfed. "When did you start saying 'reach out'?"

"And I know I'm thinking on my feet, but not bad to have a little FBI backup when you want it, someone who knows everything about the case."

"Who, you?"

"I'm retired. Laura Coleman."

"Couldn't hurt. Have some FBI resources without officially calling them in and letting them run the show. Would you talk to her?"

"I already did. She's ready."

Back at my hotel, having bundled the clothes I had been wearing into a plastic bag and stuffed them into the small trash basket by the desk, I sat in the tub, soaking the remaining odor of the scene out of my skin. Bad as it was, finding Murry, after the shock wore off I started replaying in my head what had happened with my mother that morning. I needed to go back there, to either the hospital or her apartment. I needed to figure out what to say that would return us to usual. So far I couldn't come up with anything, and that tightened the little knot in my gut.

Strung out after the day with that combination of physical exhaustion and the mental condition of a just-plucked violin string, with an extra little vibrato running through me I realized I hadn't called Carlo. I confess, the last thing I wanted to do was talk to another person, even him. That made me feel like a heel. One of the things I discovered in my late-life marriage is that, while the lover is always there, our feelings about them can change from one moment to the next. With more of a sense of duty than love, I threw on fresh jeans and a blouse and FaceTimed him.

He appeared with an unusually large grin and a Pug on his lap, clearly hoping to cheer me up. I imagined even the Pug was grinning on both sides of his lolling tongue. I could see the kitchen behind them and knew they were sitting at the dining room table, Carlo's iPad leaning up against the small pile of books that seemed to serve as our only centerpiece. I wished I could spirit myself there for a breather before whatever was going to happen next. "Which one is that?" I admitted to not being able to tell.

Carlo wagged a paw at me. "It's Al."

"Hi, Al," I said.

"What's wrong?" Carlo said, dropping the grin. He bent to the side for a moment and then came back without the Pug, having dropped him, too.

Maybe sometime I would be specific about what I'd said to my mother, and her reaction, but it would have to wait for his real presence rather than virtual. "It's a shitstorm. Everything is going to hell. Dad is getting better and out of nowhere Mom breaks down like she's not thrilled about it. I'm in the middle. What do you do with parents like this? And I have my doubts about Laura's stability after watching Creighton get executed. It's for sure she was in love with him."

He didn't look surprised. "And you're trying to fix it all."

I ignored that, took a deep breath, and said, "And this morning I found Shayna Murry's body."

He pursed his mouth in a whistle, but no sound came. "Was she murdered?"

I bit lightly at the inside of my lip. "Nothing is certain yet, but until the autopsy report comes back they're treating it like a homicide. The Vero Beach detective in charge is reluctant to admit it, but I think there's a connection to Marcus Creighton's execution. I'm pushing that theory on all fronts."

"It doesn't take a genius to conclude that."

"Thanks," I said.

Carlo's usual aspect is more ironic than sober, and you'd have to know him a while to detect the change that came over his face as he said, "I want you to tell me if you're in danger."

"No!" I didn't realize I was holding my breath until I finally let it out on that word. "That's why I wanted you to see my face. You're getting good at knowing me, and I wanted to tell you there's no danger here. At least not to me. I was on Creighton's side, remember?"

"You said you found the body. What did you see?"

The molecules of decomposition wafted back into my senses so I couldn't tell if it was imagination or coming from my clothes in the plastic bag.

"You're not talking," he said. "What are you not telling me?"

"Stop trying to be pastoral, I'm just thinking." One more pause and then, "You know, Dad used to come home and tell Mom and the rest of us everything that happened. There was one night where over dinner he told us how someone died in their Jacuzzi and the body had to be removed with a strainer when it was discovered three weeks later. Ariel spewed her Hamburger Helper. He didn't seem to have any boundaries between his job and his family."

"Didn't your mother do anything to restrain him?"

"Maybe at some point she did, I can't remember. But if she ever tried, she gave up early on. Anyway, when I grew up and knew other colleagues in the business, I found out not everyone was like my dad. Most didn't pull their families into the business, didn't subject them to secondhand violence. I admired that. This is the first time I've been in the position where I have a mate. Here's how I'm going to play it. It was really grim, but you're a grown-up. If you insist on knowing the details, I'll tell you when I'm home. I know I promised to be honest, and I know I shouldn't try to protect you, but it's the closest I can get right now."

"You need me to be there," Carlo said. "I'll get a ticket and let you know when I'm arriving."

I didn't tell him that he would just be one more person I'd feel compelled to look after. So sue me. "Oh sweetie, no, I've got everything under control and I'm in a really good place in my head, I swear. It's just like today some clown has been following me around smacking me with a pig bladder. One thing after another."

"How long, do you think?"

"I can't tell right now."

"Well, do me a favor and call every day, would you?" He leaned forward and kissed the screen, and his nose ballooning up like that made me smile even now. "I love you, O'Hari."

"Love you too, Perfesser." And then of course I had to make a joke. "And I promise I'll make it up to you. Anything you want, cowboy."

"Not a bad trade for another lonely day," he said, his voice sounding more amused than aroused. "Call your mother. Tell her how much stress you've been under."

How could I claim stress when I had no idea of hers? I picked up my phone several times that evening to call Mom, but still couldn't imagine what I would say. It wasn't avoidance. Better to have a cool-down period, I told myself. That's what I told myself, and it helped the guilts, not much, but some.

Thirty-four

I was still giving it time to cool down the next day.

It worked out well that Shayna Murry's partially decomposed body was taken to Palm Beach for the autopsy, where they had more pathology bells and whistles given the sometimes deadly high jinx of an area wealthy enough to make Vero look much less Very.

Madeline Stanley had convinced Gabriel Delgado of the sense of making the investigation a joint one from the start. Laura Coleman was included because she knew so much about the original case and could go across jurisdictions. I was included because I had gotten involved, and knew her and Todd.

We gathered in one of the conference rooms of the FBI office in West Palm Beach, the middle-class city west of Palm Beach. Paneled ceiling with recessed lighting, particle board conference table surrounded by vinyl-covered swivel chairs—the usual.

Detective Delgado led the meeting, at least ostensibly, and next to him sat Dr. Oliver Brach, the ME I had last met at Shayna Murry's homicide scene. Madeline sat next to Todd but leaned away from him, her arm resting on the arm of her chair, the way you sit next to a stranger on a plane. She was here because of her connection to Delgado and her brokering of the meeting, but she would stay respectfully detached, not get in Todd's way. Laura sat brooding by herself, erect, steely-eyed, appropriately FBI-ish, the only suit at the table. Her hands clasped on the table before three huge binders filled with all her research on the Creighton case. While Delgado seemed to have set aside any hard feelings about her attitude toward how he had handled things, Laura made a point of not looking at him while he spoke.

Correction, there was another suit. The boss that Todd had mentioned, Captain Wayne McClay, listened to our conversation without comment, corners of his mouth turned down and eyes shifting to each speaker. He didn't ask for an introduction to anyone. He was one of those commanding presences that made everyone in the room speak as if justifying their existence to him.

Delgado and Brach passed crime scene photos around the table while they took turns giving us the reconstruction of what we were now certain was Shayna Murry's murder:

The assailant entered through the front, the only door in the house, without any signs of forced entry. The victim was in the front room, which she used as her art studio. She may have known the identity of the assailant, because she reacted very quickly, throwing a metal sculpture across the room.

"I'd been to her studio previously, and saw the sculpture hanging on the wall about here," I said, pointing to the spot on the photo.

"Then let's say the victim was standing near it, maybe at the worktable in that corner of the room," Delgado said. "The assailant reacted just as quickly, attacking the victim from a distance."

"We know this because of the wounds," Brach said.

He passed around four close-up photos taken on the autopsy table. It was difficult to see with the decomposed flesh, but arrows pointed out what looked like vampire bites on Murry's chest.

"Those double-pronged tears, those are electroshock weapon marks. The assailant used a stun gun as a weapon," Brach said.

"Can you tell the distance between her and the assailant?" Todd asked.

"If it was law-enforcement issue, could have been a maximum distance of thirty-five feet. Max distance for a civilian defense weapon is only fifteen feet," Delgado said, looking at McClay.

I pointed to the photo of the studio. "Distance from the front door to the workbench is about twenty, the length of the room," I said. "But the assailant could have come in further before activating the gun."

"Do you need a permit in Florida?" Laura asked.

"Nope, unless it's concealed carry." Delgado picked up the thread from there. "She would have dropped to the floor, everyone does. Then it seems the victim was allowed to come to fully rather than be killed immediately, and with the front door blocked ran down the hall, putting herself in even greater jeopardy because there was no way out."

"Or she could have been dragged while unconscious," Todd said, more for the sake of his boss than from any strong conviction, "which would indicate a fairly strong male assailant."

Delgado found the photograph of the palm frond pulled across the hallway and slid it across the table to Brach. It was getting to seem more like table hockey. "We think it was a chase, that she went on her own steam, because someone pulled this down, possibly the victim to block the assailant. The assailant would have been close enough behind her, that is, a maximum of thirty-five feet, because the electrodes were still stuck into her."

The others could talk about victim and assailant as they did their reconstruction. Delgado and Brach told the story as detective and medical examiner, nice and dry, but my mind kept saying *Shayna Murry, Shayna Murry, Shayna Murry*. And as they spoke I watched the story.

Maybe Shayna Murry doesn't have her blowtorch to cover the sound of whoever is coming through her front door just like I had the day I visited her. He, let's call it He for the time being, doesn't stop to announce his presence, but comes as close as He can in one second and then fires the stun gun at her the moment she turns around.

Shayna Murry shouts, "Oh!" from the pain and her little elfin body gives one huge convulsion and then falls back against her workbench and onto the floor of the studio. It will be hard to see her bruises after her body is found.

He waits. He has two more charges to deliver in this particular model before needing to reload.

She's still relatively young. Within a few moments, Shayna Murry's muscles relax and she is surprisingly in good enough shape to get up off the floor. To defend herself. She tries to pull the wires from her chest, but the device has prongs in each one that anchor in her flesh. She can't go out the front door because He is blocking it.

Shayna Murry takes the metal sculpture off the wall, the one that's shaped like a Roman shield, and hurls it, Frisbee-style, across the room. He dodges it easily. She wishes she had her blowtorch turned on, because she could defend herself with that, but there's no time. He doesn't even have to come at her. All He has to do is press the lever and deliver another shock to bring her down again. Then He can finish her off.

But He doesn't.

Trailing the wires behind her that connect her to him like a deadly umbilical cord, Shayna Murry goes the only way possible, down the hall and into her bedroom. Maybe she thinks she can close and lock the door.

But He gets there first and stops the door with his foot. She finds herself trapped now. Does she know who this is? Has He told her yet why He is there? No. There is no stopping to talk, at least not now, but He thinks He has time. Shayna Murry is terrified and tries to break through the boarded-up hole that is her window. She pounds at it and hysterically claws the wood as if she can dig her way through it.

He delivers another shock. It goes throughout her body, causing all her muscles to cramp simultaneously. She goes rigid again, again shouts *OH* with the pain. Does He only want to inflict the pain? Does He want her dead, but not immediately? Or does He want something else?

Shayna Murry comes to, although this time it takes a little longer, this time it's with the help of a glass of water thrown in her face to revive her. A glass He got from the bathroom.

What now?

No matter what now, whether they talk, whether any sense is made out of an otherwise senseless act, Shayna Murry takes one more jolt. As if her body is giving up, this time she barely twitches at all. Then she is still.

He throws more water on her. But this time Shayna Murry doesn't come to. No matter how safe the weapon is for law-enforcement defense, in Shayna Murry's case the third time is the charm for death. A heart can only take so much.

Is He disappointed? Did He get what He came for?

He pulls the barbed prongs out of her, without the care that might have been taken for a living victim, leaving two tears, the same size, side by side, in her flesh. He leaves.

As if they had rehearsed for a television crime drama, Brach had ready a microscopic photo of Murry's fingertips that, despite the rawness that welcomed the earliest insect activity, distinctly showed the splinters from the wood panel over the window.

Dr. Brach brought me back from the scene reconstruction to the ME report. "Cause of death, cardiac arrest brought on by repeated stun gun shocks," he finished.

Todd was looking closely at one of the crime scene photos that he had held back as the others were passed around. These days everybody in law enforcement needs to be scientific, show off their forensics. "I'm not convinced about the stun gun theory," he said. "Could have been some sort of sharp-force trauma that broke the skin there without breaking bones." He jabbed with his index and middle finger extended. "What do you call those—"

"A meat fork?" I said. I've been learning how to cook.

Todd nodded. "Otherwise, how do you account for the blood spatter?"

"I'm sorry?" Brach answered, puzzled to know what he had missed.

"Here on the floor in the bedroom next to the body." Todd shot the photo he was looking at across the table as if he was taking Brach's queen in a game of homicide chess. Hockey, chess, the boys are always playing some game.

Brach looked again at the photo with a studied casualness and smiled. "It's a little harder to tell from the photos, but that's not blood spatter. It's tracks from insects that got to the corpse early on before the blood was fully coagulated. There was evidence of roaches in the place."

Brach had Todd in a velvet vise. McClay cleared his throat. Todd cleared his throat, too, despite his best effort not to do so, yet tried to cover his ignorance with one more question. "The weapon is silent, but what about the screams?"

Delgado said, "Murry's home is pretty secluded, in the middle of a large yard with nothing real close by. Plus the windows are boarded up."

Brach nodded. He seemed to be a man who was comfortable not

speaking, and because of that others treated him with respect and not a little gratitude.

"Was she killed before or after Marcus Creighton's execution?" I asked.

Brach smiled at me, too, this time like a professor at a student who was getting, if not the solution, at least the problem. "Ah, that's what's hard to determine given the approximately forty-eight hours between the Creighton execution and your discovery of the body, and the speed of decomposition."

"But we agree, right?" I said. "There's a connection between Creighton and Murry. At least there's a motive in there somewhere."

The others agreed with their silence, each probably thinking what possibilities could arise out of it in the days ahead.

Delgado looked at Laura with a respect he'd gained from the day they found the Creighton children's bodies. "You've been there every step of the way. You know more about Creighton and Murry than anyone else in this room. Even more than I do, and I investigated the case originally. What do you think?"

Laura, who had been hunkered down and quiet during all the talk, pushed herself upright in the chair. "I've been thinking a lot, but right now all I've got is possibilities. It seems pretty clear that there are three possible motives. A) Was it to make her talk—was the killer trying to get her to maybe admit to the role she played in the murder of the Creightons? Did he think she knew who really did it? Was he hoping that her confession would exonerate Marcus? Or B) Was it to keep her from talking? Was he trying to tie up some loose end that would lead to his discovery? Or C) Was it to finally avenge the death of Marcus Creighton? If we could answer those questions, I think we'll know who did it."

I had the sense of brain rubber burning to keep up with her. Even McClay looked impressed, which seemed to mildly piss off everyone else at the table.

Todd spoke while he passed around copies of a paper he'd kept in front of him. "If it's A or B, and Shayna Murry is the only person who could have given the killer what he wanted, this was an isolated crime, and up to the Vero Beach police and whoever they want to call in to investigate. But if it's C, if this is a vigilante killing, there's a possibility it's not over. There were quite a few people who could be blamed for Creighton's death. Agent Coleman and I got together before the meeting and compiled this list of people in my jurisdiction."

When we each had a copy of the list of names and addresses in front of us, McClay finally deigned to speak. "We keep this to ourselves for now. The media won't make a connection between Murry and Creighton unless they've dug deep into the case investigation or the appeals, and we have the benefit that most of the journalists are too young to remember all the details of the original case." He tapped his index finger on a name about halfway down. "Tracy Mack. The fingerprint examiner. I think he's the most obvious next target. And Detective Delgado, I'd take some precautions if I were you. Detective Quinn, keep me apprised." Then McClay left the room.

Delgado laughed at seeing his own name on the list, but the rest of us had been where he was at one time or another, and we all did that little look-away thing that tried not to show concern. "Why am I on this list?"

"Because you stopped investigating right after Shayna Murry lied about Creighton's alibi?" I put a question mark after that, but Delgado still took offense.

"What the hell are you even doing in this meeting?" he countered, at least for a flash dropping his small-town Lothario shtick, more comfortable after the boss, didn't matter whose boss, was gone.

"Easy there, guys," Todd said. "That doesn't get us anywhere."

"Alison Samuels," I said. Most of the people at the table looked blank. Except Todd. I was probably the only person at the table who could read his face. I saw him following some chain of thoughts before openly staring at Laura. And I watched him think something cops never want to think. An icy finger reached into my chest and flicked my heart. Oh, little brother, you're thinking of that night at Laura's place, aren't you? I regretted mentioning Samuels's name but couldn't back down now. I said, "She's the representative from the Haven, and she was hot to get Creighton dead. She's not on the list."

I felt Laura flinch beside me. "Beyond what Brigid and I know, there's nothing that formally links her to the case," she said.

"She was pretty public with that TV interview," I said.

"Couldn't hurt," Todd said, a little more slowly than he usually spoke. "We'll have a patrolman keep an eye out."

"Where's David Lancer these days?" Delgado asked. "The prosecutor."

Laura said, "I called Lancer on the way over here. His housekeeper answered and said he was on a cruise through the Panama Canal." She opened the file that she had brought to the meeting. She was the only one who brought her own materials. She wrote down the name and address of the state's attorney who had prosecuted Marcus Creighton and flipped the paper across the table to Todd. "That's for when he gets back," she said.

Madeline Stanley spoke for the first time, rocking irritably like she had a hemorrhoid. "It's too bad when people are only doing their job."

I thought, *Or taking orders. That's another good excuse.* But I said, "If it's a vigilante killer, the murders don't need a logical basis. It doesn't matter whether people in the justice system were behaving ethically at the time. It doesn't matter whether they were, as Detective Stanley says, 'only doing their job.'"

Delgado agreed with me. "It's about ultimate justice in the mind of the vigilante. Now we need to find out who still cares about Marcus Creighton."

I willed Laura to keep her mouth shut, but no dice. "Somebody cares," she said. "Enough to kill. This is partly about finding who killed Shayna Murry, and partly about stopping the killer before he can do it again. But there's another angle. Because Marcus Creighton was innocent—"

"That's not true," Madeline said, her tone sounding like a rattling saber. I remembered that she and Delgado were tight.

"Goddam right it is," Laura said. "That means that whoever murdered his family may still be out there. Maybe still in the area. Maybe he's tying up loose ends. If we want to do this right, we have to consider the second motive I raised. We have to return to the Creighton case."

Todd looked a little impatient as he held out a cautionary hand to Madeline. "In the meantime we follow the revenge motive, and get on the process of protecting other potential victims until Delgado finds this guy."

218

Laura stayed silent now, but her face took on that narrow-eyed judgment that she'd turned on me not too long ago.

I watched Todd watching Laura with a speculative look.

"Todd?" I said, to bring him back to the table.

His eyes cleared and he picked up my gaze.

"What do you want me to do?" I asked.

He wasn't ready to deal with me yet, so he said, "Detective Stanley can notify McClay that she'll be organizing the security detail down our way."

Madeline said, "If this is still ongoing we can tell Lancer when he gets back from his cruise. The others, do we tell them?"

"I wouldn't, not just yet. What do you think?" Todd said.

"Agreed," Madeline said.

Todd looked at Gabriel Delgado. "Hey, don't look at me," Delgado said, back to jocular normal. "You've got all the bases covered on the protection angle. I'm going to go home and check my security system." A grateful twitter diluted the tension in the room, bringing Laura's into contrast. But everyone would suppose that was just the FBI way. Delgado said, "Seriously, I'm not saying there's no connection between Creighton and Murry, but I think you're jumping to conclusions with this vigilante theory. You guys go ahead and worry about someone else being killed. I'm going to focus on the Shayna Murry investigation. Let's meet back here in twenty-four hours."

"Where's Will Hench these days?" Todd asked.

Laura said, "Will Hench. I think he's trying to catch up on cases he put aside because of Marcus Creighton. I'll call him. Let him know what's going on. I don't think he's in trouble."

Everybody split, leaving Todd and me in the room.

"What?" Todd said.

I gave him an opportunity to say what he was thinking, but he didn't take it. So I threw in another option. "Laura was good in her assessment, but she left out one possibility. Killer could just be a crank who has nothing whatsoever to do with the case. Nothing. Could be someone who lost someone else to the death penalty and is taking revenge on others."

"Well, that would be truly lousy," he said, but in a more formal tone than he usually used with me, added, "We should follow up. Would you ask Laura to check the FBI records to see if there are any other homicides that fit this pattern?"

"Anywhere in the country. Will do." Nothing more to do here, and I hadn't been given an assignment, so I decided to tie up a loose end that no one else appeared to notice. Something about a fingerprint. It would also keep me from thinking about what Todd might have been thinking about when he looked at Laura that way.

Thirty—five

FROM THE DIRECT EXAMINATION OF TRACY MACK

By Attorney Lancer:

Q: Dr. Mack, would you please explain these two images that have been set in front of the jury?

A: The print on the right side of this chart was taken of Marcus Creighton's right thumb at the time of his booking for the murder—

By Attorney Croft: Objection.

The Court: Sustained.

Q: Go on.

A: The print on the left was developed from the plug on the hair dryer found in the victim's tub.

Q: Would you please briefly explain the process of fingerprint analysis.

A: Print analysis, or in this case latent analysis, is performed by highlighting with a chemical process fingerprints that are not visible to the naked eye. In this case I checked the plug, which was the most likely place to have been touched by the murderer. I used a superfuming technique that revealed the print shown on the left photograph.

Q: And would you please let the court know what your analysis showed.

A: I've marked with numbers certain sections of each print. You can see on both the similarity of facets of prints we call whorls. I found twelve identical points between the prints.

Q: And your conclusion was?

A: They came from the same person.

Q: From Mr. Creighton.

A: Even though he denied he had ever touched the hair dryer.

By Attorney Croft: Objection. Hearsay.

The Court: Sustained.

Q: Would you say conclusively that the fingerprint found on the plug of the hair dryer, the presumed last person to touch it, belongs to Marcus Creighton?

A: I conclude it is a match. Yes.

Q: Thank you. Your witness.

CROSS-EXAMINATION OF TRACY MACK

By Attorney Croft:

Q: How many fingerprint analyses have you performed in your career so far?

A: I would say over five thousand. I don't know for sure.

Q: And in how many of those cases did you exclude the suspect?

A: I'm sorry. I don't understand your question.

Q: It's a forensic term, Mr. Mack. It means that you find that the fingerprint you're looking at does not match the person in custody. In how many of those five thousand cases did you exclude the suspect?

A: I understand that, I just don't have that number, sir, off the top of my head.

Q: You seem to be in great doubt over numbers, Mr. Mack, but very certain when it comes to fingerprint comparisons.

The Court: Please ask a question.

Q: Never mind. Do you know whether Mr. Creighton is left- or right-handed?

A: No, sir. I do not.

It wasn't just incompetence, even if Ronald Croft, the public defender, wasn't the smartest guy in the room. At least he made appeals possible with his objections on record, but at the time of the Creighton trial a forensic technician could get away with the "because I said so" argument. People trusted visual comparison by anyone who could identify himself as a forensic scientist. Those were the days when they were rock stars, riding high on the O. J. Simpson case. If Mack said it was a match, it was a match. These days the defense is challenging whether fingerprints are even unique. They say it's never actually been proven statistically.

Everyone else had been sucked into the clusterfuck of running hither and yon, following all leads at once, for both suspects and other potential victims. But I thought it was a good idea to return to the scene of the crime, so to speak. What really happened that night? If Creighton didn't kill his family, then who did? If Creighton was innocent, the mass murder of his family had turned from a solved crime into a cold case. And the killer could still be alive. And trying to silence Shayna Murry? What about Manny Gutierrez? Or even Derek Evers? What about any of the investigators?

Everyone else had forgotten the one piece of evidence that got us all involved in the first place. The hair dryer had finally arrived.

From the outside, on Dixie Highway, you couldn't tell that Frank Puccio's lab was a lab. It was housed in a building that looked like a Quonset hut with the long side facing the street and had three separate entrances. It shared space with a St. Vincent de Paul thrift store and a place called, plainly, Religious Articles. The lab itself was unnamed, and you could only find it if you had the address that I had given to Derek Evers. Puccio greeted me at the door.

Stocky, without a neck, Frank Puccio looked like he had had the choice of doing this or punching tickets for the mob, and had incongruously, incredibly, decided to do this.

"Dr. Puccio, I'm Brigid Quinn," I said, holding out my hand.

"Call me Frank, Brigid." He flung out his arms as if he was going to hug me and then decided against it and took my hand in his dry, warm grasp. "I feel as if I know you. Your brother and I have had some dealings."

"And not on the same side, I'd expect."

He said through a half smile, "Regrettably, this is often true. But not always. If I had some advance notice I would have prepared light refreshments."

The voice didn't go with the way his ears were attached to his shoulders, but you never know what you're going to find with forensic scientists. The only thing you can be sure of is that none of them match any of the quirky stereotypes you see on television.

His hand swept me inside with that come-on-come-on scooping gesture. I stepped through the door and found what I would have expected, a small but unmistakable place where science was done. It couldn't compete with the shiny gizmos at the county level, but good enough to get the odd piece of defense evidence analyzed.

Puccio was unapologetic but still felt the need to put any hesitation on my part to rest. "I'm certified. When the big guys get swamped I even get some overflow if urgency is needed. My setup is the modest minimum, but I do some good work now and again, and there's a thriving business in DNA analysis for paternity tests and veterinary work. I even got into pet DNA analysis in case you want to know whether your dog with a head like an anvil is part pit bull."

Assurance finished, he indicated where he had a little workstation set up for the Creighton evidence. We stood before a slab of wood laid out over a couple of two-drawer filing cabinets with cinder blocks on top to give it good height for standing. Frank picked up an eight-by-ten glossy of a smudge that just barely looked like a print.

"Is that what got him?"

He sneered. "That's the one." He picked up in his right hand a similarly blown-up image of another print, this one fairly perfect in its detail. "And here's the exemplar they got of Creighton's thumb. You can see how the one they lifted from the dryer plug is marked with twelve points? That was the minimum they needed at the time to show a conclusive match. However, only five of them actually match, in my opinion. The bastard guessed at the remaining. He may as well have pinned it to the wall and thrown darts."

"Creighton's appeals attorney should have been able to secure a stay of execution with this, then?"

"On the strength of point comparison? Unfortunately, no. Since his trial the standards have become less rigorous rather than more."

"But you're sure it's not Creighton?"

"There's no way to tell who it is. I could possibly commit to a cautious opinion that it's human."

"Thanks for doing this, Frank. I know it's too late."

"It's never too late." He dropped the hail-fellow-well-met aspect and looked as serious as anyone can get. "It may be too late for Creighton, but not for the next poor schmuck who comes up against the system."

"And it's never too late to find out who killed that family."

"Yes, indeed." As if to show me a just-discovered archaeological artifact, he turned both palms up in a balletic gesture at odds with those pudgy hands. I looked where he directed and saw a rickety metal frame covered from top to bottom with clear plastic. From a hook at a crossbar over the top of the frame hung a silver metallic hair dryer. The cord stretched out and off the platform. A plastic cup, the kind you'd keep in the bathroom to rinse your mouth, sat next to the dryer.

"I'll do the DNA test that Will Hench wants, but first I'm processing the latents. It looks like the dryer is finished, and I've vented the cyanoacrylate." He drew on a pair of latex gloves, then lifted the plastic sealing that had kept the superglue from escaping its plastic cell. "Nonporous, so it's an ideal surface," he said, with the hushed tone of a connoisseur. "The little cup of water rehydrated the prints after being in the evidence locker for such a long time." There's something about a forensic scientist that always makes them want to teach you something. "Looks like there's a lot of story here."

Still examining the dryer, which was dotted here and there with what you could tell even now were fingerprints, Puccio reached for some black dusting powder and lightly covered the spots with it, revealing them more.

"There are so many prints we'll be lucky if we can find one that's isolated enough," he said, turning to me. "I'm sure the majority of them are the victim's. But see this one? I've been looking at prints a long time, and this one looks different from the rest." He had a little smudge of dusting powder on his chin. I resisted wetting my thumb and rubbing it off, that thing mothers do. Must be hardwired.

I said, "The testimony of the examiner said he didn't look at the dryer because it had been submerged and there would be nothing to see."

"Well," Puccio said, with satisfaction, "this shows he was either ignorant or lying."

"Which is worse?"

Puccio gave a small smile in acknowledgment. "If the current isn't too fast to wear away the body oils, you can get prints off a gun that's been in a river for three weeks. Only this guy, Tracy Mack, once he found evidence to support the suspicion of Creighton he didn't look any further."

I thought of Delgado. "It appears that was going around at the time."

Puccio shook away his satisfaction and looked sad. "Poor Tracy, I heard he was a good scientist, once."

I called Todd. He said he wanted to see me.

I thought of calling Laura, but didn't. I told myself she didn't need to have her flames fanned any more than they were already.

I got assurance from Frank Puccio that he would compare the prints against the exemplars he had on file for Kathleen and Marcus Creighton, and confirm there was at least one that didn't match up to anyone in the family. He promised to call Delgado and let him know what he found. As I let myself out he was softly singing "Ruby Tuesday" and reaching for some tape to lift the prints off the hair dryer.

Thirty—six

With what followed after finding Shayna Murry's body I hadn't come to the hospital since the morning before, when I had that dustup with Mom. You can only use the cool-down reason for so long. So when Todd said he wanted to see me I told him to meet me in the Palms Coffee Shop at St. Luke's Hospital. He pulled out the chair across from mine and sat down.

"I've been thinking," he started.

"I'm sorry," I said, which didn't draw as much as a curl of his lip, he was that intent. "Want coffee?"

"Does a wild pope shit in the woods?" Todd said. Quinn family in-joke. That meant he was nervous. Nobody else could tell, but I could.

I pushed my empty cup across the table and said, "Get me some more, too, would you? Black is fine."

Neither of us got up. Instead, Todd pulled open a soft-sided brief-case and drew an eight-by-ten sheet of paper from it with names and addresses on it. It looked like the list of possible victims.

"Here's the list of suspects as it stands."

It wasn't just that Todd didn't have a good poker face. He was pretty good at covering, but you don't grow up with someone and not be able to read them, almost read their thoughts. "Suspects. I didn't know you were going to do this part. I thought it was Delgado going to do this." From the moment he sat down I could read my little brother like a book. I was just stalling the inevitable.

"He sent me his, I added a couple. We could be working against the clock. Better to have more than one person work on it. I'll share it with him."

"You haven't shared it with him yet?"

Todd's head gave an involuntary jerk. "You'll see why I wanted to find you away from the office."

I've shown self-control, haven't I? Except for when I went off on that doctor when Dad was in intensive care, but he deserved it. And maybe that thing I said to Mom, that was bad. Mostly I felt like that old poem I had to memorize in school and never forgot, where everyone was losing their head and blaming it on me. But with that, and Dad being sick, and losing the appeal, and watching Creighton being executed, and Laura Coleman's meltdown, and Mom not being Mom, and finding Shayna Murry's body, and . . . I guess that's all, but you can understand my finally flying off the handle. Before looking down at Todd's list, I knew what I would see, and I just couldn't handle any more. I tore the paper in half and tossed it, if not in his face, then pretty close. I leaned across the table and whispered, with what I consider great restraint, "Fucking bullshit."

He leaned back at me, though with his resonant man voice I couldn't swear that the candy striper sitting a couple of tables away couldn't hear. "Look at you. You're so convinced she's innocent, what have you got to worry about?"

"That's what we always say before the interrogation starts."

"Look, none of us wants to be caught with our pants around our ankles when the next victim goes down. Who said, 'This isn't an isolated case?' Who said, 'This isn't over?' You should be able to see it's a routine investigation. Nothing personal."

"Why are you even telling me about it?" I asked. "You want to interrogate me? Maybe I'm an accessory."

"Oh, can the drama. I could have done this without telling you. It's family that makes me show you my hand, and it better be family that makes you keep it to yourself."

I thought of the moment when I told Laura that I had met with Shayna Murry and was convinced she had information she wasn't giving up. I thought of Laura saying some people deserved to be punished. I thought of Laura promising not to kill anyone.

"It's not Laura," I said.

"Why not?"

"It's stupid. I know Laura, and it's not Laura."

"Well, that's a compelling argument. You spent a few days working a case with her more than a year ago."

"We were nearly killed. She saved my life."

Todd made that jerk-off gesture that guys do to show they're not impressed. "You were the one who told me she was angry that night, that she was going out to kill Alison Samuels."

"I didn't say that. And even if I did, we all think it. You can't tell me you've never wanted to exact a little justice yourself."

"Who would know better than you?"

He could have gone the rest of his life without saying that. If we were alone we would have been yelling at each other. But in public even the Quinns know to keep their voices down. I leaned across the table, and my voice got softer as the words got harder. "You self-righteous little prick."

"You're biased," Todd said. "You're blocking it out."

"And you're locking in. Just like Delgado did with Creighton."

Rather than tell me to fuck myself as he normally would, Todd reached across the table and grabbed my hand. I was too stunned to move it. Other than the usual duty hug at meeting and parting, I couldn't remember my brother ever touching me. I've mentioned we weren't a touchy-feely kind of family. "Brigid. I'm not saying anything. I'm just following investigative protocol. From an unbiased viewpoint. You know, unbiased? And remember, Dr. Brach said there was no telling even whether Shayna Murry was killed before or after the execution."

I started to object, but he put up his other hand to silence me. "You said Laura was desperate to stop the execution. Who knows what she might have done to get some truth out of Murry? I'm going to play it safe, put a tail on her."

"You're wasting valuable time chasing this. And you're risking the lives of the other people who were involved in prosecuting Creighton's case." I picked up the paper I'd torn in half, worked on it some more, and threw the pieces into the air. Maybe he was prepared for my reaction. He got up and brought us both a black coffee from the drink bar. After he put one in front of each of us, he calmly bent over and gathered the pieces that had fallen onto the floor. It was all so not Todd. I wondered again about the strain of him looking after his sick wife for nearly two decades, how it must have been greater than anyone realized. Here I was, just watching out for Dad for a week, and I'd been ready to run screaming even before this latest trouble.

I said, suddenly weary, "Do you realize our father could be dying upstairs and we're talking about a case?"

"Oh come on, you said he was feeling better. Besides, Dad's going to go sometime, and I can't stop that. This, I can stop."

"Yeah, you're right," I said. "Dad would be proud of you."

"So do you agree to stay out of the way and let me do my job?"

Instinct born of my guilty childhood years made me look toward the entrance to the cafeteria, much the same way that Dad did when she walked into his room. I said, "Shut up, here comes Mom."

I noticed Todd rearranged his face the way I always did to protect Mom from what we all did for a living. Different from the rest of us. Poor Mom, not as tough as the rest of the family. Someone to kid about. I still hadn't apologized for what I said to her. Who knew, maybe enough time had gone by and there was a statute of limitations on gratuitous cruelty. Still, my gut cinched in her presence like when I was thirteen and she caught me forging sick notes to my teacher.

Todd and I both looked up at her approach, our gently solicitous smiles in place. She took her time coming across the cafeteria. As I watched her walk slowly but relentlessly, it occurred to me this was another difference; she'd always moved deliberately in a family that was always tearing about. Literally off-beat from the rest of us, just like I'd said to her, in so many ways. I wondered whether it was by choice, depression, or simply controlling one of the few things that was in her power.

I was relieved to see that whatever cracks there had been the day before were neatly patched up, and the person who came across the room was Old Saint Mom.

Todd didn't get up, but pushed a chair out for her with his foot. The politeness I remembered from his wife's funeral, those days when we tried to guard against eruptions of our anger, was gone, forgotten in the stress of this latest case. Mom gave that look of withering disappointment at what she had spawned, and sat down in the chair. Yep, she was back to herself, someone I could safely count on.

"You haven't been up there to see him yet. What are you doing here?" She looked at the torn paper on the table between us as if to indicate she knew damn good and well what we were doing there. I wondered now if she had always known. After all, how did she know I was on birth control pills when I was seventeen? How did she know to shut and lock that window after Ariel and I snuck out that night, so we couldn't get back in? This realization, that Mom had always been more savvy than I gave her credit for, took some getting used to.

"How's he doing, Mom?" Todd asked.

I guess she figured I would have told Todd about Dad's improvement, and his getting out in a couple of days. So she just said, "Could be worse."

"Could be raining," Todd and I said at the same time, and smiled wider.

Those Quinn family in-jokes. Can't get enough of them.

I managed to take Todd aside and get him to agree to let me do a little reconstructing of timelines for means and opportunity before he destroyed someone's reputation. I got his point about motive, I said, but even an official interview could do Coleman harm. I asked him to trust me to keep an eye on Laura, not to have her followed. She'd know.

Then I did my duty and went up to see Dad, trying to tell myself he looked even a little better than when I'd visited before, even though in retrospect he did not. I should have been with him more on that day than any other. But no, the whole time I was there, another part of my brain was thinking about Laura. People I respected, people I trusted with my life, were not vengeful murderers.

Laura? Not Laura. Laura.

"Who would know better than you?" Todd had said, about my

comment on exacting justice outside the law. Okay, here we go again. Todd was right. There have always been rogues, good people with noble ideals who went into law enforcement and then over time turned into white knights who couldn't endure the endless grinding of the system, and the inherent flaws that let bad people slip through the net. Including their personal flaws that made for some instances of poor judgment in their personal life. I know all about this because I'm one of those people.

Must we really revisit this? I suppose we must. I sit here flashbulbing through all the stories of my life.

I've already told you about framing the child molester to avenge the suicide of my colleague. That Manny Gutierrez I mentioned? There was a night in the swimming pool at the Delano Hotel in South Beach. Having sex with your confidential informant is a real no-no in squeaky-clean FBI circles. But I've done worse. Back in Tucson the year before, after I'd been retired, I had killed a man. You could call it self-defense, sure, but I covered it up because I didn't think Carlo could take knowing what I was capable of. I still wasn't sure that mistake wouldn't come back someday to bite me in the ass.

Yet I've done worse.

About five years ago, I tracked an eight-time serial killer, operating exclusively in New Mexico. I followed him across the border into Mexico, following a trail of body parts that he planted just to taunt me. I finally found him in the wilds south of Nogales where he'd joined up with a drug gang who found his résumé appealing. I killed most of the gang, which was appreciated by the Mexican government, not a problem for anyone. But I was supposed to do the usual extradition process for my guy, and then watch him get a life sentence because New Mexico had just abolished the death penalty. He knew this. I knew this. So as he was surrendering, I shot him in the face, and planted one of the drug dealer's guns in his hand.

I was cleared of any official wrongdoing with a suicide-by-cop ruling. But the civil suit by the guy's family cost the FBI a lot of defense funds, and cost me my career. That's how I got sent to Tucson.

These things happen, so I got why Todd had Laura Coleman in his sights. I got it even better than he did. I saw her after her Achilles tendons were slashed, and she was kept, drugged, in a storage unit for two days. I was a witness when she made her first bones. In watching her over the time I knew her, in the way she'd been betrayed by the people who should have protected her, in her passion for clearing the innocent and catching the scumbag, in her determination never to let anyone hurt her again, in her single-minded devotion to exonerating Marcus Creighton, whether or not she was in love with him, I could see what Todd saw.

Why was I so hell-bent on maintaining Laura Coleman's innocence?

Simple. Because I'd been through everything she had been through, and in Laura Coleman I could see myself, what I had become.

Thirty-seven

It wasn't with Laura in mind that I returned to my hotel room with my gun drawn that afternoon. I was just feeling generally suspicious. After sliding my key card and opening the door with more caution than usual, I punched the button that turned on all the lights in the room. The closet door was open the way I left it. Same with the bathroom door, and the shower curtain, also left open. The thick blackout drapes with an unattractive geometric design were drawn over the sliding glass door that led to the minuscule balcony overlooking the pool. Those I had forgotten to leave open, and, nerve sparking in my neck a bit, that old warning signal, I quickly slid my gun across them to find there wasn't a body standing behind.

I relaxed a little. Tired from the day, but a little wired just the same, I threw the bolt on the door now that I didn't have to worry about a quick exit, and tossed my tote bag and pistol on the bed. Then I stripped down and stepped into the shower for a long hot one. When I'd lived here I'd never noticed the smell of the chlorine in the water. I re-dressed, planning to pick up Mom and take her out to dinner for a bit of a break from the hospital. I combed my wet hair, and decided to let it dry on the balcony.

The sliding glass door slid open easily.

It had been locked when I left the room.

Was I on someone's list after all?

I immediately tried to slam it shut again, but whoever was out there was prepared for me. A shoulder wedged in the door to stop me from closing it. I dealt that shoulder as crushing a blow as eighth-inch hurricane glass in a steel frame can deliver.

I preferred not to deal with my assailant hand to hand unless I had to, so I made a dive toward the bed, hoping he didn't have a gun and wouldn't simply shoot me before I could reach mine. I made it to the bed and clawed after the gun but felt myself jerked back by someone's grip on both ankles, and I ended up on the floor.

I kicked back like a mule, aiming for his nuts, but I think I hit him in the kneecaps. I heard him make an *oof* sound and fall back against and possibly through the open sliding glass door. While he was getting his balance, I pulled on the bedspread to help me get up, and dove for the gun again, but he had recovered from my kick and was on top of me. And he had the gun. I had started to roll over and now kept the momentum going. He wasn't prepared for my strength and how close I was to the edge of the bed. We both crashed off the side onto the small space between the two beds, but now I was the one on top of him, if on my back. The safety was on the gun, and that gave me a half second to scramble back up on the bed, stepping on his groin in the process. That must have made him lose interest in the gun, giving me another half second to grab the lamp off the bedside table and, without looking where I was aiming, swing it over the side of the bed and clock him on the side of the head. I rolled back off the bed on top of him and was about to break his collarbone with the lamp when I saw who it was.

"If I knew it was you I wouldn't have hit you that hard," I said as I patted Glen Slipher, Manny Gutierrez's accountant, down, removed the gun from his jacket pocket, and then watched his eyes refocus.

"Look at that," I said. "You did have another gun."

"I'm sorry," he said.

"I'll just bet you are." I got off him and helped him get up and sit down on one of the beds. I sat on the other opposite him. You'd think we were friends if it wasn't for the gun I was pointing at him just to be on the safe side. "I thought Manny warned you not to startle me."

"I didn't mean it to happen that way. I was just waiting on the balcony, and with the thick door I didn't hear you come in." Slipher rubbed the side of his head where I hit him.

"Do you want some ice for that goose egg?"

He fingered the small lump that was coming up at his temple and gave his head a shake to see if it ached any. "It's not that bad."

"Couldn't you just call from the lobby?" I asked him. "Or stalk me in the garage like you did the last time?"

"You weren't here when I arrived. And the balcony is a nicer place to wait than the garage. I've been waiting a couple of hours."

"How *did* you know my room? And how did you get in?" I asked, out of professional curiosity.

"Money," he said.

"Well, tell Manny I don't have time to go see him today. Marcus Creighton is dead, and so is his old girlfriend."

"He heard. He's curious about his own welfare."

"He should be."

"He says in exchange for information on the Shayna Murry case he'll talk."

Now here's the thing with Manny Gutierrez. It's true he was a scumbag of the lowest order. But all his crimes, as far as I knew, were financial. He preyed upon others' greed, and from my point of view, that wasn't as bad as, say, tricking women to come from Guatemala and then using them as sex slaves to migrant farmers. Or distributing child pornography. Or making snuff films.

No, Gutierrez was just another nonstandard lender, the technical term for a loan shark before the days when the check-cashing shops and payday loans started whittling away at the business. He was a relatively average-sized fish on the spectrum between your major whales, aka the Mafia, and chum. But he had splashed in the same water and knew more about the whales than anyone realized.

Sure, I didn't much like him, but not liking can sometimes morph into a kind of transference for people who get off on adrenaline. I owed much of my success to having Manny Gutierrez as my confidential informant.

Slipher escorted me through a vast cavern of white marble identical to that outside the front of the house, then through some ceiling-to-floor gauze curtains that beckoned flirtatiously in the offshore breeze coming through sliding glass doors.

The patio was nice, not a big yard, with a pool. A six-foot wall with decorative yet deadly colored glass shards stuck into the top hid the beach itself from sight. On the north and south sides of the yard, banana trees, hibiscus, and oleander covered high concrete walls you could glimpse here and there through the foliage. The same colored glass along those walls told me this was as much a fortress as a home.

Somewhere jasmine blossoms assaulted me with a sickeningly sweet smell that made me think of Shayna Murry.

Manny was reclining on one of two chaise lounges, in the shade now that we were in the late afternoon and the sun well over the house. He wore carefully creased chinos and a white shirt, sleeves turned up at the cuffs. Loafers, no socks. His full head of hair hadn't thinned, combed back from his face and carefully sprayed to stay that way. A small Baccarat glass of something amber rested on the table between the chaises. Snapshot: He looked costumed and posed. Waiting for me.

"Glenfarclas 1955," I said.

"You remember everything," Manny acknowledged, toasting me with the glass.

"I bought enough of it for you."

"Drink?"

"No, thanks." I sat down in the chaise next to his and took a closer look at the bad man I hadn't seen in at least twenty years. He was older than me by almost as much as Marcus was to Laura. He had been handsome, too, something of the Gabe Delgado look, a Mediterranean smolder that was one of the things that attracted me to Carlo.

Letting pleasure get mixed up with your business? I understood Laura far better than she would ever know. I thought back to that night in the pool with Manny at the Delano Hotel in South Beach. But Manny hadn't aged well. He looked like a well-preserved mummy.

"Too bad about that wall spoiling the view," I said.

"You have to compromise," Manny said.

"I wouldn't have thought there were that many people wanting to kill you. You weren't that kind of crook."

"Probably no more than want to kill you. Why did you want to see me?"

"You know it's about Marcus Creighton. You know one of the people who put him away has just been murdered. You sent Glen to get me because you're wondering if you're next, if someone will interrupt your drinking Scotch that could support a village in Ghana for five years. Was that business about knowing something just a ruse to get me here?"

He admitted I was right. "Do you think I'm in any real danger?"

"Of course you are. Unless you killed Shayna Murry yourself. But if you didn't, maybe I can help. What can you tell me that will help save your life? Did you have actual information that could have saved Creighton? Did you let him fry so you could take his business?"

"My goodness, can you make things up. How was the woman killed?"

If he had it done himself, he would know. If he hadn't done it, and I told him, it might get him to talk. I broke the rules.

"It was slow and nasty. She was shocked repeatedly with a stun gun until her heart gave out."

Manny picked up another glass of Scotch that Glen had supplied before he had drained the first. He picked it up this time with two hands, but even so couldn't hide the trembling. "Brigid, it has been a long time, at least a decade, since I retired. Maybe I've lost my nerve. All I want to do is have a little peace. Don't I deserve that?"

"No. You don't. But talk to me and maybe I can stop someone from killing you to prevent you from talking to me."

"Now you're stooping to fear tactics, and that was always your last resort. I may be lonely sometimes, but I'm not afraid. No, I keep myself safe here. You. You're the one who takes risks like not leaving history alone. I wonder which of us will die first? All my enemies are dead."

"Maybe all but one." I enjoyed the setting sun glinting off the shards of broken glass on the back wall for a moment. "Why didn't you end up testifying?"

"Both sides questioned me before the trial. I told them Marcus Creighton had borrowed a moderate sum to tide him over until some deals came through on his import/export business."

"What was the sum?"

"Moderate, I told them. And while those deals were taking more time than we both expected, Creighton was making his payments."

"Was it a moderate loan or were you lying? Did you extend funds you knew he couldn't pay back so you could take his business?"

"It was all in cash, so it was whatever I say it was, dear. The way it ended up, the prosecution didn't want me because I said he was making his payments and wasn't in financial ruin. The defense didn't want me because showing that Creighton borrowed from a nonstandard lender made him look desperate for money. Nobody wanted me in the courtroom. Oh, someone might have suspected I did it, but why risk all those investigative shenanigans when they had someone they could more easily convict."

"If you had nothing for me, why did you go to all this trouble to send Glen after me?"

"Do you remember that night in the pool at the Delano Hotel?"

"No."

He gave a resigned sigh and said, "Maybe I wanted to warn you the way you're warning me. Who knows what people out there can still make trouble for you and people you love. You're retired. I'm retired. Let's be retired. No one who's dead is coming back."

"You're stalling just to keep me here. You're a pathetic waste of time," I said. I got up, and made to leave, but heard Manny behind me in a final attempt to make me stay. The further away I moved, the louder his voice grew to reach me.

"Brigid, wait."

I stopped, but didn't turn around, just listened.

"After Creighton went to prison I did take his business. He had signed it over as collateral. I didn't have to have his wife killed. The whole thing just swung to my advantage and I took it. I sold it to someone who was looking for a money-laundering business. Huge profit."

"That's it?"

"That's it."

"That's not enough." I picked up my tote. I thought I heard him say, very softly, "Don't go, Brigid." I kept going, and Manny finally got up from his chair, caught up with me, and hooked his arm in mine. He walked me slowly across the living room and out the front door, Glen following closely, as he told a story about Marcus Creighton.

Marcus was always a nervous man, he said, and because Manny only knew him when he was in financial trouble, this quality did not surprise him. Everyone he did business with was nervous, more or less. And coming to beg for an extension on the loan, Marcus appeared to be more on edge than usual. He had a minor asthma attack, possibly due to Manny's secretary owning a cat, and took a hit from his inhaler after sitting in an armchair that Gutierrez offered. Recovered, he rested his left ankle on his right knee. Manny wouldn't have been able to tell how that foot was shaking, but the tassel on the loafer gave it away, bouncing as it did. Then Marcus switched, and put his right ankle on his left knee. Then he switched back. He leaned in and leaned out, as if trying to match Manny's own body language the way they tell you to when you want someone to be on your side. Only he was too distracted to read Manny's body. It wasn't that easy; Manny didn't express himself much with his body. He just kind of sat there, staring.

"I knew what he was going to ask before he asked it, and I already intended to give him an extension. Business was good in those days, and I could take his company whenever I wanted it if he didn't pay the loan. But you don't want to give in too fast. It makes people think they can take advantage. So I dicked with him a little while."

Manny excused himself to go to the bathroom, to let Marcus worry a little more, and when he got back Marcus was on his cell phone.

I was suddenly interested. "What was he saying?" I asked.

"I'm not sure. He disconnected when he saw me, but it was something like let it go. Or let me know. Or let them go. You see, I hesitated telling you because it was all so vague. But I swear that's all I know."

"Did he sound upset?"

"Definitely. When he saw I was listening, he asked, 'Do you have any children, Mr. Gutierrez?' When I shook my head no, he said, 'Good for you. Life is hard, and when you watch what it does to children, your heart breaks.'"

By this time we had reached the driveway. "Manny," I said, when I had gotten into the car. "You may not be a killer, but you've known your share and you've known people who hired them. You knew Creighton before I did, when he was a different man. Did I have it right about him?"

"That man on that day? He was foolish, but he wasn't bad." Manny laughed. "I may be a bad man, but I know goodness when I see it."

On the drive back to my hotel I thought about what Gutierrez had told me. How a crook could characterize Marcus Creighton better than any of us. Also about how no matter how much power we wield when we're younger, it can always come down to an old lonely man sipping on a cocktail of Scotch and self-pity behind a wall.

Thirty-eight

Sometimes even if you're convinced something isn't going to happen, that there's no chance of it, you still take precautions. That's what they sell insurance for.

After I left Gutierrez, with a phone call to make sure she was at home, would give me her address, and didn't despise me for my connection to Laura Coleman, I headed back over to an older part of Fort Lauderdale, just east of Dixie Highway and north of Commercial Boulevard, one of the few areas that was old enough so that the houses didn't all look the same.

The stone driveway crunched under my wheels as I pulled up to a carport with a tarpaper-and-gravel roof that sagged a little. A battered jeep was pulled up onto the lawn down by the street because there was no room in the carport. It was filled with metal filing cabinets, pushed up against the wall it shared with the house, presumably so they wouldn't get wet when the rains came. For extra protection the cabinets were covered with tarps.

Alison Samuels's job may have been saving children, but you could tell it didn't pay well.

She was out the front door before I had my seat belt off. She held on to my door while I gathered my tote bag and climbed out. In every other instance I'd seen her, she'd been only a spokesperson, and cold. Now she had shed the spokesperson suit and was dressed instead in jogging pants and a neon yellow T-shirt. Without Laura, or Will, without her professional persona, she was sweeter somehow, almost shy. She greeted me as if she had been the one to suggest this meeting.

"It's so great of you to come over," she said, trying not to gush, as she led me into her less-than-modest concrete-block home. Larry, asleep on a round braided rug in the middle of the wooden floor, alerted when the screen door banged shut. He came to where I'd stopped just inside the front door, stepped on my foot with his own.

"Hello, Larry," I said, remembering him from the interview. I reached out my hand tentatively, palm up, for him to check me out. He ignored the hand, and instead gave a growl that must have started at his butt and worked its way up. I just as tentatively pulled my hand back to my side.

"Larry, down," Alison said, and Larry obeyed, backing off but still watching me.

"That's some therapy dog you got there," I said.

"Larry and I meet with victimized children all the time, and he's a doll with them, but with me he's very protective. Wine?"

"Sounds lovely," I said.

Alison gestured at the couch and said, "Sit. You'll be less of a threat."

I remained standing because I'd be damned if I was going to let Larry intimidate me into cowering on the couch. While he studied me, Alison went off into the kitchen after promising to bring him something, too.

From where I stood I could see that the interior of the house had the same northern style in a petite format. Recessed bookshelves and even a little fireplace, though it had a potted plant stuck in it. The plant needed water. I heard a small curse, a cork pop, some glasses tinkling gently against each other.

Alison had a work area off to one side, a desk that only looked like Laura's in that it had sides and a flat top. The top was littered with papers and the gloss of photographs an inch thick. Her computer sat on a little table to the side, turned on. With a cautious glance at Larry, whose whole soul was glued to my presence, I looked.

It was a Web site she was on. I'm not going to describe here what I saw. All I'll say is that it appeared she was trying to match the photographs of children on her desk to the photographs on the screen.

"Spend too long doing this and it breaks you," Alison said behind me. "After just a few years I tell myself it's time to get out." She said, extending one of the glasses she held, "Sorry I took so long. Dry cork. I don't think I got any in your glass."

I turned to take the wine she offered, served in a little etched glass, clear on dark red, old-fashioned. "The glass matches the rest of the house," I said.

"Thrift shop stuff. I didn't ask whether you wanted red or white," she said. "I don't have people over much." She handed what looked like a leg-of-lamb jerky to Larry, who pulled his lips back and took it in his teeth with exaggerated delicacy.

"I'm so sorry we had to meet this way," she said. She clinked her glass against mine and took a sip. "You have no idea how much respect and admiration I've always had for you, and you must think I'm a real bitch."

I'd wondered how I was going to get to that. "Laura Coleman at . . . the prison, you mean. That was pretty nasty."

Alison nodded an acknowledgment, and at the end her chin was a little lower. "I'm sorry," she said, and without sarcasm, "Now I feel like I should punch myself in the face."

She again motioned me to the couch where Larry had wanted me to sit, and plopped herself down in an overstuffed armchair next to it, crossways, popped off her running shoes and socks with the opposite toes, and pointed her bare feet unapologetically in my direction. They were runner's feet, well calloused. She sipped her wine, then held the glass on her stomach. "That's better," she said.

I dipped my head in the direction of her computer. "I'm glad I interrupted your work," I said gently. And even more gently, "Would you like to ask me what I know about the Creighton children?"

"Were you there?"

"When they found the bodies. I was."

Alison's eyes filled and her nose went pink, but she didn't cry. She didn't cry. It seemed as if she was so in control she could even force her tears to run down the inside of her face.

"I know enough," she said. "I talked to Henry Aggrawal." She shook her head, regretting that she could say she knew a forensic anthropologist. "I guess I know everybody in the state who looks for children whether they're alive or dead."

Her phone went off, and she went over to the desk, answered it, and wandered back into what I assumed was a bedroom. When she came back out, she didn't bother to explain who it was, but when she sat down again, this time facing out from the chair with her feet tucked up under her, she kept her hand on the phone.

"It's an occupational hazard," she answered, her eyes getting hard. "You can work twenty-four hours a day and it's never enough. Sorry. How's Laura doing?" she asked.

"Angry. Depressed. She'll be all right. How are you?"

"Angry. Depressed. But that's kind of been me for as long as I can remember. And tired. I'm tired a lot. Why are you here?"

I told her about Shayna Murry. I told her about the possibility that it was a revenge killing, and that there was a fear of more.

"I had you put on the list for security," I said. "But you know how that goes, maybe a patrol car driving by a couple of times a night if you're lucky. I think you should watch out. Maybe no running after dark."

"You think I haven't had angry parents after me? Death threats from pimps? Menacing e-mails from pedophiles?" She put her glass on the table next to her chair, then swung one foot down and rubbed Larry's back with it. "You see how he protects me. He won't let anyone hurt me, will you, Larry?"

There are certain times when we, the best way I can put it, seem to be actors playing the part of ourselves. As she spoke Alison fumbled her lines and dropped her character, the one that was so well rehearsed for so many years. She swung her legs off the chair and fell down beside Larry, hugging him around the neck and burying her face in his fur.

"Alison, why the obsession with this particular man, with a family you never knew?"

"That's the only one you know about," she said, and then paused. "But that's not the whole truth. Marcus Creighton was different from the rest. I did find the photo that looked like his son, but it was more.

Of all the guys I hunted, all the ones I put away, Marcus Creighton was the only one who would talk to me. I could sit there and say things and watch him suffer. It was like he came to stand for all the men who hurt children. And now he's dead and my only feeling is frustration that I can't make him suffer anymore. Marcus Creighton is gone. The children are gone. Everyone is gone. I feel like I'm hardly here. What else do you feel when the sole reason for your existence is all gone? When everyone is gone and you don't have your meaning anymore?"

I had thought Alison Samuels was tough like me, like Laura. I didn't expect her to bleed this way, and to a near-stranger. She looked up at me. From that vantage point, sitting on the floor next to her dog, she looked like a little girl, as lost and alone as she had ever been.

Then her face sorted its features back into the kind you show company. She reached up to the end table for her wineglass, drained it, and picked a bit of cork off her tongue. Alison said, "The thing I don't get is finding you on the other side of the fence."

I said, "I keep hearing that. I'm not, really, more like on it. I'm on nobody's side. I've seen too much corruption at worst and stupidity at best by the guys who are supposed to stand for justice. So I can see the objection to the death penalty, because unless you see the smoking gun in the killer's hand and find a bullet that matches it in the victim, you really never know, and even then . . ."

Her face clouded, and I didn't want to take her back to Creighton again. "On the other hand, I hate the same fuckers you hate, and you could talk about chemical castration and I wouldn't blink. But that's the big picture. Mainly I'm trying to make sure no one else gets hurt."

Now for the hard part. I said, "I also wanted to advise you to steer clear of Laura Coleman for a while. She's angry. She might want to pick a fight, and it could get ugly. Don't agree to meet her for coffee. She doesn't really like coffee."

"What about you, can't you convince her this is all over?" Alison rubbed her fingers on both temples like a headache was starting. "Can't it be all over?"

"You and I both know it's not over."

She looked at her hand, and I realized she'd brought her phone to the floor with her, continuing to clutch it while we were talking. The hand reacted as if to a vibration. She looked at the screen. "Oh Jesus, it's an Amber Alert. I gotta go," Alison said.

"But you're hearing what I said about Laura Coleman, right?"

"I hear you. And thanks for coming to see me. Talking actually made me feel a little better."

We left together, me heading over to the Howard Johnson's, and Alison God knew where. She didn't bother to change out of her running clothes and was loading Larry into her jeep as I pulled away from the house. I guess she intended to keep going for now.

On the way back to the hotel I wondered what family Alison might have run away from, what kind of abuse might have been happening at home that drove her. I had not run away, and I reluctantly admitted one could do worse than the mother I was given.

Thirty-nine

Laura wasn't answering her phone the next day, and regarding my father I stupidly contented myself with the no-news-is-good-news logic. I called to find out what Todd was up to.

He said, "I can't talk. I'm on my way to St. Luke's. That woman from the Haven."

An officer was waiting in the lobby and escorted me to the emergency ward, where Todd was talking to one of the doctors. He turned to me without introductions or preamble. "She was assaulted. From her description to the paramedics we figure it was a stun gun."

"Where?"

"In her driveway."

You didn't have to be his sister to know the conclusion he was reaching. I have to admit it was reaching me. I said, "Do you mind if I talk to her with you?"

He nodded and pulled aside the curtain to the small area where Alison Samuels lay, looking tranquil despite the deepening bruise on her chin.

"Brigid," she slurred, and her eyes were a little unfocused.

"Did they give you some good stuff?"

"Oh yeah, better than wine."

I introduced Todd and asked if she was okay to talk. When she said yes, Todd asked, "Can you tell me what happened?"

"I was on my way to work, had my back turned to close the front door . . ." She squinted, maybe losing control of the details at that point.

"Did you see anyone?" I asked, thinking *Please say yes and describe some random guy.*

"No, and I'm usually pretty alert. I've had my share of people wanting a piece of me for something or other, dads accused of kidnapping their children, and stuff."

She was more talkative and off point, probably from the effect of whatever they'd given her to sedate her.

"So you pulled the door shut," Todd said.

"Mm, maybe, but I don't think I could have because of Larry. I think I heard a footstep behind me, but I couldn't swear to that. I felt something hit my back and then this electric shock that made all my muscles contract at once. Like a full-body cramp." Alison explained they were keeping her for observation in case she was concussed from hitting her head.

"But the assailant didn't try anything more?" Todd was the one asking the questions now. I was too busy holding my breath.

"No. I was unconscious for just a moment, I think, the doctor thinks from hitting my head. I think Larry must have saved me. He was in the house. He must have gone after the guy, or stood guard until I came to. I called nine-one-one." She smiled. "Good thing I was coherent so I could tell Larry to stand down when the paramedics came." The drugs she'd been given seemed to fail at that point, and she cried, "Oh my God, my dog. Where's Larry? Is Larry all right?"

"He's fine," Todd said. "A little tense. He's trying to gnaw his way out of the backseat of my car. But the windows are halfway open," he assured her.

She started to cry. "I want to see him. Please let me see my dog. I know they won't let him in the hospital. Let me just go see him." She started to get off the bed, but her knees buckled from the effects of the sedative. Todd kept her from falling, and held her.

"I gotta see my dog." She wouldn't stop crying, and held the sides of her head as if the crying hurt while her nose ran onto her upper lip. "You can't leave him in the car."

"Wait a second," I said. "He's a service dog, right? And Todd's a cop, right?" I went out and commandeered a wheelchair. "If we take you out to Todd's car to get Larry, could you make sure he doesn't bite me? I can take him back to your place."

Alison nodded, and when Todd got her into the chair, she grabbed her purse off a side chair. Scrabbled around in it, feeling. Took out a tissue first and blew her nose, threw the tissue onto the gurney, and reached back in the bag. "I don't think I'd taken the keys out of the lock yet. Oh, here they are, someone got them for me."

"You didn't get a look at him?" I asked.

"I couldn't even say whether it was a him."

"You said guy," I insisted.

"Brigid, let her talk," Todd said.

Alison shrugged. "Generic."

Dammit. I kept trying. "Can you think of anyone who might have witnessed the attack?"

"Yeah, Larry. If you find a suspect, Larry should be able to identify him. He's been used as an eyewitness before. Well, a nose witness." Alison had stopped crying and started hiccuping.

We went out to Todd's car, and Alison comforted Larry in short order, reintroducing him to me in the process, saying I was a friend. On the way back into the hospital I told her I'd drop her keys back off after I took Larry home.

Alison reached behind her to touch my hand that was on the bars of the wheelchair. I bent over slightly. She kept her voice low so Todd couldn't hear. "Would you also please bring me a change of clothes? T-shirt, jeans, underwear." Her voice dropped lower. "Mine are on the chair next to the bed, and they already stink. I must have pissed myself when I fell down."

The four of us came back into the hospital, Alison riding with her hand on Larry's back while he walked beside her, Todd muttering, "Police," and me muttering, "Service dog," over the fussings of the emergency room staff. We put Alison back where we found her, and she made sure we had the keys to her place.

Todd wanted to talk before he would let me take Larry home.

We were right there in St. Luke's, and I could have insisted he come up to Dad's room while we talked. He was just one floor up. That was my second chance. I told myself it wasn't because I was avoiding talking to Mom. Instead, we sat down in the emergency waiting room. Larry whimpered and looked back in Alison's direction a couple of times but understood his orders.

"When did you see her last?" Todd said. He knew he didn't have to say Laura Coleman's name; I would understand.

"At the briefing. With you," I said. I thought that much was safe to say. "I told you I'd stay out of the way."

"I'm bringing her in," Todd said. "The only people who know Shayna Murry was killed with a stun gun are part of the investigation. We withheld the information."

Well, not from Manny Gutierrez. "But it's someone who doesn't know about Larry."

Larry looked up at the mention of his name, then went back to sniffing one of the chairs, which might have held some trace scent of a wounded patient.

Todd said, "Not necessarily. She might have thought the door was shut and he wouldn't be able to come after her. I'll put someone on Alison Samuels for twenty-four-hour security. She won't know what Alison might have seen. I don't want her to finish the job."

I guess we didn't have that much to talk about after all. That made me sad. Right now he felt like just one more of those people who thought we were on different sides. We left, and put Larry in my car. I took him back to Alison's place.

Todd and I parted without him pressing the issue further. He didn't have to; despite our not keeping in constant connection, he knew how I thought as well as anyone, as well as I knew him. And he knew I'd be thinking, *What if it's Laura? What will I do then?*

Forty

I swear I had every intention of going back to spend some time at the hospital, but somewhere between the car and the lobby, who called me but Tracy Mack. He said it was because he wasn't sure who else he could trust, and he needed to talk. So I picked up Todd and headed over to his place. When Mack answered the door, he looked angry that I had Todd with me, but I assured him he was my brother and I would vouch for him with my life.

We entered one of those living rooms filled with shiny brocade furniture and the same stink I'd noticed the last time I'd been there, one of the downsides of living in an area that has the air-conditioning on all the time and the windows unopened.

Mack wasn't the sort to offer a seat, so we took one. Without pleasantries he began, "Madeline Stanley was here to see me this morning. She said I might be in danger. Some vigilante killing people who put Marcus Creighton away. Oh God." He put his face in his hands and ran his fingers through his hair. When he looked up again I noted that people really do look ashen when they're experiencing mortal fear. His skin was the color of charcoal the day after the cookout.

"I was afraid this was going to happen," he said. "All these years.

Those indictments. Then when you started investigating the case again I figured that was that, I was up shit's creek."

"What are you going on about?" Todd asked.

"I couldn't have gotten the guy off with a hand job. I was just a piece of the whole puzzle. They said they didn't even need my evidence because they had him with the alibi. That I was 'just in case.' You know what I mean?"

"Are you talking about Creighton?" Todd asked. I kept my mouth shut. This was Todd's investigation, and I had only come to allow him to gain access to the house.

Once Mack started, there was no prompting necessary. Like for most people, it seemed to feel good, at least in the moment. Later he'd think about what he said, and wonder what he should regret.

"Madeline Stanley was here this morning. You know her, right?"

"I put her in charge of security detail," Todd said, not mentioning that Mack was repeating himself. "I didn't think she was going to let you know, just make sure you had a drive-by now and then, keep an eye out."

"Hoo-boy. She told me I should watch my back, that some vigilante was going after the people who got Creighton convicted. But listen. I know it wasn't a friendly call. She was warning me to keep my mouth shut."

"Why would you think that?" Todd asked. I think it was only because I knew him so well that I could hear the edge in his voice.

"When she was working up in Vero with Delgado, they were tight. You know, like I mean tight. Delgado gave me the hair dryer and encouraged me to find the print that would convict Creighton. Encouraged, you know what I mean?" He laughed a mirthless laugh. "Stanley said she had my back, but I can't trust her. The way she said it. It's in her interest if I go away."

I did want to say *Tracy, maybe this isn't the best person to be confessing to. Maybe you should be a little more circumspect, not spill everything. Maybe one of us wouldn't appreciate you snitching on his girlfriend.* In the meantime, I wasn't sure how to shut Mack up short of taking out my pistol and shooting him in the foot to stop him from doing it to himself.

"I'm not going to risk my own life to protect her," Mack said. "But I don't know who I can trust."

In the midst of this who-struck-John clusterfuck, Todd's phone rang, and the three of us detached as if to go to our various corners and take a deep breath. He wasn't on long.

Todd said, "All kinds of intel coming in. Puccio called."

"You got Puccio to look at the evidence?" Mack asked.

Todd ignored him. "And the Maples center called. They finished defleshing the bones and laid them out pieced together. They also did a rush on the DNA, and will fax photographs down to the office first thing tomorrow."

"What about me?" Tracy Mack said softly, trying not to whine and failing.

Todd looked at him as if he was already dead, and just a piece of evidence. He looked like the sound of Mack's voice in his ear was dirty.

"You should call someone," I said to Todd.

"I'll let them know when we get to the office in the morning."

"Todd, now. Call now."

Todd walked out of the room, leaving me trying to listen to what he was saying while Mack sniveled. "I told you, didn't I? You try to do the right thing, but it gets messy. You go with the good guys. You try to do what the good guys want."

"And now people are dying," I said. "Go figure."

Todd came back faster than I would have expected. "Someone will be here within the hour," he said.

"An hour?" Mack asked. You could tell he thought that was an inordinately long time when his life was in danger. "And not Stanley, right? You didn't call Stanley."

Todd looked like it was all he could do not to punch Mack in the face. "I didn't give them any details about why you needed extra protection. Right now the three of us are the only ones who know. We'll keep it that way," Todd said.

"You understand I was over a barrel, right?"

"Were ya?" Todd asked, and then jerked his head away from Mack like he wasn't worth the words used to shame him. "Look, just keep this to yourself and you should be safe for the time being."

． ． ．

Distractions momentarily gone, I went back to the hospital. Dad was out of the room, Mom sound asleep in the chair at the foot of the empty bed. Gratefully, I went down to the end of the hall, to a visitor area with hard couches pretending to be inviting. I dug the business card out of my tote bag and got Will Hench on the phone just because I was in the mood for some cage-rattling.

"Laura hasn't been answering her phone. Do you know where she is right now?" I asked.

"I don't know," he said, and then, "She did call. She told me she thinks there's a list. That I might be on it. Am I?"

"I think you're one of the few people not on the list of potential victims."

"Maybe we're talking about different lists."

"Ah, that list. And I'm going to tell you you're a suspect? That would be highly inappropriate, wouldn't you say? Nope, afraid I can't share that with you right now. Why did you do this, Will?"

He understood and said readily, "Because I thought he was innocent."

Time to push on the white knight a little. "You already made that speech. Enough."

"Okay, okay, it was high profile," he added. "Exactly the kind of case that makes the news and gets national attention. I was honest when I told you I wanted to show the flaws in the system. One more step in creating enough doubt to make people question the death penalty again."

Push a little more. "So if he lived you win, and if he died an innocent you win more. Lucky you. I'll bet you're writing a book."

You'd think Will Hench's profession would have made him too thick-skinned to rise to that bait, but he snapped it like a bigmouth bass. He thrust the words at me. "There are four hundred people on death row in Florida. Average time spent there is thirteen years, but a hundred have been there for more than twenty. This new Timely Justice Act has the purpose of getting them executed the way most people declutter a house. Even though as many as half of those inmates, *half of them*, would be exonerated if we had DNA available to test."

"And Marcus Creighton, upper-middle-class white guy, makes the perfect poster child for your crusade. I bet you got a hefty advance, because it's gonna be a bestseller."

Direct hit. I knew it. He hung up on me. I often have that effect on people.

Forty—one

The summer downpour smacked against the windows in the hospital guest waiting area at the same time as my phone rang.

Mom.

Make it stop, I thought. Just for a little while let me worry about one life at a time. I could have gone down to the room, but I was fresh out of the emotional endurance it required to get up from the armchair, walk down the hall, and face her judgment or whatever was the Mom du jour.

"Hi, Mom," I said, wary about what she might have to say.

"It started raining," she said. "Is it raining where you are?"

"Mm, must be raining all over," I said, looking out at the same sky she must be looking at. "How are you holding up?"

There was a pause before she answered with a little tremor I'd never noticed before, "Not real well, Brigid. I'm feeling a little blue. You're the only person who's come to visit, willingly, that is. Sitting here so much, I've been thinking about how not even the priest at our church knows my name."

That was code for *I forgive you*. Before I asked for it. There was something different in her voice, a tone more vulnerable and yet more brave in its frankness, not like Martyr Mom at all. She spoke as if to a contemporary rather than a child, which made her voice all right.

"It's hard to keep going, isn't it?" I said.

"Yes. It is."

"Is Dad still on track to go home tomorrow?"

"I'm not so sure now. He doesn't look as good today. The doctor looked a little concerned when he stopped by. He's off having some tests run. But so far he didn't say Dad had to go back to ICU, or even stay here. Things are up in the air, and I've made arrangements to put him in the Canopy for a while."

The Canopy was the area of their assisted living facility where people got extra attention.

I said, "That's smart. It will be a little less stressful for you, too, not having to do all the work taking care of him." I didn't offer to stay and do it, but she didn't hint at my neglect the way she might have in the past.

She said, "I was thinking about Todd just now, and how hard I've always been on him. Even when he was taking care of Marylin all those years. How did he do it?"

"He loved her."

"And I don't. Your father, I mean." She didn't sound defensive. It was more as if she was truly asking for corroboration of her own feelings.

"He's a hard man to love," I said. "But listen, he's tough. He's going to get through this, and you'll have to tolerate him for a good ten years more."

"You might think that's a comfort. But it's especially hard when the choice is a good ten years for him or a good ten years for me." Pause. "I shouldn't have said that, should I?"

I didn't know what to say. There were so many things in life where you didn't get to choose.

"Are you still there?" Mom asked.

"Sure I am. Mom, I—"

"When will you be coming by?"

I couldn't admit now that I was just down the hall.

"I'm in the car on my way. I'll be there in fifteen minutes or so. I'll spring you for early dinner."

"I'd like that. Drive carefully, it's raining harder here."

. . .

I told Mom we could go wherever she wanted, but she opted for Boston Market. The most I could do was get her to drink a glass of wine. There was no huge thing with Mom, no bringing up of past or recent grievances, just a sane and gentle conversation about how she appreciated me being there, how much longer I'd be staying, and would I help to bring Dad home on the morrow. I spent the evening at her place again, and stepped out into the hall when my phone rang.

Finally, Laura. And it was not for a friendly chat.

"Where have you been?" I started.

"Your brother called and asked me to come into the office."

I waited. So did she. Both of us trying to determine what the other knew.

"When?"

"This evening. This evening? I get the urgency of the situation and all but, seriously, does he think I'm naïve?"

"What did he say, exactly?" I hedged.

"Exactly, he said he wanted to talk to me because I know more than anyone else who had investigated people connected with the Creightons."

This was it. Once she entered that office, without an attorney, she could get herself into all kinds of trouble that even a fully seasoned professional couldn't foresee. She was super smart, but Todd had a good twenty years of experience on her. Now, did I stand with my brother on the side of law and order, or did I stand with someone I owed my life to?

"Did he mention Alison Samuels?" I asked.

"No. What's she got to do with it?"

You threatened to kill her, I thought. And then someone nearly did.

"When was the last time you saw her?" I asked.

"The night Marcus was executed. You were there. Why are you asking me this?"

"You've got a GPS in your car, right?"

She knew why I was asking. "Yes, but it doesn't automatically record where I've been." She laughed one of those laughs that isn't funny. "I can't use it as an alibi."

259

Then I decided. "Don't go see Todd just yet," I said.

"No shit. I'm not stupid, and I know a setup. But I was taken off guard and agreed to go."

"Get a flat tire. Tell him you'll go tomorrow. Contact Will Hench and make him go with you. And just remember, people don't mean to do things. Things get out of control. Accidents happen."

I heard a soft gasp. "How did I get here?" she asked.

"I don't know."

"Sure you do. I'm a suspect in Shayna Murry's murder, and I can tell you knew it."

"That's what I'm saying," I said. "It probably wasn't murder. Accidental manslaughter. No one uses a stun gun as a murder weapon; it's not guaranteed effective."

"They might if they don't want the bullets traced," she said bitterly. Then she hung up on me and wouldn't answer the phone after that. I figured she wouldn't let me into her apartment either. I took a sleeping pill with a shot of Dad's bourbon because I suspected the next day I'd have to be on my game.

Forty-two

Todd had told me there was a meeting at the Fort Lauderdale Police Department for discussion prior to the meeting with Delgado et al in Palm Beach. I wasn't sure if I was invited, but showed up anyway the next morning, and found Todd already in his office frowning at the small pile of pages faxed from Gainesville. He had dark bags under his eyes.

I didn't give a shit if it was because he was worried about getting his precious Madeline in trouble because of what Tracy Mack had said. I said, "You told me you'd stay off Laura Coleman, give me some time to talk to her."

"But you didn't talk to her. And then we almost lost Alison Samuels. Coleman was supposed to drop by the office yesterday. Then she called to say she had a flat tire, and she'd see me today. You break a promise to me, Brigid?"

Instead of answering that directly, I said, "Have you talked to Madeline yet? Or Delgado? I wouldn't be too hard on them. It's not our fault if the lab guys can't stand up to a bit of encouragement from the detectives. Though you have to admit, with Madeline going to visit him despite her saying she would not, and coming across like threatening him, and the possibility that she knew Delgado dicked around with the evidence . . ."

Todd thrust his index finger in my direction as if it was loaded and he knew how to use it. "You suggest one more time that Madeline is a dirty cop and I'll—"

"Okay, okay, I take it back about Delgado. All I'm trying to say is that people, like Laura Coleman, for instance, can be totally innocent even if at first they appear to be suspicious. Nobody wants Madeline Stanley's reputation muddied by some misunderstanding."

Little brother knew what I meant beneath my words. Take extreme care with Laura Coleman or I counter with Madeline Stanley. Simple. Just because you're family doesn't mean you don't fight dirty sometimes.

He did have one parting shot. "Other than some battle loyalty, what do you know about Laura Coleman? Have you considered what you would do if you found out she was involved in Shayna Murry's death? And Alison Samuels's assault? Just how far would you go to protect someone?"

I couldn't answer that because I was too busy thinking about how I could minimize the harm someone might do.

When we went up to the meeting room, Dr. Brach was already standing over some color photographs at the conference table.

Laura, of course, was not there.

McClay was back and more involved this time now that Todd had briefed him regarding the attack on Alison Samuels. When McClay spoke, he had that softly quiet style that you have to watch out for because it's deceptive. In a lazy drawl, McClay informed us he wasn't interested in some Indian River County cold case. The only reason he was in the room was to prevent anyone else dying in his jurisdiction over an Indian River cold case. McClay wanted to see the forensic anthropology reports on the Creighton children because of who they might lead us to.

Most of us had been in the business long enough to know what we were looking at, without needing a forensic anthropologist to interpret, but the center in Gainesville had sent along a typed report, and the faxed photos were all numbered and labeled. They were very efficient up in Gainesville.

Dr. Brach read from the report he had in his hand, while pulling out each photograph identified by a letter and passing it around the table.

"Photograph A, a canvas tarp wrapped with nylon rope, measuring forty-six inches long by thirty-two inches wide. More rope used to tie off each end. Both knots were in place when found, and remains were secured within the tarp.

"Photograph B, inside the layers of the tarp as unfolded: leaves, several peanut shells, animal fur, and biological residue from fish. And some feathers, assume pelican, but white. Vegetation has been turned over to a forensic botanist to determine if bodies or tarp traveled. Somebody looking at the fur and feathers, too, a lot of that. No report back on that yet. Multiple commingled skeletons found. Photograph C, human remains one: disarticulated skeleton, juvenile male, age range eight to eleven years based on development and eruption of the dentition—."

Fur, I thought. What's wrong with that picture?

"—some perimortem trauma to the skull, but cause of death uncertain.

"Photograph D, human remains two: disarticulated skeleton, juvenile female, age range eight to eleven years—"

Animal fur. Asthma. Laura was right on that point, too. Marcus Creighton couldn't have done it himself. He couldn't even have had contact with the person who did it.

"—with a crushed skull indicative of massive blunt-force trauma postmortem, possibly from construction equipment. Skulls not reconstructed at this time. Right fifth metatarsal shows what may be rat bites, suggesting possible animal scavenging. Due to the secure seal of the tarp, scavenging would have occurred preburial. This indicates bodies not buried immediately, but possibly stored somewhere, possibly the primary or a secondary murder site. Photograph E, reconstructed—"

"Can we just cut to the DNA to see whether these are the Creighton children? Were they able to get that yet?" Captain McClay interrupted impatiently, as bosses are wont to do.

Dr. Brach shuffled the papers. "Here's a page with the DNA analysis. They kept a tissue sample at time of death from the mother, Kathleen Creighton, and they were able to find a certain match to her via mitochondrial DNA from the bones."

"All right, then," McClay said. "Let's talk about this Samuels woman. Whoever is getting revenge on Marcus Creighton got her because she wanted him executed, right?"

Everyone nodded obediently. McClay was the kind of person who required that. "So why didn't they kill her? Why didn't it go down like it did with Murry? I know, I know, the dog," he said, not waiting for the expected response. "But let's say this killer is organized. He doesn't know there's a dog? He doesn't take steps to ensure he gets her without the dog?"

We all listened. It's what he expected. He gave a half-lid glance at each of us in turn. "Why?"

"Maybe he wanted to send a message," Todd said. "Taunt us that he could pick who would die, and when."

"Sounds like a good movie," McClay said. "What about this? What if she did it to herself?"

"Why the hell would she do that?" I asked.

McClay rocked his head back and forth in thought and said, "For attention. Todd says she's a media hound."

Brach cleared his throat in preparation for suggesting McClay was an idiot. "I think it's very difficult to stun-gun yourself on the back," he said.

"Yeah, I think there are probably easier ways to get attention than shoot yourself in the back," I said, trying to keep my voice as bland as possible so as not to set McClay off.

A knock came at the door. Without waiting, a uniform opened the door and handed a piece of paper to Todd, who was sitting closest.

Todd glanced at it. "It's the report from Frank Puccio." He scanned it and repeated the salient points. "Found a print on the metal part of the hair dryer that didn't match the Creighton exemplars . . . ran it against IAFIS . . . came up with a match from an arrest in 2008 . . . nothing significant . . . public drunkenness, brawling . . ." He looked at me. "Erroll Murry."

"Erroll Murry," I said to myself. And to the rest of the room, and to the photographs before us, "Shayna Murry's brother murdered these children."

While the rest of the room gasped, McClay asked, "Who's Erroll Murry?"

I said, "He's the brother of the mistress who blew Marcus Creighton's alibi."

"Is there any logical reason at all why he might have handled the wife's hair dryer at any point in time?"

"I've met Erroll Murry, and I can say there's no way Kathleen Creighton would have let him through the front door. There's no way that an independent examiner would identify the print and match it to the brother of Creighton's mistress. I don't know the motive, but I tell you, he's the man who—"

I thought about how I had seen Erroll Murry at Cracker's Café before Creighton was executed. Before Shayna Murry was killed. If only I knew the true story, what could I have prevented? Before that, if the case had been more thoroughly investigated, what Delgado could have prevented? Everything, or at least much of it, clicked into place. I blanked.

"Yes?" McClay asked.

What's done is done, I heard Mom say, and finished the sentence. "Sorry. Murry is the man who started this whole chain of events. And I tell you we have to start there because all this is linked somehow."

"Are we positive he's the one? Is there a motive? What was this guy's motive?" McClay asked, while his very calmness implied that someone had damn well better come up with a motive fast so we could establish him as the Creighton killer and move on.

"Okay, what are the possible motives? Jealousy," I offered. "He loved his sister."

No one spoke. "He loved his sister too much," I said. "Hated to see her with Marcus Creighton."

McClay gave a lazy nod but didn't seem to go for it.

"Money," Todd said. "There was a life insurance policy on the wife. Erroll saw a chance to wipe out Creighton's family, and install Shayna in their place," Todd said.

"Money always makes a good motive," McClay said.

"Maybe Shayna knew beforehand he was going to do it, and maybe she didn't. But she lied about Marcus Creighton being with her in order to save Erroll," I said. When you're in law enforcement you can make this stuff up faster than a scriptwriter with Tom Cruise on the clock.

McClay took his time considering our ideas, then remembered his original goal. "Actually, the only reason I could care about Erroll Murry right now is if he killed his sister. Is it a neat package? Could we be looking at this guy for Shayna Murry's murder?"

I remembered what Delgado had told me about the Murrys, how she had raised her brother and how devoted he was to her. I remembered meeting him at the café and how he appeared ready to go at it with me if I even tried to talk to her. I remembered how genuine his hysteria was when he arrived at his sister's homicide scene. "Nothing is impossible, but I think it's pretty improbable given their relationship. Sixteen years of keeping the secret, I can't see Shayna giving up her brother now, so he wouldn't kill her to keep her silent."

"Then we're back to the vigilante theory, aren't we?" McClay asked, in that voice that makes you feel like you're on the witness stand being cross-examined.

Todd said, "If it *is* a vigilante we're looking for, they're going to want Erroll Murry more than anyone."

"So where's Erroll Murry right now?" McClay asked.

Everyone did that little look-away thing.

"Step one," McClay said. "Send out an APB to find Murry, but don't touch him. Just put him under surveillance. And somebody go over to this lab, what's his name?"

"Frank Puccio," Todd said.

"Step two, triple-check his results. Step three, don't wait for Puccio, info goes out to the media that Erroll Murry is wanted for questioning in the murder of the Creighton family. I want this in a local TV bulletin and on the Internet within the next thirty minutes."

"You realize if you do this you're going public with the fact that we executed an innocent man." This was Madeline, speaking for the first time, and apparently without thinking it through first.

"I don't recall executing an innocent man," McClay said in the same calm voice.

Madeline was staring at Todd, and her shoulders were rounder than the first time I'd seen her, making her look more like a girl. McClay turned to Todd also. Todd was carefully silent. Everybody plays these things very carefully.

"What about bringing Murry in for questioning, without putting him on the news?" Todd suggested.

"Because it's not about Murry," McClay said.

"You're trying to draw out the person who killed Shayna Murry," Todd said, and, realizing who the big fish might be, looked at me when he said, "You're making Erroll Murry bait."

McClay seemed unperturbed by this bluntness. "What would you rather do, put a twenty-four/seven armed guard around that entire list of potential victims you showed me? We're not going to be that passive. I'll call the Vero chief of police to put a watch on Murry once they locate him and not let anyone get near him. And I'll put the state bureau on notice in case Murry goes into the wind." He looked at me with some suspicion. "You're the agent from the FBI working with us, right?"

Todd said, "Actually, that's Laura Coleman you're thinking of. This is Brigid Quinn, former FBI but also assisting in the case from the start. She's the one who found Shayna Murry's body."

"Quinn," McClay said.

"My sister," Todd admitted.

You could see McClay flashing back through the immediate conversation to see if he'd said something that made him look bad, something he would regret. "Dandy," McClay muttered.

Forty-three

Laura had provided Henry Aggrawal with photographs of the children from the files, and the Gainesville anthropological center had done a computer reconstruction of the boy's face using the intact skull. The reconstruction matched the photo of Devon Creighton. I stayed behind in the conference room after everyone else left to read the full report. But I discovered something was missing, and it wasn't just that McClay had interrupted the description of the condition of the second body. I called Aggrawal and asked about the other child.

"That's all there was," he said. "Everything is in the report."

"But there were three children."

"There were only two at this site. The third must have been buried somewhere else. It's all in the report."

"I can see that."

He started to hang up, but I stopped him. "Wait a sec. The bodies you did find. What ages would you put them at, again?"

"They were both eight to eleven." He sighed audibly. "Like the report says."

I looked at the photograph with the three children that had been used in the aging. "Henry, would you do me a quick favor?" I asked him to do a simple computer aging on the oldest child, who was maybe about ten years old when the picture he had was taken. "That ten-year-old would have been around fourteen at the time of the crime. So age her . . . seventeen years."

I heard something in the close background, like he was doing something else while he was talking to me. His patience was wearing thin. He said, "Don't you people ever talk?"

"What, who else asked you to do this?"

"Laura Coleman, the agent who was there with you when the remains were found. She's been calling the whole time we were assessing the remains. She already asked for the same thing."

"Okay, what was the result?"

"Result? Some woman. I just did what she wanted and sent it on. I assumed she'd share it with y'all. Ask her, I'm late to class. And figure out who's in charge, for cripes sake."

What was Laura doing? Now I was getting mad. Sure, I may have killed someone on impulse and felt good about it. But I'd never plotted it, never descended on someone out of cold vengeance. That makes a difference. I needed to go after Laura Coleman myself, and I still had so much doubt of Laura's guilt that I went to Todd's office and told him where we were going.

On the way over to Laura's I filled Todd in on what I knew. That Laura had been in touch with Aggrawal the way I had about only finding two bodies at the site. That she had beat me to it. And that when I asked Aggrawal to age all the photos, he told me Laura had already asked him to do that.

"Sounds like she's conducting her own investigation," Todd said.

"Just stick with me in this, little brother."

Laura's car wasn't in its parking spot, but you never knew. She didn't answer the door, and that breaking-in business was getting to be typical of our visitations. I'd taken one of her keys, so I didn't have to break in this time. Besides, second-floor with front entrance and a large kitchen window—I would have made more of a mess and possibly been spotted.

She wasn't just being inhospitable, she wasn't home. I looked around quickly and saw the unrepaired hole in the wall where she threw the medicine ball, and Marcus Creighton's personal effects still littering her desk in a very un-Laura-like mess. I pointed it out to Todd, who went over and picked through it. "There's a letter here," he said.

"The one Alison Samuels wrote to Creighton," I said without looking. "Laura has probably read it a dozen times and gotten madder and madder."

"This letter isn't to Marcus Creighton," he said. He wandered in the direction of Coleman's bedroom.

"Where are you going?"

"I got cause here," he said.

I turned to look closer at the letter and saw that it wasn't typed like Alison's letter to Creighton, it was handwritten. On top of that, it had been torn up into small pieces and was taped back together. I remembered what Wally said about finding some "bits and pieces of stuff" under his bed and putting them into the box with the rest of the effects. It was my guess that Creighton must have ripped it up himself and Laura pieced it together. I read, *Dear Kirsten.*

In denial to the last, I thought. But then I was distracted by the photographs lying next to it. Hopefully the photographs I had come to find.

There were the photographs of the exploited child Alison Samuels had found on the Internet, and the photograph of the same child aged in reverse to about eight years.

The other photograph showed the three children from Creighton's album, the one on the boat, that must have been taken a few years before the murders.

A final photograph was the one Laura must have requested from Henry Aggrawal. It took the boat photo and aged all three children about sixteen years. The photo showed Sara and Devon, the eight-year-old twins, as they would have looked upon graduation from college.

And there, at approximately age thirty, with longer hair and brown eyes, was Alison Samuels.

Todd came back into the room with a Victoria's Secret gift box. The pink satin ribbon used to tie it was untied.

"What do you think?" he asked.

"It's either perfume or where she hides her vibrator," I said, covering the quaver in my voice with a joke.

"Neither," he said, and opened it to reveal a very unladylike collection I'd seen before: pepper spray, rape whistles, a set of brass knuckles, and . . . wait for it . . . the stun gun.

"Well?" he asked.

"Coleman is really big into self-defense," I said. I opened the desk drawer where the stuff had been before. She had moved it all to a safer hiding place. But her gun was neither in the drawer nor in the box. I took my cell phone out of my tote bag.

"Who are you calling?" Todd asked.

"Alison Samuels," I said, showing him the photo. "This just got more complicated."

"Why did Coleman have this photo?" he asked.

"Because Alison Samuels is Kirsten Creighton." I stopped denying that Laura Coleman might have gotten herself into trouble and shifted into protecting whoever might get in her way. I heard Alison's phone ringing and her voice telling me to leave a message. "Dammit, doesn't anyone answer their phone anymore? Why carry a cell phone if you're not going to answer it?"

I snapped my phone shut and picked up the Dear Kirsten letter. "Marcus knew it. He knew it all along, but he never told anyone. Not even Alison Samuels. Maybe this says why."

I dialed another number. "Hey, Frank. Thanks for sending that report on the print ID so quickly. Yeah? Yeah? I figured. Thanks."

I turned to Todd. "Let's go."

"I'm a little confused," he said. "Where are we going and who are we going after, Laura Coleman, Alison Samuels, or Erroll Murry?"

"I think all of them," I said. "Puccio was employed by Will Hench, so he sent that print ID to him first. Will Hench would have called Laura immediately. And because your Captain McClay leaked the news and also because Alison gets police broadcasts, I imagine they'll both be going to the same place."

Now it was Todd's turn to take out his cell phone. I asked him who he was calling. When he told me, I said, "Sometimes backup is good and sometimes it gets people killed. Trust me on this, would you?"

"Protocol," he said.

"I know, I know. But right now we don't know why we're calling backup or even where to direct them. I think it's a strong possibility that Alison has found out about Erroll Murry and has gone to Vero for a confrontation."

"I can't picture Alison Samuels hurting a fly."

"Maybe not. Maybe Kirsten Creighton would."

"Where does Laura Coleman fit into all this?"

"To tell you the truth, I'm not positive anymore who Laura is after or why. Let's see if Alison is home before we do anything else."

We got back in his car and headed out, passing by Alison's house again to see if her car was still there. It was not.

"Vero?" Todd said. "I got the location at the briefing."

"Yup," I said. "I'll tell you what I know for sure and what I'm thinking on the way."

Forty-four

Now that we were in forward motion, I took out the letter from Marcus Creighton written to his daughter the night before his death.

Dear Kirsten,

Even with what will happen in a few hours, the overriding feeling at this moment is relief that I can finally call you that, if only in this letter. I'll give it to Laura Coleman and tell her it's for Alison Samuels. I trust her not to read it, and smile thinking of how similar the two of you are in your passion for justice.

If you didn't identify yourself to me, I suppose there must have been a reason.

I've wondered what you knew about that night, if anything. Where you were that you escaped (that's what gave me hope that Sara and Devon might be alive), why you were convinced I was guilty. It's a mystery to me. But I'll keep your secret. You have such a strong sense of right and wrong, I fear that if you were truly convinced the real killer was still out there, you'd do anything to find him, even if it meant sacrificing yourself.

What I want to be very specific about, is the certainty that neither you nor I are responsible for the death of our family.

I see you have grown into the kind of person who won't stop trying to get what you believe is justice. In your case this is too dangerous. Stay Alison Samuels. Keep doing your good work to save children. I'm proud of what you do, and I don't want to do anything to hinder it.

I am guilty, not of murder, but of lust and greed and selfishness. Maybe this last thing, keeping your identity secret, will redeem me.

~~Your loving father~~
~~Respectfully~~
~~Dad~~

I folded up the letter and put it in my pocket.

After both of us paused, for thought, I figured, Todd said, "He tore the letter up. At the end he decided not to tell her he knew."

"There was that line, 'I see you've grown into a woman who won't stop trying to get justice.' I bet that's what made him change his mind while he was writing the letter. Marcus had an inkling that if Alison was convinced the killer was still out there, she wouldn't stop, and might reveal that she was Kirsten Creighton in order to flush him out. Speaking of bait."

"Makes sense," Todd said.

"I think Alison thought her father was guilty. But then she found out about the fur in the burial tarp from Aggrawal, and figured her father at least had an accomplice, because of his asthma. And you know what else? She heard Will Hench say at the interview that they were looking at evidence that one of the witnesses perjured *herself.* Accomplice. Perjury. Wouldn't take a genius. She didn't know the truth, but she thought Shayna Murry did. And Shayna Murry died rather than rat out her brother."

"But wait. Alison Samuels got tasered."

"Did she really?" I tried to remember our conversation the night I visited her, and wondered if that had made her nervous enough to cover her tracks. "Or was she just deflecting suspicion to Laura in case I was figuring it all out? Even Captain McClay suggested that she could have done it herself. I nixed that idea, but maybe he was onto something." I stretched my right hand over my left shoulder and touched my mid-scapula. "Young limber person could take off the cartridge and reach her upper back. We didn't ask exactly where the contact occurred. What we do know for sure is that only the person who killed Shayna Murry would know that a stun gun had been used."

"Laura knew," Todd said. When I didn't answer, he went on, "Erroll Murry hasn't been at his place since they put out the APB. Now they've put a dragnet around the area, all roads north and south monitored, Coast Guard watching the waterways for his boat."

"But if you were looking, and you had a tracking dog, where would you start?"

"At his place. Pick up a scent."

"That's where Laura and Alison, together or separately, are headed."

"They're both after Murry?"

"How should I know? Maybe Laura wants to question Alison on her own. I still can't believe Laura tasered Alison out of revenge. Oh, frankly, I don't know who did what, or what their next step is, I only know we need to get there before the three of them connect, like the mythical Furies, only destroying each other."

"What if you're wrong?" he asked.

"You mean what if we go to Vero and our two gals aren't there? I may have been totally off the mark with Laura, but I think I know this. And if that's not enough, I can't afford to be wrong. Look at the situation. You got Laura. You got Alison. You got Erroll Murry. You got an attack dog. It's a perfect storm."

"I've met Larry," Todd said. "Working on a missing-child case. He's not an attack dog."

"Not even Larry is telling the whole truth. So you got Laura, Alison, Murry, and Larry. On top of that you got who knows what surveillance."

"I'll alert Delgado, my boss, and the FBI on the way."

We'd already pulled onto I-95, and Todd was moving pretty good, not too much traffic in the early evening. I touched Todd's arm as he reached out for his car radio.

"My point is, you call in all those people and you've got a bloodbath waiting to happen. Or a textbook scenario for suicide by cop. I could go on. Look, we're on our way and it's going to take a couple of hours to get there. And we can't be far behind the others. We've got a little time to think about a strategy."

"What we need is SWAT."

"Less is more," I said.

"I've heard that, but I never got it. As far as I'm concerned, more is more."

"On top of what I already named? And us? No, you do that and you've got a mess. We need to finesse this."

"Oh yeah, the FBI has always been good at that," Todd said.

"It always comes down to this, doesn't it? Your metro-cop inferiority complex on top of short-man syndrome."

"Waco. Ruby Ridge—"

"Ancient history. You want to get Laura or Alison killed?" There was something there that wouldn't let me lose either of them no matter what they had done.

I took a deep breath. Being a Quinn, what Mom called bull-headed, wouldn't get us anywhere. What we needed was compromise. Todd was clipping along at eighty miles per hour in a sixty-five zone. We were already passing the Hillsboro exit, but it was agonizingly slow.

"Lights?" I suggested.

"Nah, someone gets on the radio and asks if I need help. Easier to flash a badge if we're stopped. I'll speed up once we're past West Palm."

"Watch out."

"I see him."

"Todd."

"What?"

"Madeline."

"I told her, I get any inkling of dirty business she's going down for it. Right now I don't think they can pin anything on her. All they would have is what Mack says she said."

"Can you trust Delgado?"

"Do we have a choice? My boss called his boss, so Delgado knows."

"Okay, tell me what you think of this. You call Delgado and tell him about Alison. Tell him we're coming up. But tell him that Laura is on Alison's tail and she should be left alone so as not to raise suspicion. That she's got ranking jurisdiction since she's FBI. That we'll keep him posted of any changes."

"That's not altogether the truth," he said.

"Yeah, well," I said.

"But it could work," he said.

Quinn after all. "Good brother. When this is all over I'll buy you a doughnut."

"Fuck you," he said amiably, and kept driving. We passed the Glades exit in Boca Raton.

Forty-five

Todd called Delgado and told him what I suggested. Then I filled Todd in on the story I either knew or conjectured. Here's the way I was thinking that day on the way up to Vero Beach:

Shayna Murry had known it was her brother who killed the Creightons. I'd seen the guy, and what Todd and I had proposed for his motive sounded right. He was just stupid enough to think he could remove the wife and insert Shayna into the house. But the two kids showed up.

Atlantic Avenue exit at Delray. Boynton Beach.

Where was Kirsten that night? I don't know. What I do know is that she didn't take the twins to the community sleepover. And I do know that Shayna wanted to protect the brother she had raised when her parents left them. So when Erroll told her he'd just killed the family, she lied for him. Said Marcus hadn't been at her house.

Palm Beach exits. Four of them. Todd jumped to a hundred miles an hour, safe on this part of the highway where there was less traffic.

The thing with Shayna Murry was, lying made her an accessory after the fact, and she would have gone down for murder one herself. She was trying to save not just her brother's skin but her own. When she saw Creighton convicted, and getting the death penalty, the guilt had tortured her, but not enough to make her confess her perjury.

Jupiter exit. As if the god himself was fucking with us, the thunder clapped loud enough to vibrate my dental fillings, and the rain started.

"Oh, terrific. This is just fucking terrific," I said, leaning forward to try to see anything out the windshield. All I could see was the wipers doing their best against what looked like we'd slid into a river.

"Actually, it is terrific," Todd said, increasing his speed. "It'll hinder anybody ahead of us in or out of their cars, and no cop will be out to stop us. Help me watch the road for other cars."

I clamped my jaws as if that would help. Now I knew how Laura felt when I drove through the storm.

Exit for Vero Beach. The rain stopped.

It was a good thing Delgado agreed to withdraw the surveillance. There was one dirt road leading to Murry's place, and with the number of people potentially converging here, it could turn into a parking lot of mud. Figuring they were still ahead of us, though hopefully not by much, Todd parked the car far enough away that it couldn't be seen from the house, and at the same time blocked vehicles from getting away.

I got out of the car first and immediately jumped back in again before Todd had time to holster his weapon. Without looking in the mirror I could feel my lips plumped like a bad Botox job. Todd swatted one of the mosquitos that had gotten in with me, then reached into the glove compartment for some repellent. "I didn't think I needed to tell you," he said.

"I'd forgotten what this place can be like."

He gave me and himself a good spraying, and then we got out of the car and let the doors ease back without closing them entirely, just in case we were closer than we thought we were.

Weapons in one hand, flashlights in the other, though turned off for now, we made our way down the dirt road between growth that still dripped with the downpour. It all hung close, feeling as if it resented that gash that had been cut in the middle of it, the strangler figs that crawled up the oak trees threatening to close in at any moment.

My eyes grew slowly accustomed to the darkness, so I was able to spot a turnoff narrower than the road, and a glint of a red rear reflector. I nudged Todd and pointed to it.

"Laura," I whispered.

We continued on for ten minutes, walking as quickly and as quietly as we could, our shoes sucking into the sandy mud in places where the water had pooled and we didn't see. Then a small clearing and a smaller house.

I knew Laura from her build and the limp, so I turned my flashlight on her coming out of a house that was more like a shed. She didn't close the door behind her, but stood looking at me as if she could see who I was even with the light in her eyes. Her stillness said she belonged there. I was the one whose presence was odd. Having been caught in the rain she was soaked, which she didn't seem to notice any more than the mosquitos that flocked to her.

My skin crawled, watching them on her and her lack of reaction to them. I wanted to slap at them. I wanted to slap her. I had a feeling from the way she left the shack that there was nothing urgent to deal with here. "How about I talk to her while you check the perimeter," I said. He nodded and moved off around the left of the house.

"Why are you here?" I called, getting closer but not too.

"I'm not sure," she said, engagement with me somehow bringing her out of a daze. "Why are you here?"

"Looking for you," I said. "What's in there?"

"Nothing," she said. "I think I saw a few rats."

I went past her into the shack, weapon drawn. Laura didn't turn around to watch or warn me. Todd had circled around the other side of the house, giving me an all-clear, and standing, watching Laura who didn't look at him.

Inside, with the night and the rain hiding the moon, it was all darkness. I switched on my flashlight and pointed it randomly around, hoping that Laura had told me the truth, that there was no one here. I saw a sty of a dwelling. A raw half-eaten fish, dried animal feces, and plates of what looked like the stuff they put out on a bar next to your beer littered the floor. In place of a bed, Erroll had been using an old couch that someone sometime had dragged in. Besides a light blanket there was a pillow, waxy with grime.

I caught something in the corner of my eye and flashed my light on a skittering along the edge of the wall. Like Laura, I assumed a rat, but it was too big to be a rat, too thin, too slinky. I found it again. A ferret.

So Murry keeps ferrets, I thought. That explained the shit and plate of kibbles on the floor, and also the animal scavenging of the bodies, and maybe the fur that had been found in the tarp used to bury the Creighton children. Murry had kept the bodies here, possibly even murdered the children here, before he wrapped them tightly in the tarp and took them by boat to the island. Only not before the ferrets got to them.

But where's Murry? I checked the bathroom, a toilet and a shower stall big enough to be on a small boat. Filthy like the front room. I left.

"Where did they go?" I asked her.

Laura didn't pretend to not understand that by "they" I meant Alison and Erroll Murry. She shrugged.

"I should call for backup now," Todd's words said.

What my brother meant was *You got Laura. That's the best I can do.*

I nodded my agreement. Then he said, his tone casual, "How about you give me that, Laura." He had gestured to her side, and then I saw the gun she held in her right hand, angled away from me and tucked against her thigh.

"What?" she said to Todd, and then to me, "What?"

I saw her anger flare the second time she said it, and heard the accusation in it. I didn't try to coddle her. I treated her like she had all her wits with her. "Coleman, we know where to go. We need to get a move on, and my brother won't go without that gun."

She looked at me like I had betrayed her, but let Todd take the gun out of her hand.

"Are you sure Alison has been here?"

"Yeah," she said. "Pretty sure."

"There's a truck parked behind the shack," Todd said. "It's registered to Murry. And a jeep."

"That would be Alison's," I said.

Todd said, "Murry's boat is at the dock."

Knowing what I knew now, it didn't take genius to figure out the next move. "Todd, how about dropping us off at Coleman's car, then you can go somewhere to get a signal and alert Delgado we'll be at Shayna Murry's place. We won't do anything but keep an eye on them until you get there, so hurry." I gave him the address.

"Why there?"

"I bet Alison has been all over this area with Larry a million times looking for the children's bodies, so she knows. Murry went on foot because he knows they'll be keeping an eye out for his truck and the boat. Alison is tracking him with Larry. Where he went is secluded and private, boarded up, and not too far from here. Shayna Murry's house. It's a guess, but it's the only one I've got, and we don't have a tracking dog to confirm it."

"Why you instead of me?" Todd asked. Again, I could hear what he wasn't saying: *Why Laura?*

"Because I know Alison better than either of you. She's got some respect for me. I'm the most likely to keep everyone alive. And Coleman is FBI. If the shit goes down before backup, she has more jurisdiction in this county than either of us." *She's unarmed and I'm not going to let her out of my sight until this is finished.*

I may have gone from insistence on Laura's total innocence to preventing worse things from happening, but that's how it goes.

Forty—six

Laura was too silent on the short drive over to Shayna Murry's place. She may have been cold from the drenching, and I kept the AC off in her car as I drove (she was still eerily passive and didn't object to my driving), but I didn't like the way she sat bent over pressing her hands between her knees. For what we were about to do she appeared a little too lethargic.

I pulled in to a grassy lot a little ways down from Shayna Murry's place.

"Are you going to let me go in there unarmed?" Laura asked. As with Todd, I heard what she was saying underneath her words. *Don't you trust me?*

"Alison won't kill Murry until she gets him to confess. So what I'm going to do is make sure they're in there, and if I can, talk Alison down. You catch the backup when it arrives and let them know. Okay?"

Whatever Laura heard underneath my words that made her eyes narrow, she got out of the car but stayed put, leaning against it. I came up behind the house and saw the smallish window, not boarded up like the ones in front. Standing on tiptoe I could just barely look in from the bottom right corner of the window, the dark hiding me from whoever was inside.

I thought I smelled something burning and hoped it wasn't Erroll.

From this vantage point I could see the rod for a shower curtain. I was looking over the bathtub shower stall. I nearly slipped when I looked down and saw Larry looking back at me. His lips pulled back in a snarl.

But then I saw he was not actually looking back at me. He was laser focused on someone in the tub. Alison stood at the door of the bathroom, her back turned to me. With Larry keeping guard, she didn't have to be cautious about whoever was in the tub. I needed to confirm it was Erroll Murry, and for her sake, I hoped he was still alive.

I thought I could talk to her, and no time to waste, with Todd and Delgado probably on the way. I quickly made my way around to the front door.

Crime scene tape had been stripped away from the front porch, and the door was unlocked. Alison must not have thought she needed too much time to get the whole truth from Erroll.

Unlike the shack we'd just left, this place had electricity, of course, and a gooseneck desk light had been turned on in the front studio. The boards over the windows kept the light from showing outside. The powder the crime scene techs used to dust for latents after Shayna's murder still coated much of the surfaces, and the place still carried the disgustingly sweet odor of decomposition. It always would.

So far neither Alison nor Larry was alerted to my presence. Maybe the smell prevented it. I had been here before and knew that the hallway led to the bedroom led to the bathroom.

I hadn't seen a firearm, at least not in the bathroom. And I didn't want to approach Alison with mine pointed at her. It sends the wrong kind of message when you're trying to negotiate. I put mine in my back waistband. In the bedroom I noticed a heavy comforter on the bed, and I grabbed it, doubling and doubling it again as quietly as I could. I'd seen this sort of thing with K-9 trainers and thought it should work. I wasn't sure when Larry would hear or smell me and shift his focus from Erroll in the bathtub.

Not a moment too soon.

Larry appeared at the bedroom door, his lips now curled up over teeth that were meant for me. He didn't look much like a therapy dog right now. Then Alison was behind him, her thoughts so hard in her eyes I couldn't tell if she saw me or not.

Maybe the comforter wasn't enough.

We stood-off like that until I was aware of Laura standing beside me. I felt her reach behind me and pull out my pistol. "Don't," I tried to say without moving my lips too much and setting Larry off. But Laura did anyway.

So I hissed out of the corner of my mouth, "Shoot the dog," and backed up a bit out of the bedroom into the hallway.

"I can't shoot the dog," Laura hissed back.

That was enough for Larry. Without waiting for a signal from his mistress, he attacked.

Braced for the impact, I met him with my body and kept the padding of the comforter between us. His jaws snapped for my face, close enough to feel his breath. Wrapping the comforter around him felt like putting a straitjacket on a hundred-pound meth tweaker. He nailed me on the forearm, but I was so bent on not getting killed I hardly felt it at the time. Luckily he wasn't real good at balancing that long on his hind legs, and tripped. I fell on top of him, pinning him on the floor with the whole weight of my body, his teeth brushing my cheek, vaguely hearing Laura shouting, "I'll shoot the dog! I'll shoot the dog!"

I couldn't have shot the dog either. He wasn't your basic junkyard dog, he was a colleague. But Alison didn't know that, and enough of her came back to care for the only family she knew. She couldn't save the others, but she could save this one.

"Larry, down," she said.

Larry went limp under me, and whimpered like a good therapy dog. I had enough adrenaline pumping, though, that if he had tried to lick my face I would have punched him. I rolled over next to him, and rose cautiously, saying, "Good dog, good boy, Larry," knowing that coming from me it probably had no effect.

With Larry less of a threat, Laura turned her attention back on Alison, giving her the same order Alison had given the dog. "FBI," she said. "Get down." I wasn't sure about the legality of her law enforcement claim, but she was the only one in the room with a gun.

Alison ignored Laura's gun, turned, and moved back into the bedroom, out of sight.

Laura looked at Larry, who sat quietly but at attention. "I couldn't shoot the dog," she said.

"Don't waste time," I said, and, "Give me the gun."

Which she did not. She followed Alison to the bathroom. I closed the door that would keep Larry in the hall, and followed Laura.

We stood at the entrance to the small bathroom and observed her sitting on the edge of the tub. Holding up his head by the hair with one hand, in the other she held a knife to the throat of Erroll Murry. There were puncture marks in his arm and a tear in his face where he had been mauled by Larry. Otherwise he was aware. He was too aware for his own good, his eyes bugged out with terror. A stun gun was on the floor next to the tub, but it hadn't been fired. I wondered if he'd told her what she wanted to hear. When he saw us he started to wiggle, but the knife at his throat made him stop.

"Alison, what are you doing?" I said, knowing the answer, but stalling for time, and wondering if Laura would get in a head shot before the knife sliced through.

"He killed my family," she said. "He let my father die in his place."

"I know," I said. Not caring about Erroll except in an abstract sense, but caring about Alison, who had been so good and endured so much, I wanted to stop her. I wanted to save her. And I wanted to save Laura from killing her.

I said, "Alison, don't do this."

"He says he's scared, but not as scared as he was all those years after he found out there was a kid he missed killing. He deserves to die."

"I know, I know. All the scumbags in the world deserve to die. But this, this doesn't look to me like righteousness anymore. It doesn't have that noble a name. This guy's not worth it. You don't want to do it, not with us watching like this."

Having an audience didn't seem to bother Alison. Her head wagged back and forth an inch, like she was hearing her own thoughts instead of my words. She pressed the blade into Erroll's neck where the water from the shower flowed down. I could tell the knife was pretty sharp from the thin line of blood that crept to the surface and washed down the front of his T-shirt. She didn't look at Erroll as she did this. She watched Laura, or more precisely, the finger that Laura held against the trigger of her gun.

Alison said, "If you shoot me, the last thing I'll do is slash his throat. That's really all I want. So you do what you have to do."

The air crackled with uncertainty. I took a chance, reached into my pocket and drew out the letter Marcus Creighton had written but failed to send. Alison's focus was so fixed on Laura, though, I was unable to distract her with it.

"Alison, your dad wrote you a letter the night before he died. He addressed it to Kirsten. He knew it was you. Read the letter, Kirsten."

Alison wouldn't fall for it, wouldn't take her eyes off Laura's trigger finger. "Alison," I said. "Come away now. Read the letter."

"He took my family. He took my life," she said. "Isn't that right, Erroll. Tell the woman what you told me."

While we talked, Erroll's mind had been concentrated on nothing but gauging the pressure of the knife. If he wanted to nod he was too terrified to do so, with the blade pressed just gently enough against his throat. He reached his hand up to ease the pressure, and Alison nicked the hand. Erroll moaned and tears flowed.

"Never mind," Alison said. "I'll tell them what you told me. You just nod, okay?" When he didn't speak she pressed harder. "Okay?"

Erroll gave a nod that pressed the knife just a little deeper.

"Alison, please let Erroll go now," I said.

"You never ever talked to my father, did you, Erroll? You didn't know him."

Alison eased up the pressure of the knife to encourage him.

Erroll shook his head.

"Erroll felt bad for his sister, that she was poor and the Creighton family had everything she deserved. Nod if that's true, Erroll."

Erroll nodded.

"Alison, the police are on their way. They'll deal with Erroll," I said.

"Erroll says he didn't know there were three of us until Shayna told him. And Shayna loved her brother more than my father, so she protected him. But what he won't tell me is how it happened. I have to know. Erroll, tell us."

Erroll struggled but the way his head twisted I had the sense if he could have freed his hands he would have covered his face.

"No."

"Alison, put down the knife," I said. "Can you just put down the knife."

"Erroll," Alison chided, as a mother would her naughty son.

I gasped as he turned his head toward the shower wall and the blade entered, a thin sheet of blood emerging down his neck.

"Erroll," murmured Alison, quietly. "What did you do to the children?"

His eyes closed and that long ago memory finally seemed to explode from his mouth. "I'd never kill kids. Never. But he came in and tried to pull me away and then she came in too and they both started screaming. I only wanted to shut them up. I'd never kill a kid, I'd never kill a kid."

"But you did," Alison said.

Then she slit his throat. The blood gushed and mixed with the water, turning pink before it got to the drain.

Laura and I leapt forward simultaneously in that futile gesture to stanch the blood that can't be stopped. But Alison was already standing, now between us and Erroll with the knife still in her hand. She waved it back and forth and took a step forward. "It's okay, it's okay," she said in the tone of reassurance that she meant us no harm as long as we cooperated. "I just needed to make sure he died this time. Before."

I knew what she was thinking, that she herself had been one of the people responsible for her father's death, and now it was her turn. "Alison, don't do it," I said. "We can get you help. It doesn't matter what you've done, the law will be sympathetic."

"I don't want sympathy," she said. "I want my life to have been different."

Laura kept her gun trained on Alison as they did a little dance in a mirror image of each other.

"I don't want to kill you, Alison," Laura said, taking careful aim at a spot I couldn't guess.

Oh yes she did, I thought. She sort of wanted to kill Alison. And Alison wanted to be killed. These two women both wanted the same thing. And if Laura succeeded, I knew I would have lost them both.

"Don't worry," Alison said to Laura. "I'll kill you instead."

"Not necessarily," Laura said, and, as Alison lunged with the knife upraised, fired.

The knife flew away and bounced off the bathroom wall, but Alison wasn't stopped. After her surprise and pain she lunged again, this time with nothing but her will to die. Laura stepped back and away from her, further into the bedroom.

"Don't," I half-whispered, afraid to tip the scale in the wrong direction, but unable to resist. "Don't be so sure of yourself."

"I won't," Laura said. I couldn't tell if she was talking to me or trying to convince herself.

From the first shot I could hear Larry barking in the hallway. Now he threw his body against the bedroom door, trying to get to his mistress.

"I won't," Laura said again, and fired.

Alison dropped to the floor.

But the blood I was expecting, from one taken through the heart, did not come. My eyes slipped over her form and found that she'd taken it in the shin, probably shattering the bone, and her forward motion tumbled her over. She lay on her side, writhing with pain, clutching her improbably bent leg while Larry whimpered and whined and barked beyond the door.

Laura had already slid down the wall and was sitting with her knees up, holding the gun in two hands but not exactly aiming it at Alison. That looked good to me, and I slid wearily down, too, feeling my back against the door, feeling the bumps as Larry hit it on the other side with his body. Laura didn't bother to speak to me. I didn't bother to tell her I was sorry to doubt her.

I didn't hear Todd and Delgado drive up, but I heard them in the hallway comforting Larry, who just sounded sad and uncertain at this point. Then I moved my butt away from the door so they could come in. Delgado secured Alison and called an ambulance while Todd went into the bathroom. "You can call the ME and a meat wagon, too," he said to Delgado when he came out.

Delgado looked at Laura, who still sat holding the gun. "Thank you, Agent Coleman," he said.

Not being able to resist one little snark, I said, "For solving the Creighton case, you mean." I was watching Todd as I said it.

You didn't say anything about Laura to Delgado.

No.

When the ambulance arrived, I finally got up off the floor and walked out next to Alison's gurney. Delgado went to stop me, but I pressed Marcus Creighton's letter to Kirsten into her hand.

"You go real easy on her," I said to Delgado. "I'm going to find out if you don't."

"I'm going to have to make something up here."

"People like us are good at that."

"I'm serious. With SWAT we could have saved Erroll," he said.

"No you couldn't. You would have just lost Alison, too," I said. "And maybe Laura or me. I think we got a good deal on that."

Alison was understandably ungrateful. She called out to me. "Brigid! What about Larry?"

"Laura will take care of Larry," I called back.

Laura had followed me out, and I felt her flinch beside me, but she had the good sense not to say anything. I turned to her as Delgado pulled away. "It'll be good for you, force you to be a little less compulsive," I said. "Plus you get a guard dog."

"You're bleeding," she said, pointing out a trickle that ran down my forearm to my wrist. "You should get a tetanus shot."

That was pretty much all that was said of the evening's events at that point.

Forty—seven

Early the morning after her arrest I visited Alison in jail, where she was being held in hospital lockdown without bond. I had to give up my cell phone while I was visiting her, so the call from Mom went to voice mail.

When I sat down next to Alison's bed, with a guard stationed discreetly just outside the door, she first asked how Larry was doing, and I told her he was getting along well with Laura. I didn't mention that he had eaten the couch, and Laura was going to have to get used to not having her house quite as tidy as she had been accustomed.

Alison asked about Laura, too, said she was sorry for trying to force her hand that way. I told her Laura was going to be fine. It was part of Alison's innate kindness, to be thinking of Laura.

Then I asked her to tell me about her and her father, what really happened that night.

She ignored that. She started to lift her hand in my direction before she remembered she was cuffed to the side of the bed. "Do you want to know where I was the night my mother and brother and sister were murdered? I had run away. How pathetic is that? If I'd been home that night, I know I might not have been able to save my mother, but if I'd done what my father told me to do, gone to the sleepover, Sara and Devon wouldn't have died. I've always known this."

"You were only fourteen," I said. I pleaded with Alison, Kirsten, savior, killer.

As she told her story I saw them all:

It started with a fight the night of the killings. Kirsten had come into her parents' bathroom to ask her mother about dinner. Her mother had already started on her first glass of wine. Kirsten's father was gone for a brief out-of-town trip, who knew where, and would be back in a few days. Before he left, he said Kirsten was in charge. That was the only acknowledgment he ever made of the family being in ruins. She was to take Sara and Devon to a community sleepover that night.

"I'm not going," Kirsten said to her mother.

"Your father told you to do it. You're supposed to stay there with them. They're too little to be left alone overnight."

"Oh, like you care about any of us," Kirsten said, looking at her mother's back and at the reflection of them both in the bathroom mirror. Seeing herself seemed to encourage the drama. "Look at you. You're a mess, Mom. You didn't even get dressed today."

"I get dressed," Kathleen said, as if, already beaten by the familiar argument to come, this was at least one point she could verify.

"You slept in those yoga pants and T-shirt, Mommy," Kirsten said. "And you *could* wash your hair once a week." She turned to leave. "I'm outta here."

"You better not be going to that boy's house," Mom said, in an effort not to appear totally out of control of the situation.

"What difference does it make where I go?"

"He won't respect you."

"Where'd you get that line, out of the Middle Ages? You're talking about sex, right? Well, get this. I don't want his *respect*. Why don't you at least be honest and admit you don't give a fuck who I sleep with? I know all you're worried about is whether I take the twins out tonight so you don't have to be their mother."

Mom leaned back on the counter as if the words had struck her. Kirsten saw her sober on the instant, her eyes narrowed. Mom said, "You think you're so grown up, that you know everything there is to know. Well, then, get this, Kirsten. Your father is fucking somebody else."

Kirsten had turned to go, but this stopped her. Or rather it felt as if she had stopped but all the blood in her body had kept going and now she was drained of everything. It was a lie; her mother was just trying to be vicious. And yet, a child is really no match for an adult. All Kirsten could think of to say was, "He is not."

"He is."

"You're nuts, Mom. You're just drunk and talking."

"I know her. Her name is Shayna Murry. She thinks she's an ar-teest." Mom tried to look all cool and uncaring when she took a sip of her wine, but Kirsten saw her hand shake.

"I saw them," Mom said.

Kirsten wanted to cover her eyes and ears like at the worst part of a horror movie, but couldn't bear not to see what was in the basement. Like an accusation more than a question, she said, "When?"

"Long time ago. He doesn't know I saw. They were in the bar at Harrison's. They were turned toward each other on their stools. Their knees were interlocked, one of his between hers—"

"No."

"And the inside of her other leg tucked against the outside of his leg. Like this." Kathleen bent her fingers and interlaced the knuckles of her right hand with the left. She rubbed the fingers slowly together and apart.

"No."

"He swiveled his stool back and forth real slowly. His knee rubbed the insides of her legs."

Kirsten didn't say anything.

"She picked up her wine from the bar without taking her eyes off his, and she took a tiny sip. She didn't swallow. Then she put her index finger on his jaw and ran it down his neck until it hooked into his shirt under this little depression at the bottom of his throat where the first button of his shirt was buttoned."

Kirsten didn't say anything.

"Then she pulled him to her so his knee pressed against her crotch, and her knee against his. Then she kissed him. She must have tasted like wine. When they pulled away I saw his tongue pull out of her mouth. Then she swallowed." Kathleen stopped to see the effect she had had. "I bet you understand what she was promising."

It was true, Kirsten was old enough and had enough personal experience to understand what she was being told. She didn't realize that she wasn't old enough yet to judge the ugliness of a mother telling her child these things, let alone about her own father. She couldn't sympathize at the time that there was too much pain built up in one person, so much pain it spilled over this way. It would take years for her to come to this understanding of her mother, and by that time it would be too late.

On that afternoon Kirsten reeled a bit, dizzy without knowing why.

Adults always know when they've won. With a mixture of satisfaction and a dash of some remaining regret in her voice, Mom said, "Yeah. You're a real big girl now, aren't you?" She turned on the faucet in the bathroom sink. "Go ahead and go. I think I'll wash my hair."

Kirsten walked into the living room and then into the family room, turning off a rerun of *South Park*. "Don't you guys watch *Dora the Explorer* anymore?" she asked. The twins looked up expectantly. Kirsten felt the warmth of love wash through her that she had been feeling more and more no matter what she told her mother. She expected this happened when little ones turned that needy look on you.

"What's for dinner?" Sara asked, ever hopeful, because very often there was dinner.

Kirsten put on a smile and knew they couldn't tell it was fake, because they were already used to this pretend life, and they wouldn't notice the wet sheen coming up over her eyes. "It's Raisin Bran night," she said.

Sara and Devon both brightened. Raisin Bran night was one of their favorites.

There was actually a chance that Mom would get her act together enough to fix a bag of frozen P. F. Chang's for the kids, but just in case, Kirsten went into the kitchen and took the cereal box and two bowls down from the cupboards because she knew they couldn't reach them. They could get to the milk all right, and maybe this time they wouldn't dump it on the table.

Kirsten went into the garage to get her bike.

She pedaled over to her friend Adam's house on John's Island. The Lupitskys were in the Caribbean for spring break and she had the key for their poolhouse. She had had it with being a mom. Didn't she deserve to be a kid? Life was supposed to be happy, fun. Let her parents stew over where she was when she didn't come home for a couple of nights.

She took one call from her Dad, on the cell phone she took from her mom's purse.

I remembered what Gutierrez told me about that phone call. Now I knew who Creighton was talking to. "He called to remind you to take your brother and sister to the sleepover, didn't he? He said, 'Let them go.'"

Alison looked surprised. "How did you know that?"

I shrugged. "What did you say back to him?"

"I told him I'd take them. But I didn't."

That night she stayed in the Lupitsky poolhouse, on the couch. It was no big deal; she had done this before, stayed out all night. Once she'd slept on the beach. Word had gotten around school that she was a slut. Maybe she was.

But not her dad. He was a good husband and father. He hadn't done the things her mom said he did. He called again, but she didn't answer.

She fell asleep watching TV on the couch, and the news woke her up in the morning. As she came awake, she saw on the television screen what looked like her house in the early-morning light. It was her house. Then she saw the front door open and her father led out with his hands cuffed behind him. The reporters swarmed in but were kept from asking any questions by attending policemen. One of them opened the back door of the police car parked in the driveway and helped her father inside.

Alison said, "They reported everything that we now know. Mistress. Blown alibi. Taken in for questioning regarding the murder of his wife and family."

As she watched the broadcast, Kirsten was at first just dazed. Murder. Mistress. Her father was screwing around after all. This was a true story, and the rest of the story he lied about. He knew Kirsten had run off again, and he took Sara and Devon somewhere. He took them somewhere. Kirsten's imagination circled around that thought but didn't dare go any further. Her father couldn't be her father. Her father wouldn't . . .

He knew she wasn't dead. Yet. If he got out, he'd be looking for her. She had to run.

Alison made that circular motion with her finger at the side of her head. "Nutso, huh?"

"Obviously. You were traumatized," I said.

What were her other choices now? Go home to an empty house? Turn herself in to child protective services? Or just head out.

Alison said, "I was just like the rest of the children who run off or get lured. Angry, lonely, and frightened. I rode my bike to I-95 and hitched a ride with a trucker heading south. By the time I got to Miami, Kirsten Creighton had been wiped out of existence."

Years later Kirsten Creighton would think back about how it's done, this running away, about how easy it all is and how to a child it seems the only option. Kirsten would make it her business to know the numbers she was a part of. All those tens of thousands of children who run away every year, and one in seven ending up in the sex trade.

"That was the worst time," Alison said, closing her eyes to block out some particular memory. "Then somehow I got my act together. In my late teens I escaped the life, cleaned up, went to school and got a degree in social work.

"Then I got started working for the Haven. Last year I found an old porn photo of a child I was convinced was my brother. He looked to be about ten years old when the photo was taken. I started to think that maybe they weren't dead, that they had been exploited somehow. After all, that's what happened to me, and I was still alive. Oh, Dad and I were a pair, all right, feeding each other's denial. But that's not how it was at first. I took the photo to Dad, to get him to admit what he had done."

"And you didn't tell him who you were . . ."

"I gave him every chance to recognize his own daughter. But he didn't, and I hated him the more for it."

"He did recognize you."

"I only know that now. He let me stay Alison Samuels because he thought it was best for me. The bastard."

"You had to realize, if he was there that night, he had to know you weren't."

"I didn't think he was actually there. I ultimately thought Dad contracted Mom's death. I figured that's why he was forcing me to get the kids out of the house that night. I didn't. I'm the one to blame that they died. I might as well just say I'm guilty and be done with it all."

I'd be damned if I let that happen, I thought, damned if I'd allow her to be lost again, even if I had to get involved myself. "You killed Shayna Murry before we found out that Erroll Murry had killed the family. Did you think she knew?"

"I didn't." Alison confirmed most of what I had already conjectured when I was laying out the possible scenarios for Todd. That she heard about the fur from Henry Aggrawal, and knew her father couldn't have gone near the tarp. That she remembered Will Hench claiming during the TV interview that a witness had perjured *herself.*

"I was convinced Shayna Murry had to know something, and I kept zapping her. Even then she wouldn't betray her brother. Then I heard on the police radio that they were looking for Erroll Murry."

When she was all talked out, I started to leave and then thought of one last question. "How the hell did you manage to taser yourself in the back?" I asked.

"Easy. I took the cartridge off that has the prongs in it and pressed the gun to my upper back just to make sure I duplicated any physiological effects the jolt might produce. Hurt like hell."

"You're quite a good actress," I said.

"Thanks. Besides being able to tolerate pain, I learned how to pretend when I was very young," Alison said.

Forty-eight

I got my tote bag back from prison security and checked my cell phone. I swear that's the first thing I did. There was a call from Mom; it sounded like she had started to leave a message and then just sat there silently. She forgot to disconnect, so I couldn't call back. No one answered the phone in Dad's room.

I was near collapse myself, reeling with fatigue, but I hightailed it to the hospital. Rather than sitting upright in a chair by his bed, I found her waiting at the door to Dad's room, more like a guard.

"How is he?" I asked.

"Everything is fine," she said.

"You called and didn't leave a message."

"You knew it was me?"

"Yeah, you can tell who's calling."

She nodded like she'd just learned something new. Rather than going back into the room, she took my arm, which I never remembered her doing before, and suggested we sit someplace else, that nice visitor area at the end of the hall, she said.

She chose one of the unforgiving chairs that faced down the hallway we had come from. She patted the seat next to her, even more gentle than when we had talked the afternoon I called her from this same spot. She put her hand over mine, glancing at her watch as she did so. I couldn't remember her touching me like that since I was a very little girl, when she would sit on my bed at bedtime and grasp my foot through the covers and give it a playful shake. I couldn't remember when she stopped.

"What's up, Mom?" Feeling ever more weary, trying to focus a vision that was a little blurry. "Is there something wrong?"

"I want to tell you a story," she said.

"Why here? Is it something you don't want Dad to hear?"

She smiled as if I'd meant to be amusing. "Oh no, Dad knows." Then she turned her head to the side and waved her hand as if warding off a stinging insect.

"So what's the story?"

She started, "You were five years old. Ariel was little, and I was in my first trimester with Todd, so I wasn't showing yet. You remember Uncle John?" She spoke a little more slowly than usual, as if we had a lot of time to kill and she wanted to make the story last. Or as if she was telling me something complicated about economics and it was important I understand.

"Sure. Dad's older brother by ten years. Battle of the Bulge. World War II prisoner of war. Serious alcoholic. Used to go out to the car to take an extra nip during family get-togethers."

"He was always after me. John was."

Whoa. Not the story I was expecting. "As in sexually?"

She nodded. "For a while it was pats on the bum that no one else saw."

"Why didn't you tell Dad?"

"You think Dad would have believed me?" Mom looked at me with her face closing together, as if speculating whether I was smart enough to get what she was about to say. "I was able to avoid John most of the time by never being alone with him. But there was a birthday party, your fifth. You were in the kitchen with me, watching me put candles on your cake. Uncle John came up behind me."

Mom stopped, and took a deep breath. She looked at her watch again.

She said, "I thought it was Dad when he put his hands on my hips and turned me around. John kissed me before I could dodge away. Your father came in and saw us."

I remembered things from when I was five, but I couldn't remember that and told her so.

"Of course you don't remember. This was my life, not yours."

I pictured instant throwing. Maybe the birthday cake against the wall. What else could there have been? "What did Dad do?"

"He was quiet, but after everyone left he blamed me. He was so angry." She stopped again, crossed her arms over her elder belly in remembered pain, and added, "I almost lost Todd that night."

"Did you lie when you told me he never hit you?"

"He didn't hit me."

We both stopped, and our eyes connected for longer than they ever had before. I didn't call it marital rape. Fifty years ago no one did. Fifty years of knowing how a man could hurt a woman, but I had never known my own house. Five years old, what would I have done? I asked, "What happened to Uncle John? I remember seeing him every holiday and family celebration after that."

"Dad never blamed John. He was the heroic big brother. I was only the wife. Blood—"

"—is thicker than water," I finished for her.

Now there's a piece of intel I never had. Over something so small. A kiss. Can the course of life turn on something so small? There was something in me that wanted to go back and view our family past differently from the way Mom knew it, the way she was telling me. Stupidly, still a child in some respects, I wanted to salvage us, to force her to remain the old Saint Mom I knew. "He didn't divorce you. And he was pretty good to us kids, roughhoused with us, taught us to shoot, even the ride-alongs as soon as we were old enough." But it sounded lame even before the words finished.

"After that night he never touched me again. But that's not all. Among your father's many qualities is the ability to hold a grudge." She glanced down the hall as if feeling at a distance the tug of anger that connected the two of them. "You think I wanted you to grow up into such a hard person? You think I wanted you to become bait for sex maniacs?" Then she calmed herself down as the rest of us would not. She looked at her watch. "I tried to keep it out of the house, but the more

I protested, the more he brought home the stories, left the photos lying around for you to see. Giving you a copy of *In Cold Blood* for your thirteenth birthday. Looking at me as he did it with a little smile and a twinkle in his eye, daring me to challenge him. He treated it all like a joke between us, and I hated him for it. Oh, I don't think he had a specific plan to avenge my kissing his brother." Mom nearly chuckled. "He's not that clever. But it was after that night that he started to change. I got so tired of fighting him. So I let him suck you into his world. And that's what happened, didn't it? He took all of you."

I was caught partway between adult sympathy and protecting anything good in my memory of childhood. "You gave up easy. Those photograph albums that don't have pictures of me after the age of ten. That's why you stopped taking pictures of us, because you'd given up."

Mom must have been able to tell this was hurting me even if I swore it wouldn't. She stroked my arm as if it would calm me. I was surprised that it did.

She said, "What possible good could have come out of making you love me, but hate him? And I didn't give up. I tended the house and sewed little dresses and listened to the occasional sly remark about how I wasn't like the rest of you. I never gave up, I only kept trying to show what normal looked like. Even now I'm not sure there isn't a good reason for keeping my mouth shut." She looked at her watch again. We had been sitting there about fifteen minutes. "But you know, dear, there comes a point when you've had it with self-sacrifice."

I felt my heart speed up, still not knowing why. I always thought I knew Mom. I still did. "So why are you telling me this now?"

"Because I want, just once, for you to know me. *Me.* This is my one chance to either win you back or lose you forever. I know I don't have your love, but oh my dear, I deserve it. I deserve it."

I held up my hands as in giving up. "I don't understand. What do you need me to do?"

"I want you to give him up," she said.

"It's not up to me," I said.

"No. It's up to me," she said. She looked down the hall toward Dad's room, and I looked, too. A nurse had gone in. She wasn't in there very long. As Mom and I watched, she came back out, moving faster now, back to the nurses' station. Immediately there came a voice over the PA system, "Paging Dr. Sinclair. Paging Dr. Sinclair."

Mom looked at her watch again. "I've spent so much time here I know that code. We can go now," she said. "I think we can go." But she didn't move.

I jumped up from the chair, wanting to run down the hall and stay by Mom's side in equal measure. "You're telling me Dad is dead."

"He wasn't altogether, when you arrived." Mom didn't stand. She placed the hand that had been holding mine over the other, which rested in her lap.

In a voice too small to be Brigid Quinn's, I said, "Mom. What did you do?"

She took my hand in hers and pressed my palm to her cheek as if she was forcing me to reassure her rather than the other way around. "If you know nothing else, you have to know I did nothing. I just let him go. Maybe it was a heart attack. I only know I watched his breath get lighter and slower, and with each one I felt this lightness growing in my chest, like a response. I couldn't force myself to stop the lightness. So I did nothing, didn't call someone to bring him back. I wanted to let a little time go by to make sure he was gone. That's all I did." Maybe later reality would hit her, but for now she seemed ethereally calm as she said, "I've never watched someone dying before. I suppose you have."

Forty-nine

Two days later . . .

I kept in constant touch with Carlo as we arranged for the funeral and picked out a casket. I told him how the hospital had said the tissue of Dad's lungs was thinner than we thought, too thin to withstand his coughing without rupture. They said he died peacefully and rather suddenly, probably of heart failure, and there was no sign of distress. They appeared to be relieved that Mom was not going to sue them for moving Dad out of ICU, where his life would have been prolonged.

We couldn't reach Ariel, my sister in the CIA. So the wake at Kreller's Funeral Home was the rest of us and whoever knew Todd. After everyone had left, I heard a mild commotion out front. A voice said, "Service animal," and then Laura walked into the viewing area with Larry, who didn't have his uniform on. I bent over to pet him.

"Am I forgiven?" I asked them both. Larry wagged his tail, apparently letting bygones be bygones.

Laura paid her condolences to Mom, and we sat down for a moment in one of the empty chairs. I could tell she hesitated to talk about the case, with my father having just died and all, so I started for her. "Hey, it was really really nice that you didn't kill Alison."

"I couldn't kill his child," she said, and added, "I've been to see her."

"That's good," I said. "I'm hurting for that kid."

Laura didn't point out that she and Alison were about the same age. She said, "I took her Marcus's photo album."

"Also good."

"And Will Hench is going to take her case. He and I will make sure she gets the best defense possible. The prosecutor loves her because of her work, and we'll make a deal. Maybe parole after five years."

"Good for us all," I said, taking a deeper breath than I had all day. This time I felt more confident that Laura would win.

When she left, I noticed Todd down on the kneeler they put out for anyone who wants to pray in front of the casket. The thing reminded me of an immense silver bullet, kind of appropriate for sending off a cop. And Quinn-like, we weren't talking about Dad, but no one was there to notice, as this was the family time before the casket was finally shut. I don't recall that any of us cried that day, or the day before or after, but maybe in the privacy of their own homes the others did.

"It was nice working with you, little brother," I said.

"Likewise. We should do it again sometime."

"Better we shouldn't press our luck."

Todd placed his palms together in that pious way they taught us as kids and raised his eyes to the crucifix on the wall behind the casket. He said, "Listen, I talked to Delgado and Madeline together. They tried to remember what happened back then with the fingerprint examiner and the Creighton case. Best I can piece together after all this time is that they remember acting in an upright manner. No threats, no coercion of any kind to get Mack to interpret those prints. They said why bother, they had Shayna Murry blowing the alibi to get the conviction. As upright as you and me, I guess."

Maybe more so. "It's hard enough to remember exactly what you say, let alone try to figure out what the other person heard. Chances are good Mack is funneling it all through his own warped sense of what he was called to do. And it was a long time ago. You're going to just let it go, right?"

"Right. If Mack wants to stir the shit if and when he comes to trial, that's up to him."

"Good call. Delgado express any regret about sending an innocent man to his death?"

"Not to me, but no telling what a man thinks to himself."

The kneeling was for show; Todd thought Mom would like it. I was the only one who knew how Mom really felt, and I didn't think I'd tell Todd. No need to make him hate Dad more than he already did. I got up from the kneeler and moved to the head of the casket. They had Dad in the same suit he wore to Todd's wife's funeral. He had lost so much weight in his final illness I could feel his bones through the padded shoulders. I leaned over and kissed his screwed-up head, not out of forgiveness, but with the thought that if I didn't, maybe someday I'd wish I had. I turned toward Todd, but he had already moved away.

There was a startled cry behind us, and I turned to see Carlo had arrived and taken Mom by surprise, wrapping his long arms around her with arm to spare. I didn't know if Mom would ever take to hugging.

"You came," I said. "I told you not to come."

"Yet here I am," he said, and wrapped his arms around me next.

We invited Mom to come out to Tucson, but she said she wanted to stay at Weeping Willow, join the choir at her church, maybe make some friends. And, with that new lightness that had appeared when Dad died, she said that one Quinn was more than enough for Carlo to have on his hands. She said she was going home now to throw out Dad's clothes.

The best part of the funeral was when everyone went to their own places and Carlo and I were sharing a bottle of wine on the balcony of my hotel room. At first it was that beloved small talk, nothing where the stakes were life and death. Who was staying with the Pugs. Whether he had eaten the chili. But then the wine opened me, and I talked about Mom and Dad and their embattled life, and forming the words wondered whether, after all, it was sadder than any other life. I told how I had arrived at some understanding, if not love, as far as my mother was concerned. How it made me sad that I had never loved her.

"Sure you do," he said. "I'm having another. Want one?"

I drained my wineglass and lifted it to him. I can't remember if he noticed, or pretended not to notice for now, the bite mark on my fore-arm where Larry nailed me.

"Depends," I said. "Can we have drunk sex?"

He took my glass and lightly ran the base against the side of my neck. When he came back with two refills, he handed me my glass and, with that small frown that said he'd been continuing our conversation without me, said, "Maybe we get it wrong sometimes. I'm not sure love is a feeling. Maybe it's more like a decision. Like the decision your mom made to stick by the family."

Other than that bit of pith, he just listened to me some more, asking questions to get beneath what I was saying, but otherwise not speak-ing. This, too, was a great gift.

Admittedly, gifts were rare this time around. A man executed for murders he didn't commit. His guilt-ridden daughter driven to ven-geance by her own unwitting culpability in the crime.

And where's the justice in the story? That Erroll found his, certainly. That Laura learned something about the limitation of her own power and chose to not kill Alison when she had the chance. That my mother could have fought the battle against my father with her children as the spoils, but she surrendered us to him for our sake. This was her story, and mine, too, that I never knew.

The fact is, you may think you know someone else's story, but you don't. How can you, when you don't even know your own? Maybe we're all mysteries that can't be solved.

Acknowledgments

Thanks to what has become a treasured team of editors principally led by Hope Dellon of St. Martin's Press in the U.S. (oh, your patience and wisdom!), and including Helen Smith of Penguin Random House (Canada) and Bill Massey of Orion UK. I'm also grateful to India Cooper, the brilliant copy editor who occasionally "discorrects" Brigid Quinn's speech.

Helen Heller, my agent. One hour's conversation with her is worth an MFA program.

The following experts were always there, to answer any questions and make valuable suggestions. If you want to know more, I urge you to look up these names, as they've all written excellent books on their specialty:

Dr. Jan Leestma and Dr. Scott Wagner, forensic pathologists.

Peter Stephenson, digital forensics.

William Bodziak, impression evidence expert, actually, but we talked about wrongful convictions.

William Bell, correctional facilities.

Barry Fisher, forensic science.

Ted Vosk, law.

Diane France, forensic anthropology.

Sue Stejskal and the real Chili Dawg, human remains searching. Thank you to:

Julie King, for helping me *see* Vero Beach, Florida.

Dr. William Martin and Nadine Martin, for help with medications.

Readers and authors William Bell, Victoria Bergesen, Ruth Davey, Mickey Getty, and Pat McCord. You were all right. About everything.

My friend Aimee Graves, recipient of the 2016 Paladin Award for the fight against sex trafficking, and people like her. I have respect and admiration for all the heroes of our justice system, for law enforcement, for the Innocence Project, for the National Center for Missing and Exploited Children, and for the Academy of Forensic Science. My story explores the limitations of science, legal systems, and the individuals within them. This is not to further any cause, but only to discover how complicated is the pursuit of justice.

And always finally and forever, Frederick Masterman, with whom I look forward to many more years of sharing stories real and fictional. I'm making spaghetti tonight.

blog and newsletter

For literary discussion, author insight,
book news, exclusive content,
recipes and giveaways, visit the
Weidenfeld & Nicolson blog and
sign up for the newsletter at:

www.wnblog.co.uk

For breaking news, reviews and exclusive competitions
Follow us 🐦 @wnbooks
Find us 📘 facebook.com/WNfiction